The Shadow Universe III
Dawn of Darkness

William G. Davis, Jr.

Published by
William G. Davis, Jr.

ISBN: 978-1-959880-07-3
Library of Congress Control Number: 2022920913

First Edition: January 2023

Acknowledgments

Special thanks to Pastor E. C. Fulcher, Jr. for his support. To Ursula Crouse, Linda Shoaf, and Alyx Bliesener for feedback on continuity, spelling, and grammar corrections. Finally, to Sergeant 1st class Marc Schenker, his valuable help explains certain unclassified army procedures and jargon specifics.

The cover design is courtesy of www.Pixabay.com.

Chapter 1

Earth

The Regime - Washington, D.C. - Fort McNair

May 17, 2452

Yanamai's new alien alarm clock woke her from a sound sleep; she fumbled, trying to silence it. Unable to find the *off* button, she threw it, intending to send it across the room, hoping it would break into tiny pieces; the electric cord caught it, landing only a few paces from her. It was her first Terrestrial Rotation away from Akil, and she already felt homesick. Back in Argi, soft Akilian music would have awakened her, not some loud buzzing sound that had ripped her violently from a deep sleep cycle.

Sitting on the edge of the bed, she saw that the face of the clock, staring back at her, displayed numbers showing 5:30 AM. In a few Terrestrial Revolutions, she would adapt to the conversions. She set the clock back on the nightstand and performed her morning ritual with an added step. The females in this new world painted their faces. To blend in, she had a makeup kit delivered, along with a video tutorial. It took a few tries and more than a few thousand heartbeats to complete the process until the outcome satisfied her.

The colors blended in with her natural skin tone, and the black eyeliner did seem to bring out the blue in her eyes, as the instructor showed. She considered using her shapeshifting ability to replace the morning ritual of painting her face and decided against it because Zorion insisted that all Akilians hide this ability from their hosts as a precaution, giving them a fighting chance if they chose to turn on them.

If anyone within the Regime caught her using it, she knew Zorion would be disappointed in her, so she completed her new persona using the makeup and stepped into what the Earthians called a living room. She heard Garbi talking to someone on the wall communicator in the kitchen. *It must be that idiot she was with last night.* With her new Earthian purse in hand, she started to leave, but Garbi caught her attention before reaching the door.

"Oh, good, you are still here."

"What is it, Garbi? It is 6:47 AM, and I have a lot to do this work cycle."

"I was hoping you would do me a favor."

Yanamai sighed, "What do you want this time?"

"I need you to pretend to be me for," she paused, calculating the new time measurement, "about a half-hour this morning."

"I do not have time! *You* do not have time! You know what we are here to do and what is at stake! What could be more important than getting another portal machine up and running?"

"I have two dates this morning."

"No way! Not going to happen," Yanamai firmly responded, walking toward the door.

"Name your price," Garbi almost regretted it as the words left her mouth.

The terms stopped Yanamai in her tracks, "All right. If I do this, you will grant me any favor I ask in return with no end date this time!"

"Done."

"Not so fast. I want an Akilian oath from you."

"Fine, I swear as your fellow Akilian that I will perform any favor you ask in return for this one, with no end date."

"I accept. What am I supposed to do?"

"After Michael left, I contacted someone I met earlier that Terrestrial Revolution. I thought he did not like me during our first encounter, but we talked until morning. I just got off the phone with him."

"Who?"

"His name is Jason."

"You should call Michael and reschedule."

"I do not want to discourage him because he had a terrible experience, and canceling our date would send him the wrong message. My dilemma is that I saw Jason first, so I think it is only right to go out with him before Michael; this way, if it does not work out with Jason, I can still pursue Michael."

"Michael does not know about Jason?"

"And Jason does not know about Michael."

Yanamai shook her head, "You are here one Terrestrial Rotation, and already you are acting like an Earthian tramp."

"Hey! I am embracing their culture. It is perfectly acceptable to date more than one Earthian at a time."

"Yes, except I am sure you should let them know what you are doing."

"That would take all the fun out of it!"

"You will get into a lot of trouble here, Garbi."

"Oh, relax. You are such a killjoy."

"What did you call me?"

"A killjoy. It means someone who spoils the joy or pleasure of others. That is you."

"Fine; do not say I failed to warn you. Now, when will Jason arrive?"

"*You* are going out with Michael. I have been talking to Jason for hours, so you will not know anything we have discussed. It will take too long to fill you in."

"You know how I feel about Michael. He is clumsy."

"Oh, he just spilled a little soup on you. Get over it."

"Get over it? Where are you picking up these Earthian slang terms?"

"You must learn to be more sociable. It is easy to talk to Earthians. You must be willing to be nice for a change."

"I am nice."

"Ha! I am your sister. You cannot lie to me."

"You better tell me when Michael will arrive before I change my mind."

"He will be here in a few minutes, so you have enough time to change."

"What do you mean change? What is wrong with what I am wearing? It is only breakfast."

"It is a date, Yanamai. You should dress up. I do not want you going out with Michael looking like that. He will think *I* do not care."

"By asking me to take your place, you prove that you do not care about him. Besides, who goes to breakfast on a date?"

"I suggested it before I realized that most dates occur in the evening here. Now I know better."

Yanamai exhaled loudly, "Fine, what do you want me to wear?"

Having convinced her to help, Garbi waved for Yanamai to follow her to the closet, pushed several garments out of the way, and picked out a casual blue dress with matching shoes, one of many recently bought sets. She put the outfit's top under Yanamai's chin and studied it.

"Yes, I will look great in this."

"How did you find time to shop?"

"Stacy helped me during lunch yesterday. You should see the stores, Yanamai; there are thousands of distinctive styles. It was hard to choose, so I selected a few I liked. Now put this on."

"It is very blue."

"They call it royal blue."

"Just because it has royal in the name does not make you royalty."

"I can pretend," Garbi smiled playfully.

Yanamai rolled her eyes, left to change, and fidgeted with the material.

"It is too snug. You can see every curve of my body."

"That is the point, killjoy," Garbi pulled out the pin that held Yanamai's hair up.

"Hey! That took me fourteen hundred heartbeats to fix!"

"Start using the Earthian terms. It took you twenty minutes. Besides, you do not have to wear it up here. Remember? We are on a different planet, with different rules."

Looking in the mirror and seeing how different a few changes could make in her appearance surprised Yanamai. She liked wearing her hair down yet would never admit it to Garbi. Also, the dress matched her eyes perfectly, just like Garbi said it would, except going out in public wearing Garbi's blue dress made her feel naked. Yanamai continued to fidget with the dress, prompting Garbi to help straighten a few minor wrinkles and tease her hair to give it direction.

"I think Michael will be pleased with the dress," Garbi paused to look at Yanamai's reflection in the mirror, "I look great!"

"You mean I look great."

"No, you are me for a half-hour. I am only glad you decided to put makeup on. I would hate for him to see me without it."

"You are vain, Garbi."

"I am just telling the truth."

"Just remember, I expect you to honor your promise," Yanamai warned.

"I gave you an Akilian oath, so be nice to him."

"I cannot make any promises. Michael is liable to spill something on me again; at least this time, it will be your clothes he ruins, not mine."

"You are such a baby."

There was a knock at the door, and they froze until Yanamai mouthed, "Is it, Michael or Jason?"

Garbi shrugged her shoulders, "There is only one way to find out." "Who is it?" she yelled.

"Michael."

The door muffled his voice.

"Be right there," Garbi replied.

"Remember, be nice and be affectionate."

"That was never in our agreement. I will try to be nice, and that is all."

Shaking her head, Garbi walked into her bedroom to hide. Yanamai opened the door and saw Michael's eyes widen, taking in her whole image.

"Garbi, you look amazing!" he paused, "You are Garbi, right?"

Yanamai liked his reaction to her new appearance even though he thought she was Garbi; it gave her the confidence she needed to wear it out in public. Still, Yanamai would never admit it.

"Do not worry. Yanamai already left. You are safe."

Reflexively, Michael peaked over her shoulder into the room to make sure. Before he could see anything, Yanamai, still pretending to be Garbi, stepped out into the hallway and closed the door behind her.

"Are we going to the cafeteria for a quick bite?" she asked, looking at her watch, hoping the date would be over soon.

"If you don't mind, I have a small surprise planned that I think you'll like; if you have the time."

She bit back a curse. *I will never get that portal machine up and running at this rate.* Remembering her promise to Garbi, she smiled pleasantly at him.

"I have plenty of time. Where would you like to go?"

"I'd like to keep it a surprise until we get there."

"Great, I love surprises," she lied with a fake smile.

As they walked beside each other, she noticed a pleasant fragrance. It reminded her of the sweet strawberries she had eaten the day before.

"Did you bring strawberries with you?"

"No, why?"

"No reason. I smell them."

"Maybe someone took a plate back to their room, and the aroma still lingers in the hallway."

"That must be it."

As they continued, she could tell he was nervous because he kept looking at her oddly. First, he would smile and look away, clear indications of shyness and uncertainty. Qualities like that would ensure a solitary life on Akil, yet he made it seem alluring and sweet. Her conclusion was puzzling. In her peripheral view, she could see that he kept his head facing down. It was another sign of insecurity; for reasons unknown, she found it attractive. *Strange.*

"You surprised me yesterday," he blurted out.

"Yes. I have a bad habit of doing that sometimes. My sister often reminds me of that fact, but I do not seem to care."

Confused by her response, Michael furrowed his eyebrows, "It sounds like she's bossy."

"She is the head of the science division and must be bossy."

"That doesn't give her the right to tell you what to do in your personal life," he noted and paused briefly, wondering if it was an unknown social difference, "Unless it is her right as your older sister."

"No. She does not have that right. I think you have the wrong impression of Yanamai. She is only looking out for me."

"From my brief encounter with her yesterday, she seemed ill-tempered. I don't know how you have put up with it for so long."

"You did drench her with hot soup and ruined a clean uniform. I would think any Earthian would give you the same response in a similar circumstance."

"Hey, I would be happy to reimburse her for it; she never gave me a chance. The moment it happened, she didn't stop swearing at me. Also, she was testy when I took a sample of her blood back at the Sahara Base, so it wasn't just one time. It's clear she doesn't like me."

Abruptly, she stopped walking to face him, "Look, Yanamai has many responsibilities. She has the fate of her people lying on her shoulders and does not have time to coddle the feelings of everyone she meets."

"Ok…Ok!" he raised his hands in surrender. "I didn't mean anything by it. I'm sure Yanamai is very busy."

Her anger faded, so she turned and started walking again, "Besides, I am sure if you ever got to know her, you would find that she is caring, genuinely sincere, and pleasant to be around. I, on the other hand, can be whimsical at times."

"I'm glad you are, or else we would have never walked home together last night, and you would have never kissed me," he blushed.

"Humph," she voiced her opinion with a disapproving sound.

"I'm also impressed by how well you speak our language. I've noticed that you don't use the translator very much."

"I only need it sometimes. There are still some words or phrases that are tricky for me. Still, I have learned enough to communicate my thoughts."

"Akilians must be smart people. I've never known anyone to learn a language so quickly."

"Perhaps it is born out of necessity."

"That certainly makes sense."

He led her through several hallways until they entered a large glass dome. The sun was still low in the sky, yet there was enough morning light to see everything.

"Where are we?" she wondered.

"It's an aviary. General Saunders put me in charge of it."

"It is amazing," she inhaled the sweet, floral aroma.

Deep within the volary, he set out a table with a white cloth. He carefully placed the colorful foods on plates to make them beautiful and appealing.

"During dinner last night, I heard you tell Alex how much you loved fruit, so I gathered an assortment for you to try."

"That is very thoughtful," she answered, surprised that he was so astute.

He pulled out a chair for her, "Please, have a seat."

Yanamai was unaccustomed to such pampering and found herself enjoying the dating ritual. She sat and inhaled the fruits' scent.

There were different varieties, and their fragrances made her eager to try them all.

"How do you like them so far?"

"Oh, their fragrance is very pleasing. I sampled a few fruits yesterday, but I am impressed at how you gathered such a vast assortment. I never knew so many existed."

He handed her a fork, and she tasted each to discover her favorites. Watching her eat them for the first time gave him immense pleasure. Even more pleasing was hearing the soft moan she made eating them.

"Do you have any favorites yet?" he queried.

"It is difficult to decide. Each one has its distinct, rich flavor; if I had to choose one, I would say the strawberries are still my favorite."

"Interesting."

"What is interesting?"

"You smelled them earlier in the hall, remember?"

"So?"

"I just thought that since they are your favorite, if you think of them, you smell them."

"No. Someone must have walked by earlier with a plate, as you said. My sense of smell is precise."

"Ok, I'm just offering an idea."

After eating, he showed her the aviary, including the different plants and trees his team planted and nurtured. They approached a small bridge arching over a handmade stream and stopped to look around. The sound of moving water reminded her of home. She watched with delight as the small stream emptied into a large pool. Continuing his tour, he explained that the Regime built the aviary to preserve endangered species of birds; as if on cue, several landed on a willow tree near the pond where they were standing. At first, she was frightened until he told her they were not dangerous.

"What is that noise they are making?"

"We call them songs or chirps, depending upon how they do it."

"Are they singing to each other?"

"Yes."

"Oh, how romantic."

"I come here sometimes to think. Their song helps to soothe me."

"It is a very pleasing sound."

Without warning, a sparrow landed on his shoulder. Seeing an opportunity, he told Yanamai to hold her index finger so the bird would rest on it. As the sparrow stood on her finger, he showed her how to gently stroke its feathers. It stayed briefly and flew away, leaving behind one of its feathers floating in the air. As it gracefully fell to the ground, he cradled his hand under it until it landed in his palm, placed it inside a small, clear plastic bag, and gave it to her as a keepsake. The experience and the gift left her teary-eyed.

While walking on the green grasses, passing lush flowers and trees along the way, they talked about their childhood, compared things they liked and disliked, and discovered they had many things in common. On the east side of the building, rays of sunlight struck her face through the leaves. She moved to a small clearing to see the Earthian sun, in person, for the first time. To express her joy, she closed her eyes, held out her arms, and spun in the warmth of the shiny orb. Again, he enjoyed watching her experience something new because it enabled him to share that emotion, at least in some small part.

"I have been so busy that I have not had the chance to see it yet. It is warm."

Her watch chimed. She frowned and turned it off.

"I am sorry; I must go."

"I understand. Your work is important to the survival of your people. I hope I didn't take up too much of your time."

"No, it was wonderful. You are wonderful. Thank you for showing me this place. I would love to come back sometime."

"You're welcome to visit anytime you'd like. I've already taken the liberty of giving you clearance just in case you did enjoy it. You can come here alone if you want. I don't have to be with you."

"Thank you. That is a tremendous gift."

"Would you like me to walk you home?"

"Yes. I would," she commented, surprising herself.

Along the way, she could not stop smiling at the experience. In only a half-hour, she sampled several new foods, saw live vegetation of all sizes and colors, touched a bird's feathers, felt the sun's warmth, and had a keepsake to remind her of the Terrestrial Revolution.

At her apartment, she turned to face him.

"Did you bring strawberries back with you?"

"No. I can get some if you'd like."

"I only asked because I smell their fragrance even stronger than before. I thought for sure you brought some along as a surprise."

"Maybe some of the juice is still on my hands from preparing them this morning."

Resolute in solving the mystery, she took his hand and sniffed.

"Yes. Your hands are rich with the sweet aroma."

"I'll be sure to wear gloves next time."

It occurred to her that she might be sensing something other than food on him, so to satisfy her curiosity, she gently took a strand of his hair, leaned in, and sniffed.

"Your hair smells like strawberries too."

"I don't remember touching my hair as I put together the food. I made it a point not to touch any part of my body until I finished preparing the meal. It might be my shampoo, except I don't think it's supposed to smell like strawberries. If it did, it would also explain why my hands smell like strawberries."

Even though the lingering fragrance seemed to be a logical explanation, the answers did not satisfy her. There was only one way to know for sure, so she took a deep breath, leaned in, and kissed him. The very moment their lips touched, she knew. He smelled and tasted like sweet strawberries; she forced herself to pull away and felt flush.

"Wow! It seems like every time we kiss, it keeps getting better and better," he smiled.

Stunned by the new revelation, she could only manage to stare at him in disbelief.

Since she did not respond, he offered, "Um, if you're interested, I'd like to take you to dinner tonight. There's a restaurant I think you'll enjoy just as much as the aviary."

She was quiet for a moment, "I would like that. Yes, I would like that very much."

"Great! I'll make the reservations. I'll meet you here at 5:30 PM after work."

"I will be ready."

Before he could leave, she kissed him again, hoping to prove that her first analysis was wrong; it only reinforced her findings because the longer she kissed him, the more difficult it became to pull away. *I am in big trouble.*

She gently pushed him back, "I think you better go, or neither of us will get any work done today."

"I can't argue with you there. I'll see you tonight," he added, slightly out of breath.

She stepped inside her home, leaned against her door, and licked her lips, still tasting strawberries. Although late for work, she could not resist savoring the moment. She closed her eyes, enjoying the taste and smell until it finally faded.

Chapter 2

Akil

Argi City

The 22,281st Terrestrial Rotation of the Second Summer

With just over eight thousand heartbeats of rest, Olan struggled to wake as soft music played overhead. Having insisted on staying by Julie's side, they spent most of the sleep cycle awake, practicing her swordplay, which Urki allowed because Julie insisted on exercising with Olan. He had fought some of the best warriors the Akilian military had trained in his business, except none came close to what Julie could do.

She claimed to be a novice yet moved faster than anyone he fought. Also, her strength far outmatched his or anyone else he knew. The practice exhausted them, but he noticed a vast improvement. Urki still criticized her skill, saying it was not enough to defeat the Skeans. His warning meant that the Skeans posed a more significant threat than he initially realized. Julie rested, so he decided to seek an answer to the question burning inside him since speaking to Dolas.

He dressed, quietly left the shared apartment, and headed to the northern section of level three hundred fifteen, where Dolas spotted Broll. Upon finding the home, he picked open the lock by connecting his communicator to the electronic door. Soon, he heard the bolt moving. Not knowing what to expect, he unsheathed his sword, gripped it tightly, and carefully entered.

The room was dark, and the glow from the avenue did little to brighten it, so he shut the door behind him and turned on the lights. The doors of a nearby closet opened with great force. The attacker swung violently, knocking Olan backward. He caught himself before falling, saw the attacker's face, and smiled.

"It is me, Olan!"

Announcing his name did nothing to stop the attack. Having no choice, Olan defended himself against the onslaught. Although the attacker fought well, he was not as good as Olan.

"I am not here to hurt you!" Olan yelled.

The attacker did not relent. Instead, he fought more forcefully. Since the assailant would not yield, Olan worked to disarm him; it was not easy, especially since Olan did not want to hurt him. As the fight continued, the attacker hit Olan with every piece of furniture in the room, throwing them between strikes. Olan saw an opening, knocked the assailant's sword from his hand, and put the blade's tip to his throat, ensuring he could not grab it.

"Get this over with, *putok*!" the attacker snarled.

The words cut Olan to his heart. Knowing there was only one way to convince the assailant that he could trust him, Olan knelt before him. With both hands, he lifted his sword above his head in surrender.

"I came here to help, but if you do not trust me, take my life."

The attacker took advantage of Olan's weakness and grabbed the sword from his hands. He raised the blade above him and swung, stopping a hair's width from Olan's neck. Zorion stayed quiet for a few heartbeats.

"Stand up."

Looking up at his Sovereign, Olan rose with tears in his eyes. For a long time, Zorion studied him until returning his sword.

"What are you doing here?"

"Broll is clumsy. One of Dolas's agents followed him here, and they still do not know whom he is sustaining in this apartment. It is only a matter of time."

"You have not answered my question; what are *you* doing here?"

"I learned that Broll was bringing moss here, and I needed to confirm my suspicion that you were still alive."

"Now you have, so leave and tell no one what you saw, or the next time we meet, I will not hesitate to kill you."

"I swear, your secret will die with me. Still, there are some things you must know."

"Like what?"

"I have killed Elzer."

"You fool! Now his heir will attack Argi and drag us into an intercity war that we cannot fight right now?"

"You do not need to worry. I have sent his secretary the video of Igon's confession. The Information League has already reported that he died from the sickness."

"It was a risky move."

"It was necessary. Molo did not attack you. It was one of Elzer's guards disguised to look like him."

"Is Molo still alive?"

"Yes. Dolas cleared him of all charges. Nevertheless, Elzer was not responsible for the latest attack, which killed your double."

"Who was it?"

"I am convinced a Skean tried to kill you."

Upon hearing the news, Zorion sat, and his face went pale.

"Did I say something wrong?" Olan wondered.

"No. You just confirmed my worst fear. Lately, many oddities have been occurring in my life and those close to me."

"Where did those suspicions lead you?"

Since someone killed his double, Zorion had plenty of time to research and think about the matter during his confinement. He researched all the information at his disposal and found reports about Skeans with similar circumstances of recent events. Still, he could not find any record of a drug that caused Yanamai and Garbi's symptoms. He discovered a legend about a female Skean, who secreted a pheromone that gave her the power of suggestion over anyone she touched. Zorion came to the only logical conclusion: Kraeth is a Skean. Further research led him to diagrams of Skeans making potions of all sorts, and his failed relationship with Thea made sense.

"Based on my analysis and observation, I believe Kraeth and Thea are Skeans; I cannot prove it yet."

"I know of two Skeans, Nayrah and her Skean mother, Gecheana. Gecheana tried to kill you. Nayrah, on the other hand, either drugged me or used her powers to force me to kill you."

"If you can prove it, I will reinstate you after we catch them."

"One Terrestrial Revolution, I might welcome your generous offer; for now, I can get more things done as a rogue agent. Having me back in the field again helps us, and we will need every advantage if we plan to rid ourselves of these Skeans."

"How can we? They have powers beyond our grasp."

"When Gecheana attacked your double, many saw a bright light."

"Yes. The Information League said it is a strange unexplainable phenomenon."

"That light is a Saiph."

"Are you sure?"

"Yes. We have met."

"How do you know this Saiph can be trusted? It may be another trick by the Skeans."

"I can only tell you that I trust this individual. The bad news is that the Saiph is a novice. Even though a novice is faster and stronger than you and I put together, it will take more to defeat the Skeans."

"I will take any help at this point."

"Our fight will not be easy. The Saiph said that there are eleven Skeans on Akil."

"Eleven?"

"Yes. Even more interesting is what one Skean told the Saiph earlier; she has four sisters."

Zorion's eyes widened, "That means all the sovereigns have joined houses with Skeans! It means my assumption is correct; Thea is a Skean!"

"It would seem so, but I believe the other Sovereigns do not know their companions are Skeans."

"Do you remember what happened after my coming of age ceremony?"

"Yes. The one you chose died tragically of the sickness. When the mourning period ended, you took Thea in her place."

Zorion's face turned red with fury, realizing what she had done.

"That *putok* killed her to take her place by my side! She made my life miserable!" Enraged, he threw several pieces of furniture across the room until his anger subsided, "This means they have been manipulating us for a very long time."

"Yes, now Gecheana is advising Otsoa."

"They have taken everything from me!"

"I agree, so it is time we take it back," Olan replied, leaving.

"Where are you going?"

"I have much to do and little time to complete it."

"Before you go, I need to know if you have seen Julie. Is she safe?"

"Yes. She is safe, for now. I have hidden her because Otsoa is looking for her."

“I had hoped that Dolas would help her.”

“Otsoa has him occupied, searching for any signs of a rebellion. Even if Dolas did have her in his custody, Otsoa would force him to turn her over. If he refused, Otsoa would convict him of treason.”

“How did you find her?”

“Tionah tried to hide her. I located her easily and moved her to one of my safe homes.”

“Do not tell me her location because if Otsoa’s agents capture me, I do not want to risk revealing her location.”

“Agreed,” Olan looked at his timekeeper. “I must leave. The avenues will be busy soon. I do not want anyone seeing me exit this apartment.”

“Before you go, I have one more thing I need you to do. You must get a message to Yanamai.”

“Where is she?”

“Earth.”

“That will be difficult. Otsoa has the Interstellar Transport Bay locked down.”

“I need you to find a way to warn her. Tell her not to come here for any reason. Tell her that Otsoa is Argi’s Sovereign and will stop at nothing to bring her back.”

“I understand. I will do my best to get her that message.”

Before Olan left, Zorion placed his hand on his shoulder, “Thank you for everything. I promise things between us will return to normal once this is over.”

“Thank you, my friend,” Olan remarked and left.

Chapter 3

Earth
Scotland - Edinburgh - Clone Replacements Facility
May 17, 2452

During the night, Dawn closely watched Blair prepare Ethan's new body. The speedy process in which Blair produced a clone impressed her. Blair placed it inside a glass womb tank and poured a liquid that simulated natural amniotic fluid. It had added nutrients, proteins, perfluorocarbon (an oxygen-rich liquid), and patented drugs to speed up the growth process.

Dawn stepped into the room at the top of every hour to check the growth progress. By 7 AM, the embryo grew into an exact duplicate of Ethan at twenty-one years old; the protein and drugs within the amniotic fluid ensured the clone's muscles would be healthy so that Ethan would not need physical therapy to walk. It would have taken weeks to complete without them, which Dawn did not have.

Satisfied that the clone was ready, Blair drained the tank, used a suction machine to remove any fluid obstructing the clone's airway, grabbed two paddles, and shocked him. The first jolt made it gasp its first breath, and it started breathing on its own. She checked the clone's pulse, blood pressure, and pupil reflex and washed away any excess amniotic fluid from its skin.

She attached four chains to the corner of the plate where he rested and used an electric crane to lift him out of the tank and onto a gurney, where she and Dawn dried the body and covered it with a blanket. Blair wheeled the gurney into the MR room, and Dawn left to retrieve Ethan. She found him sitting in his wheelchair, peeking outside through the blinds. He heard the door open and turned to face her.

"I see you're already up," she smiled pleasantly.

"I couldn't sleep."

"Understandable. Don't worry; I promise this will be painless."

"Is the new body ready yet?"

"Yes. That's why I'm here. It's time."

"Let's do this. I'm tired of living in pain."

"I'll take you to see your new body."

Moving behind him, Dawn grabbed the handles on the wheelchair and pushed him to the room with the clone, where Blair was giving it an injection.

"What is she putting in my body?"

"It's for the memory transfer. The chemical allows the machine to imprint your consciousness. We'll also give you one before we start, so it can easily identify the memories in your brain."

"May I take a closer look?"

"Sure," Dawn replied, pushing him close to the gurney.

"Amazing," he touched its skin, "My hands haven't looked like this in years."

"I take it you approve?"

"Yes. I'm very anxious to get started."

"Good. Here we go," Dawn pushed Ethan into the adjoining room, where a second MR machine sat. With Dawn and Blair's help, Ethan got out of the wheelchair and into the cushioned seat under the MR helmet, where Blair gave him the injection. They strapped his legs and arms to the chair, lowered the dome over his head, and put the other one onto the clone's head in the adjacent room.

Dawn began the startup protocol. The motor whined louder and louder until it reached its highest speed. Soon, lights started flashing, showing that memory transference had begun. Dawn and Blair watched Ethan and his clone during the whole session. About two hours later, the MR shut down, and the whining motor faded to silence. In the adjoining room, Dawn and Blair removed the clone's helmet.

"Ethan. Can you hear me?" Dawn asked.

The clone did not move until his eyes rolled underneath its lids; he opened them and gasped.

"It's all right; the process will leave you disoriented. It's normal. Just breathe slowly until your mind adjusts," consoled Blair.

Ethan panicked until his thought process acclimated to the new body; within a few moments, he felt whole again. The first thing he noticed was the absence of pain. The second, his energy level returned; he sat, looked down at his new body, and smiled.

"It worked!"

"Excellent! Just sit tight, and we'll be right back," Dawn responded as she and Blair stepped out into the hallway.

Dawn frowned because Blair handed her the syringe, "I can't do this. You must give him the injection."

"We have an agreement, Blair. Now do your job."

"No. I won't do this. I can't."

"Fine. I'll do it, but you better keep the clone occupied until I finish with him."

"I'll wait for your signal," Blair confirmed, returning to where Ethan's clone waited.

Dawn smiled and walked into the adjacent room, where the original Ethan sat. Before removing the helmet, she injected the contents of the syringe into his arm.

"Ouch!" he protested from underneath the helmet.

"Sorry, I didn't mean to hurt you."

"Is it over?"

"Yes," she assured, removing the helmet.

As it lifted off his head, Ethan smiled with anticipation yet could not hide his disappointment seeing his old body.

"Why didn't it work?"

"It did, Ethan. You're in your new body in the other room."

"I don't understand. You said you would transfer my memories over into a new body."

"Your memories *were* successfully transferred."

"Why am I still in this old body?"

"Because Ethan, the machine doesn't delete your original memories. Those must remain intact if there is an error during the transfer. Don't worry; the machine successfully transmitted your consciousness. Your clone has all your memories. He *is* you."

"You bitch! You tricked me!"

"I did no such thing. I told you I would transfer your memories, which I did."

"What will happen to me?"

As the words left his mouth, he felt a sharp pain in his chest.

"I'm sorry, Ethan. There can't be two of you. One must go."

The pain was so severe that Ethan could not call out for help. With his limbs still restrained, he could not even grab his chest. Dawn watched him writhing in pain for thirty seconds as the drug moved through his body, destroying everything in its path until he succumbed to the serum and took his last breath. She checked his pulse to ensure

Ethan passed and stepped into the adjoining room. Wearing the same warm smile, she found his clone wearing a hospital gown, moving around to assess his new body.

"How are we doing in here?" Dawn queried cheerfully.

"Great! I've never felt better!"

"I'm glad to hear it; now, put some street clothes on, and we'll get you started in your new job."

His smile faded, "Am I still in the other room?"

"Yes. Your old body is there; I suggest you don't go in there."

"Is he dead?"

"The original body doesn't survive the transfer."

"I would still like to say goodbye if you don't mind."

"Take all the time you need."

Ethan approached his old self. Standing over him, it felt like he was looking down at a stranger. *The mirror didn't lie, but it's worse looking at myself through young eyes.*

"Goodbye, old friend," he whispered and returned to change.

Dawn sent him ahead to her car, and before leaving, she spoke to Blair.

"Make sure you burn the body, and Blair, if anyone finds out about this, I will hold you solely responsible."

"Don't worry. I have no desire to repeat what happened here today."

"Good. I'd hate to lose a reliable resource."

"I want to be clear; I have paid my debt to you in full," Blair insisted.

"I should charge you for not killing the original; since the clone turned out to be everything I expected, I'll consider us even for now. Just know that you'll hear from me if Ethan experiences any problems."

"He won't. I used the best materials available."

"Good. For now, I will consider our business complete."

Abruptly, she spun around and met Ethan in her vehicle. Already buckled up in the passenger seat, he was anxious to get moving.

"It feels good to be back in action. So, what's on today's agenda?"

"I'll tell you when we arrive at my home."

Chapter 4

Earth
The Regime - Maryland - Eastern Shore - Jared and Sonya's Home
May 17, 2452

Unable to sleep, Sonya lay awake in bed, staring at the clock. About an hour before, she felt Jared get out of bed. The fact that he woke when his alarm sounded put her mind at ease. Having drugged him the night before, she would never forgive herself if something happened to him. Pretending to be asleep, she allowed him to prepare for work alone this time. Later, she would pretend to have been ill. The thought of lying to him tore at her heart, but this would be the last of it. Once the spy received his money, she would never have to deal with President Martinez again.

While staring at the clock, she heard his footsteps at precisely 9:09 AM. Their sound became louder, so she pretended to be asleep, hoping he would kiss her on the cheek and leave. Instead, he gently shook her, trying to rouse her from her sleep. She faked waking up, their eyes met, and she smiled lovingly.

"Hey, you."

"Sorry to wake you; Supreme Commander Porter requested our presence."

She felt a cold sweat break out, hearing the summons, "Why does he want to see me?"

"He wants to see *us*, Sonya. He didn't say why. All I know is that we must be there before 10:56 this morning. I can only guess that he wants to meet you in person and welcome you to your new home."

"Boy, he is precise with his appointments, isn't he?"

"I must admit, this is unusual, even for him. You better hurry; we don't have much time."

Jumping out of bed, Sonya dressed. Visiting the Supreme Commander required professional clothing, so she wore one of the business suits from her days as governor. She put on her jacket and walked downstairs. High-heeled shoes tapping the wood floor echoed throughout the house, making her even more apprehensive.

"Are you ready? We should go," Jared remarked nervously.

"Yes. We don't want to be late."

As he drove the hovercar to the Interstate Transportation Facility, she wore her best poker face, but inside, she felt terrified. In her experience, there was no such thing as coincidence. Her gut told her that she slipped up somehow, and the Regime found out. She contemplated last night's events and could not figure out where things went wrong because she thought to have covered every contingency.

Also, the meeting time of 10:56 AM was very unsettling. Since it is an odd time to make an appointment, she hoped he did it out of necessity and not scare tactics. Although, either way, she was afraid. Try as she may, it seemed impossible to believe this was a simple meet and greet with the Supreme Commander, as Jared supposed. As he slowed the hovercar, she felt a lump in her throat. *I'll find out soon enough.*

Chapter 5

Earth
The Regime - Georgia - Fulton County
May 17, 2452

Ashley drove off to the local police department alone early in the morning, insisting that Wendy and Kenny stay behind just in case something went wrong. Upon arriving at the barracks, Ashley used her NYC credentials to enter the building and requested a visitor's workstation. She logged in to her virtual desktop within a New York server, uploaded the file Kaleb made for her, sent it to Scott, a trusted TBI agent, and started a video chat with him.

"I just read your email and sent it to Special Agent Reed, the agent in charge of the investigation. I don't know when he'll see it."

"I appreciate your help. Is there any way you can send information on the case to me?"

Scott hesitated, "Promise you'll delete it after you read it."

"I will."

"I've sent it over."

"Thank you, Scott. It's a huge help."

She read one of their witnesses' testimonies and found several contradictions in what Kenny told her. At Wendy's home, she interviewed him to clarify what happened.

"Didn't you say they laid you off from work?" quizzed Ashley.

"Yeah. Why?" Kenny acknowledged.

"Your boss said you quit."

"What?"

"Here's a copy of your resignation notice," she handed him the statement.

Kenny read it in disbelief, "When they laid me off, I had to sign many forms; that wasn't one of them. Great, no wonder I couldn't collect unemployment."

"Read your boss's statement."

Kenny read it, "He's lying. I didn't do or say any of that."

"I didn't think so. It looks like your boss needed a patsy, and he chose you."

"Why me?"

"Look at your background. You're single. You don't make much money, and you're in debt to several casinos, so you're the perfect dupe."

"I'm not in debt. I don't gamble!"

"Their records say you owe them quite a bit," Ashley noted.

"How did this happen? I've never been to a casino in my life!" Kenny exclaimed.

"Based on what I've read about your boss, he doesn't have the skill to set you up like this. He must be getting help from someone connected. Let's visit him," Ashley offered.

"Shouldn't we wait until the TBI contacts you?" Wendy offered.

"We don't know when Special Agent Reed will look at it; if we wait too long, Kenny's boss could leave the country," Ashley explained.

"We better get over there. I don't want to be his patsy anymore," Kenny commented.

"It will be another long ride. His home is in Thomasville," Ashley warned.

"Great. It'll be dark by the time we get there," Wendy remarked.

"At least he won't see us coming," Ashley reassured.

Chapter 6

Akil
Argi City
The 22,281st Terrestrial Rotation of the Second Summer

Like Zorion, Olan had never been religious. The myths of Gau, Izar, and Lehoi did not speak to him before; now, things have changed. Seeing Julie's abilities made him a believer. Gau's creed was the most popular of the two. Last he checked, only a few thousand resolute acolytes worshipped Lehoi. They hid their temple in the lower part of the city, disguised as a business to prevent Gau's followers from destroying it.

As a Lehoi follower, Tionah knew its location. Olan and Tionah stepped off the elevator onto the one hundred and fifth level. Inconspicuously, he scanned the avenue. It was mostly vacant, except for a few Argians rushing to work at the last moment. Olan always did what was necessary to fit in, no matter where his job took him, so he and Tionah moved quickly, pretending to be late like everyone else on the boulevard.

Having never met a Lehoi follower before, he consulted with Tionah to figure out how to make an appointment with their High Priest. Since High Priest Kexel would only meet with a long-time acolyte, Olan had to bring her along. A few heartbeats later, he regretted his decision because paranoia kept her looking around, which caught the attention of many on the avenue. He grabbed her hood, threw it over her head, and insisted she focus on the walkway ahead.

At their destination, she knocked on the door. Moments later, a prominent business owner, whom Olan suspected of being a guard, answered in a deep and throaty voice.

"What do you want?"

"I am Tionah. I have important news for High Priest Kexel."

"Wait here."

Olan felt exposed on the avenue, which made him apprehensive; he even caught himself looking around at strangers like Tionah did on the upper level. He scolded himself, calmed down, and remembered his training; the business owner returned moments later.

"Follow me."

Inside, he touched something underneath the counter. A hidden door opened, where shelves and inventory hung. Their journey led them through a series of corridors, similar to those Olan used moving throughout the city. The rock was freshly carved, which meant the architects did not record them on any original apartment designs; he almost smiled, admiring their attention to safety and covertness. At the end of the corridor, the guard stopped to knock on a thick, metal door at the end of the passageway, using a sequenced pattern. The latch clicked open, and the guard motioned for them to enter, where several Lehoi disciples, dressed in red robes, greeted them.

As a precaution, they restrained Olan and Tionah to chairs before a screener verified Tionah's identity. Afterward, Tionah vouched for Olan, telling the disciples that he was now fighting for Lehoi. Skeptical of her claim, they kept them bound until the High Priest arrived a few hundred heartbeats later. Olan admired his elaborate white robe, with gold embroidering, in a decorative pattern around the edges and across the back.

"Tionah, my dear. It is good to see you; it has been a while," High Priest Kexel remarked.

"Forgive my intrusion, High Priest Kexel, but the prophecy mentioned in the scrolls has begun to unfold, and I am involved with the outcome."

"What do you mean?"

"A Saiph has come to our world. I am her Domestic."

"Are you saying she has returned to us?"

Olan raised an eyebrow, "Who has returned?"

"Lehoi," Tionah asserted.

"You are mistaken. The Saiph's name is Julie. She is from Earth, not Akil," Olan insisted.

"He is correct, High Priest Kexel; she does not claim to be Lehoi because she knows nothing of our faith."

"The scrolls are clear on this point. When Lehoi returns, she will fight to save our people from the present and past Skeans. She does not have to believe she is Lehoi; only we do," High Priest Kexel answered.

"Present and past?" Olan inquired quizzically.

"Yes. Lehoi fought during the days of Gau, and just as the scrolls have prophesied Gau's return, they also foretell Lehoi's appearance in the last Terrestrial Revolutions of Akil before the sun finally explodes."

"You believe that Julie is Lehoi?" Olan inquired.

"Yes," High Priest Kexel responded.

"Good. We need your help," Olan commented.

"We do not have great riches or influence with the government, yet I will give you what I have to help in her effort. My only request is that you take me to see her."

"No. It is too dangerous. Otsoa is hunting her. We risked getting caught by his agents just trying to see you," Olan warned.

"I have heard of your disgrace; you tried to kill Zorion, and now you have no sovereign. Even though I trust Tionah, I must consider the possibility that you have deceived her with your trickery. Therefore, I will only help you if I see Lehoi with my own eyes."

"Fine, except only I will take you to her," Olan asserted.

"It is a trap," one of the disciples commented.

"Why would I want to trap a Lehoi High Priest? Zorion is dead, and Otsoa will kill me when he finds me. There is no benefit in turning you in, even for someone without a sovereign."

"Tionah, why do you trust this, Argian?"

"Because Lehoi trusts him."

"Very well. I will go with you alone."

"You must change your clothes, or someone will recognize you. We are going down a few levels. Now hurry and untie us."

Chapter 7

Vincent returned home from Madrid, leaving a Regime crew behind to sift through the debris made by the explosion, hoping they would find Dragon's corpse. Since the process took time, Vincent decided to debrief Wu Luli about her pursuit of Dragon. Later, he stopped by to see Sofia and check on her progress.

He entered her room and found the shock trauma team trying to revive her. Although they had stabilized her, a nurse told him it was the second time her heart had stopped. Worried that she would not make it through the night, he slept in an uncomfortable chair by her side until the doctor arrived in the morning. Vincent was still asleep, holding her hand, so the physician nudged him, and he woke.

"How is she?"

"I haven't examined her yet. I need to take her blood pressure, which is why I woke you. Would you mind moving out of the way for a moment?"

"Oh, sorry."

The doctor checked all her vitals as Vincent watched until the physician completed his exam, hoping for some sign that she was finally out of danger.

"What do you think?" Vincent asked.

"Her injury is severe. The DNA stimulus drug we gave her is working as expected, but as the brain cells regrew, the neuro impulse to the heart stopped. A nurse on duty said you arrived during the second event."

"Yeah, it was unnerving. Will she be all right now?"

"The damaged part of her brain will grow back, so I'm confident that she will fully recover physically, except the memories stored in the damaged area of the brain are lost forever."

"How much of her memories did she lose?"

"It's hard to say. When Sofia arrived, not only did she have a severe brain injury, but it also took our shock trauma team a couple of minutes to bring her back. The moment her heart stopped, it deprived her brain of oxygen for too long. As a result, she may never wake up."

"Uh," a croaky voice moaned.

The doctor moved to her side, checking her vitals as she came out of the coma. As he worked on her, Vincent sat in the chair near the window, anxiously waiting for him to finish. She opened her eyes, rolling them uncontrollably until she focused on her doctor.

"Relax," the doctor remarked. "You've been seriously injured."

A few minutes later, he gave her a series of questions; at the end of his exam, she saw Vincent and smiled.

"Do you recognize me?" Vincent wondered.

"Naturally, you're Vincent, my boyfriend."

"Do you remember what happened to you and why you're here in the hospital?"

Frowning, she shook her head.

"What is the last thing you remember?"

She smiled, "We had made love and were lying beside each other in bed."

"You don't remember what happened next?"

"No. I don't."

"You don't remember trying to kill me?"

"What? Why would I kill you? I love you," she asked, trying to sit up.

She attempted to move until handcuffs prevented her from getting too far.

"Why am I in restraints?" she nervously inquired.

"You were convulsing last night. We borrowed a pair of handcuffs from police officers who were in the vicinity. Don't worry. I'll have a nurse put softer restraints on you until we're sure you are feeling better," her doctor lied, trying to soothe her.

He faced Vincent, "Step outside for a few minutes. I need to ask her a few questions. I'll meet you there shortly."

"Please, doctor, don't make him leave," Sofia pleaded.

"Don't worry. I'll be back in a moment," Vincent assured.

A few minutes later, the doctor met Vincent in the hallway and whispered, "Obviously, she has memories of you; it's still unclear how much she's lost. She knows her identity, her parents, and where she lived as a child, which means that at least some of her long-term memories have stayed intact. Still, I must perform a complete MR and have it reviewed before determining how much damage she sustained."

"I heard you ask her what she did for a living. She is employed and doesn't live at home with me. I just met her last night, so how can she possibly have memories that don't exist?"

"Her mind is trying to fill in the blanks by joining other memories. Since she doesn't remember what she did for a living, her mind created the thought or perhaps an actual memory of living with you."

"She tried to kill me; why in the world would she think we're together?"

"The memory of her mission to kill you has been replaced with the intimate encounter you shared just before her attempt on your life. She now believes you are a couple with only that memory to work with."

"Wow! I've heard of shotgun weddings, but this one takes the cake."

"It would be best if you played along, for now, until I'm sure she's stable enough to endure the truth. If she lost the memories of her crimes, I'm not even sure the Regime would prosecute her. It would be the same as convicting an innocent person."

"The MR will show if she's pretending or not. Right?"

"Exactly. It'll show us all the memories Sofia has left. If she's lying, the Regime will move forward with her trial. If she's not lying, we must gently break the news to her."

"All right, I can pretend to be her boyfriend for a little while; if she isn't faking, be sure to let me know the moment I can tell her the truth."

"You'll be the first to know."

The doctor left, so Vincent returned to Sofia, "I'm sorry; I must return to work. I'll come back as soon as I can."

He started to leave until Sofia called out to him, "Wait! Aren't you going to kiss me goodbye?"

He approached her with a fake, apologetic smile, "I'm sorry. I've been in such a rush lately with everything at work."

Leaning down, he kissed her cheek. Before he could pull away, she gently grabbed his head, pulled him toward her, and kissed him.

"Now hurry back to me," she smiled seductively.

As he left the room, his thoughts returned to his recent, failed mission. Even though he took every precaution, Dragon discovered she betrayed him. The memory of seeing Dragon shooting Sofia haunted him, so he replayed that event, hoping to find something they did that had revealed their plan to Dragon. He came to the only conclusion that made sense; there was a mole in the Regime, leaking top-secret information to Dragon.

Chapter 8

Earth
The Regime - Washington, D.C. - Capitol Building
May 17, 2452

Having hurried through the Interstate Transportation Station and a line at the metal detector, Jared and Sonya arrived at the Capitol Building with little time to spare. Due to his high-level clearance, Jared passed through security without examination; the sentries scanned Sonya from top to bottom, which did not help ease her concerns. Jared checked in with Supreme Commander Porter's assistant at 10:45 AM., and they waited in the lounge for him to call them.

Sonya smiled, pretending nothing was wrong, but her instincts screamed for her to run. She often wondered why time seemed to slow down during the most painful trials in life, yet if things were good, the moments passed quickly. The following eleven minutes were no exception to that rule. Holding Jared's hand for comfort, she focused on her breathing to prevent hyperventilating, which would give away her real emotions.

At 10:56 AM, the assistant called their names. Sonya hoped to keep it together long enough to get through the meeting. As they entered, she saw Supreme Commander Porter standing behind his desk with a warm smile. It did little to calm her fears because, as Texas' governor, she used the same practice before giving some unsuspecting person terrible news. She knew it was a form of control, yet did not show her hand and smiled to greet him.

"Governor, it's a pleasure to meet you," Supreme Commander Porter greeted her pleasantly.

"Please, call me Sonya. The pleasure is mine."

"Jared, good to see you again," Supreme Commander Porter shook his hand. "I apologize for the late notice; we have a dilemma on our hands, and I was hoping that Sonya would help us."

"I will do my best," she answered, keeping a mask of confidence over her terror.

Supreme Commander Porter's communicator beeped.

"You said to remind you that President Martinez is on the video com, waiting to speak with you."

"Thank you, Mrs. Miller. I'll bring him up now."

To her left, Sonya saw a massive monitor rise from within a cabinet; it stopped, and the image of her stepdad appeared on the screen.

"How dare you keep me waiting, Porter!"

"I can assure you; it was unavoidable."

"You've only hurt yourself by making me wait," President Martinez smugly commented.

"Exactly how have I done that?"

"I want my disc, Porter."

"I've already told you. I don't have it."

"If you don't produce it in two minutes, you can say goodbye to your Market Place."

"I warn you; we have defenses against your attacks."

"You can't stop this one. It's already there."

"Interesting. How did you get the device on Regime soil?"

President Martinez smiled fiendishly, "How is not important. The fact that you now have only ninety seconds *is* important. The explosion will wipe out everything within a fifty-mile radius. If I'm not mistaken, I believe your office is within that range of the Market Place, which means it will wipe you out as well."

"Just a moment," Supreme Commander Porter muted their communication, moved out of the camera's eye, and faced Sonya, "He can't hear or see you, so I want you to answer me honestly. Is what he says true? Is there a weapon of mass destruction somewhere near our Market Place?"

Sonya almost fainted but held herself together enough to respond, "No. At least, I don't think so."

On a different monitor, Supreme Commander Porter played a video. Sonya believed a satellite recorded it by the video quality and the angle directly from above. It showed someone tossing a metal case into a garbage container.

"That is you. Isn't it?" Supreme Commander Porter asked.

Fidgeting in her chair, Sonya knew Porter had her dead to rights and took a moment to consider her answer very carefully. Feeling Jared's gaze, Sonya fought not to look at him. It hurt her deeply to believe that Jared would think she could do something so horrific, even though Sonya would feel the same way in his position. Sonya was guilty of delivering a suitcase full of Regime Talons; she was not guilty of delivering a nuclear bomb. That detail would not matter to the Regime. Her clever stepdad put her in a no-win situation, like many times in the past. At this point, denying her involvement would only make her look like she volunteered to be part of the scheme. Convinced that only the truth could save her, she took a deep breath.

"Yes. It is me in the video."

She faced Jared, "He threatened your life. I had no choice."

Returning to Supreme Commander Porter, she continued, "I swear, I thought it was only money. He told me he was buying information. Please, you must believe me. I had no idea it was a bomb. I even tried to pry the lock; it would not open."

"I will deal with you in a moment," Supreme Commander Porter commented, moved back into the camera's eye, and reopened the communication.

"You've wasted precious time, Porter; now you only have thirty seconds. I'm warning you; I'm not bluffing," President Martinez informed.

"I suggest you disarm the bomb, Martinez."

"Why should I do that?"

"Because, if you don't, you're going to blow yourself up."

"Now, you're bluffing."

Supreme Commander Porter looked at his watch, "I guess you'll know in ten seconds."

Sonya looked from Supreme Commander Porter to President Martinez and back as the clock counted down. Even with all her experience, she could not tell who was bluffing, and with only two seconds left, President Martinez laughed.

"Goodbye, Porter."

"Goodbye, Martinez."

At zero, the monitor lit up with a bright white flash, replaced by static. With a loud gasp, Sonya sat. It was hard to believe that he was dead. She never dared to even dream of such freedom. Still, she had to be sure.

"Is he dead?"

"Yes. It wasn't what I wanted; he left me no choice," Supreme Commander Porter answered.

Unexpectedly, Sonya laughed hardily. Jared and Supreme Commander Porter looked at each other quizzically.

"What's so funny?" Jared inquired.

"That stupid bastard finally got what he deserved!"

She continued to laugh until she remembered the reality of her situation.

"What will happen to me?" she frowned.

"I'm afraid you've also left me with no choice. The Regime will charge you with terrorism and treason. The Regime will sentence you to death if you're found guilty of terrorism."

Entreatingly, she looked to Jared, hoping he would believe her, "I swear to you, Jared. I didn't know it was a bomb."

With a grim expression, Jared removed restraints from his belt, "Turn around and put your hands behind your head."

Turning, she placed her hands up as Jared commanded, and as he adjusted the bands, she looked to Supreme Commander Porter, "How can I prove to you I'm not guilty?"

"Since the Regime will seize all your assets, a court-appointed attorney will guide you through the process. If you agree to an MR, it would be beneficial to your case, assuming you're innocent."

"I will do it. Please, record whatever memories you want."

"In either case, I won't see you again, so I bid you farewell, governor."

Sadly, Jared guided her out of the office. All Sonya could do was look at the floor and sob.

After they left, Supreme Commander Porter hit the button on his communicator, "Mrs. Miller, I'll need to send a copy of the recent video to the U.N. They're going to want to know why the White House vaporized."

Chapter 9

Earth
The Regime - Washington, D.C. - Police District
May 17, 2452

Sonya changed into the orange prison jumpsuit while the prison officials processed her. The female guard placed her clothes and personal belongings into a bag with her name, handed the package to a clerk for storage, grabbed Sonya's arm, and guided her to a cell for holding. Hearing the cold steel bars close behind her made Sonya flinch.

"Back up and put your hands through the opening," the guard ordered.

She removed Sonya's restraints as Jared approached the cell.

"As your arresting officer, I'm here to advise you that your trial will begin tomorrow morning, right after your MR. The Regime will execute you immediately if you're found guilty of terrorism. If you're found guilty of treason, you'll spend the rest of your life on the moon."

"I'm guilty of many things, Jared, but I'm not guilty of terrorism or treason. What I did, I did for you. I did it to protect you. I did it because I care for you!"

"I don't believe you."

"It's true. Please, review the MR tomorrow. I want you to see it."

"It doesn't matter, Sonya."

"Why?"

"Because it's over between us. Tomorrow morning I'll get the divorce agreement together. I expect you to sign it before your MR. After that, you're on your own."

Although she fought to stay strong, her eyes pooled with tears, "Please, Jared. Don't do this. I swear I didn't do anything to hurt you. I would *never* do anything to hurt you."

"And yet, you did. When I woke this morning, I could tell there were drugs in my system. I had my blood checked, very potent stuff."

"I hated doing it, but it was a necessity. I didn't want you to find out."

"I think it's fair to say that you just threw trust out the window and ran over it several times with heavy machinery."

"You don't understand. Your life was in danger!" she disputed.

"Yes, I know, the moment I met you."

Hearing his hurtful words forced a tear down her cheek, "Jared, life is seldom black and white."

"Today, it is, at least for me."

He stared at her with righteous indignation as a black stream flowed from her eyes.

"Please, forgive me, Jared! I need you! I can't do this alone!" Sonya begged.

"I want you to listen to me very carefully. I am leaving."

"No!" she protested, trying to grab hold of his arm, shirt, or anything she could reach to prevent him from going; Jared pulled away from her grasp.

"Once you sign the divorce agreement, you will never see me again."

Knowing she had lost him forever felt like someone punched her in the stomach. The dire circumstance brought up old feelings, reminding her how it felt to lose her first husband. As everything came crashing down around her, a river of tears streamed down her cheeks, leaving several black, wet trails of makeup. Having failed to convince him of her good intentions, she cried even harder, causing her body to shake and convulse while struggling to breathe.

Every breath was a desperate gasp, which she released again as another violent sob. She pleaded and begged with outstretched arms, yet Jared would not hear her. Anger, rage, frustration, and hate dominated her emotions in response to his cold reply. President Martinez's final act of manipulation had cost her everything: the man she loved, her freedom, and her life. If ever there was a time she needed a friend, it was now, but Jared kept his word and walked away without looking back. She watched him leave, fell back onto the floor, doubled over, and wept.

Chapter10

Earth
China - Hong Kong - Lam tin Park
May 17, 2452

Wu Luli left the Regime at 6 AM and landed in China a second later at 6 PM. The time difference put her twelve hours ahead. Entry into China was a little trickier than the average transport. Due to the large population of six billion, opening a portal at the usual places could kill someone. The only alternative was to enter from above. The Technician opened a vortex facing the ground amid the tree branches in Lam tin Park.

Landing this way helped hide Wu Luli's entry and prevented the Regime from accidentally killing a pedestrian. Hanging by a rope, she swung from the event horizon to the nearest branch that could support her weight. Anyone who saw her would think she hung out of thin air. After letting go of the rope, she watched it disappear into the vortex, which closed and disappeared. She propelled herself down through the branches until reaching the ground.

She secured her gun before taking the Wilson Trail toward the nearest mall, where she stopped to contact a former colleague to collect an old debt. Yang Shing told her to meet him at the Wong Tai Sin Temple. Since the temple was more than a walk away, she took a taxi. As Wu Luli stepped out of the cab, her eyes watered from the thick smoke of burning incense from the sanctuary; she made her way to the small bridge nearby and understood why Yang Shing chose the temple grounds to meet.

There were droves of people arriving from every direction. It was a suitable place to hide out in the open. Although she arrived on time, Yang Shing was late as unusual. She knew he was careful. In his position, she, too, would ensure no one followed her. About a half-hour later, Yang Shing grabbed her arm from behind and pulled her alongside him as they walked. As if they were in a well-rehearsed dance, Wu Luli automatically fell into place beside him, putting her hand into his, making it seem as if they were a couple.

"You're crazy for coming here. Everyone is looking for you," Yang Shing whispered.

"It's important," Wu Luli answered.

"I could be killed just for speaking to you."

"I promise, once I have what I need, you'll never see me again."

"What do you want?"

"I need to know where General Ming-tun Fu is hiding."

Yang Shing laughed, "General Ming-tun Fu doesn't hide. He doesn't have to."

"Then, this job will be easy for you. My intel says he's building something that will need lots of power."

Yang Shing scratched his neck nervously, "I've heard that there has been activity at the Black Point Power Station. They just completed a new hall with two new turbines; it has restricted access to military personnel only."

"I need to get inside. I know that General Ming-tun Fu divides his projects, putting different scientists in charge of each. I'll need the identifications and addresses of all his current staff."

"I've told you where he is. I've paid my debt to you."

"Not so fast. I need this information to get to him."

"If he catches you, he will know I helped you and kill me."

"Not if I catch him first."

"What will you do with him once you have him?"

"The Regime wants to question him."

Yang Shing sighed, "It will take at least a week to hack the system."

"You have four hours. Meanwhile, I'll find someone on his staff that I can replace. Also, I'll need enough time to ensure she won't show up for work tomorrow."

"You ask the impossible!"

"I risked my life for you, and this is a small price to pay. Besides, I'm sure someone who can hack into his system owes you a favor, so it's time to collect."

Yang Shing exhaled loudly, "How do I contact you?"

Wu Luli handed him a burner phone, "It's untraceable; when you get the information, send it to me, and I'll leave you alone."

Yang Shing took the phone from her and disappeared into the crowd. Knowing where General Ming-tun Fu planned to build a portal machine was only her first step. For now, she needed to disappear until Yang Shing contacted her. She looked at her watch; it was 9 PM. The local nightclubs were open now. They offered shelter and cover because the crowd did not leave until early morning; it would be the perfect place to vanish. Ninety-nine spies had thousands of contacts, which meant she had a small army looking for her, so she had to be careful.

Chapter 11

Akil
Argi City
The 22,281st Terrestrial Rotation of the Second Summer

Julie woke to hear a door close and did not feel a sense of urgency yet still detected an unknown presence in the adjacent room. Exhausted from last night's practice, she got out of bed, changed, and attached her sword to her belt. She stepped into the living room and saw Tionah with a basket full of moss in her hands. Beside her stood Olan and a stranger.

"Why is he here? I thought you were supposed to keep my location a secret."

Hearing her voice, Edur ran out of his bedroom and saw High Priest Kexel, so he bowed.

Seeing his obeisance, Julie frowned, "What are you doing?"

"This is High Priest Kexel. He is here to meet you," Olan answered.

"Is she the one you spoke of?" High Priest Kexel wondered.

"Yes," Olan confirmed.

High Priest Kexel studied her, "You are the alien from Earth."

"Yeah, why?"

"This one, named Olan, came to me for help. Tionah says he is a defender of Lehoi. I insisted on seeing you myself," High Priest Kexel explained.

"Who is Lehoi?" Julie questioned.

"*You* are Lehoi," Olan noted.

"I think you have me confused with someone else."

"Your sword, may I see it?" High Priest Kexel inquired.

Not sensing any danger, Julie removed it from her belt and handed it to him without extending the blade. High Priest Kexel studied her artisanship carefully and handed it back.

"The markings are Lehoi's; can you wield the weapon?"

"I built it, so yes, I can wield it," Julie asserted.

"Please, ignite the sword for him, Julie," Tionah requested.

"Sure."

With a thought, the handle in her hand came to life. The blade shot forth, glowing brilliantly. High Priest Kexel gazed with fascination. A brief time later, Julie turned it off and sheathed it. Upon seeing her demonstration, High Priest Kexel knelt to the ground.

"Lehoi, I am your humble servant."

"Ok, stop kneeling. I'm not a god. I'm a person, just like you," Julie irritably clarified.

Reluctantly, High Priest Kexel obeyed, stood, and excitedly responded, "What can I do to help you?"

"I have read there is a necklace that can hide an ordinary Akilian from the senses of a Skean," Olan noted.

"Ah, you speak of the Cloaking Gem," High Priest Kexel acknowledged.

"Yes. That is the one. Do you have it?" Olan requested.

"I carry it with me at all times," High Priest Kexel exposed the gem hanging from his neck.

"Would you be willing to let me borrow it?" inquired Olan.

"It is yours, defender of Lehoi," High Priest Kexel responded, removing it and handing it to him.

Olan faced Julie, "This should prevent any of the Skeans from sensing me while I follow you."

"It looks like the Sapphire in my sword. How can a gem cloak you? I had to practice for hours to hide, and it still isn't easy," Julie articulated.

"A long time ago, there lived a Saiph who could conceal himself and others around him. He transferred his power into the gem on his deathbed; we do not know how far his abilities can reach. Nevertheless, it should shroud the wearer from Skeans and Saiphs alike," High Priest Kexel explained.

"If you no longer have it, won't that put you in danger?" Julie asked.

"I will hide until you or one of your defenders call me. It is a bad time for you, Lehoi. You must be brave. Our future is in your hands."

"At least there's no pressure," Julie quipped.

Olan put on the necklace, "Thank you. It will help me protect her. Now, we must eat. We do not know if there will be another chance."

As they ate, High Priest Kexel solicited Julie with questions about Earth and her life there. They briefly talked, and as High Priest Kexel was about to leave, Julie stopped him.

"Please explain to me why all this is happening?"

"Before the beginning of time, there was the High Lord, who rules the high kingdom of light. The High Lord created the Night Lord and gave him dominion over the Shadow Universe. The Night Lord was not happy having only the Shadow Universe. He wanted the high kingdom as well. There was a great war between the two deities, and the High Lord cast out the Night Lord. Then, the High Lord created our universe and set it as a gulf between the two realms. Now, the Night Lord must conquer this universe, turning it into total darkness, before even attempting to enter the high kingdom again to take it," High Priest Kexel explained.

"This universe is mostly dark space. How can the Night Lord make it any darker?" Julie wondered.

"The scrolls do not comment on how the Night Lord accomplishes this task; some believe Gau tried to destroy the Akilian sun, hoping to bring darkness to our solar system."

"That would be suicide. Without the sun, the planet would die," Julie remarked.

"I agree. I am sorry; we do not have all the answers."

"What can you tell me about Lehoi?" Julie asked.

"Lehoi is the Saiph who defeated Gau."

"Who is Gau, and how did Lehoi defeat him?"

"Gau is the first Skean mentioned in our Sacred Scrolls. More than ten thousand of your years ago, he first appeared at the bottom of Mount Gaurette, sent by the Night Lord to destroy the sun. When Gau descended, Argi and Vlor were at war with each other. He joined the battle and fought for Argi. Many Akilians have written songs about his strength and bravery; Lehoi's followers do not sing them because Gau served the Night Lord.

"The Sacred Scrolls that detailed his life were destroyed in a fire. A few hundred Earthian years after his death, his acolytes wrote down the myths about his last days. They tell us that he and Izar, his mate, ruled Akil with an iron fist. Since the Night Lord instructed Gau to build a pyramid, he worked diligently to accomplish the task and succeeded. Shortly afterward, he held an elaborate ceremony and ascended to the summit at midday.

"He reached toward the sun with his hands to destroy it. Some claim to have seen a dark stream of energy shooting upward from him. His most devoted followers surrounded the pyramid as he worked to consume the sun, preventing anyone from approaching. Had it not been for Lehoi, he would have succeeded in blotting out the star completely. Instead, with the help of her army, she fought her way through Gau's acolytes to the pyramid," High Priest Kexel explained.

Julie interrupted him, "Upon reaching it, she ascended to the top, where she fought Gau and stopped him."

"Yes. Have you heard the story before?" High Priest Kexel questioned.

"No, I've dreamt that part. I keep dreaming about it," Julie frowned.

"Yet, you still do not believe you are Lehoi," High Priest Kexel shook his head.

"I could be seeing the past through her eyes. It's only a dream."

"There is one more thing you must hear. Within the Sacred, Scrolls is a prophecy that says: during the last days of Akil, Lehoi, Gau, and Izar will return."

"That must be why you think I'm Lehoi," Julie surmised.

"Yes, because you are a female Saiph, and you are here in the last days of Akil. Everything the Sacred Scrolls foretold has happened," beamed High Priest Kexel.

"Except, my name is Julie, and I'm not from Akil. I never heard of Gau, Izar, or Lehoi until I arrived here."

"The Sacred Scrolls only tell us what we must believe. I am positive that you are Lehoi."

"What if I don't believe it?"

"You will when the time is right," High Priest Kexel advised.

"Enough talk about prophecies," Olan interrupted. "It is time for us to begin our work."

"Of course, you have been gracious," High Priest Kexel commented, bowing.

Olan faced High Priest Kexel, "Wait for me outside and hide your face under your hood. I will be out soon."

High Priest Kexel left, and Olan handed Julie a generic communicator, "You must contact Nayrah. Set up a place and time to meet. When I return, I will follow you. Use the generic communicator I gave you. She cannot trace your location."

"I guess this is it," she remarked, with butterflies in her stomach.

He placed his hand on her shoulder, "You will do fine. I will be with you the whole time."

Chapter 12

Earth
Scotland - Dunnottar Castle
May 17, 2452

Ethan changed into military fatigues, followed Dawn's butler to her office, and found her sitting behind a large, oak desk. Once inside, the butler left them alone to their business.

"Have a seat," Dawn gestured with her hand.

"I'm anxious to begin my first mission," Ethan said excitedly.

"Before we begin, I want to ensure you understand our agreement's perimeters."

"Don't' worry. I owe you a great deal. I plan to work hard to earn your trust and to pay off my debt."

"Good. I'm glad to hear it, except you aren't the first person I've helped."

"You mean you've cloned others?"

"Yes, and each one, at some point, betrayed me, so as you can imagine, it's been difficult finding someone with the right temperament."

"I can assure you that I'll do anything you need."

"I've heard those words before, so to be clear, you *will* do as I say, or you will not live to see tomorrow."

"Excuse me?"

"In the first stages of your clone's growth process, we inserted a small cyanide capsule into the clone's brain, which grew around the capsule without injury or consequence. It will open and release its contents if it doesn't receive a signal by 9 AM daily. I'm currently transmitting that signal from within this office."

Ethan stood and pointed at Dawn, "You booby-trapped my clone!"

"I consider it a protection plan for my investment. It guarantees that you'll return after a mission and ensures your loyalty. I'm sorry, Ethan; you just can't trust anyone these days."

"Starting with you!" he yelled angrily.

"Now, now. I know you're upset, but you will grow old and rich if you follow my orders. Once I've decided that you have earned the clone's cost, I'll give you the transmitter, so you can live the rest of your life the way you want."

"Once I've earned the right to own my new body, you will remove it, right?"

"I'm sorry. The capsule is deep in the center of your brain. Surgical removal would be too risky."

"What if the transmitter's battery dies?"

"It won't. Now please, have a seat."

With a glare that could kill, Ethan sat.

"Now, to your mission. We have a few deliveries to make on behalf of President Martinez," Dawn explained.

"Wait. I heard he's dead. Someone blew up the Capitol Building."

"He already paid me, so I must honor the contract to keep my reputation intact. Now, we must fill twenty warehouses with crates of weapons and ammunition, some of which sit in my transport station waiting for you. Before his demise, the President planned to support the rebellion's opposition in Texas. I've assigned four mercenaries to help you. They are in your charge. You will land in a warehouse in Houston first to find this man," she handed him a photo and continued, "His name is Tucker. My intel says that he is very temperamental, so do not provoke him in any way. I'm sending you to this warehouse because it was the last place my sources saw him. Once you've found him, offer him the weapons President Martinez paid us to deliver, and I want you to tell him they are from me."

"Why?"

"Tell him it is a goodwill gesture and that I'm interested in speaking with him face to face. We can meet here or in Texas; I need to know when and where."

"What do you want with him?"

"That is "need to know" information. Right now, you do not need to know. Now, please, get going. I want him to have the weapons before it gets dark there. Take the dossier with you because it may help you identify him. When you return, I'll send you to other locations, where you'll leave the weapons and come home. And Ethan."

"What?"

"You have twenty-four hours, or the capsule will explode."

Ethan left to meet with the others in the transport station and tried to think of a way to remove the capsule or find the transmitter. Ethan contemplated every conceivable scenario yet could not think of anything; he would spend every free moment trying to find a way to rid his brain of the capsule and be free of her.

He was thankful for her gift before their talk; now, Ethan wanted to kill her. He entered the transport station, where the mercenaries were waiting for him, along with a couple of forklifts. The operators were ready to move the boxes of weapons and ammunition. One of the men walked up to him and saluted.

"Sir! Corporal Boyd at your service."

Ethan studied his crew and noticed that they were all young, making him wonder if they were also clones; it was not the time for questions.

"Relax, Boyd. We're not in the army."

"Dawn demanded we treat you with respect, Sir!"

"Call me, Ethan."

"As you wish, Sir. Are we ready to go?"

"Yes. How do we get back?"

"I have a transmitter. When we're ready to return, I'll contact our technician, Mitch," he pointed at him.

"All right. Let's get going," Ethan ordered.

Corporal Boyd signaled Mitch to open the portal. Seconds later, a vortex appeared, and Boyd sent two of his men to guard the warehouse while the forklift operators moved the boxes. A few minutes later, all the crates were on the other side, so Ethan led Boyd and the other soldiers through the event horizon.

Chapter 13

Earth
The Regime - Texas - Gang Occupied Suburbs
May 17, 2452

After the vortex closed behind him, Ethan scanned the dimly lit warehouse, looking for an exit. Standing in a protective formation, Corporal Boyd and his team surrounded Ethan as they walked toward the building's west side door. The dossier Dawn gave him did not have much. It included a satellite map of known locations that Tucker frequented. They were so far apart; it would take time to get there on foot, which made him wonder why she did not give him a vehicle to use.

As he contemplated the following site on his list, the west door opened, and the silhouette of a large man stood on the other side. The bright sunlight of the setting sun behind him prevented Ethan from seeing the man's face. Once inside, the man approached him and his men. The door closed behind him, and the warehouse returned to the dim lighting. A few moments later, Ethan's eyes adjusted, allowing him to see the other's face; it was Tucker.

"Mr. Tucker, you're just the man I'm looking for," Ethan smiled pleasantly.

"What the hell are you doin' in my warehouse?" he asked in a loud, deep, threatening tone.

"I came here to bring you a gift," Ethan answered.

"Who the hell are you?"

"My name is Ethan Brun."

"Never heard of ya."

"Who I am isn't important, but I'm sure you will be interested in what I've brought."

"Yeah, what's that?"

"The crates behind me contain weapons and ammunition, enough to last you and your men a few months."

"What exactly do you want me to do in return?"

"You don't have to do anything. My employer only wishes to speak with you as soon as possible."

"Who is your employer?"

"Her name is Dawn Pierce."

"Never heard of her. What does she want with me?"

"I can only tell you that she wishes to speak with you at the time and place of your choosing. You can meet at her Scotland Office or somewhere here in Houston, whichever you prefer."

"Is she pretty?"

"Yes," Boyd chimed in.

"Boyd, take your team and open the crates, so Mr. Tucker can see the gift our employer sent him."

"Yes, Sir!"

Tucker rubbed his chin, thinking, "I guess I can hear what she has to say."

Turning to ensure his team was out of ear reach, Ethan returned to Tucker's gaze and whispered, "She is the most lethal person I've ever met. If I were you, I'd take the weapons and disappear."

Tucker looked at Ethan quizzically. By now, the mercenaries were returning and were within earshot. Ethan returned to speaking at an average volume, hiding his betrayal.

"Yes. As I said, Mr. Tucker. All she wants is a quick chat. What do you say?"

"I don't know," he remarked.

Tucker walked toward the crates, removed one of the automatic weapons, examined it, loaded it, and pointed it toward the east wall. He turned on them and started shooting. Ethan and his team ran out the west door, returning fire and dodging from left to right, hoping Tucker would not kill them. When they were outside, Ethan faced Boyd and shook his head.

"I guess he doesn't want to talk to her."

Chapter 14

Earth

The Regime - Texas - Houston - Resistance Head Quarters

May 17, 2452

Larkin checked in with his Lieutenant and headed straight for General Bailey's office. Doctors still had General Bailey's forehead wrapped with a bandage from the attack at his home.

"How you feelin'?" General Bailey questioned.

"Ah, my wrist and ankles are sore; they'll mend soon enough. You've looked better, though," Larkin answered.

"Yeah, I'm gonna have a headache for a while," General Bailey added.

"By the way, thanks for puttin' those soldiers outside my house."

"Until we get this Rico character, I want her under guard at all times."

"You should let me find him alone. I work better that way."

"I know you do, except if somethin' happened to you, Sarah would never let me hear the end of it."

"You can't let Sarah dictate our strategy."

"I'm not. I have another plan. The Regime is gonna use satellites to watch Rico's territory, and once they know where he's staying, they're gonna send in a quick airstrike and take him out."

"I've heard about those Regime airstrikes. You never hear 'em comin'."

"Tell me about it. It gives me shivers just thinking I could ever be on the receiving end of one of those. The last one they did was in Florida. They popped in and out of the kill zone before the bombs even touched the ground, laying waste to the Florida resistance in seconds."

"The only problem with trying to get one person like that is, you never know for sure if you got 'em 'cause there's too much debris to confirm a kill."

"I agree. I'd feel better if they'd let us take care of him ourselves; there's still the matter of your brother. I know he was mad at you but telling Rico to send in men to kill Sarah and Sable doesn't seem like the man you described to me. I know he's got a grudge against ya, yet killin' your family seems extreme, even for him."

"Rico explained what his men planned to do to Sarah and Sable; all Tucker did was make fun of me."

"That must have made you mad."

"Let's just say I'm looking forward to our next encounter."

"Just keep it together for a little longer. I'm working on another plan to find him. Once I do, I'll give you his location, and you can have 'em all to yourself."

"Good. It's time to put that threat to rest."

"Until then, you better get back. You'll be walkin' the border tonight."

Chapter 15

Earth
The Regime - Washington, D.C. - Fort McNair
May 17, 2452

Yanamai returned home from work and called for Garbi, who was not there. Not having enough time to shop for new clothes, she went to her sister's closet and selected a formal dress for the evening. She spent most of her workday thinking about Michael and the kiss they shared that morning. During her lunch break, she ate in front of her computer and read about Earthian dating etiquette and fashion. Since going to a restaurant required more formal attire, she selected one of her sister's little black dresses.

Yanamai looked in the mirror and realized her sister focused on the *little* too much. *Each dress seems to be getting shorter and tighter.* She tugged on the dress, trying to make it go down her leg farther; there was insufficient material. The front was just as bad, leaving most of her chest exposed for the world to see. She tried on all the other dresses in her sister's closet; it was the only one that seemed right for her date with Michael. She styled her hair until hearing the front door close.

"Garbi, is that you?"

"Yes."

Having known her sister all her life, Yanamai could tell by her response that something was wrong and stepped into the living room to console her. She found Garbi sitting on the arm of the couch, moping.

"What is wrong?" Yanamai wondered.

"Jason and I did not work out," Garbi lamented.

"Oh."

As her gaze met her sister, she frowned, "Where are you going in my dress?"

"Uh, out."

"With whom?" Garbi suspiciously queried.

Yanamai hesitated, "Michael."

"He asked me out tonight?" Garbi smiled.

"We are supposed to go to a restaurant," Yanamai informed.

"That is perfect! I will take it from here. Change out of the dress, and I will get ready."

Again, Yanamai hesitated.

"Why are you not moving?" Garbi questioned.

"Because we need to talk. I spent some time with him this morning and changed my opinion; if you do not mind, I would like to go out with him tonight."

"No! Michael is mine! I saw him first!"

"You did not even want him this morning because you were fascinated with Jason."

"That is not true. I asked you to go out with Michael in case Jason and I did not get along. Well, it did not work out; now you no longer have to pretend to be me."

"You leave me no choice; I am calling in the favor. I want you to give up Michael because I want to pursue him."

"What? No way! The whole reason for the favor was so I could still go out with him!"

"I am sure that would not make him feel good if he ever found out."

"He will not find out."

"You made an Akilian oath. I expect you to keep it."

"But…but…I thought you hated him. That is the only reason I had you to take my place."

"As I said, I changed my mind. I got to know him a little better."

"Please! Do not do this, Yanamai! It is not fair!"

"I am sorry, Garbi. I did not plan this; I must insist."

"Fine. I will not pursue him," she paused and smiled. "I wonder how he will take the news?"

"What news?"

"That you are Yanamai."

Yanamai did not think that far ahead and imagined the conversation with him. At some point during the evening, she had to reveal her identity to Michael or pretend to be Garbi for the rest of her life, which would be impossible. The only obstacle blocking her future happiness with him was how he would take the news. Putting herself in his place, he obviously would not be happy with her, which meant she needed a plan.

"I will tell him you cannot make it tonight and that I will go instead; during the date, I will seduce him with my charm, and he will go out with me instead of you."

Garbi snickered, "I cannot believe you think that will work."

Blast, she is right. This morning, Michael revealed his impression of her: bossy and ill-tempered. Knowing his low opinion of her, the chance of Michael taking her out in Garbi's place was zero to none. Still, there had to be a way to tell him without angering him; she had to think of something fast because there was a knock at the door.

"Who is it?" Garbi yelled.

"Michael."

"Go hide in your bedroom," Yanamai whispered to Garbi, who vengefully smiled, walking away.

Yanamai opened the door and saw Michael wearing a suit and tie, making him look even more attractive than this morning. *I am in big trouble.*

"Wow! You look amazing!" Michael complimented.

Yanamai did not respond because of her dilemma; although she had kept her emotions in check from her earliest memories, she found herself nervous around a boy for the first time.

"Garbi, are you feeling all right?"

His voice brought her out of her brooding.

"I am fine," she forced a smile.

"You don't look fine. Have you and Yanamai argued again?"

"No. It is not that."

She did not elaborate further, so he stood quiet for a moment and added, "I planned to show you the world tonight; if you are not in the mood to go out, we can reschedule."

"No. I want to go," Yanamai responded, closing the door behind her.

She spent a long pause contemplating the best time to reveal her identity, and after taking great pains, she decided to go out with him one more time and tell him the moment she summoned enough courage. Yes, it was selfish to lie to him just to have one more fond memory, but once he knew the truth, she did not know if he would ever speak to her again.

Along the way, she cleared her throat and puzzled, "How can you show me the world?"

Her voice was just above a whisper because the stress had caused her to choke.

"The restaurant is mobile."

Yanamai nodded absentmindedly because her thoughts focused solely on his inevitable reaction when she revealed her identity. They stepped through the event horizon and landed in a lobby full of people dressed in formal attire. The wait in line was minimal. Michael gave the Host their names, and she promptly seated them near a window. Adamant to focus on the date and have an enjoyable time, Yanamai took a moment to scan the dining area.

"The room is circular," she noted.

"It's shaped like a flying saucer. There is a deck outside that surrounds the entire restaurant."

"How fast does the restaurant move?"

"Not fast at all."

"How can we possibly cover the Earth?"

"The restaurant is built over a large, sturdy electromagnet. At each landing site, there are thick metal plates. The operators charge the magnet, which raises the restaurant. When it reaches its full height, the conductor will open a vortex at each site, allowing us to move from one destination to another. Compressed air pushes and spins the restaurant through the portal.

"Once we arrive at each stop, the restaurant will pause for fifteen minutes. Long enough for us to eat one serving and have a short walk outside to take in the view. The whole tour lasts an hour and forty-five minutes. We'll have eaten seven courses and seen seven different countries."

As if on cue, the restaurant rose from its resting place. The motion was subtle, so they barely felt it lift them. It began to spin as it rose, giving each patron a 360-degree view of each destination. She looked outside as a vortex opened, and the restaurant started moving toward it. Before they entered the event horizon, the restaurant rotated her seat to the opposite side. At their destination, she heard rushing water.

"Where are we?"

"Niagara Falls. It's in Canada."

Looking out the window, she saw a beautiful waterfall, which reminded her of home. Moments later, a waiter brought them their first course and a glass of wine.

"What is it?" she inquired, looking at the colorful dish.

"Tomato bruschetta."

"It smells wonderful."

The portions were small, so it only took them a couple of minutes to eat the Hors d'oeuvre. Later, they walked out onto the deck. A large steel rail prevented anyone from falling, and they sat on a bench that fastened to the floor inches from the edge. They were very close, and she could feel the spray from the water dancing on her skin. The air was cold, giving her goosebumps. Michael saw her arm and motioned for one of the attendants to bring them a blanket. The steward laid it on her lap, she thanked him as he left, and they sat in silence until he reached over and took her hand. Feeling guilty, she again had to force a smile, hoping to hide her fear.

"I can tell that something is troubling you. I want to help; please, tell me what's wrong, and I'll do whatever I can to make things right for you."

"I need to…."

A warning bell chimed, interrupting her confession. The alarm alerted the patrons that the restaurant was about to move again. Yanamai had to wait until another opportunity presented itself. They stood and returned to their seats inside. As the evening progressed, she pretended to enjoy herself. They visited some strange and beautiful places. The restaurant took them to Egypt, Brazil, Hawaii, Great Britain, and Japan. Finally, as they moved toward the Eiffel tower in France, she could not hold back her feelings anymore, and her eyes welled up with tears.

"Please, tell me what's wrong. I hate to see you upset."

She blinked them away and whispered, "I need to tell you something, and you will not like it."

Oh boy, here it comes; you're a nice guy, but... Or it's not you; it's me.

"I am not Garbi. I am Yanamai."

"What?" Michael's jaw dropped.

Yanamai took a deep breath, "Garbi had somewhere else to be this morning," she paused. *It is even more challenging than I thought.*

He put the pieces together during her pause, "That was you this morning!"

"Yes."

The warning bell chimed again, alerting the patrons that the restaurant was about to move. *Oh, will you stop ringing that bell!* Without warning, he walked away, leaving her alone on the deck. She followed him to their table; he had positioned his chair to face away from her; the restaurant passed through another portal.

"Michael, please talk to me," she begged.

He angrily spun around and whispered, "Congratulations, you fooled me. I guess you two had a long, hard laugh at my expense."

"It was not like that at all."

"This is very petty for something as trivial as spilling food on a jacket. I told you this morning I would have paid for it."

"This has nothing to do with the accident."

"Then why play these games? If Garbi had to be somewhere else, all she had to do is tell me."

"She was with Jason."

"Jason?"

"She met him before you."

"Are you saying that Garbi was dating Jason when she asked me to walk her home?"

"I do not know if *dating* is the right word. She met him before you. After asking you out for breakfast, he called her. Having met him first, she thought it only fair to go out with him before you."

"Are you saying she wants to date both of us?"

"Just until deciding which one of you she preferred."

"Since you're here, it's obvious she likes him more."

"Well, not really. It did not work out between them, and since you asked me, I mean her, out for dinner, she planned to be here."

"Why are you here instead?"

Yanamai swallowed hard, "Well, during our date this morning...."

Michael interrupted her, "You know what, it doesn't matter. I don't want to know, and I don't care."

The restaurant stopped moving, and an announcer told everyone to exit. Michael stood, threw his cloth napkin on the table, and briskly walked away.

Again, she followed him, "Wait, you have not heard my side of the story!"

"I think we covered it all," he replied, without breaking his stride.

"Not everything," she insisted, reaching out to grab his arm, stopping him.

Reluctantly, Michael turned to face her.

"What else is there?"

"Something unexpected happened to me."

"Oh, do tell."

"I discovered that I like you a lot."

"Ha!" he blurted out loudly, drawing the attention of other patrons passing by.

He turned and continued walking. Again, she ran to catch up with him.

"Why did you laugh? I had hoped my feelings for you would mean something."

"Um, no. Why should your feelings matter to me because it is clear you don't care about mine?"

"I do care about your feelings. I struggled all night, trying to figure out a way to reveal my identity and how I feel about you."

"Meanwhile, I paid for an expensive meal at one of the most sought-after restaurants in the world. I discovered that the woman I thought I was dating wasn't here. Instead, it's her sister who hates me."

"I do not hate you, and I did not tell you earlier because I just wanted to have another fond memory of you."

"Wow! You are something else. It's all about you and what you want. Isn't it? Look, just leave me alone."

"Can we see each other again?"

"You must be joking."

"No, I am not; I *really* do like you."

"Since you don't understand the obvious signs, let me clarify so that even an alien will comprehend. I wouldn't go out with you if you were the last person on Earth!"

"Why?"

"Why?" he repeated in disbelief.

"Yes, I deceived you, and I apologized because when I agreed to stand in for Garbi, I did not have these feelings for you."

"So, it's all right to deceive someone if you don't like them?"

"That is not what I meant."

"That's what you did."

"You are twisting my words around. I did it as a favor for my sister. I never thought you would find out."

"Ah, so it's all right to deceive someone if they don't find out."

"Michael, stop this. I am trying to explain that I never meant to hurt you. All I am asking for is forgiveness. I want us to go out again tomorrow. We can start over fresh. How about another breakfast in that beautiful aviary? I will bring the fruit this time."

Shaking his head, he spun around without saying another word and walked away, leaving her alone. She watched him leave and was more determined than ever to figure out a way to get back into his good graces. Since he was too angry to speak with her, she would wait a few Earthian minutes and try to reason with him again.

Chapter 16

Akil
Argi City
The 22,281st Terrestrial Rotation of the Second Summer

Having achieved his goal, Otsoa sat in Zorion's old chair. Before the cities moved underground, Artisans made the seat cover from the skins of a long-extinct beast. While sliding down onto the leather surface, he reveled because it felt good beneath him. Although it was not much different from any other seat, the sheer power it represented excited him. Now, everyone in Argi had to obey *his* commands; in his mind, it was long overdue.

The only downside was the number of forms he had to review, sign, or reject. He did not expect or like it and decided to find someone else to do the mundane tasks, leaving him free to follow other pursuits. At the top of that list were Yanamai and Nayrah. He finished work and noticed someone had opened the side door without his knowledge. Standing within its frame, he saw Gecheana watching him. He stood, waving at her to come inside.

"I see you have settled into your new position as Argi's Sovereign quite well."

"Yes. Thanks to you."

"Elazar has been telling everyone that you did indeed ignite the sword. Soon, public opinion will side with you, and then we will make our grab for power, making you Akil's Supreme Sovereign within a few Terrestrial Revolutions."

"You have been true to your word so far. I am Argi's Sovereign, but I still lack two things: Nayrah's head and Yanamai by my side."

"I am close to finding Nayrah; it will not be long until I give her head to you. As for Yanamai, I will make myself look like her mother and record a video pretending to be ill; seeing it, she will come home at once."

"Even if she finds out I am in charge?"

"She loves her parents, which is one of her many weaknesses, so trust me; she will return, and you may do with her what you will."

"Our social laws will not permit me to have Durnah and Yanamai simultaneously. If I change the law, my advisors tell me the elites will withdraw their support. How do I fix this problem?"

"Simple, kill Durnah with this," she handed him a potion.

Taking it from her, he examined the clear liquid inside.

"Do not let it touch your skin, or you will perish with her, allowing Va'ron to take your seat in the Argi House."

After hearing that his younger sibling would replace him, Otsoa decided to kill him as a precaution. He heard stories about siblings killing one another to take control of the city's House and would not allow that to happen to him.

"Will it look like she contracted the sickness?"

"It *is* the sickness. I created it to eliminate anyone who opposes me."

"I will be careful with it."

"Good. See that you do. Now, there is one more thing."

"Yes."

"I want you to set up a meeting with the ambassador from Earth. Inform him that you are now in charge. I will go with you as an advisor. We must ensure our new allies that the agreement between our two worlds will remain intact."

"I will have Shilda contact him right away."

"After the meeting, I will resume my search for the Saiph and Nayrah. There will not be a place in Argi they can hide. Once I eliminate them, no one can stop us."

Chapter 17

Earth
The Regime - Texas - Houston - George Bush Park
May 17, 2452

While Larkin met with General Bailey, Sarah and Dr. Grant worked together to convince Sable that the evil man in her dreams could not hurt her. First, they tried telling her he was either too old or 'had gone to heaven,' as Sarah put it. They were unsuccessful and discussed their options in the adjacent room, out of Sable's hearing range.

"Sable clearly understands what we've told her yet insists that she didn't see him on the television until yesterday," Dr. Grant explained.

"Where could she have seen him?" Sarah asked.

"I think she did see him on television, but she doesn't remember watching it because of her young age. Since the images she saw were disturbing, I'll leave a very mild sedative for her. Use it for a week, and if she doesn't have the dream in a few days, maybe she'll forget about it," Dr. Grant responded.

"All right. I'll give it a try and let you know if it works or not."

After he left, Sarah sat thinking of Larkin's abilities. For years, she knew that the things he did during patrol were not typical human behavior. Still, it never occurred to her that Sable would have similar skills. Also, Larkin never talked about seeing the future, making her wonder if Sable inherited some of his traits with different gifts. The only problem with her theory was that Ethan Brun had to be in his eighties by now, assuming he was still alive.

Even more confusing is why he would want to hurt them. They did not even know him. Frustrated, Sarah pushed the thoughts out of her mind, gave Sable her medicine, and put her down for the night. She watched her fall asleep and stepped outside, where two soldiers sat in a Jeep about a hundred feet from the house. Knowing her dad, two more were hiding in the brush behind the house for support.

Their presence did little to comfort her. Sable's insistence, combined with Larkin's strange abilities, made her feel uneasy, so she locked the door behind her, opened the closet, removed the 12-gauge shotgun and the flare gun, and sat in the living room with the television on, hoping to shake off the dreadful feeling.

Chapter 18

Earth - Scotland
May 17, 2452
Dunnottar Castle

Dawn read Ethan's report while tapping her oak desk loudly; it was a clear sign that she was not happy with the results of his mission. At least he was careful; Corporal Boyd was unaware of his betrayal and confirmed his account of Tucker's sudden attack on them.

"I don't understand. Are you sure you didn't provoke him in any way?"

"I'm positive. Boyd was there and saw the same thing I did."

"What a waste. I needed to meet with him. At least there's someone else I can try to speak with."

"There is?"

"Yes," she handed him another dossier. "Larkin is Tucker's younger brother. He works for the resistance."

"The report on him is light. All you gave me was a grainy photo and an address. Do we know anything else about him?"

"I haven't had time to work up a complete background on him. I've heard a rumor that he's married; you might run into his wife at home."

"What are my orders?"

"By my calculation, Larkin will be at work soon. Hopefully, you'll catch him before he leaves. If not, I'll send you early tomorrow. You'll land about a hundred yards from his house. Take the dirt road to his front door and knock. Be polite. I don't want anything to go wrong this time. When you speak to him, ask if we can meet. Get the place and time of his choosing. Are those instructions clear?"

"Yes; what if he refuses to meet with you?"

"Give him my card and tell him I'll give him a pure gold brick for his trouble."

Ethan raised an eyebrow, "You mean a solid gold brick, like the ones that used to be in Fort Knox?"

"Yes. Why?"

"I'm just curious what these men have that you want so badly."

"They don't *have* anything, and why I want to meet with them is none of your concern. Your job is to set up a meeting. Now hurry. It's 11:30 PM here, which means it's 5:30 PM there. The sun will set in about fifteen minutes. I want you to catch him before he leaves for work."

"What about our weapons?"

"You won't need them for this mission."

"You're sending us into a war zone unarmed."

"Fine. Let your men take their weapons but leave yours behind. You cannot approach Larkin armed."

"I understand. Is there anything else?"

"That's all. Now get moving."

Ethan left her office and hurried to the Transportation Station, where his men waited for him. During their short break between missions, Ethan made it a point to know the four men under his command. The best way to bond with colleagues such as these was to buy them a beer or two. Since they spoke more freely after the second round, he decided to tell Boyd that Dawn cloned his body. There was a long moment of silence until Boyd confessed the same secret.

He also told him that the rest of his team, Colin, Ben, and Scott, had accepted Dawn's generous offer, so it was no surprise to find out that they each had a cyanide capsule implanted in their brain. The discussion changed to figuring out how to find the transmitter or someone who could remove it. Ben mentioned hiring a Regime doctor because they used portal technology in certain surgeries. The idea gave them hope of escaping Dawn one day.

Knowing they had the same dilemma formed a bond; they became brothers, fighting for a common goal. His team's help made the odds of their success more in his favor. Ethan removed all his weapons at the Transportation Station and briefed his team on their new mission. Later, he nodded to Mitch, who opened a portal to Houston, and they walked through the event horizon.

Chapter 19

Akil
Argi City
The 22,281[st] Terrestrial Rotation of the Second Summer

On the one-hundred-fiftieth level, Julie waited in the shadows of the southern courtyard for Nayrah to arrive. Olan selected the location to ensure the meeting place was far from their safe house and that no one was in the area, guaranteeing their discussion would go unnoticed. As an added precaution, he told Julie to arrive at least one hour early. If Nayrah saw her leaving the hidden tunnels, they would lose the advantage of moving about the city secretly.

Julie glanced in the general direction of where Olan stayed hidden. Hopefully, the artifact High Priest Kexel lent them would keep Nayrah's Skean senses from detecting him. *We'll know soon enough.* She took a deep breath, pulled the headpiece down to cover her face, hiding her identity, stepped out into the light of the courtyard, and using the High Lord's power, searched the area for any sign of Nayrah. Moments later, she sensed her approaching.

She smiled underneath her headpiece at Olan's prowess. Nayrah arrived forty-five minutes early, as he predicted. Julie did not get a good look at her the last time they met because her mind focused more on Zorion's death. Seeing Nayrah's pale, thin face, combined with short, straight, black hair, giving her a gothic look, made Julie shiver. Also, her smile reminded Julie of old paintings depicting witches stirring a cauldron, eerie and wicked.

"You are prompt. I like that in a colleague," Nayrah smiled.

"We're not colleagues," Julie articulated through her mask, which distorted her voice.

"For the moment, we are."

"Let's get one thing straight. We're not friends or even casual acquaintances. We're enemies, working toward a similar goal. Once we reach that goal, you will try to kill me, so don't bother acting like we're best friends. You will not trick me."

"My, someone is irritable. Having a bad Terrestrial Revolution, are we?"

"Just tell me what your plan is, Nayrah," Julie hoped to confirm her identity.

"Now, I wonder where you heard that name," she marveled, searching for a familiar presence until her scan failed to detect anyone. With a knowing grin, she returned her attention to Julie and said, "Very well, since we're putting away pretenses, please be kind enough to remove your headpiece, Julie."

"Fine," Julie removed her headpiece.

"Ah, that is better. That suit of yours is quite blinding."

"That's the idea."

"It will be a good distraction when we attack my Skean sisters."

"Are they coming?"

"As promised. I contacted them earlier. They think Gecheana has called the meeting, which means they will not suspect an attack. I set it up in my old apartment. Please, follow me."

"Where is your old apartment?" Julie asked before moving a step.

She wanted to ensure that Olan, who was nearby, could hear where they were heading if it was a trap.

"Why, at the lowest level, where it is darkest. Where else would a Skean live?"

Julie put the headpiece back on and followed her to the nearest elevator. As the doors closed, Julie felt nervous in such close quarters with a mortal enemy. She moved her hand on top of the hilt of her sword, just in case Nayrah changed her mind and decided to kill her Skean sisters alone.

"I do not want you to be surprised when you see them. My sisters look like I am now," Nayrah remarked.

"You use your shapeshifting abilities to hide your numbers."

"Very clever, Julie. Yes. That is why we do it."

"How did you figure out who I am?"

"It was quite simple. Gecheana (our soon-to-be former Skean mother) ensured that any Akilian with the potential to become Saiphs died as infants, and around the time you and the ambassador arrived, we felt your presence, so it had to be one or the other. Since the ambassador could never fit into the tight outfit you have on, I knew it had to be you."

"You can see the outfit through the reflection?"

"Do not worry. It is only visible at certain angles if you pay close attention, which I have practiced for some time. If you remember, after Gecheana attacked Zorion, we spoke for a few hundred heartbeats. I used that time to work past the reflective glow and briefly saw your outfit without the glare. Only someone your size could fit into something that small, yet Gecheana thinks the ambassador is the Saiph, a mistake that will cost her life."

"I'd rather not talk about Zorion if you don't mind."

"I am sorry. Were you two friends?"

"Yes."

"In any event, I understand she is having a meeting with the ambassador at the same moment we will be dispatching my Skean siblings, so she will sense them leave this world and know it is not him."

"That means she'll start looking for me."

"At least this way, the ambassador will still be alive. I thought you would appreciate the gesture."

"You need him alive too. If she kills him, Supreme Commander Porter will end relations with Akil, leaving us on a dying world."

Nayrah smiled, "You are very astute, and you are correct; it would not help me if she killed him. Since birth, I have known that we must leave this world, but I would rather go as a queen than a pauper."

"You'll have to beat me before you can leave."

"In time, my dear, in time."

The elevator doors opened, and Julie felt cold, damp air rush over her body, giving her a chill. Following Nayrah, they moved through the thick fog that made it hard to see more than ten feet in any direction. Even the lights struggled to shine through such a dense gloom. Since maintenance workers did not replace the burnt-out lamps, there were long unlit sections between them, so Julie had to rely on her instincts to guide her through. As they walked in the dark, Julie found it peculiar seeing Nayrah because it was like looking through someone else's eyes.

They reached the apartment, and Nayrah showed her where to expect her Skean sisters to sit. In their custom, Nayrah sat near the door, which would help with her trap. The others would sit around the small table, equally spaced apart. Two would have their backs toward the door, where Julie would enter adjacent to the dining area. Nayrah explained the seating arrangements, told Julie whom to attack and led her to hide.

"Cloak your presence, as you did at the ceremony, because they will be here shortly.   They will eat first. Traditionally, Gecheana sets out food for everyone, which means they will expect it. Once they finish, their eyes will be heavy with sleep."

"I didn't know that moss can make you sleepy?"

"It does with poison sprinkled over it."

"You're going to drug them?"

"Why not? It is two against four; we need the advantage. Besides, it is how Gecheana slew the Akilian Saiphs."

"Why don't you give them enough to make them sleep and kill them yourself?"

"Their Skean sense will tell them something is wrong with the food if I put too much on it. On the other hand, if I put just enough to make them sleepy, the shadows will not alert them of the drug."

"Damn! I have much to learn about Skeans."

"Yes, except you will not live long enough to find out."

"I guess we'll see."

"Gecheana did not call the meeting. Therefore, she will not arrive. After they eat, my sisters will question her tardiness, and at that moment, I will say, '*I will contact her.*' That is your cue to come out of the room with your sword in hand and ignite. Allow your cloak to fall, so it will surprise and scare them when they sense your sudden presence. Do not hesitate to kill them, or you *will* die."

"Don't worry. I understand the situation."

"Good."

"If you and your Skean sisters will look exactly alike, how can I distinguish between you?"

With her right hand, she reached into her pocket, pulled out a small red ribbon-like piece of material, and tied it to her right wrist.

"If you see this red string, you will know it is me.   Any questions?"

"Nope. I'm ready."

"Good. Now cloak yourself. I sense them at the elevator."

Using the technique Urki taught her, Julie concentrated, and her presence faded, making it impossible for Nayrah or her Skean sisters to sense her, so Nayrah closed the door, and a few minutes later, Julie heard the others arrive.

"Why are you here?" Julie heard one of the Skean sisters ask.

"Jadell did not wish to attend and ordered me to take her place. I am sure you can understand the reason," Nayrah answered.

"Gecheana should kill both of you. We would not be in this mess if you had done your job correctly," another Skean sister added.

"Maybe this is why Gecheana called us together," Nayrah lied.

Nervous, Julie felt her heart pounding and slowed it using a calming technique as Nayrah offered the others some food. Julie heard dishes clanging for a few minutes as they filled their plates with the drug-coated moss. There were mumblings of conversations too low for her translator to interpret. The waiting was difficult. Thinking Nayrah may have deceived her (to get her in a room with five Skeans) nagged at her continuously. She wiped her sweaty palms from time to time until they finished their last meal. Finally, Julie heard Nayrah clearing the table.

"Where is Gecheana? She is never late," Julie heard one of the Skean sisters ask.

"I will contact her."

Springing from her hiding place, Julie released her cloak and ignited her sword. All Nayrah's Skean sisters turned to look at Julie with fear and surprise. The looks on their faces were priceless. It almost made her laugh. Knowing she was moments away from the fight of her life brought her back to reality.

Nayrah stood, pointed at Julie, and yelled, "Saiph!"

Taking advantage of the surprise, Julie swung her sword at the nearest Skean. She quickly brought her sword down at a sharp angle, slicing from the left side of her neck to underneath her right arm. Simultaneously, Nayrah brought her sword horizontally through Udara's neck, killing her instantly. Julie and Nayrah moved to strike down the remaining two sisters, but they drew their swords and blocked the attack. *Damn, Nayrah said they would be sleepy by now.*

Nayrah fought her opponent, and Julie concentrated on hers. Each battled feverishly. Their swords arced in semi-circles as they hummed through the air to attack and block. Since the room was small, their glowing blades cut anything in their path. For example, Julie cut off a large chunk of the table that was the room's centerpiece without realizing it. The wedge fell to the floor as she spun to block another attack in a series of swings. On the other side of the room, Nayrah and Kemena fought fiercely.

Kemena used her power to knock the door off its hinges, hoping to escape; Nayrah did not allow it. Nevertheless, as they fought, Kemena managed to maneuver herself to the door and back out onto the avenue. Their blades cut new openings in the door frame as they passed through. Outside, Nayrah struck Kemena with hate and rage, making her powerful. Kemena owed her a debt, and this Terrestrial Rotation Nayrah planned to collect it.

"What is wrong, Kemena? You seem scared," Nayrah continued to fluently swing her sword through the air at a blinding pace.

"I am not afraid of you!" she spat.

"Gecheana is not here to save you this time, you little wretch!"

"I do not need her help. I can defeat you all on my own!"

"Ha! We will see!"

Unlike their last encounter, Nayrah did not wait long for Kemena to tire because the potion was already working. As they fought, Nayrah pushed forward, edging Kemena increasingly backward into the darkness. The invisible hands that guided her kept the blade moving faster than the eye could see and quicker than she could even think. A few hundred heartbeats later, Kemena started faltering. Waiting for just the right moment, Nayrah paid close attention to Kemena's balance. Once Kemena overstepped her attack, Nayrah brought her blade down, severing the wrist that held her sword.

"Ah!" Kemena exclaimed.

Hovering the blade's tip, a finger's width from Kemena's throat, Nayrah pushed her back until reaching a support column, where she stopped.

"We should have killed you," Kemena hissed.

"What stopped you?"

"Gecheana forbade it."

"It looks like I am not the only one around here who makes mistakes."

Without warning, Nayrah pierced Kemena's neck with her sword. Unable to fight back or run, Kemena had to endure Nayrah's wrath. As the hot blade pushed its way through cartilage and flesh, Kemena gurgled with wide, frightened eyes and reflexively reached for the sword with her other hand in a desperate move to pull it out. Her fingers could not withstand the sharp, hot blade as it severed them on contact.

Nayrah wished there had been more time to torture Kemena but had to ensure Julie was still alive. Before Nayrah moved the blade sideways to end her life, Kemena frantically used her bloody stubs to grasp at Nayrah, hoping to stop her. At long last, Nayrah flicked her wrist, severing Kemena's head. Gravity pulled it to the ground, and Nayrah watched it roll off into the darkness. Now that she satisfied her thirst for revenge, it was time to see how Julie was fairing with Domeka, Gecheana's favorite of the five Skean sisters.

Nayrah returned to the room, surprised to see them still fighting. By now, the drug made Domeka slow and careless; Julie being a novice, was still no match for her. Nayrah did not intervene because she wanted to see if Julie had improved from their last encounter. Watching her move, Nayrah almost felt disappointed that Julie had not progressed. Her form had no grace; her defense and attack looked sloppy. Still, she kept Domeka from getting past her defenses, which was something.

Domeka noticed Nayrah watching and yelled, "Betrayer!"

"It takes one to know one," Nayrah chided.

"Would you mind giving me some help?" Julie requested, her voice still muffled through the headpiece.

"How else are you going to learn? What will you do when you face me? Do you expect me to help you defeat me?"

Underneath her headpiece, Julie frowned, furrowing her lips in frustration yet keeping her focus on Domeka.

"Gecheana will destroy you for this!" Domeka yelled.

"I am sure she will try."

"Siding with a Saiph is heresy!"

"Yet, I can trust the Saiph more than my Skean sisters. Is that not also heresy?"

"You *putok*! I told Gecheana to destroy you at the last yellow harvest."

"All my Skean sisters have hard feelings toward me, yet you look surprised at my actions. You must be getting dim of sight, sister."

"After I kill this Saiph, I will hack you into pieces," Domeka threatened.

"Hey, if you two want to fight, I'd be glad to step outside," Julie quipped.

"You will not get away from me that easy," Domeka challenged vengefully.

As they continued to fight, Nayrah watched Julie closely, using her gift of keen observation to figure out her problem, debating whether to tell her until she could not stand to see the imperfection any longer.

"You continue to let your power dictate every move. You will never progress if you do not put yourself in the fight," Nayrah instructed.

"I'm doing my best," exasperated Julie.

Nayrah shook her head, "No, you are not. It is what I mean precisely. I know you are capable of much more, even as a novice; you either lack confidence or are afraid."

"Yes, I'm afraid! I've never fought to the death. Now, if you don't mind, I need to focus."

"As you wish," Nayrah responded, waving her hand dismissively.

The fight continued for a few hundred heartbeats, to the point that Nayrah was getting bored, so in the interest of ending the mind-numbing event, she decided to help. With a motion of her hand, she sent an invisible wall of power toward Domeka's left ankle, making it snap. Stumbling, Domeka had to support her weight with a nearby chair, crippling her ability to fight at full strength.

"Now, will you please end this? I have things to do," Nayrah commented impatiently.

Taking advantage of Nayrah's help, Julie cut through Domeka's wrist and spun around to sever her head. It bounced on the floor before rolling into a corner. Julie sheathed her sword and removed her headpiece, trying to catch her breath, which took several minutes.

"Why did you wait so long to help me?" Julie wondered.

"Because I had hoped you would have shown improvement. You should be embarrassed at your display, even as a novice."

"You realize I've only been doing this for a couple of days, right?"

"Do not let this feed your ego; the power I sense coming from you should have been enough to take down a drugged Skean. The only one, who is making you fight horribly, is you."

"I'm sorry to disappoint you."

"I had hoped you would be a little more challenging. I should not complain because once we finish our joint mission, I will end you and claim the spoils."

"Thanks for the warm and fuzzy feeling."

"Enough chatting. We still have their children to dispatch before we take on Gecheana."

"And, I guess you still need my help for them too."

"Do you think their children are any less dangerous?"

"No. I'm sure they're all deadly."

"Exactly. No sense taking any chances, now, is there?"

"No, but I'll need some rest before we go."

"Very well, go home and get your rest. I sense Gecheana approaching anyway, so you must take a different elevator up. I will see you on the following Terrestrial Revolution at our last meeting spot at the same time as before."

Without another word, Nayrah left the apartment and disappeared into the darkness. Before leaving, Julie stared at the corpses on the floor and shook her head. *How did I get here?* She sensed someone approaching, looked outside, and put her hand to the hilt of her sword. As he came closer, she realized it was Olan and relaxed.

"Come, Julie. We must leave now!"

Chapter 20

Earth
The Regime - Texas - Houston - Border to Gang Territory
May 17, 2452

While patrolling the border, Larkin sensed imminent danger. He raised his fist to signal his men to stop and motioned for them to find a safe position. As they moved to a secure spot, Larkin felt dread coming over him. The sensation was like when Sarah and Sable were in trouble and Tucker trapped him in the *Pit* with Rico. Gunfire erupted across the road, so Larkin and his men returned fire.

Yelling over the noise of gunfire and explosions, he told his Radio Telephone Operator to call for backup. Having the high ground, the attackers kept Larkin's platoon pinned at their location. Hearing the sound and frequency of their bullets pass by, Larkin knew they were using different weapons than before. The steady flow of slugs, accompanied by a more precise aim, was a clear sign that they had upgraded. *Someone has been shopping.* The bombardment was so extreme that even he did not feel safe enough to move through the barrage, as in times past. Still, he had to do something.

Instinctively, he reached for the grenades strapped to his uniform. One at a time, he removed their pins and hurled them to where his intuition guided them. Explosions, followed by horrific screams, made him grin with satisfaction, but the grenades did not kill enough attackers because they had him and his men pinned down. Minutes seemed to pass like hours until the sound of tank cannons filled the air. The hill, on the other side, lit up like July 4th.

As the attackers retreated, Larkin and his men came out of their hiding places, filling the air with return fire, killing many. Once the gang raiders were no longer within range, Larkin yelled over the cannon fire to his Radio Telephone Operator.

"Call off the tanks so that we can pursue!"

The tank cannons stopped, so Larkin ordered his men forward. They chased the others, firing their weapons. Before going too far, Larkin stopped because the feeling of dread heightened to a sickening level. Looking toward his home, he saw a flare rising in the sky. *Oh no, Sarah and Sable are in trouble*! Larkin put Murphy (who recently

returned to active duty) in charge of the platoon, and before Lieutenant
Blake could stop him, he disappeared into the night to save his family.

Chapter 21

Earth
Regime - Texas - Houston - Burke Farm
May 17, 2452

Ethan and his men landed about a hundred yards from Larkin's home with the sun low on the horizon. To make time, they started running as the portal closed behind them. Their goal was to speak to Larkin before work. Nearing the home, they spotted a military vehicle parked in front of the house and stopped. Ethan motioned for his men to crouch as he surveyed the area through binoculars.

"I see two soldiers sitting in the Jeep; if there are any more, they're well hidden," he whispered.

"What do you want to do?" Boyd questioned.

"I'll talk to them unarmed; I won't pose a threat. I'll approach and ask to see Larkin; they'll frisk me and hopefully call him outside."

"I don't like this. Why would he have soldiers at his home?"

"We're near the line between the gangs and the resistance; I think it's obvious he wants to ensure they're protected. I can't blame him for that," Ethan explained.

"It's too risky; we should come back tomorrow," Boyd advised.

"No. Dawn wants us to make contact tonight. If I'm not a threat, nothing will happen."

"All right, it's your call."

"Take a position here in the brush. We're about a hundred feet from the house, which should be far enough away so that the soldiers won't see you. No matter what happens, don't shoot anyone. Dawn wants this to be a peaceful meeting."

"Roger that."

With his hands raised, Ethan walked toward the soldiers' vehicle. Seeing him, one spoke into the vehicle's loudspeaker. He stopped, and they rushed out of their Jeep, pointing their weapons at him, yelling.

"Get down on the ground, now!"

"Easy men. I'm unarmed."

"I said, get down on the ground!"

"Ok, relax. You're in control."

Kneeling, Ethan kept his hands raised and was careful not to make sudden movements. He lay prone on the ground, and one of the soldiers secured his hands with a plastic restraint; others searched for weapons, lifted him onto his feet, and began questioning him.

"I'm here to speak with Larkin," Ethan spoke calmly.

"What business do you have with him?"

"I'm here on behalf of Dawn Pierce. She would like to meet with him. Now, please, let him know I'm here so I can deliver the message."

"What's all the noise?" Sarah asked, walking out the front door with her shotgun in hand.

"Please stay inside, ma'am," one of the officers warned.

In her usual fashion, Sarah did not obey and studied their visitor, "He looks familiar."

"Do you know him, ma'am?" the soldier inquired.

"Mrs. Burke, my name is Ethan," he started to say until one of the soldiers hit him in the stomach with the butt of his gun to silence him.

Since they restrained him, Ethan had to absorb the blow, making him double over in pain.

"That's enough," Sarah ordered, moving closer to get a better look.

"I recognize you. You're Sergeant Ethan Brun, the Butcher of Logan County," Sarah commented.

She remembered her daughter's nightmares and felt all the blood rush from her face, turning her skin white.

"Sable was right," she whispered to herself.

The soldiers looked at her quizzically, uncertain whether to release him.

Sighing at how his past had caught up to him, Ethan frowned, "I didn't kill those people; I'm only here to speak with Larkin."

The sound of the soldier's radio caught his attention. Although hearing distorted words, he surmised that others were guarding the home. It became apparent that they discovered his team on the east side. Gunfire erupted from the west side of the house, sending bullets in their direction.

Knowing his men were under attack, Ethan yelled, "Do not return fire! Retreat!"

Turning to Sarah for help, Ethan hoped to convince her to stop the soldiers from slaughtering his men; before he could speak a word, she shot a flare into the sky and joined in the shooting, using the shotgun in her hand.

"No, please! We're not here to harm you!" Ethan yelled.

"I'm hit!" the cry came from where his men were hiding.

To Ethan, it sounded like Scott's voice; abruptly, his men returned fire. Bullets soared past Ethan from both sides, forcing him to crouch to stay out of their path.

"Please, Sarah, go inside the house!" Ethan yelled; she ignored him.

Aiming, she repeatedly fired into the bushes, where the soldiers discovered Ethan's team hiding.

"Grenade!" a distant voice yelled, just moments before the explosion.

The blast's concussion left Ethan momentarily deaf, with a loud ringing in his ears. Stunned, he fell to his knees, watching the battle continue without him. The grenade exploded near the house, setting it on fire, and Ethan saw Sarah dash toward the building for unknown reasons. Before she reached the front steps, he saw her head snap.

Blood spattered everywhere, even onto his face and clothes. As the events unfolded, it was as if the explosion put everyone in slow motion, and in the same gradual manner, she fell lifeless to the ground. Flashbacks of the Logan massacre haunted his thoughts. Still disoriented from the grenade, he struggled to reach her and kneeled awkwardly to check for a pulse because the guard had left his hands tied behind his back.

He tried to find evidence that she was still alive, unaware that the shooting had stopped; someone grabbed him underneath his shoulder, lifted him to his feet, and cut his hands free from the plastic restraints.

"Two men hid in the bushes on the west side. We neutralized them. One soldier is dead, and the other ran off into the woods," Boyd reported.

Ethan had begun to regain his composure, shook off some of the effects of the concussion, and yelled, "What the hell is wrong with you? I told you not to shoot!"

"We didn't until Scott got hit. We were trying to get the hell out of there; he took one in the back, so while Colin treated him, Ben and I had to return fire, hoping they would take cover, which would take some of the pressure off us."

He looked back at Sarah, "You killed his wife!"

"It must have been friendly fire. Ben and I aimed for the ground."

Replaying Sarah's death in his mind, Ethan tried to remember how her head moved as the bullet hit her; with everything going on at the time, he could not recall it. Ethan approached the soldier, who restrained him, and checked for a pulse but found none. He examined the body and saw a bullet hole dead center in his chest. Boyd inspected the others to see if there were survivors.

"I found two in the brush. They're dead."

"Damn it! How did this happen?" Ethan yelled.

"I saw the soldiers on the road wearing night-vision goggles. They must have scanned the area, seen us hiding in the brush, and thought we would attack."

"Is Scott all right?"

"I put a bandage over the wound; he's going to need surgery soon," Colin urged.

"Should I call for extraction?" Boyd inquired.

Watching the house burning bright in the darkness of the night, Ethan sighed, "Yeah. I think we've done enough damage for one night. Don't you?"

*****

Running and teleporting himself forward, Larkin moved fast. The closer he came to his home, the more nauseous his stomach became. At one point, Larkin felt a sharp pain in his head that nearly tripped him. Ignoring it, he pushed forward even faster. He saw smoke and flames rising above the trees a quarter-mile from home.

He desperately drew upon the unseen power within his mind, which increased his abilities, allowing him to teleport the remaining distance in one jump. The scene was horrific. He checked a soldier lying near a Jeep for a pulse and did not find one, so he moved on to another lying on the ground until he recognized a familiar form.

"Sarah!"

He checked for a pulse, did not find one, and began CPR. Moments later, several military vehicles arrived. Bolting from his seat, General Bailey ran to Larkin's side, with paramedics close behind. Moving aside to let them work, Larkin looked to General Bailey for an answer.

"I heard them talkin' on the radio. Someone was here. I came as fast as I could."

Distraught from the pain, Larkin's voice trembled, "Why did they do this?"

"I don't know. Where's Sable?"

"I don't know. I haven't had a chance to look for her. I found Sarah and started CPR."

General Bailey ordered his soldiers to search the area; firefighters extinguished the fire. By now, the flames had spread throughout the whole building, making it that much harder to quench. Yelling for Sable at the top of his lungs, Larkin called for her in every direction, hoping she had made it out of the house. He searched all the secret places she knew to hide and returned to find General Bailey sobbing beside Sarah's body. Moving closer, he saw a more petite frame lying on the ground alongside her.

"No…no!" he yelled, running toward them.

He fell to his knees, wrapped them in his arms for a final embrace, and cried uncontrollably. Sometime later, he set them down, stared at their lifeless bodies in disbelief, and felt the void. Everything he held dear in this world had disappeared. Whoever attacked the house took away his happiness in this life, leaving only darkness. Rage overshadowed his pain. Unable to hold it, he touched the abyss within his mind, hoping it would relieve his agony, but instead, it only fed the anger, causing it to grow.

It came to the surface, making his eyes as black as night, even though he tried to push it away. Within him grew a reservoir of power that swelled until he could no longer hold it; with no one there to take the brunt of his rage, his only choice was to direct the energy into the ground. As it passed through his body, he let out a fierce, primal scream that echoed throughout the valley. Simultaneously, the Earth groaned and shook as if one of its plates were shifting until all the power drained from him, and he collapsed, face down, unconscious.

Chapter 22

Earth
The Regime - Washington, D.C. - Fort McNair
May 17, 2452

Having left Yanamai at the restaurant, Michael returned to his apartment angry and frustrated. He tossed his keys into a bowl and slammed the door behind him. On his way to the kitchen, he saw the bedroom light peeking out from under the door. *That's strange; I don't remember leaving it on.* He opened it, only to find a naked woman posing seductively on his bed. She smiled.

"Care to join me?"

"Mai Li! How did you get in here?" Michael asked.

"I have a visitor's pass."

"No. I mean, how did you get into my room?"

"A friend."

"Why are you here?"

"I thought that was obvious."

"You shouldn't be here."

Moving sensuously, she got out of bed and walked toward him. Backing away, he tried to keep some distance between them until reaching the wall, where she caught him and pressed her naked body firmly against his.

"You don't really want me to go, do you?"

Before he could answer, she leaned in and kissed him. At first, he resisted but decided to surrender to her advances after thinking about Wu Luli, Garbi, and Yanamai. Just as Mai started to pull him back toward the bed, there was a knock at the door.

"Don't answer it," she whispered into his ear and nibbled it.

"Michael!" Yanamai yelled through the door.

"I can't believe she followed me home!" he turned to look at the door.

"Ignore her. She'll go away. Come, lie down with me," Mai pulled him on top of her on the bed.

This time, Yanamai pounded on the door, demanding he answer. Yanamai's persistence distracted him, causing him to look at the door; meanwhile, Mai reached under the pillow and retrieved a syringe. Before she could stick him with it, he got up.

"Sorry, Mai, I can't concentrate. I need to get rid of her."

Without looking back, he started toward the front door. Mai got out of bed to follow. The floor squeaked, causing him to turn around and face Mai, who held a syringe in her right hand.

"What the hell are you doing?" he yelled.

Instead of replying, Mai tried to stick him. Reflexively, he grabbed both her wrists to stop the attack.

"I'm trying to apologize," Yanamai yelled through the door, thinking he was talking to her.

Mai knocked the wind out of him using her knee; still, he held her wrists tightly. Yanamai continued to pound on the door and call for Michael as they struggled. Trained in the Martial Arts, Mai threw a series of kicks at his legs, trying to take him down. Since his knees and shins could not take many more of her attacks, he let go of her left wrist to free his right hand, made a fist, and punched her in the nose, knocking her backward onto the bed. The force of the blow made her roll over the bed, causing her to land on the other side. He shut the bedroom door and ran to let Yanamai in for help. Seeing him, she smiled.

"No time to talk. Get in here and help me!" he yelled.

Yanamai obeyed and stepped inside, smelling perfume, "Is there another woman in here?"

"Yes, in the bedroom. That's why I let you in."

"Excuse me?"

"It's not what you're thinking."

"Why is she in your bedroom?"

"Because Yanamai, like all the women I've met recently, she's crazy. First, she tried to seduce me, then attacked me!"

"I'm not crazy, Michael. You don't understand."

The bedroom door opened, and Mai walked out, wearing a summer dress. She walked toward the front door and kissed Michael on the way out as if nothing had happened.

"Thanks, babe. I had a wonderful time," she smiled smugly at Yanamai and closed the door behind her.

Yanamai stared at him in disbelief with a raised eyebrow, "She does not strike me as someone trying to attack you. My English must not be as good as I thought. Are you sure you do not mean she tried to pounce you?"

"No. She held a syringe in her hand. She was either going to sedate or kill me with it," he explained.

He dialed the number for security, hoping they would catch Mai before leaving the Inner Circle. Yanamai listened to his conversation and realized he was serious about the attack. Later, he ran out into the hallway and chased Mai, hoping to catch up. Removing her high heel shoes, Yanamai followed him.

"Why are you chasing her?"

"I want to know why she attacked me?"

"If you catch up to her, she will try to assault you again, so you should let the security team deal with her."

"I don't plan to capture her; I only want to ensure she doesn't disappear. Soon, every floor will have a security guard patrolling to find her. If I see her, I'll call them," Michael clarified.

They finally reached the elevator as it opened, and a security guard stepped out.

"Did you see her?" Michael inquired, breathing heavily.

"No," the guard answered.

He checked with the other guards on patrol; they had not seen her yet, either.

"How did she escape?" Michael wondered.

"Go back to your apartment. We'll check every floor and knock on doors until we find her. If we do, we'll call you," the sentry stated.

"Thanks," Michael responded distractedly. He returned home, checking every room in his apartment to ensure Mai had not returned until noticing that Yanamai waited for him in the hallway.

As he approached, she questioned, "Can we please talk now?"

Without a reply, he pushed the door closed, leaving her outside.

"That is not very forgiving, Michael. If I had not arrived, she might have succeeded," she yelled through the door.

"Go away before I call security on you too."

Exhaling loudly, she left to go home; his rejection did not deter her because tomorrow, she would have another chance to change his mind.

Chapter 23

Akil
Argi City
The 22,281st Terrestrial Rotation of the Second Summer

With Gecheana by his side, Otsoa entered the meeting room, where Ambassador Reynolds sat patiently at the end of the table, waiting for Zorion to arrive. As they entered, Ambassador Reynolds stood to greet them; Zorion's absence surprised him.

"Forgive me; where is Zorion?" Ambassador Reynolds asked.

"I am Otsoa, Zorion's heir."

Putting his palm forward, Ambassador Reynolds smiled politely and reached out to salute him with a formal Akilian greeting, "I hope you don't mind me asking what happened to him?"

"There was an attack earlier today; he is dead. Therefore, as his heir, I have taken his place as Argi's Sovereign."

"That's terrible news. I'm sorry for your loss," Ambassador Reynolds glanced at Otsoa's companion.

"This is Gecheana. She is my advisor," Otsoa remarked.

Turning his attention to her, Ambassador Reynolds greeted her in the typical Akilian fashion. She touched the palm of his hand and searched for any sign that he might be a Saiph but found none.

"I must notify Supreme Commander Porter of the change," Ambassador Reynolds advised.

"I will escort you to the Interstellar Transport Bay, where you can send a video message unless you prefer to return to Earth to deliver the news personally."

"I need to know whether you plan to honor Zorion's agreement with the Regime."

"Absolutely. It will be a smooth transition. Everything Zorion agreed to, I agree to as well."

"Excellent. I'll be glad to relay the news to our Supreme Commander."

Still unsure whether the ambassador was a Saiph, Gecheana had to assume the worst. While reaching for her sword, she sensed the Saiph at a distance and felt the deaths of two Skean daughters, Udara and Tesol. The shock was devastating, forcing her to sit.

"Is everything all right?" Ambassador Reynolds inquired, seeing the distress on her face.

"Yes. I will be fine. Just give me a moment," Gecheana answered, closing her eyes to search for Domeka and Kemena, hoping they were still alive.

She sensed their presence in Argi. *Why are they here?* Using her connection to her Skean daughters, she focused on them and sensed that they were in a battle for their lives, except Kemena fought against another Skean. Knowing how each one felt through her power, she could tell it was Nayrah. *You Putok! You will pay for this betrayal!* She focused on Domeka and saw her fighting the Saiph. Reflexively she raised her hand to cover her eyes, sensing the glaring light of his or her power because it was like standing in Domeka's place.

"I must leave right away," Gecheana walked toward the door.

"I hope you'll feel better," Ambassador Reynolds responded; Gecheana ignored him.

She approached the elevators and used the Night Lord's power to push those waiting in line out of the way. Alone on the elevator, she closed her eyes as it descended to see if Domeka was still alive. It pleased her to sense her life source, so she focused on Kemena. Through their bond, she felt the pain of Nayrah's blade as it sank into Kemena's throat. Still descending, she fell to her knees, choking and coughing until Kemena died and the link faded.

With Kemena gone, Domeka was her last, loyal Skean daughter. Returning her focus to Domeka, Gecheana watched her fight the Saiph using the Night Lord's power. Hoping Domeka would stay alive until reaching her, Gecheana cursed the elevator for not moving faster. She felt Domeka's left ankle break; the pain was short-lived because her bond with Domeka had also disappeared. Now, she was dead too. Having reached the bottom, she darted out of the elevator to the apartment.

She stopped several paces from the door and saw Kemena's body lying on the moss. With her sword in hand, she walked into the apartment and saw the carnage. Rage overwhelmed her, and she screamed. Every Skean daughter was dead, save one, the betrayer. Sensing Nayrah and the Saiph fleeing, Gecheana stepped outside into the dark fog.

Using her powers to magnify her voice, she exclaimed, "I will find both of you! When I do, I will repay you for what you have done! Do you hear me, Nayrah? Do you hear me?"

Her voice echoed through the lower level's darkness and into the secret passages. Hearing her voice, Olan and Julie paused to look at each other.

Olan smiled, "If she is angry, we are doing our job correctly. Now we must return home."

Chapter 24

Earth
Spain - Madrid
May 17, 2452

Vincent approached the crime scene and saw Alex standing about two stories high on a platform. A Regime crew worked all night, sifting through the debris, trying to find evidence of a body. They did not find anything, leaving him with only two possibilities: the blast disintegrated Dragon's corpse, or he escaped and was still alive. After Wu Luli's debriefing, Vincent asked for Alex's help hoping to find the portal's point of origin. Vincent would not accept any excuses this time. He let Alex know within twenty-four hours, so tracking the vortex should not be a problem.

Before exiting his van, he turned on all his surveillance equipment that recorded every inbound and outbound call within the vicinity. Automatically, an application would send the data to his base computer back at the Regime. Later, he would review it with the hope that it would reveal a lead. Diego stepped out of the van and brought him a bottle of water.

"Here, my friend. It's going to be a hot one today."

"Thanks. How close is he?" Vincent nodded toward Alex.

"I don't know. He's been working for several hours now," Diego noted.

"Damn it! What's taking him so long?"

"Relax, Vincent. You'll find Dragon soon enough."

"I don't know. This guy is way too slippery."

"I don't mean to insult you, but is it possible you have a mole in the Regime?"

"Normally, I'd argue against that point, except lately, I've begun to think it's possible. I need to find out who it is and fast if there is."

"If there's anything I can do, please, let me know."

"Thanks; I've got it covered. I watch every email, text, voice, and video communication; something will turn up."

*****

Standing on a portal tracking platform, Alex waited all morning for a response. Vincent was getting restless for information, and Alex could not do anything until receiving approval; it was a necessary downside part of his job. His phone rang, so he answered and heard the familiar voice on the other end.

"I received your inquiry. You have my approval to release the information," a female voice remarked.

"You realize that it will lead him directly to your warehouse," Alex explained.

"Yes, I'm aware. I've already moved everything. Give him the information."

"Ok, I will."

Alex disconnected, stepped down from the platform, and handed Vincent the coordinate.

"It's about damn time," Vincent snapped.

"I'm sorry. It's a lengthy process."

Vincent studied the data and finally discovered a solid lead.

"It looks like I'm going to Edinburgh, Scotland," he paused and faced Diego, "Thank you for all your help. I'll let you know when I get 'em."

"Just be careful. This character seems dangerous, even for you."

"I will. See you soon," assured Vincent.

Chapter 25

Earth
Scotland - Dunnottar Castle
May 17, 2452

Dawn fumed, reading Mai Li's report, and would have killed Mai on the spot if she had been standing in the same room. Failing once was bad enough, but twice was simply unacceptable. Dawn could not pursue her now because of other problems. She briskly walked down the hall, stopped by the weapons cache room to pick up a gun, tucked it behind her jacket, and stepped into the recovery room, where Ethan and his men watched over Scott, who had just got out of surgery. As she entered, they all stood, except for Scott, who was sleeping off the anesthesia.

"Twice, I sent you to complete a simple mission, and twice you've failed me," Dawn growled through gritted teeth.

"I know you're upset; I put all the details in my report. They fired at my men, who were a hundred feet away. They had to lay down cover fire to get out of there."

"And now Larkin's wife is dead!"

"I don't think it was us. I believe it was friendly fire because her head snapped forward."

"I don't care who killed her! If you knew soldiers were guarding the home, your men shouldn't have been near that place!"

"I had no idea things would turn out this bad. I was unarmed and thought it would be enough to show that I wasn't a threat. Please don't blame my men; it's all my fault. I'm the one who decided to move forward."

"You're right. I don't blame your men. It *is* all your fault," she removed the weapon from underneath her jacket.

Before they knew what hit them, Dawn shot each team member in the head, including Scott, killing them instantly. Lastly, she aimed at Ethan and paused. While staring down the barrel of her gun, he almost wished Dawn would pull the trigger. Had he known she was this ruthless, he would have never agreed to work for her. Unexpectedly, she holstered her weapon.

"Come with me. I must take care of something."

Chapter 26

Earth
Scotland - Edinburgh
May 17, 2452

Before leaving, Vincent completed an official request form and sent it to Deputy Chief Constable Brice at St. Leonard's Police Station in Scotland. Alternatively, he could have gone to Scotland by portal without sending the form, except they would put him in prison for life if they caught him. Not to mention the strain it would put on the Regime's relationship with Scotland's government.

He met with General Green in the monitoring room while waiting for a response where he received the mandatory tracer injection, and the General explained how the bacteria worked. Since Regime personnel would continuously watch him, knowing his location twenty-four/seven made him feel safe and violated. Considering the dangers of this kind of mission, he could not argue with the General's logic. This way, if trouble comes, all he must do is signal for help using his watch communicator. Considering Dragon was one of the most dangerous and slippery targets the Regime had ever chased, he welcomed the support. An hour later, there was still no response from Deputy Chief Constable Brice, so Vincent contacted Chief Constable McDaniel.

Going over Brice's head was the last thing he wanted to do, but time was running out. A few minutes later, Chief Constable McDaniel gave his approval. Vincent landed at St. Leonard's Police Station in Scotland; Deputy Chief Constable Brice was not there. Instead, a police officer greeted him. Brice's absence was a message that Vincent offended him by involving the Chief Constable. Without a response, he left him no choice. Later, he would send him a gift basket to smooth things over.

Although the officer offered to help, Vincent declined, saying, "The fewer people involved, the better. Whoever sponsors Dragon is powerful, so I'd appreciate it if you'd keep my visit here a secret."

The officer gave Vincent a knowing nod and escorted him to the parking lot behind the station, where he gave him the keys to one of their undercover vehicles.

"I filled the tank. Leave the keys at the desk when you finish," the officer said, leaving without saying goodbye.

Not familiar with anyone at St. Leonard's Police Station, Vincent did not know whom to trust. After the cold greeting and even chillier farewell, Vincent realized it would have been better to land unannounced; now, it was too late. Taking the Edinburgh bypass, Vincent drove to a place called Old Wood. It was a forest until businesses industrialized the area like most of Scotland. He turned onto Old Dalkeith Road and left onto a dirt road with no name.

He stopped at a locked steel gate and double-checked his GPS. He was heading in the right direction. The gate sign read *No Trespassing*, proving that he had found the right place. He pushed through the small blockade using the police vehicle's front bumper guard and pulled up to an old warehouse. The owner chained and locked the door, so Vincent sent enough electricity through the metal chain to melt it.

He opened the rusty, creaky door. Inside, it was dark, so he removed the flashlight from his belt and walked in. The echo of his footsteps was the only sound; it made him nervous. He found the breaker box and flipped a few switches until the lights came on. A quick scan of the area revealed that whoever owned the building left in a hurry. The floor showed signs that something had been here recently.

Desperately needing to find some clue as to Dragon's whereabouts, he decided to walk the floor. About a half-hour later, he found a flush steel trap door and pulled it open. Below, he found a set of stairs leading down into pitch black. Using his flashlight, he cautiously took each step until reaching the bottom, where he found another door and opened it. Shining his flashlight toward the ground, he saw a metal grid. With his right foot, he assessed its strength. Satisfied it would hold him, he secured the door behind him so it would stay open and walked in.

Like the warehouse above, the basement was empty. The difference was the dirt floor and walls. It appeared that someone had dug a tunnel. *Where does it go?* He took a few steps and stopped, seeing a reflection from his flashlight. Reaching out with his hand, he touched a thick, transparent wall in front of him. He stepped to the right and heard something click under his foot. Another translucent barrier dropped down behind him.

He turned around to find his exit blocked and frantically checked the transparent wall for a breach. Having searched it, he did not find any. He kicked at the enclosure; the panels were too thick for him to break. Lights flickered to life, illuminating the room, and out of the shadows, a woman appeared.

"Welcome, Vincent. It's a pleasure to meet you. My name is Dawn Pierce," she spoke through an intercom fastened to the inside of his clear cell.

Realizing she trapped him, he used his watch to signal for help; the red, flashing light showed that something blocked his signal.

"I'm jamming this whole area," she said indifferently.

Pushing his hand forward, he shot a burst of high voltage energy toward his captor; the fingers of electricity moved downward to the grid.

"By now, I hope you realize there is *no* escape. Your physical enhancement is useless over a grounded, metal grid, and there are walls of aluminum glass, one inch thick, surrounding you."

"What do you want?"

"You're very persistent, Vincent. I admire that. However, it's become a nuisance, so I'm afraid it's time for you to retire."

"If you kill me, the Regime will send every agent they have to apprehend you."

"I expect nothing less, except they will not find your corpse, neither will they find any leads; it will force them to start from the beginning. That will give me the time I need."

"For what?"

"It doesn't concern you. I am sorry for what it's worth; I have only the highest respect for someone with your ability, but this is business."

"You bitch! You won't get away with this!"

"I already have."

A yellow-green gas filled the translucent cell, and Vincent began to choke.

"It's chlorine gas. I'm sorry. It's the best I could do at such short notice. I had hoped the explosion would have derailed your pursuit; you're just too determined."

Through unwavering eyes, she watched Vincent struggle against the toxic fumes. The gas worked quickly, making him fall to his knees, coughing and crying as it burned his eyes and airways, and in a matter of moments, Vincent disappeared within the foggy toxin. Patiently, she waited until venting the tank several minutes later and saw his lifeless body lying on the grid. Turning, she called for Ethan, who waited nearby.

"Dissolve his flesh and put his implants into the briefcase I gave you; it will prevent his generator's nuclear signature from broadcasting its location. Give the box to Mitch, my transport technician, and he'll send it to our team in Livingston, where they have the skills to deactivate it."

"Anything else?" Ethan asked.

"When you finish, get rid of the police car and get some rest. We have a busy day tomorrow."

Ethan ensured the pump cleared all the gas and opened it. Since she killed his team for ruining the mission, Ethan believed this assignment was punishment for his failure. This was the worst of all the things he ever had to do. Grabbing the corpse by his feet, he dragged him to a tub and dowsed him with acid.

Ethan watched through a gas mask as the body disintegrated into a liquid and pumped the gooey mess into a container. Having dissolved Vincent's remains, the only things left were his implants. Using rubber tongs to prevent shock, he placed them into the small briefcase, locked it, and left to finish the rest of his work, with the case in one hand and the container holding his liquid corpse in the other.

Chapter 27

Tionah and Edur sat with Olan at the table, watching Julie eat as if it had been days since her last meal. The fight with Domeka had been exhausting, physically and emotionally. Julie did not talk about what happened during their journey home, even though Olan was interested in hearing the outcome. Instead, she finished eating and stared at the plate, lost in thought.

"How did it go? Did you kill the Skean's sisters?" Tionah asked, breaking the silence.

"They're dead, except for Nayrah."

"I knew you could do it!" Tionah exclaimed.

Julie got up from the table and walked outside. Before the door closed behind her, Olan followed.

"What is wrong?"

"Everything. Yesterday I killed two soldiers, and today I killed two more people," Julie worried.

"The soldiers were traitors, and the ones you killed today were not people. They were Skeans; there is a difference. Even if they were humanoid, you had to do it. They would have killed you and anyone else who stood in their way."

"Have you ever killed someone?"

"Yes, but like you, it is not something I take lightly. My actions recently caused the loss of innocent lives; I would not change it, even if I could, because it was necessary."

"I don't know. It just doesn't feel right."

"Your parents did not raise you for this purpose. Still, it is your calling to fulfill it. The evidence is the power you wield. If you quit now, the lives you took would have been in vain because their offspring will take their place," Olan warned.

"You're saying to justify killing four people; I must kill more."

"No; sometimes killing is necessary. *That* is what justifies it."

"Even if we're successful in killing the rest of the Skeans, I can't beat Nayrah. I wouldn't have even killed Domeka if Nayrah hadn't helped me."

"When the time comes, you will be ready."

"How can you say that? You don't understand what I'm going through. Although these powers allow me to beat you in a fight, it's nothing compared to the Skeans."

"I have never believed in the myths of the Skeans and Saiphs until I met you. Now you must believe in yourself. I know you can defeat her; just remember that if *you* do not believe it, she has already won."

"I want to believe because they will control Akil if I fail. Still, it's too much pressure; I'm not that strong."

"You are. I can see it in you. Give it time; you will see."

"That is something we don't have; I must meet with Nayrah again tomorrow, same place and time."

"We will face her together."

"I do appreciate your help and support."

"It is my honor to assist you," he paused. "The Information League has been reporting that Otsoa is Gau reborn."

"What does that mean?"

"It means he has Gau's sword. The High Priest claims he ignited it in a private meeting."

"Great, another Skean I have to deal with."

"Considering the circumstances, I am not completely convinced he is a Skean. The legend insists that only Gau or his descendants can ignite his sword. I find it very strange that it appeared during the current political turmoil, and even more unbelievable is Otsoa igniting it. In either case, you must be ready to fight him. If he is Gau reborn, you must defeat him too. If he is not, he is lying, and by using Gau's reputation, he will do great harm to Akil."

"Sure, let's add him to the list. Is there anything else?"

"That is all I know; I must leave for a brief time."

"Where are you going?"

"It is better if I do not tell you."

"You would keep secrets from me?"

"Only so you will have deniability."

"Just be careful. I don't have that many allies."

"I promise that I will be diligent. I will see you soon," he responded and left.

*****

Argians filled the avenue on the one-hundredth level as they looked for a place to eat. In his usual fashion, Olan blended in, looking like a random Akilian that passed by him on his way up. It was dinner time when he arrived at the restaurant, so he sat in the back and waited for Dolas. With Otsoa in charge of the city, it had not been easy for them to meet in a public venue. To make things even harder, they wore disguises, and neither would recognize the other physically.

By wearing a black string on his right index finger, Olan hoped Dolas could spot him in the restaurant. Moments later, someone Olan had never seen before sat at his table. The other tapped his finger twice on the table without saying a word. In response, Olan did the same once; the other tapped three times, and Olan answered by knocking twice.

"What do you have for me?" Dolas inquired.

"I need a favor," Olan requested.

"I will do what I can."

"I need to get a message to an Akilian on Earth."

"Anyone I know?"

"Her name is Yanamai."

"You mean the one from the science division?"

"Yes. She is the one."

Dolas thought momentarily, "I have a few agents watching outgoing messages. Otsoa is paranoid with good reason. There are whispers of a rebellion, so I will do my best to keep it from him."

"Can you trust the agents?"

"I will not risk it. Instead, I will send them on a break during a lull in the work cycle, post the message and erase any evidence. What do you want to tell her?

With his right hand, he covertly gave him a data chip.

"Send this video. It will tell her not to return to Akil. I believe Otsoa may try to lure her back here for the sole purpose of taking her for his own."

98

"He has Durnah. As beautiful as she is, why would he want Yanamai?"

"Because the little *putok* has obsessed over her since his youth."

"How will he get around our social laws?"

"I am uncertain. Since a very lethal Skean is counseling him, I am sure he will figure it out."

"I have seen the Skean with him before," Dolas noted.

"Stay away from her if you can. She may sense your betrayal and kill you," Olan warned.

"I will try; Otsoa demands constant updates, and she is usually with him."

"Cloud your mind with the details of the reports. It should be enough to fool her."

"Thanks for the advice. I will get your message out soon. I promise."

"Thank you, my friend."

Olan placed a generous tip on the table and left the restaurant. At his first opportunity, he changed his features once again. Now, Olan's appearance matched another random Akilian that caught his eye on the way up. Simultaneously, he removed his outer jacket, turned it inside out, which changed his coat's color, and disappeared into the crowd. Dolas stepped outside and looked for him but did not see him anywhere.

*****

Landing on the six hundredth level, Olan, still in disguise, walked into Gau's temple. A few yellow harvests ago, he investigated one of the temple's acolytes, which gave him familiarity with the building's layout. The temple was Akil's wealthiest and most lavish sanctuary on the six hundredth level. It was where they kept the Sacred Scrolls that prophesied Gau's return. Once inside, Olan requested to speak to High Priest Elazar; that it was an emergency.

A few hundred heartbeats later, the acolyte returned. While the disciple escorted him to the High Priest's office, Olan noticed how well they decorated the corridors. Hundreds of red, gold, and black tapestries, depicting Gau's different expressions hung on either side.

The votary showed him into the High Priest's office, closing the door behind him.

High Priest Elazar stood behind an expensive and rare, large wooden desk made from an extinct tree. The polished surface that protected and preserved the wood reflected the light in the room. Olan approached the High Priest, who wore a seamless robe made from the highest quality yellow moss. The cloak was black, and the borders had many soft, golden threads woven into the fabric.

Olan discovered that the robe took about an entire yellow harvest to make. The price of such a garment equaled a new apartment on the one-hundredth level. Also, the headpiece he wore weighed as much as seven hand size stones. Artisans made the frame from silver minerals found only in the deepest caverns of Akil's underground city. They melted the metal, formed it into an elaborate headdress, and fastened several rare jewels into established settings. Olan stood in front of his desk, and the High Priest held his right hand, palm forward.

"Greetings, my fellow believer."

Olan returned his salutation, "It is an honor to meet you, son of Gau."

"Tell me, my child. Why are you here?"

"I have the information you need to know."

"What does this information concern?"

"Skeans and Saiphs, my guide."

High Priest Elazar raised an eyebrow, "You have my attention. Please, have a seat."

High Priest Elazar sat and pushed a shiny golden bowl toward Olan, who tossed in several Sovereign Cubes. It was their custom to bring an offering whenever meeting with the High Priest, even if you were there to help him. High Priest Elazar pulled the shiny golden bowl back.

"Do you believe in Skeans?" Olan queried.

"Yes, Gau was the first Skean."

"Do you believe that these Skeans have supernatural abilities?"

"Yes. Our tradition says that they can do many miraculous things."

"Do you believe in Saiphs too?"

"You cannot believe in one without the other."

"Has a Skean approached you for help?"

High Priest Elazar did not reply immediately. Instead, he studied Olan cautiously.

"Why are you asking me such things? I thought you had information for me."

"I do, my guide. Please, forgive me. I came here to warn you that I have seen a Skean in Argi."

"Gau's High Priests do not fear Skeans. We serve them."

"It is the calling. Still, there is more than one Skean, my guide."

High Priest Elazar moved forward in his chair, "Are you sure?"

"I have proof," Olan insisted, using his right hand to retrieve a portable video recorder from his jacket.

He replayed Nayrah's fight with Kemena earlier during the Terrestrial Revolution. As the video continued, Elazar watched with amazement.

"Why are they killing each other?"

"As you well know, Skeans lust for power; the victor is making a move to wipe out the others."

"How many others?"

"I know of eleven."

"Oh dear, that is terrible news. Skeans do not do well in groups."

"Correct, and since you must serve them, the others might use you as leverage," Olan said.

High Priest Elazar swallowed hard, "I am glad you came to me with this information. You may have saved my life."

"It is an honor, my guide. At least you have Otsoa to protect you."

High Priest Elazar snickered, realized his mistake, and frowned, "Since you have shown profound loyalty, I will share something with you, only if you swear not to tell anyone."

"I swear, my guide."

"Otsoa is not the son of Gau. A Skean has approached me and demanded I vouch for him, so his transition to Sovereign would be smooth."

"I understand. You serve our master well."

"Except, I am unsure which Skean spoke to me. Based on your video, they appeared identical, which means they are disguising themselves to hide their numbers."

"I suggest you conceal yourself, my guide; once the fight for supremacy is over, you can appear and serve the victor," Olan advised.

"You have given me sound advice. I will leave at once."

"Before you go, there is another matter of grave concern."

"You have more bad news?"

"Yes, my guide. I also saw a Saiph on Akil."

"Hmm, this does pose a problem. Allowing a Saiph to roam Akil unchecked would be disastrous for the Skeans."

"I agree; we must warn the other Skeans that a Saiph is on Akil."

"I cannot do it. I must hide, as you have said," High Priest Elazar answered.

"I would do it, except I have no way to find them. You know as well as I that they live in secret places."

High Priest Elazar rubbed his chin, thinking, "There is an artifact I have that should help you find them."

"What is it?"

"It is a compass. According to legend, a Saiph created the device to track and kill Skeans. The Skeans captured and killed him before the Saiph found all of them. Once in their possession, the Skeans discovered they could use it to find others like them. To ensure none would use it against each other, they agreed to give it to Gau's High Priest for safekeeping and to ensure no other Saiphs could use it again."

"I thought they could sense each other?"

"They can, which is why it is possible that the Skeans already know the Saiph is here. However, Saiphs and Skeans can cloak themselves; their sensitivity range varies based on the individual's ability. The compass should enable you to find the Skeans and warn them about the Saiph even if they have a cloak. Maybe they can find a way to reverse it to locate the Saiph."

"Do you have it here?"

"Yes, except it does not work because the power source has depleted. I had our best technicians examine it, yet they could not get it to work."

"I would still like to borrow it. Perhaps I can get it to work."

"I will lend it to you if you give me a copy of the video."

"It is yours, my guide."

Chapter 28

Using his credentials as Chief Administrator of Argi's Intelligence Department, Dolas entered the Interstellar Transport Bay on Argi's upper level. It was a short walk to the room where he stationed his agents. Otsoa ordered him to scan all incoming and outgoing messages between Akil and Earth. In turn, he ordered his agents to report anything suspicious to the senior staff. Since it was in its beginning stages, only two agents were necessary. With only a handful of Akilians on Earth, there were not very many communications to review. He hoped that would change soon. He stepped inside, and the two agents on duty stood out of respect; he nodded for them to have a seat.

"I am only here to conduct a brief audit of your work," he advised.

When his Information Terminal sprang to life, Dolas downloaded Olan's video earlier for Yanamai and inserted it with the daily bundle of messages the agents already approved to go to Earth. Before leaving, he used personal software to erase any trace of his involvement with the correspondence and performed a quick audit of their work to support his visit.

"Everything seems to be in order. Keep up the good work."

Having completed the task Olan gave him, he returned to his office and finished several reports that his paranoid sovereign expected.

Chapter 29

Earth
China - Hong Kong
May 17, 2452

Standing in the back of Club 51, Wu Luli sipped a club soda, waiting for Yang Shing to deliver the list of names and addresses. With so many vengeful colleagues looking for her, she could not take the chance of returning to any familiar places. She knew some agents made fatal mistakes by hiding in safe houses or known rest stops during a crisis. In her experience, once you become a target, any of your known hideouts become a hunting ground, even safe houses.

Therefore, having never stepped foot in this club, she hoped no one would look for her. The club played loud house music, which kept most of the patrons on the dance floor, making it easier for her to watch the door. Occasionally, a server stopped by, asking her if she wanted something to drink. She knew from experience to order something every fifteen minutes (even though she would not drink them), so the owners would leave her alone.

It would have been the perfect spot, except that she attracted a male suitor, who sent her a drink, hoping for a response; the server set it on her table and pointed to her admirer. Wu Luli did not touch the glass, sending the universal message of disinterest. The full glasses were starting to accumulate on her table. Knowing it would draw attention, she decided to move to another seat.

Along the way, she saw a familiar face walk through the front door, Chow Dai. It had been years since she collaborated with him; he was an excellent agent. Over time, he developed a reputation. Even some of her peers called him the ultimate assassin. Rumors spread fast about how he could kill a person in a pinch with anything, such as a pen or paper clip. He was also exceptionally efficient with his bare hands. Of all the agents to find her, Chow Dai was the last one she wanted pursuing her.

As he scanned the club, she turned her head to hide; her instincts told her it was too late. Hoping to escape unnoticed, she headed for the side door, keeping her back to him. Outside, she risked craning her neck to look back and saw him glaring at her. Her brisk walk turned into a sprint as Chow Dai raced to catch up to her. Fear drove her to run faster toward some vehicles stopped at a traffic light.

She leaped in the air on the street, kicking a motorcyclist off his bike. Before he realized what had happened, she was on it and sped away. In her rear-view mirror, she saw Chow Dai open the door of a stopped vehicle and pull the driver out onto the street. In a moment, he was inside the car and in pursuit. Shifting through the gears, she reached top speed in seconds, zigzagging through traffic, hoping to lose him; Chow Dai continued to follow.

He often moved to the sidewalk to pass stopped vehicles on the street. One time, he even pushed another car through a traffic light. As it inched forward, oncoming traffic hit him, sending shreds of fiberglass everywhere. All the cars stopped at the intersection to help as he sped past. Eventually, he caught up to her and used the bumper to slam into the back of her motorcycle. The bike bucked and swerved, but Wu Luli kept from falling.

Leaving one hand on the throttle, she used the other to retrieve her gun. Seeing no one in front of her, she looked back, aimed, and fired. She put holes in the driver's side windshield with cold precision; Chow Dai ducked below the dashboard moments before the bullets hit the glass. Unable to injure him through the vehicle's frame, she put her last two shots in the car's radiator, causing steam to billow from the front. Chow Dai sat up and knew the vehicle would soon be out of commission.

He accelerated to ensure his prey would not escape, slamming into Wu Luli one more time. The motorcycle's rear wheel went sideways, forcing her to lay the bike down and ride out the skid. Keeping his speed, with the vehicle's heat gauge in the red, Chow Dai moved closer to the motorcycle as it fell. Wu Luli's torso landed on the car's bumper, and her legs rested on the skidding bike. The motorcycle slowed from friction, causing it to slide under the pursuing vehicle. It lodged in its undercarriage, causing it to slow down too.

Steam gushed from under the hood, burning her skin, so she used the protruding part of the bike as footing and pushed herself off the dangerous ride. The momentum forced her into a roll that led onto the sidewalk. She stopped tumbling and ran for the wooded area nearby. Behind her, the sound of screeching tires let her know that he was still in pursuit. He jumped out of the car to see Wu Luli disappear into the woods, so he chased her.

Hiding behind a large tree, she took a moment to catch her breath. Heavy panting would give away her position, so she took slow, deep breaths, even though her lungs were burning for more. She focused on her breathing and used her hands to check for injuries, working from her legs up. Wu Luli did not find anything serious besides a few rips on her clothes and possibly a few cuts, which she could not confirm in the dark. However, there was one major problem: she could not find her gun.

Thinking back to the collision, she remembered he hit her from behind the last time, and the crash knocked it out of her hand. To her disappointment, the crescent moon did not offer enough light for her to see any shapes, making running farther into the woods impossible. Her only choice was to hide. In the distance, she could hear his footsteps in the grass. Occasionally, she heard branches breaking as he came closer to her position. Taking a chance, she peeked around the tree. Seeing a small green light moving toward her, she swore. *Damn it; he's wearing night-vision goggles!*

She ran deeper into the woods, holding her arms up to protect her face from hidden branches. Shots echoed from behind; she zigzagged back and forth, hoping to give him a hard target, until her foot lodged under a large, fallen branch, causing her to fall. Unwittingly standing on top of a ravine, Wu Luli uncontrollably rolled until landing in a small creek. Without having to check, she knew the fall injured her knees and elbows because they throbbed.

Stunned, she lay in the creek as chilly water soaked her clothes, cooling her skin. She tried to get up, but the fall made her dizzy, making it hard to stand. Looking up at the ravine's top, she saw the green light approaching as he made his way down the hill. Although General Fu trained her never to accept defeat and never give up, her body would not move. She heard his gun click and knew the only way to survive was to convince him of her innocence; it was a long shot.

"I didn't do it," she spoke calmly as her instructor taught and briefly paused before continuing, "General Ming-tun Fu killed your mother and faked the video to frame me."

"Lies."

"Think about it, Chow Dai. How does killing the parents of all my colleagues benefit me?"

"I don't have to think about it. You wanted to take over General Ming-tun Fu's operation. To do so, you had to remove his control over us to weaken him, except you didn't know he recorded your betrayal until it was too late."

"That's not what happened. Somehow, he discovered I would rescue my dad and leave his organization."

"Impossible. Even I didn't know where he kept our families."

"He kept them on Po Toi Island. General Ming-Tun Fu only took me to see him because I refused my next mission."

"Even so, there are too many guards. Even I couldn't get past them all, so you certainly could not have saved him."

"I defected to the Regime. They used their portal technology to free him. Please, come with me, and I'll prove it to you."

"Stay where you are."

"Don't you believe me?"

"No. General Ming-Tun Fu said you would tell stories to save your life."

"You're making a big mistake."

"Enough! It's time for you to die, Wu Luli, and time for me to collect your bounty."

Even though it was dark, she reflexively closed her eyes and put her hands out as if they would somehow stop the bullet. Her thoughts turned to Michael. She wondered if he would mourn her death after what happened between them. Bang! Reflexively, she flinched, expecting the bullet to penetrate her head or heart.

Since she was still alert, the bullet must have penetrated her heart, so she waited for the end. *It won't be long now.* She tried to find the bullet hole in her chest, knowing that her blood was gushing out. While searching, her hands trembled from fear and the cold; unexpectedly, she heard a body hit the ground.

"Are you all right?" a familiar voice asked.

"Yang Shing?"

"Who else would it be?"

"How did you find me?"

"You crashed just outside my apartment. It was a good thing I recognized you."

Sensing danger had passed, she opened her eyes, saw another set of night vision goggles staring at her, and smiled, "I owe you one now."

"You are correct. Now come with me. I have the information you requested."

*****

Wu Luli stepped out of the shower, put bandages on her knees and elbows, and changed into a fresh set of clothes from Yang Shing's wife, Yang Mei. It was the first time they met, and for a good reason. Mixing work and personal life was never a good idea for anyone in their line of business, so it had always been her top priority to keep that from happening.

Today's circumstances were beyond her control. Now that Yang Mei was aware of his odd work companions, he had some explaining to do. She dried her hair, pulled it back into a ponytail, and walked into the living room, where Yang Shing waited for her.

"Here is the list you requested," he handed it to her and gave her another gun for protection. "I'm sure you're going to need this."

"Thanks. I'll need some other things too. I'm assuming you still have your old contacts."

"What do you need?" he inquired.

She handed him a list.

"This will cost a great deal of money," he warned.

"You get the items, and I'll ensure the Regime reimburses you."

"They better."

109

Chapter 30

Earth
The Regime - Washington, D.C. - Capitol Building
May 17, 2452

Standing in front of Supreme Commander Porter, General Green grimaced while patiently waiting for his call to end. Images of their gruesome discovery flashed through his mind, nearly bringing the battle-hardened army veteran to tears.

"I can see by your expression something is wrong," Supreme Commander Porter's words brought General Green out of his trance.

"Yes, Sir. I'm afraid I have some sad news. At 1335 hours, Vincent's signature disappeared from our monitors. I sent a team in to find him."

"Is he injured?"

"No, Sir. He's dead."

Standing in shock, Supreme Commander Porter asked, "How?"

"It appears to have been a trap. Our forensics team found a small room underneath the warehouse. My men found chlorine residue on the walls and floor. They must have gassed him."

"Where's his body?"

"Whoever killed him liquefied his remains. My men thoroughly examined a nearby tub. Someone carefully cleaned it, but they found a jelly-like substance in a small crevice. They performed a DNA test and confirmed it was him."

"Do we know if Dragon did this?"

"We're uncertain. Since Vincent pursued him, we think Dragon is responsible. We'll know more once my team reviews Vincent's data on the case. The last file he added to the folder included every in and outgoing communications from the crime scene in Madrid."

"I want to know who owns that warehouse!"

"We're already investigating it."

"When we catch this killer, I have something special in store for him."

Just as he finished speaking, General Green's communicator beeped. Supreme Commander Porter nodded for him to answer.

General Green finished and said, "Our agents have confirmed that someone on the Regime Madrid team contacted an outside source. I had them forward the communication to my tablet."

As General Green played the conversation, their eyes widened.

"That's Alex asking for approval to release information!" Supreme Commander Porter exclaimed.

"I don't recognize the woman's voice on the other end."

"Find out who she is. Use the whole damn department if needed; I want her name!"

"I've ordered my team to compare her voice with everything we have in our database."

"I want this person apprehended at any cost!"

"Yes, Sir; in the meantime, what do we do with Alex?"

"It's obvious this woman used the MR machine to coerce him into feeding her information. Have him screened at once using the same protocol as before. I don't want him committing suicide."

"I'll take care of it myself."

Supreme Commander Porter was alone with his thoughts. Although Vincent's occupation often invited danger, Porter hoped the Regime's enhancement would keep him alive. Sadly, it did not. While staring at Vincent's picture within his dossier, Porter felt the loss of an agent and a friend who had saved his life more than a few times. Now, he had to tell Vincent's parents about the tragedy of their son and dreaded the responsibility.

Chapter 31

Earth
The Regime - Washington, D.C. - Fort McNair
May 18, 2452

Although her alarm rang out loudly, as it did the prior morning, Yanamai was already awake. Due to everything that had happened between her and Michael, she barely slept. She groggily got out of bed, prepared for work, and met Garbi in the kitchen.

"How did your date go last night?" Garbi questioned curiously.

"Horrible. He does not trust me and does not want to see either of us again."

"I told you that would happen. If you wanted him so badly, you should have just traded places with me."

Yanamai scoffed at the idea, "You only want to trade places to become the head of the science division."

"You would have Michael in exchange."

"I will find a way to win him back."

Garbi chuckled, "I am sure that even Gau could not change his mind."

"Very funny."

"I did warn you, Yanamai," Garbi walked toward the door.

"Thanks for nothing."

The door slammed, leaving Yanamai alone to ponder her situation. *How does someone undo a betrayal?* Not knowing where to begin, she thought about who would be best to help her with the dilemma. It had to be someone from Earth. A memory of a woman helping Michael when she landed in Fort Levan came to mind. *Oh, what did she say her name was?* She went to her computer and searched the directory to find her name and apartment number. Yanamai headed to Lisa's home on her way to work, hoping to catch her. Yanamai found her just as she stepped out the door.

"Lisa! You are just the person I need to see."

"I am?" she queried, looking at Yanamai quizzically.

"Yes. May we step inside your home to talk?"

Lisa hesitated, "Well, all right."

Yanamai asked a few quick questions and discovered that Lisa had not spoken to Michael yet, allowing her to first relay the previous day's events from her point of view.

"Yikes! You really messed things up!"

"How do I get him to like me again?"

"I don't know if he'll ever want to see you again, let alone like you."

Yanamai sighed, "I know. He will not even talk to me."

"If he will not speak to you, you should give him some time before trying again."

"Or maybe *you* could speak to him?"

"No way, sister, not after what he's been through with Lian. I like my job."

"Lian?"

"She's his ex-girlfriend. She put him through hell."

"Hell is not good?"

"No. It isn't."

"Hmm, she must be the one he referred to as a relationship full of lies."

"Yep, that would be the one."

"There must be something I can do. I cannot accept that he will never speak to me again."

Lisa thought a moment.

"I know that he's going on an expedition today. He won't return for a few hours. If you get approval, I could add your name to the team."

"I do not know anything about what he does; how could I be of any help?"

"You're not there to help. You're there to be by his side and to support him. You may not even get to say anything, but just being there would be a good start."

"Thank you, Lisa. I really appreciate it."

"Just promise me you won't hurt him again and don't mention my name."

"I never intended to hurt him in the first place, and I promise not to hurt him or speak your name."

"You'll need General Saunders's approval to get on the list, so you better get moving."

"I am going, and thank you again!"

*****

Fifteen minutes later, Yanamai convinced General Saunders, with much groveling, to allow her to join Michael's expedition; it was worth it to get on the list. She received several vaccination shots, leaving her arms sore, and visited the mall to buy clothing proper for the jungle. On her way home, Yanamai called Garbi for help and met her at their apartment, where she stood in front of the mirror, wearing the light, fast-drying, camouflaged clothing; she faced Garbi.

"How do I look?"

"Meh, it is very brown and green. It makes you look plain."

"It is not a fashion show, Garbi. It is the jungle. General Saunders said I needed this kind of clothing, or else I could end up sick."

"You should let your hair down."

"The internet said that the jungle has many trees and branches. I do not want to risk getting my hair tangled."

"At least put it in a ponytail instead of leaving it all balled up on top of your head."

"Fine, you win," Yanamai exasperated, unraveling her hair and wrapping it into a ponytail.

"How many are going on this expedition?"

"There are three of us: me, Michael, and Dr. Young."

"A doctor?"

"Yes. Just in case someone gets injured or sick. It is only a precaution."

"I could think of other ways to get back into his good graces."

"What would you do?"

Garbi smiled, "All I will say is that he would not be able to resist me."

"You think sex is the answer to everything."

"It is. I guarantee, if you seduce him, he will forgive you."

"I want his forgiveness to come from his heart and nowhere else."

"I would have him in my arms at dinner."

114

"Would you please go check my messages? I do not know how long I will be out. I do not want them piling up," Yanamai requested, hoping to change the subject.

"Sure; what is the password?"

"It is," she hesitated, "Michael and Yanamai."

Garbi raised an eyebrow, "You must be joking. That is so childish."

"Just check them for me. Forward anything important to my phone."

"Fine, now get out of here, or you will be late."

Garbi put in the ridiculous password, reviewed her messages, and opened one from Akil. The screen filled with the image of someone she had never seen before.

"My name is Dolas. I am passing this message along from Olan. It is important that...."

Knowing that Olan betrayed Zorion, Garbi removed the message. There was no way she would let him draw Yanamai into whatever scheme Olan was plotting. Garbi reviewed her other emails, sent the important ones forward, and returned to work.

Yanamai arrived at the International Transportation Station, and a brief time later, Dr. Young entered the room. Having practiced the Earthian greeting, Yanamai extended her hand and introduced herself. While waiting, they talked and became fast friends. Hoping she had gained an ally, Yanamai took the opportunity to explain the true nature of her presence. She finished just as Michael stomped into the room.

"I don't know how you got onto the list; I thought I made myself clear that I want you to stay away!"

"General Saunders approved me for this expedition. Besides, I told you I would not give up on you, Michael; I plan to earn your forgiveness. I do not care how long it takes."

"Neither of us will live that long," he quipped.

Turning to the Transporter Technician, he signaled for him to open the portal.

Before stepping through, he faced Yanamai, "Just stay out of my way!"

He faced Dr. Young, "We shouldn't be gone long."

"It doesn't matter to me, Michael. I get paid the same no matter how long we stay."

Michael stepped through; Dr. Young looked at Yanamai and extended his elbow, "If you would allow me."

Smiling, Yanamai took his arm and walked through the event horizon.

Chapter 32

Earth
South America - Brazil
May 18, 2452

The expedition team landed in Brazil. Yanamai thought the humid jungle air felt good until it became oppressive within a few hundred heartbeats, causing her to sweat; now she understood why General Saunders recommended fast-drying clothes. During their journey, Michael made it a point to keep some distance between them. Dr. Young stayed behind with her to continue their conversation.

"How far do we have to walk? We should have arrived at the site by now," Yanamai noted.

"The camp is still a couple of miles away. The agreement between the Regime and Brazil is specific. We can only open a portal at certain designated sites. I'm afraid we must walk to our destination, no matter how far it is from our landing."

"It seems like we will never get there," she whined.

"You seem fit to me. I'm sure you can make the journey without any problem."

"It is not the distance; it is the," she paused to swat a mosquito, "it is the insects and the humidity."

"Did you remember your mosquito repellant?"

"What is that?"

"Michael, wait a moment, please," Dr. Young yelled.

"What's wrong?" Michael yelled his reply from about forty feet ahead of them.

"I need to spray Yanamai with repellant. They're eating her alive."

Even though he was far ahead, Yanamai could hear him exhale, and knowing that it would delay them, she said, "It is all right, doctor. I will be fine."

"Nonsense. I will not allow a pretty young woman to suffer in my presence. Now, hold out your arms so I can spray them."

As the mist surrounded her, she started coughing.

Dr. Young chuckled, "You may want to hold your breath and close your eyes until I finish."

She held her breath and waited for Dr. Young to stop. Upon opening her eyes, she saw Michael standing a few feet away with his hands firmly pressed on his hips and a frown on his face. She did not have to guess that he was angry with her again.

"Are you done with her yet, doc?"

"There's no need to be rude, Michael. She's taking the journey to be by your side."

"Did she tell you what she did?"

"Yes, and you are correct, it wasn't a kind thing to do, yet I know other couples who've met under worse circumstances and overcame them."

"What did she give you to say that doc, a date with her sister?" Michael scoffed, turned, and moved up the trail.

"Come. We better follow him before we get separated," Dr. Young warned.

"He is furious with me," Yanamai lamented.

"Give it time, deary. I've known Michael for many years. He is forgiving, only in this case, he'll need time to overcome the pain you've caused him."

"I hope you are right, doctor."

"I am right, most of the time."

"I truly feel terrible about what I did. If I could relive that moment, I would undo everything."

"Don't fret. His reaction at the International Transport Station tells me he's still fond of you."

"I do not understand. He yelled at me the whole time."

"He was dramatic if you ask me, but if you consider that he's allowing you to join us…."

Yanamai interrupted him, "General Saunders approved me for this expedition, so Michael *had* to let me come with you."

"No. Michael could have done many things to keep you from joining us. For example, he could have canceled the trip, rescheduled, or contacted General Saunders and protested."

"General Saunders would not change his mind. Would he?"

"Michael and General Saunders are close. If Michael didn't want you here, you wouldn't be."

"Thank you, doctor. You have given me hope."

"Don't worry. He'll come around."

They walked for about half an hour, and Dr. Young yelled to Michael, "If you don't mind, I'd like to rest. I'm not as youthful as my name may have you believe."

Michael stopped and turned around, so Dr. Young sat on an old fallen tree trunk and retrieved his canteen to have a drink. Yanamai sat beside him and did the same; Michael sat on the other side of the clearing.

"It is much more comfortable here, Michael. Why don't you sit alongside Yanamai?" Dr. Young suggested.

"Mind your own business, doc."

"Have it your way."

As they rested, Yanamai craned her head, listening to the sounds of the jungle.

"The Amazon is full of life. That sound you're hearing is coming from howler monkeys," Dr. Young explained.

"Where are they?"

"It sounds like they're about a mile or so away."

Yanamai heard another sound, "What was that?"

"Some birds nearby. There's no need to be alarmed; we're quite safe."

Just as she relaxed, they all heard a loud, booming sound.

"What was that?" Yanamai nervously inquired.

"That was thunder, which means we must go before we get wet," he warned.

Reaching out with his left hand, he grabbed a nearby branch and used it to pull himself up.

"I agree," Michael stood.

She reached out to grab a branch with her right hand, like Dr. Young did only moments before, and fastened her hand on what she thought was a wooden branch; it felt strange. Yanamai pulled on it to stand; it fell to the ground and hissed. She instinctively jumped from her seat and ran behind Michael, who shook his head, laughing.

"Yuck, what is that?" she wondered.

"It's a snake. A boa constrictor, to be precise," Dr. Young described.

"Yeah, constrictors strangle their prey until it stops breathing and swallow it whole," Michael added, hoping to scare her back home.

"Will it try to eat me?" Yanamai worried.

"Yes, so you should run back to the landing site and go home," Michael grinned at Dr. Young.

"No," Dr. Young corrected. "Michael is just trying to scare you. This one's only a few months old. Some can reach sizes big enough to eat humans; I don't believe we will run into any today."

The thought of a snake strangling her and eating her whole made Yanamai tremble.

"You can turn around and go back if you want," Michael teased.

Just looking at the snake made her want to run, full out, back to their landing site and the safety the Regime provided; seeing Michael's fiendish grin, Yanamai had to overcome her fear or return home defeated.

"That is all right. I will keep going," she said, sticking up her chin defiantly.

Although she tried, her apparent concern about snakes remained unhidden to Michael and Dr. Young. She carefully searched the ground to ensure there was not another one nearby before each step.

"At this rate, you'll never get there. Come on! Step it up!" Michael shouted.

"Stop being mean to the poor girl!" Dr. Young yelled.

"I'm just telling her the truth, doc. It's more than she did for me," he walked ahead toward the site.

"Come, Yanamai. You'll be fine. Just stay with me."

Before reaching the site, the skies opened with a torrential rainstorm. Yanamai slipped and fell, face down in the mud. Unable to help her, Dr. Young called for Michael, who hysterically laughed, seeing her mud-soaked face.

"You see, Doc, there is such thing as karma."

"I'm disappointed in you, Michael. I see a side of you I don't like," Dr. Young sadly stated.

"Relax. It's just a little mud. She'll be fine," Michael helped Dr. Young lift her onto her feet.

When she stood, they saw mud covering Yanamai's face and front. Dr. Young tried to wipe as much off as possible using a cloth; it was only smearing.

"Look up," Michael instructed.

Yanamai looked at him quizzically.

"The rain will help wash the mud off your face."

She looked up as rain splashed on her face like her shower on Akil and smiled, realizing it was her first experience with rain.

"What are you smiling at?" Michael irritably questioned.

"I have never seen rain before."

Dr. Young frowned, feeling sad for her. Michael reluctantly grabbed the cloth from Dr. Young and wiped away the rest of the mud from Yanamai's face.

"Thank you, Michael," she smiled sweetly.

He ignored her and handed the cloth back to Dr. Young, "Let's get moving."

At the campsite, Yanamai and Dr. Young were wet to the skin from the rain. Michael arrived a little before them and was already greeting his colleague inside the large tent. Yanamai stepped inside and commented to Dr. Young about being grateful to have a roof over her head.

"Cliff, you remember Dr. Young," Michael remarked.

Dr. Young and Cliff shook hands.

"What did you find?" Michael asked.

"Hey, aren't you going to introduce me to your other companion?" Cliff nodded toward her.

"Huh…Oh…that's Yanamai. She's the comedic relief on this trip. See the mud," he grinned to make fun of her.

"Michael," Dr. Young snapped. "Yanamai is one of our leading portal scientists. She's here to support you, except at this point, I can't imagine why."

Cliff shook hands with her, unable to hold back a smile, noticing all the mud on her.

"I see you lost your footing," Cliff noted.

"I will be fine once I return to my tub."

"If you leave now, you could be relaxing in warm water before lunch," Michael hoped to dissuade her.

"I am not leaving, Michael."

Cliff noticed mud on his palm, so he wiped it on Michael's jacket.

"Hey!" Michael protested.

"You're right, Michael. Karma does exist," Dr. Young chuckled.

Ignoring him, Michael faced Cliff, "Where is it?"

"Follow me. You'll want to see this."

Michael saw a small glass-covered tray behind the tent with a dim light over it. The plant inside looked familiar.

"I've never seen this before," Cliff remarked.

"I have," Michael noted.

"Did you identify it yet?"

"I'm sorry; it's classified."

"Really?"

"I suggest you don't report what you found here to the Regime. At least, until I figure out why someone tried to destroy the ones I grew in the lab."

"Sounds serious."

"I'll let you know when I find something out; in the meantime, keep this discovery off the Regime's radar."

"Do you want to see the cavern where I found them?"

"Absolutely."

On his way, he turned to Dr. Young and Yanamai, "You two stay here."

Yanamai started to follow, ignoring him, until Dr. Young gently grabbed her arm, "Stay here with me. He won't be gone long."

Heeding Dr. Young's advice, Yanamai watched them disappear into a small cavern.

Thirty minutes later, she faced Dr. Young, "Should they be back by now?"

"Give him a little more time. He loves to explore."

Another thirty minutes passed, so Dr. Young stood from his seat, "I think we should look for them. They may be lost."

Using a small lantern to light their way, Dr. Young held it in front of him as they carefully walked the rocky surface of the cavern. Yanamai walked into the cave a short distance, stopped, and pointed to an object lying on the ground.

"What is that?"

Moving his lantern, Dr. Young saw him lying on the ground and yelled, "Cliff!"

Yanamai frantically searched for Michael but did not see him, so she called out for him, and her voice echoed throughout the cavern. Dr. Young knelt beside Cliff, checked his pulse, and put smelling salts under his nose to wake him.

"Uh, what happened?" Cliff groggily woke.

"That's what we were hoping you could tell us," Dr. Young responded.

"Where is Michael?" Yanamai desperately questioned.

Struggling, Cliff searched his memory, "He was by my side until everything went dark."

Dr. Young examined the back of Cliff's head and found a bump where someone had hit him.

"We must help you back to the tent and get some ice on that wound. I suggest you return to the landing site with us for a full examination."

"What about Michael?" Yanamai exclaimed.

"I can do many things; searching the jungle for an abductor is not one of them. Before we do anything, we must contact the Regime and have them send in a rescue team."

"I will not leave him!" Yanamai insisted.

"Help me with Cliff, and we'll figure out what to do about Michael," Dr. Young instructed.

Yanamai helped Cliff to the tent, returned to the cavern, and looked for Michael while Dr. Young examined him. Having focused all her attention on finding Michael, she did not notice that the rain had stopped. Later, she returned.

"How is he?"

"I had to stitch him up. For now, the ice should prevent more swelling; he should get to a hospital soon."

"I found something. Please, follow me."

Dr. Young reluctantly accompanied Yanamai into the cavern and instinctively grabbed his medicine bag before leaving. They walked through a series of tunnels and returned to the surface at a different location; she found a road only a hundred paces away.

"You did very well. Those fresh tire tracks will lead the Regime rescue team to the abductors. Let's return and call for help."

"You can go back if you want. I plan to follow those tracks."

"What will you do if you find them? My guess is whoever took him will have weapons. In case you haven't noticed, we don't have any."

"I will figure out something," she followed the tracks on the muddy road.

Dr. Young looked back at the cavern, then to Yanamai, and exhaled loudly, "Wait up, Yanamai! If there is any chance of rescuing him, you will need my help."

Chapter 33

Akil
Argi City
The 22,282[nd] Terrestrial Rotation of the Second Summer

Having returned to the cave where she first met Urki, Julie explained everything that had happened the previous day. He seemed pleased that she dispatched four Skeans yet was unhappy with her decision to work alongside one.

"I have said this before; she will betray you," Urki warned.

"Yes, I know. She told me so herself. I've kept up my guard around her; since I fought so poorly yesterday, I don't think it'll matter much. Once we destroy the rest of them, Nayrah *will* kill me."

"You can defeat her with more practice."

"She said I allow the source of my power to control me too much. Is that why I'm having problems?"

"Be careful, Julie. It sounds as if she is trying to train you. If you listen to her, she could seduce you into joining her; you would serve the Night Lord, and darkness will rule your thoughts forever."

"I have no intention or desire to join her; still, I need to know if she's right."

"She is, except the collaboration between the High Lord's power and Saiph takes time. In the beginning stages, your power source controls your every move. In time, you will learn to control it as well. Together, you become stronger, faster, and for some, unbeatable."

"I'm guessing it takes a long time to achieve that unity."

"Yes. It takes many of your Earthian years. Therefore, you must stay and continue with your lessons."

"I've made up my mind. I must go. Today, we will destroy their offspring."

"What if she kills you after dispatching the last Skean child?"

"I don't have a choice."

For a little longer, they argued until Julie left abruptly, returning to her hiding place, where she slammed the door startling Olan, Tionah, and Edur, causing all three to run to the apartment's front.

"Oh, it is you," Tionah said, relieved.

"Sorry. I just argued with Urki. Stupid computer."

"About what?" Olan asked.

"He doesn't like me working with Nayrah. He wants me to abandon the idea of helping her. I can't get his thick, computer chip brain to understand that I need her help now. I can barely hold my own against one of them, let alone seven."

"I agree with your decision because their numbers do not give us any choice. Urki cannot think as we do," Olan noted.

"I'm tired of arguing with him. I'm not going back until we get this done." Julie looked around, "Where is my communicator? I want to contact Nayrah and get this over with."

"Right here," Tionah answered.

Julie spoke to Nayrah, and Olan handed her the artifact High Priest Elazar gave him.

"Before you go, I want you to look at this."

"What is it?" Julie inquired.

"I am told it is a compass. It is supposed to heighten a Saiph's ability to locate Skeans."

Staring at the artifact in her hand, she concentrated. Moments later, the gem inside glowed brightly, and a three-dimensional hologram of Akil appeared above the compass. Within the planet's image, several red dots appeared.

"Touch that area," Olan advised.

With her right index finger, Julie touched the red dots. They magnified.

"I recognize the layout. These are the five underground cities. They are Vlor, Krek, Nord, Drard, and Argi," Olan pointed to each one, naming them.

"I see three red dots in Argi and one in each of the other cities. I guess those four dots will disappear soon. Assuming Nayrah and I are successful," Julie pointed to the uppermost red dot, "This one must be Gecheana. That is the Argi House."

"Agreed. The second one is on level ten," Olan rubbed his chin in thought.

"What's wrong?" Julie questioned.

"That is a very wealthy district."

"So?"

"That area is very populated. I thought Skeans preferred the dark."

"Although Nayrah does like darkness, she is hiding from Gecheana. What better place to conceal yourself than where your enemy least expects it?"

Nodding his agreement, Olan made a mental note of the address for future reference and focused on the other red dots.

"Who do you think that is?" Julie queried.

"It must be Nayrah's Skean child."

"I wonder who Nayrah's better half is."

"I have been thinking over the details of what Nayrah told us. She had four Skean sisters, so including Nayrah, Gecheana had five Skean daughters," Olan concluded.

"Nayrah said they were not biologically related. I think Gecheana stole them as infants and trained them from their youth," Julie added.

"It is the ways of darkness," Tionah remarked.

"No matter how she obtained them, Gecheana has five daughters, one for each Sovereign," Olan commented.

"That would mean Nayrah is Thea," Julie surmised.

"What?" Tionah blurted out.

"I have had my suspicions; now I have proof," confirmed Olan.

"Your ability to transform your appearances leaves much room for deception," Julie noted.

"Yes, Nayrah has deceived all of us," Olan lamented.

"Poor Tionah, I feel terrible for her. She worked for Thea a long time," Julie sympathized.

"If I am right, it would explain many things that happened recently," Olan added.

"This would also mean that Otsoa is a Skean too."

"Unlikely. I have watched him grow. He is more of a dupe than a Skean. No, I think Yetta is a Skean. She and Nayrah must have been controlling Otsoa until Gecheana arrived in Argi," Olan explained.

"It would make sense. If Otsoa had their powers, he would be harder to control."

"Precisely, and just in case Otsoa gets out of line, they have Va'ron as a backup."

"Do you think Zorion knew Thea was a Skean?"

"If Tionah did not know, I am sure Zorion did not. Using her powers, Thea must have controlled his mind. Like when she manipulated me to attack him."

"He did leave her. How could Zorion break from her control?"

"I believe you are the one who freed him. Remember his dreams of you?"

"It didn't do him any good," Julie responded sadly and looked at her watch. "I must go. I don't want her seeing me step out from those secret passages."

Olan took the compass from Julie and tested it to see if it still worked, "You must have charged the gem somehow."

"Urki said the High Lord's power makes our swords glow. It goes through a transfer Sapphire, so the one in that compass must retain power."

"Good. Now I can use it," Olan put it in his utility belt for safekeeping, "I am ready; we can go."

Tionah haphazardly handed Julie her cloak, "If you plan on traveling, you will need this."

Julie took the cloak from her, put it on, and pulled the hood over her head to hide her face, "If I don't come back, Olan will watch over you."

Tionah sobbed, "You will do fine. I believe in you."

*****

Arriving earlier than the last time they met, Julie appeared from the secret passage a few blocks away, wearing her headpiece just in case Nayrah was already waiting for her.

"Remember, I will be watching you from the shadows," consoled Olan.

"I appreciate it. Thank you for all your help."

Julie approached the meeting place and saw Nayrah standing near the courtyard fountain. She had to suppress a natural urge to attack whenever they were near.

"I see you're early," Julie said underneath her headpiece.

"I could not let you beat me here a second time," Nayrah paused, "Are you ready?"

"As ready as I'll ever be."

As they walked toward the elevator, Nayrah handed Julie a small metal token.

"This is your ticket for the intercity train. We will start at Vlor and end in Drard. That is where Kraeth lives. He will be the most difficult to kill, so we must be cautious during the fight."

"Kraeth is a Skean?"

"You seemed surprised."

"I helped him on Earth. He could have killed me."

"He must not have sensed your power. I assumed you hid them as you do now."

"I didn't have these abilities at the time."

"Interesting. He must have seen the blue haze around your aura; I wonder why he did not kill you?" Nayrah wondered.

"What?"

"Does your instructor teach you anything?"

"Enough to survive."

"I disagree. Anyway, if you see someone with a blue haze around their aura, he or she has the potential to become a Skean or Saiph. It is how Gecheana found us."

"Since there are no Saiphs here, she must have killed anyone else who had it."

"Naturally."

"You guys are hardcore; I'll give you that."

"Oh, my dear, you have no idea what we are capable of doing."

"I'm getting a pretty good picture."

"Since Kraeth did not kill you, it can only mean one thing. He had mercy on you."

"In my opinion, it isn't a bad thing. I'm still alive."

"Indeed, you are, but many plans were in motion before your arrival. Someone close to me thwarted a few assignments Gecheana gave to me. Now I see that none of the failures are mine. Thank you, Julie. I needed to know this information."

"Glad to help," Julie quipped.

Nayrah smiled pleasantly, missing Julie's sarcasm, "Kraeth is extremely dangerous because he can produce the Night Lord's venom."

"What the hell is that?"

"His body secretes a naturally made drug through his hands. You will do whatever he tells you if it touches your skin."

Julie gulped, "If I know about it, won't that prevent it from controlling me?"

"No. The drug is too powerful. It suppresses any rational thought and stimulates the primitive part of your brain. Once it is in your system, you will kill for him without hesitation, even if you know about its effects, and you will not remember it. Assuming you survive."

"My suit should prevent him from touching my skin."

"Yes, if it stays in one piece."

"Do all Skeans have that ability?"

Nayrah laughed, "No. Like you, each of us has similar combat abilities, and some have rare gifts. For example, Kemena, the one I killed yesterday, could send waves of pleasure into another's mind. It allowed her to take control of her subjects. I also learned that she stimulated the growth of some missing digits on Elzer's hand following an accident."

"It sounds like she was powerful."

"We all are."

"If you're so powerful, why do you need my help?"

"Concerning my Skean sisters and their offspring, it is a matter of sheer numbers. Gecheana is different. As my Skean Mother, she placed a veil between us, making it impossible for me to kill her.

"A veil?"

"It is metaphorical. Whenever I face her, I feel like a frightened child. It consumes me and causes me to question my abilities. I have no choice; I back down."

"I see. It makes sense. To survive, she put in a failsafe to keep her children from attacking her, which you all do at some point."

"Exactly. To heighten our fear of her, she told us how she killed her master."

"Why is it scary?"

"It has to do with love, my dear. Gecheana was training to become a Saiph and fell in love with her instructor; he led her on only to reject her. The pain she felt caused a void allowing darkness to enter her, and she killed every Saiph on Akil."

"Yikes!"

"To remind herself of what he did to her, she merged part of his sword with hers. That is why you will see one side crimson and the other white; do not allow the white side to fool you. Gecheana is ruthless."

"I believe you."

"I have been loyal to her from my youth. It came with a price because I have given up many things for her, yet she tossed me aside like a used cleaning comb, and now it is time I have my revenge."

At the train station, Nayrah separated herself from Julie, intending to ride in a different car. Meanwhile, Julie kept her hood over her headpiece, her head down, handed the conductor her token, and boarded the train.

Chapter 34

Earth
Scotland - Dunnottar Castle
May 18, 2452

Ethan waited for Dawn to finish reviewing his report and discreetly searched the room for any signs of the transmitter that kept him alive. After a quick look, it was clear that he would not find it out in the open; she could have hidden it anywhere amongst the hundreds of knick-knacks scattered about the room, or inside a safe, somewhere behind a picture or cabinet. The possibilities were endless, and she would kill him if he looked for it.

Having read the report, she looked at him, "I hope you were thorough cleaning up the tub Vincent was in."

"I wiped it down twice."

"For your sake, it better be spotless. The Regime forensics team will search every nook and crevice. If they discover any trace of Vincent's DNA, they'll have evidence that I killed him in my warehouse. I do not want to speak with a Regime committee about why he died there."

"I would have taken it with me if I had time."

"My source was clear. They have a new way of tracking their agents. Regime soldiers arrived just minutes after you cleared out."

"It's a good thing I left when I did. Now, what's on my agenda for today?"

"I'll be leaving for Brazil shortly, and I want you to be ready in case I need backup. I have a squad of mercenaries on my payroll, ready to fight anyone, anywhere. I also have a tank in case things get out of hand, so have them armed and ready to go if I call."

"Understood," he replied.

"Oh, there's one more thing. I want you to think of a plan to kill Deputy Chief Constable Brice."

"What?"

"Did I stutter?"

"He's Scotland's Deputy Chief of Police; why do you want me to kill him?"

"I paid him a great deal of money to keep the Regime out of Scotland, and he failed to hold up his end of the deal."

Ethan sighed, "How am I supposed to kill him?"

"Here's his dossier. Inside, you'll find his home address, favorite bars, and daily habits. Find a weakness and use it. I want it public and bloody."

"When do you want me to do it?"

"Once I return from Brazil."

"Anything else?"

"Yes. Before you kill him, let him know I was the one who sent you."

*****

Dawn walked to the medical wing of the castle. She stepped inside a room and found Dragon lying in bed, still asleep. As she stood at his bedside, he opened his eyes.

"How are you feeling today?" she asked.

"A little sore."

"That should go away the more you move. We borrowed some of the Regime's DNA stimulant powder. It accelerates cell growth and repair. Wounds such as yours recover in a fraction of the usual time. Try sitting up."

He moved to a sitting position, wincing from sore muscles, got out of bed, and stood. He felt a dull ache in his belly from the gunshot wound Wu Luli gave him. The more he moved, the easier it became.

"How long was I out?" Dragon inquired.

"Almost two full days. It's about 2 PM here in Scotland."

"Scotland?"

"Yes. I brought you to my private medical wing in my home."

"The last thing I remember was seeing a bomb drop into the room. I thought you decided to end my employment."

"Believe me; it crossed my mind. You have really messed up this one. How could you have allowed Sofia to turn on you like that?"

"There are always unexpected variables during a mission. Don't worry; I took care of her."

"Yes. I heard. Still, there are more loose ends."

"I'm ready to get back to work."

133

"If circumstances were different, I'd give you another day to heal fully, but things are moving fast now, and I don't have that kind of time. I've been watching Special Agent Reed's progress. He's dangerously close to linking the comptroller to Sanya Electronics."

"Jim Price?"

"Yes. He didn't cover his tracks very well, either. I want to ensure we destroy any evidence he might have of our involvement, including him."

"I'll need my things."

She pointed to the closet, "You'll find everything you need in there. When you're ready, my assistant will escort you to the Transportation Station; my technician will send you to Jim's home. Before you leave, I've authorized a personal portal device for you to use. Guard it carefully, Dragon, and don't try to keep it like you did the last time I let you use it," she paused, letting the warning sink in, "This is your last chance; don't screw this up."

Chapter 35

Earth
The Regime - Georgia - Thomasville
May 18, 2452

The ride from Fulton County took a long time; Ashley, Wendy, and Kenny arrived at Jim Price's home early in the morning before sunrise. Tired from the long journey, they stepped out of their vehicle to stretch. Leaving the other two in the car, Ashley walked to his house to see if he was inside. Stepping up to a window, she saw movement behind the sheer curtain.

Ashley took a closer look and saw Kenny's boss packing several suitcases. Afterward, he sat in front of his laptop and began working. Thinking Jim would leave shortly, she moved to the front door to wait on him. He did not show, so she looked back inside and saw him still working. Since it appeared it would be some time before Jim would leave, she returned to her hovercar and got back inside.

"What did you see?" Kenny asked as he and Wendy got back in their seats.

"He's in there. I saw him packing; it means he's planning a trip. Right now, he's working on his computer."

"I bet he's erasing his tracks," Kenny noted.

"Can't you go inside and arrest him?" Wendy inquired.

"Not without a warrant; I can stop him if he gets into his car, make him get out, and restrain him."

"How long must we wait?" Kenny queried.

"Your guess is as good as mine."

As the sun appeared on the horizon, Ashley took another sip of coffee that helped keep her awake during the night; sadly, the other stimulus source was snoring loudly in the back seat. Even though her eyelids tried to close several times, Kenny's loud breathing was enough of an annoyance to prevent her from drifting off into a restful sleep. Taking a moment to check on Wendy, Ashley wondered how she could sleep through such a ruckus.

Returning to the house, she saw the garage door open, and a hovercar backed out. Before he could reach the end of the driveway, Ashley started her car and pulled up behind him, blocking his exit.

All the commotion woke Wendy and Kenny, who searched to see what was happening.

"You two stay inside, and Kenny, keep hidden. I don't want him to see you; it'll tip him off, and I don't feel like running this morning."

As she approached Jim's vehicle, he stepped out and slammed his door. Obviously, her maneuver upset him.

"What the hell are you doing? I'm trying to get out of here!" he yelled.

"I'm with the police department, Mr. Price; I need to ask you a few questions."

Seeing her badge, he calmed down and, in a quieter tone, questioned, "What is it?"

"The Kenny Barnes case."

"I've already spoken to the TBI; why would the local police have any questions for me?"

Seeing his luggage in the rear seat, she nodded toward them, "I'm sure the TBI told you not to leave town until we can resolve the matter."

"My washing machine broke down; I'm heading for the Laundromat."

"Seeing that it's a workday, it's a strange time to go, isn't it?"

"Look, why are you harassing me? Barnes is the one you're chasing!" he growled.

Using his response as an excuse to arrest him, Ashley retrieved her weapon and pointed it at him, "Put your hands on the hood, now!"

"What? Why? I haven't done anything!"

"I said, do it!"

Jim placed his hands on the hood, and Ashley handcuffed him. With Jim in restraints, she went through his pockets, took out his keys, and brought him back into his home, so no one in the neighborhood would see them. Before stepping inside, she motioned for Wendy and Kenny to follow her; Ashley made Jim sit in a chair. Although Jim protested and threatened to sue the department for false imprisonment, Ashley ignored him. Then, he saw Kenny and his face went pale.

"What is *he* doing here?"

"I'm here to make sure you clear my name," Kenny glared at him.

"Watch him. I'll see what I can find in his car," Ashley returned to Jim's vehicle, still parked in the driveway. She looked through his luggage and found the laptop he had worked on the night before. Inside the house, Ashley heard a scuffle. She returned to the living room and saw Wendy trying to pull Kenny off Jim. Kenny had him on the ground, punching him in the face. When she got to him, Jim was bleeding badly.

"Stop!" she exclaimed, finally pulling him away.

As Jim spit blood, a tooth shot to the floor.

"Serves you right, you son of a bitch!" Kenny yelled.

Ashley pushed Kenny into the adjoining room, "Why don't you do something productive?"

"What?"

"Search his rooms. He may have left something behind."

With a huff, Kenny spun around and disappeared upstairs. Ashley returned to the living room and put Jim back into the chair. Now that he sat upright, blood dripped from his mouth from where Kenny hit him.

"Wendy, see what you can do to stop the bleeding, and I'll check the computer."

Wendy returned with a towel and some ice while Ashley gained access and searched the hard drive.

"How did you get in without a password?" Wendy wondered.

"Jim offered it. I told him if he didn't, I'd let Kenny come back and beat him to his heart's content."

Wendy shook her head, "You two are a pair."

Wendy wiped the blood from Jim's face, and Kenny returned, "I couldn't find anything."

"There's nothing on his computer. He must have wiped it last night," Ashley remarked.

"Did you check the cloud?" Kenny quizzed.

"Yeah; he wiped that too."

"How am I going to prove my innocence?"

"Don't worry. The government keeps a backup of everything on the internet, so all I have to do is access the server with my ID," Ashley explained.

A few minutes later, the monitor lit up with the records of all the transactions Jim made on Kenny's behalf.

"This is the computer he used to set you up," Ashley noted.

The computer shattered in front of her. Turning to see what caused the destruction, Ashley saw a man holding a gun with a suppressor on its muzzle, pointing at Jim Price. Before she could react, he pulled the trigger twice. Blood spattered in every direction from Jim's head, giving everyone in the vicinity dripping red freckles; Ashley reached for her weapon, but the intruder turned the gun on her.

Just as he fired, Kenny came running toward her, pushing her out of the way. She heard two more whispery shots from the intruder's gun as they fell to the floor. Kenny fell on top of her and stopped moving, and his weight on her right hand prevented her from grabbing the weapon, so Ashley tried to push him off. As she struggled to move Kenny, Wendy ran to the adjacent room.

Before she could escape, the intruder shot her right shoulder, forcing her to fall forward. At the same time, Ashley pushed Kenny off her midsection, which freed her gun hand. The intruder pointed his weapon at Wendy as she lay face down. Before he could shoot, Ashley aimed her gun at him from the floor and yelled, "Hey!"

The distraction stopped him from killing Wendy. Seeing Ashley with a gun in her hand forced him to turn his weapon on her. Before pointing the barrel in her direction, she repeatedly fired until he fell, motionless. Ashley stood and ran to the shooter to ensure he was dead. She kicked his weapon out of reach and cautiously leaned down to check his pulse, keeping her gun trained on him. Having confirmed he was dead, she ran to Wendy's side.

"Are you all right?"

"My shoulder is killing me. What happened?"

"The intruder shot you, but you'll survive. Can you get up? We need to check Kenny."

"Yeah, sure, just give me a hand."

Placing her shoulder under Wendy's left arm, Ashley helped her up, and they walked to where Kenny lay. She checked his injuries, felt his neck for a pulse, faced Ashley, and shook her head.

"I'm sorry, the bullets went through his heart."

Ashley lamented, "He saved my life."

"He was a good man, after all."

"At least there's evidence on the government's server proving he was innocent."

TBI agents came rushing into the house. Ashley dropped her weapon and raised her hands until they verified her credentials. Once they secured the area, Special Agent Reed stepped inside. He handed Ashley a towel to wipe away the blood and debriefed her as medics worked on Wendy's shoulder.

"Sir, look at what I've found," one of the TBI agents handed over a small backpack to Special Agent Reed.

"Ah, the personal portal device," he remarked with admiration.

He faced Ashley, "You just brought down Dragon, who was an international hitman."

"I did?"

"Yes. Someone leaked the schematics for these devices, and we're still looking for him or her."

"Jim fried the computer; I located the government backup file that proves he set Kenny up."

"I'll have my men review the data right away. If Barnes was innocent, I promise to clear his name."

"He barely knew me yet gave his life to save mine. I can't even thank him."

"In that case, I will clear his name and ensure everyone knows he was a hero."

"Thank you. It means a lot to me."

As paramedics took Wendy out on a gurney, Ashley walked over and held her hand.

"Thank you for your help," Wendy smiled warmly.

"Next time, I'd appreciate it if you would call the local authorities," she smiled.

"There better not be a 'next time,'" she warned as the paramedics took her away.

Ashley faced Special Agent Reed, "Am I going to lose my job over this?"

"You did bend the rules, but my agent said you tried to notify me of the situation the moment you were aware."

"I didn't want to do this on my own."

"Don't worry. I'll speak to your captain and put in a good word for you."

"I appreciate it. I need my job. I have a two-year-old daughter at home."

"I think we have everything. You're free to go home. If I need additional information, I know how to get a hold of you."

"Thanks, I'm already missing her."

Chapter 36

Akil
Vlor City
The 22,282nd Terrestrial Rotation of the Second Summer

Julie exited the train and found Nayrah; their familiarity made it easier for her to locate Nayrah in a crowd. Before entering the city, Julie went through a screening booth like everyone else and passed without incident with Nayrah's help. Along the way, Julie noticed that there were sentries everywhere. It made her feel uneasy, mostly since she was there to kill the heir of a Sovereign. Nayrah forced the doors closed as they boarded an elevator, just as a couple was about to enter. One of them pounded on the door in frustration. Nayrah looked at Julie and smiled.

"Isn't that petty?" Julie asked.

"Sometimes, it is the little things that make me happy."

"Why does that make you happy?"

"Seeing someone suffer, even a little, brings me joy."

"I shouldn't be surprised," Julie shook her head, "How are we going to get to…what is his name again?"

"Stron, he is Elzer's second heir. Otsoa killed his first heir, Tuso."

"Otsoa, isn't he Thea's son?"

"Yes, he is."

"Do you know him?"

Looking at Julie suspiciously, she inquired, "Now, why would you think I know Otsoa?"

"You know everyone else around here. Your goal is to control Argi and, in time, Akil itself, so it seemed logical that you have dealt with him at some point."

"You are very clever. Yes. I know him. He is a means to an end."

Since Nayrah did not give a clear answer, Julie changed the subject, "Why is security elevated here?"

"Because someone killed Elzer yesterday."

"Really? How?"

"Someone got close to him and removed his head."

"How will we get close enough to Stron to kill him?"

"Without Kemena, there is no one here to stop us. Just follow my lead."

Even though many Akilians walked on the upper level, Julie watched Nayrah move through the crowd effortlessly. It did not take long to sense her using the Night Lord's powers to push them aside; they got through the city capitol screening post without incident with Nayrah's help. On the avenue outside the capitol, Nayrah took Julie to the side.

"It is still early, which means he has not left his home yet. On the way to his office, we will attack him on the avenue about a block before the capitol steps. There will be two sentries with him. The place where we will attack has two more posted within eyesight of each other. Before he leaves, we will dispatch them and hide in the shadows until he arrives. As they walk by, we will strike down the other two separately, and together we will attack Stron."

"When you say, dispatch. You mean kill, right?"

"Yes, slice off their heads and be done with them. If you delay, Stron will have time to defend himself."

"You must promise me that only the Skean will die."

"I do not leave witnesses. What if one of the guards sees us?"

"I have my suit to hide me, and you can make yourself look like whomever you want, keeping your identity hidden."

"It is still too risky. I say we kill them to be sure."

"Nayrah, promise me you will only kill the target and no one else, or I'll turn around and go home."

Hearing Julie's defiance sent a flash of anger through Nayrah that would have flourished into a fit of rage if it were anyone else; since she still needed Julie's help to kill Gecheana, she refrained. Instead of lashing out, Nayrah took a deep breath, pushed away from her anger, and growled through gritted teeth.

"Fine, we will do it your way."

"Thank you."

As they moved toward the private avenue, Julie wondered how her life went from teaching gymnastics only a few days ago to killing Skeans. Thoughts of Zorion moved to the forefront of her mind, and she felt a desperate need to mourn him but stopped. She had to push everything aside or risk losing her focus on the task.

"The two sentries are just fifty paces from us," Nayrah brought Julie out of her brief trance.

"I'll take the one closest," Julie remarked.

With a raised eyebrow, Nayrah gave Julie a look like - who put you in charge?

"I'm still a novice, remember?"

"Very well, I will take the one farthest away."

"When do we strike?"

"Do not worry; you will feel it."

Nayrah moved almost faster than the eye could see without a countdown or warning. Somehow, Julie sensed her movements in slow motion. Feeling the nudge, Julie also started running for her target, unsheathed her sword, and pierced his heart. The shock and pain on the guard's face made her feel terrible; he collapsed but would survive. Julie looked at Nayrah to ensure she kept her promise. At that moment, she stood over the other sentry, who was still in one piece.

Nayrah nodded, signifying he would recover. Julie noticed a slight smile on Nayrah's face. Remembering the earlier incident at the elevator, she knew Nayrah enjoyed the bloodshed, a little too much for her comfort. Nayrah looked down the avenue, waved Julie over, and they waited patiently in the shadows for Stron to leave his apartment. As time passed, Julie kept checking her watch; the minutes felt like hours.

"Is he ever going to leave?" Julie finally questioned.

"Any moment, and will you please shield your powers? You are like a beacon of light. He will sense you before getting twelve paces from us."

"Sorry, I was distracted," Julie answered, pulled her headpiece down, closed her eyes, and focused on cloaking her powers as Urki trained her.

Nayrah waited for a few heartbeats, "That is better. Now keep quiet. Here he comes."

Julie peaked around the corner to see him and paused; his youthfulness surprised her. *He can't be more than fourteen.*

She whispered, "He's just a boy."

"Even at his age, he could kill you. Do not let your motherly feelings get in the way, or I will have to finish this alone."

"I certainly don't want to make things harder for you," Julie responded sarcastically.

"I appreciate the sentiment," Nayrah remarked, not catching her mocking tone. "I still need to know if you can do this or not."

Julie groaned, "Yes. I can do it."

Walking in front of the guards, Stron was first to pass. Julie and Nayrah pressed firmly against the wall, hoping to hide their silhouettes. Julie felt Nayrah attack less than a second before moving and charging at the other sentry. They brought them down in mere moments, except it was not quick enough, as Nayrah warned. Sensing the attack, Stron unsheathed his Skean sword. Spinning, he stopped their blades just as they brought them down to kill him.

Even though the odds were two against one, Stron fought exceptionally well. Being young gave him a slight advantage because he was agile. Julie sensed that his power flowed through him effortlessly. As the trio fought, Julie struggled to avoid hitting Nayrah because her instincts urged her to kill them. By now, they positioned Stron between them. They swung at him fast; his quick reflexes kept them from making contact.

At least he was on the defensive. That is, until he jumped over Julie's head, putting her in the middle and attacking her. While Julie fought him, Nayrah moved to get back on the other side, except Stron went in the opposite direction, using Julie to block her. Nayrah stopped trying and watched them fight. In her peripheral vision, Julie noticed that Nayrah had pulled herself from the confrontation. Standing only a few feet away, Nayrah shook her head disappointingly.

"You must get involved with the fight. You are letting your powers do all the work."

"Stop trying to instruct me," Julie countered with a distorted voice that came through her headpiece.

"Fine, I can let the child kill you. It does not matter to me."

As much as she hated to admit it, Nayrah was right about her fighting, but there was not enough time to learn. The longer the sparring ensued, the faster Stron moved. Julie's defense seemed to be just enough to keep him at bay. She struggled to figure out how to turn it around and go on the attack. Stron's absence got the attention of a few staff members, who sent guards to check on him. Upon their arrival, Nayrah took them down and yelled to Julie.

"You better hurry, or we will have more sentries than we can manage."

Frustrated and tired, Julie fantasized about returning to Earth and forgetting about ever landing on Akil. At home, she would just be getting into a nice warm bath. Not fighting for her life with some stranger she had never met before. Although her mind drifted, her powers moved her body in an evasive pattern. She ducked, blocked, and spun in a smooth, fluid motion, all at the right time; one of his strikes unexpectedly landed, cutting the sleeve of her suit.

Looking down at her arm, she saw a nasty gash. Anger raced through her mind like a heated furnace. It was all she could take. Ignoring the pain, she used her rage to take control of the power that flowed through her. She instantly went from defense to offense, attacking him with a vigor that surprised Stron and Nayrah. She moved faster with each swing. At one point, she sent a wave of invisible power out from her hand, pushing Stron into the wall and stunning him.

Not waiting for him to recover, she pounced and sliced through his neck, killing him instantly. The intense heat of the blade cauterized the wound, preventing any blood from escaping. As she stood over him, her headpiece veiled the look of rage and satisfaction on her face. Nayrah sensed her feelings and applauded.

"Excellent. You used your anger to control your power. Now you understand how to wield it."

Leaning down, Nayrah picked up Stron's sword, "We cannot leave any evidence that he was Skean."

Julie continued to pant, "Damn; he was fast."

"I told you he was lethal."

"You were right."

Nayrah smiled, "I do like the sound of those words. Now come. It is time to go. We still have a few more to dispatch before we finish for the Terrestrial Revolution."

"I'm injured. I won't be of any use until I recover."

"Do not worry. I know how weak Earthians are. I brought some ointments with me, just in case. I will fix you up before we board the train. You will be good as new by the time we get to Krek."

After killing the Skeans in Krek and Nord, they headed for Drard to find Kraeth.

Chapter 37

Bereaved of his daughter and granddaughter, General Bailey sat at his desk to personally debrief the only soldier who survived the attack at Larkin's home, Corporal Wade. Even though he felt deeply distressed over their loss, his need for revenge overshadowed his need to grieve, so he listened to Corporal Wade's account of last night's events and questioned him several times.

The goal was to discover any inconsistencies or unearth some detail he might have overlooked the first time. At least he had two names to assign the blame, Ethan Brun and Dawn Pierce. The first name was familiar because Larkin told him about Sable's nightmares. Corporal Wade described Ethan as a young man. The only conclusion that made sense was that he was Ethan's grandson. Three hours later, General Bailey finally let him go. He promised to return if he remembered any detail, no matter how minute.

Now that he was alone, thoughts of Sarah and Sable occupied his mind, making him sob. With his left hand, he wiped away tears from his cheeks while pouring himself another drink. The whiskey burned his throat, helping to numb the emotional pain. Someone knocked at his door as he set the glass on his desk.

"I said I didn't want to be disturbed!" he yelled.

Colonel Scott cautiously opened the door, "Sorry, General; you're going to want to see him."

As the door widened, General Bailey saw a tall figure standing outside, holding a box. General Bailey thought it was Larkin until he recognized Tucker. Reflexively, General Bailey stood, pulled his sidearm, and pointed it at Tucker's head.

"Wait, General! Listen to what he has to say," Colonel Scott pleaded.

"There's nothing he can say to keep me from puttin' a bullet into his skull."

"Do it after you hear him out."

"Then start talkin'. If I don't like what I hear, you're dead."

“I heard what happened to Sarah and Sable last night. I brought a peace offerin’, just so you’d know I had nothin’ to do with it,” Tucker handed the box to Colonel Scott.

Colonel Scott set it on General Bailey’s desk and opened it. Seeing the contents made him take a few steps backward.

“What is it, Colonel?” General Bailey wondered.

“Rico, at least part of him. It’s his head.”

General Bailey looked inside the box, “You think this lets you off the hook? Larkin told me you laughed at him when he sent his soldiers to kill Sarah and Sable.”

“I know what I did was mean-spirited, but I swear, I had no idea he sent those soldiers to Larkin’s home until later. I told Rico to tell Larkin that story to scare him. If I’d known he sent ‘em, I would have stopped ‘em myself.”

Pulling the hammer back on his gun, General Bailey yelled, “Lies!”

Tucker kept his hands up as a sign of surrender, “I swear, General, I would never hurt Larkin or his family.”

“You damn near killed him in the pit, idiot!”

“I knew he’d win, even chained up. I know my brother. Sure, I was mad at him for leavin’, so I took the opportunity to get my revenge. I swear I’d never hurt ‘em, and I’d never attack his family. At least now you’ve got the man responsible.”

“Except that Rico ain’t the one who killed them.”

“Huh?”

“Someone named Ethan Brun came to the farm last night wantin’ to speak with Larkin. Said he was representin’ a woman named Dawn Pierce.”

“Wait, I know those names.”

“How?”

“Yesterday, Ethan showed up in my warehouse with weapons and ammunition. I asked him what he wanted in exchange. He said his employer, Dawn Pierce, wanted to speak with me.”

“Have you seen her?”

“Just after persuading me to meet with her, he sent his men away and said, ‘*She is the most lethal person I’ve ever met. If I were you, I’d take the weapons and disappear.*’ He sounded sincere enough, so I pretended to examine the weapons, loaded one, and started shootin'. They left with their tails between their legs."

"He never told you why she wanted to meet with you."

"Nope, sounded to me like he didn't know."

"All right, I've heard enough; now get out of here."

"I was hopin' to see Larkin."

"You don't want to see him in his current condition because he might decide to take his aggression out on you. The information you've given me will help us find whoever did this."

"Before I go, I want you to know I'm goin' to quit the gang and turn it over to Bruce."

"Why? I thought you lived to rule the gangs?"

"I did, but Larkin needs me now that he's alone again. I know he's mad at me, so I want him to know he can come to me for help if he wants."

"I'll pass it on; don't expect a warm greetin'."

"I won't. Just be sure to tell 'em I'll be at the warehouse if he wants to talk," Tucker replied and left.

General Bailey paused for a few moments in thought, "Colonel, I want to know where this Dawn Pierce lives, and I want to know now! Also, I want to know about Ethan Brun: if he had any children and where they are."

"Yes, Sir! Right away!"

Chapter 38

Earth
The Regime - Washington, D.C. - Federal Courthouse
May 18, 2452

Early in the morning, Jared returned to Sonya's cell and found her curled up on the floor, with her hair scattered about in every direction. Although a part of him felt sorry for her, he could never trust her again, especially after betraying him. Knowing her trial would resume in an hour, he whispered, "Sonya."

Hearing him, she stirred, opened her eyes, and smiled, thinking he was lying in bed beside her until realizing her reality, and the smile faded. She forced herself to face him and put on a rehearsed cheerful face using sheer willpower. Her appearance surprised him. Her lips were severely chapped, her hair was in complete disarray, and the makeup she wore was either gone or smeared.

She seemed genuinely happy to see him, and he could still see a glimmer of hope in her eyes until she saw the tablet in his hand. Her smile faded along with any dream she may have had of them reuniting. He turned the tablet sideways with his right hand and pushed it halfway through the opening between the bars for her to take.

"You promised to sign this if it didn't work out between us. I hope you'll keep your word," Jared spoke sincerely.

"I can't believe you're going through with it. I'm facing life on the moon, or maybe even a death sentence, and all you care about is getting a divorce!" Sonya yelled.

"Sonya, you promised."

She wanted to cry but had no more tears to respond to the pain, which was killing her inside. She walked over with a zombie-like motion, took the tablet from him, and scrolled through the pages until reaching the end. Before signing, she looked at him, hoping it was a test. She dreamed he would tell her to stop at the last moment, but he did not flinch. She reluctantly signed the tablet and handed it back to him.

"You have what you want. I'm no longer your problem," she collapsed back to the floor.

"I didn't see you as a problem until you betrayed me. Your actions are despicable."

"Sure, trying to save your life is reprehensible, so thanks, Jared, you really are a dear."

"I *am* sorry it didn't work out between us," he answered, turning to leave.

"Ha!" she blurted out loudly.

"What's that supposed to mean?" he asked, turning back toward the cell.

Standing to face him, she came close to the bars. She was close enough that he could see the salty residue of tear stains on her cheeks; anger had replaced the sad look on her face, and she yelled.

"You're not sorry! On the contrary, you're relieved that it's over!"

"That's not true. I gave you a chance."

"Some chance. I wondered why you refused to review my memories; now it makes sense. I messed up. It's my entire fault that you can't trust me, even though I risked everything to protect you, and now you have a way out."

"Don't try to put this on me because you didn't do the right thing."

"You're afraid. Aren't you?"

"I'm not afraid of anything."

"Yes, you are. I can see that now. You're afraid of intimacy. You're afraid of loving me or anyone for that matter."

"That's not true. I had a girlfriend before you."

"All right. How long were you together?"

"A couple of years."

"What happened?"

"We drifted apart."

"Uh, huh. Why?"

"I don't know. We just did."

"I bet you broke up when the Regime accepted you as an agent."

Jared was silent.

"That's what I thought," Sonya commented.

"I didn't break up with her. It was her idea."

"Of course, it was. She saw the same look in your eyes as I do. She knew staying with you would change your mind about the job. Right?"

Again, Jared was silent.

"Let me enlighten you, Jared. That poor girl, who I'm sure loved you very much, let you go so you wouldn't end up hating her."

"No, she was studying to be a lawyer and had to focus all her attention on her classes."

"All right, Jared. You're right, and I'm wrong, and after you leave, when you catch yourself smiling and feeling relieved that you don't have to deal with me, at least be a man and admit that I'm right."

"Let's examine you. You let all those people in Texas suffer while *you* lived in the lap of luxury! You were their governor; you could have done something!"

"I was under the President's thumb! I couldn't do anything contrary to him, or he would kill me, yet I did do something! I gave it to the Regime at the first opportunity!"

"Don't you mean you sold it to the Regime?"

"You know very well I wouldn't be able to work here. Who would hire the ex-governor of Texas? I had to have something to live on."

"You have an answer for everything, don't you?"

"I just call it as I see it."

"Fine, let's talk about your first husband. You know the one who died in a mysterious car accident."

She pressed herself against the bars, "I loved my first husband more than you will ever know. We were on track to having a family and growing old together. I planned to resign from my position and leave the U.S. with him, except he died the night before. I thought it was an accident until I discovered he decided to publish an article before leaving the country. That article was a formal accusation of the President, and on his way home, a tractor-trailer hit his car, killing him instantly. By the way, I did confront the President, and you know what he said?"

"No, what?"

"*You're next if you ever try to leave me again.* That bastard controlled me since I was a child."

"All right, he had control over you, but you *were* leaving. You should have told me about his plans."

"I didn't have time to calculate all the variables to the situation; I had to act quickly. He threatened to kill you right there in my office! Can't you understand the position I was in?"

"I know you faced tough decisions and didn't make the right choices. Had you come to me, I could have helped you; now, it's beyond my control."

"I guess there's nothing left for us to say. I failed you. Blame me. You have what you came for, your freedom. So, go." He did not leave immediately, so she yelled, "Guard, please escort this man out of here. We're done talking!"

Jared left, and her eyes somehow found a new source of tears. She wept, collapsing to the floor. Before turning the corner, Jared looked at her one last time.

Chapter 39

Earth
The Regime - Texas - Houston - George Bush Park
May 18, 2452

General Bailey read the report Colonel Scott recently brought him while Larkin waited. It had taken Larkin all night and most of the day to regain consciousness. His reaction to the loss of his family overwhelmed his body. The pain of losing them struck him hard when he woke, yet he restrained his rage for now. It was about two hours until he managed to get out of bed. Never in his life had he felt such a profound loss, and never in his life had he felt such rage. General Bailey put the report down.

"Sir, I want permission to find Tucker and Rico. I know they're responsible for this,"

"No, Larkin, they're not."

"How can you be sure?"

"Corporal Wade survived the attack. It wasn't them; Ethan Brun was looking to speak with you on behalf of Dawn Pierce."

Recognizing the name, Larkin stood more out of instinct than purpose.

"Ethan is the man Sable saw in her nightmares, so how is it possible he's still alive? He should be dead by now or too old to be conducting missions."

"I have Colonel Scott trying to find him now. I think it was Ethan's grandson. Corporal Wade described him as in his early twenties. If we find the older Ethan, we should find his descendant. Colonel Scott thinks Ethan may have moved to Panama and lived under an alias; there hasn't been time to confirm whether he's still alive."

"I'll go to Panama and see if I can locate 'em."

"No. He was just a messenger. Dawn Pierce is the person we want to find. Besides, if Ethan works for her, you'll find 'em with her."

"That's fine by me."

"Have you ever heard of her?"

"No."

"Neither has your brother."

"You spoke to Tucker?"

"This morning. After hearing what happened, he brought us Rico's head in a box, hoping to prove his innocence."

"He had something to do with the first one. That's enough for me to kill 'em."

"He claimed he had Rico tell you that story to scare you. Once he found out Rico sent men there, it was too late. I guess by bringing us Rico's head, it was his way of apologizing."

"To hell with 'em. Next time I see him, I'm gonna kill 'em."

"I won't argue with you, but if he kills you, who's gonna find Dawn?"

"He ain't gonna kill me. He ain't got the strength. Not now."

"Anyway, I mentioned Ethan's name to him. He said Ethan met 'em earlier yesterday at his warehouse. Brought 'em all kinds of weapons and ammo just to have a meet and greet, yet before Tucker could agree, Ethan warned him that this Dawn character was dangerous and not to go."

"Do you know where Pierce is?"

"Scotland."

Having a lead, Larkin became focused and spoke with an eerie calm, "I need to get to Scotland, now."

"Aren't you going to stay for the funeral and pay your respects?"

"I pay my respects by finding the son of a bitch who did this."

"I understand. Colonel, is there a way Larkin can use Regime International Transportation Station to get there?"

"Yes, Sir. I expected he would want to go to Scotland, so I requested his passport. It should be ready in three days."

"I ain't waitin' three days, General."

"Your only alternative is to fly, except we don't have anything that can get you that far," Colonel Scott added.

"What about Houston? They have an airport," General Bailey suggested.

"Assuming I could find a jet, I don't know how to pilot it," Larkin replied.

"I know someone I can send with you. He's a local crop duster."

"All right, where is he? I'm ready to go."

"Slow down, Larkin. We still need clearance to fly over Regime territory, and you'll need a contact in Scotland."

"I just need to do something."

"Don't worry. Colonel Scott will work to get everythin' set up. Just give 'em some time."

"Yes, Sir."

"Take the night off and try to get some rest. I want you ready to go once everything is in order."

"I just hope I can get there before she decides to leave the country."

"Don't worry. We'll find 'em and make 'em pay."

Chapter 40

Akil

Drard City

The 22,282nd Terrestrial Rotation of the Second Summer

After they disembarked from the train, Nayrah checked Julie's wounds. Satisfied that she mostly recovered during their ride, Nayrah led them through the screening post. They headed down to the lowest level, where Kraeth lived.

"Gecheana trained Kraeth very well in the Skean arts. He will not be as easy as the others," Nayrah remarked.

"You think they were easy? I barely survived. Before we go any farther, I want to know why you keep letting me fight them alone?"

"As you have mentioned before, you need the practice. There is nothing like a life and death contest to bring out the best in a fighter; that should not upset you. Ever since your fight with Stron, I have seen improvement."

"It's not enough to beat you."

Nayrah chuckled loudly, "No, it would take a few yellow harvests before you could match me."

"I guess we'll see soon enough."

"Until that time, I need you at your best. Fighting should not be a struggle. It should be a fluid motion. It should come naturally from within," she patted her belly. "It should be something you *enjoy*."

"That'll be a problem. I've never enjoyed fighting."

"Desires can change over time. I do not know much about Saiphs because Gecheana ensured they could not thrive here. I have read that they are fierce fighters, but you, my dear, hesitate too much. You must engage in the battle. Stop letting your powers do all the work."

"I still can't believe you're giving me fighting tips, especially knowing we will face off one day."

"Oh, I am not worried. I *will* beat you."

"How much farther does Kraeth live? I need to put my headpiece on," Julie remarked, changing the subject.

"Not far, except I do not think he is in his apartment."

"Why not?"

Nodding, Nayrah pointed to a silhouette several paces down the avenue.

"That is far enough," Kraeth extended his scarlet-colored blade.

"Why Kraeth, you have surprised us," Nayrah mocked.

"I know why you are here."

"You do?" Nayrah queried.

"Yes, Nayrah. I have felt the loss of my Skean cousins. I know you have betrayed us."

He faced Julie, "Had I known that you would have followed me to Akil, I would have killed you on Earth."

"Had I known what you were, I wouldn't have taken you in."

"Even though you were kind to me, Julie, I will not show you mercy if you attack, and I will use everything I have learned to destroy you and Nayrah, so I suggest you return to Argi and forget about me."

Julie faced Nayrah, "Maybe he's right. He doesn't seem like a threat."

Nayrah faced Julie with furrowed eyebrows, "You are supposed to be a Saiph; your mortal enemy is standing in front of you. How can you not kill him?"

"I haven't killed you."

"You are weak, Julie," Nayrah shook her head disapprovingly.

Nayrah lunged at Kraeth, who expected her attack, and moved to block. Their swords clashed when they met. As Nayrah's blade moved toward Kraeth, Julie put on her headpiece, unsheathed her sword, and moved to strike as well. Kraeth sidestepped from his position, placing Nayrah between them.

Julie repeatedly tried but could not find an opening to attack, so she gathered enough power within her to enhance a jump that sprung her over Nayrah and Kraeth; the move surprised them. Kraeth had an opponent on either side, forcing him to work twice as hard to defend and attack. As their fight continued, Kraeth struggled until seeing a weakness.

He unleashed an invisible wall of energy toward Nayrah, sending her flying into a nearby fountain, where she struck her head on the concrete footing. Having dazed Nayrah, Kraeth had time to focus all his attention on Julie. Their blades arced as they moved them to block and attack. Kraeth was too fast for Julie. Seeing an opening, he swung hard from above his head with a downward motion.

Julie blocked it, preventing him from splitting her head into halves. Kraeth did not relent and used his weight to press forward. Their blades locked together, sending tongues of energy back and forth as Kraeth backed Julie against a wall. Using it for support, Julie held the hilt tightly with both hands and pushed with all her might. It was enough to keep the hot, glowing swords from contacting her face; Kraeth continued to press toward her.

Glancing down at her arm, Kraeth noticed a tear in her suit. With a smile, he moved his left hand to touch her skin; the tips of his fingers held the Night Lord's venom. The moment he made contact, Julie felt it enter her veins. Nayrah had warned her of his unique ability, yet it did not seem to matter. Knowing that he drugged her was not enough to stop its effect.

She became listless as the warm, soothing sensation moved through her body. With every ounce of her strength, she fought against the drug as it activated the primitive part of her brain, giving Kraeth control. She removed her headpiece and gazed at him like a Zombie with red, puffy eyes, waiting for his instruction.

"Kill Nayrah," he ordered.

Nayrah had awakened a moment before and sat on the fountain's cement perimeter, trying to collect herself; seeing Kraeth touch Julie's arm, she knew the situation had worsened. While walking toward Nayrah, Julie covered her face with the headpiece, knowing the suit would create blinding, reflective light, giving her an advantage. Even though Nayrah knew Julie would not hear her words, she said them anyway, only out of principle.

"Stand down, Julie."

"I *will* kill you," Julie responded with a muffled voice.

Looking to Kraeth, Nayrah spat, "You little *putok*!"

Kraeth smiled, "You should have left when you had the chance."

Nayrah faced Julie, "Use your powers, Julie. You can purge your blood of the toxin."

"No. Kraeth said to kill you."

"Do not make me destroy you!"

"Don't worry. You won't."

Unable to dissuade her, Nayrah attacked. Julie was ready and blocked Nayrah's strikes. As their fight heated up, Nayrah discovered that Julie's skills had dramatically sharpened. It seemed like Kraeth's drug gave her the focus and determination needed to become a better fighter. The speed and strength she parried and attacked nearly matched her own.

Julie's blade made several contacts, leaving deep gashes in Nayrah's arms and legs. Nayrah had an idea; if she could cut Julie, it might allow her to drain the toxin from her blood. She had to withhold power to her blade to prevent cauterizing the wound to achieve this goal. The objective seemed simple, but it was much harder to get past Julie's defenses with the Night Lord's venom in her blood.

Nayrah struck her at first chance, slicing the wound Julie received earlier, making it bleed; the move cost her dearly because Julie's sword sliced open her gut. The hot blade cauterized the wound, leaving her in a lot of pain. It was enough to slow Nayrah, who backed up, hoping to keep Julie's attacks from landing until her body recovered. Kraeth smiled and, knowing Julie had won, left.

Nayrah sent a wall of invisible energy at Julie, who somehow managed to redirect the power, forcing it to go around her. Gritting her teeth, Nayrah spat a curse and tried to figure out another way of stopping her. As Julie pressed forward, Nayrah decided that pulling her forward might work since pushing did not. Nayrah sensed a wall behind her. Her life was over if she reached it before stopping Julie. That would end her plans to rule Akil.

Nayrah sent another energy blast in Julie's direction with her left hand. As before, Julie redirected it around her. This time, Nayrah was still in control of it. Just as it went by her, she pulled it back toward her. From behind, the wall of energy surprised Julie, pushing her forward. Dodging for the floor, Nayrah moved out of the way just as Julie flew overhead. She hit the wall, knocking the sword out of her hand.

Nayrah ran to her, removed her headpiece to stop the reflective light, and grabbed her wrist. Using her powers, Nayrah drew out the toxin in her blood. Julie regained consciousness and struggled against Nayrah's grip. Nayrah fought hard to keep her from moving, so she could drain the Night Lord's venom from her body. A few hundred heartbeats later, Nayrah removed all of it from her blood, and after Julie was herself again, Nayrah released her.

Julie shook her head, "It was too powerful for me to resist, and I blacked out at some point. Do you know what happened?"

"Yes. He ordered you to kill me. You almost succeeded," Nayrah added, showing the wounds she gave her.

"Sorry."

"Do not apologize. You fought better against me than you did against any of the others."

"I don't know how."

"It is simple. Kraeth's drug gave you focus and determination. You took control of your power, using it in its proper balance. You even redirected a power push, which is very advanced."

"Since I can't remember what I did, it will not help me; what do we do now?"

"When you sliced open my gut, I saw Kraeth smile, and moments later, he left, thinking you won the fight, so we must take advantage of his presumption."

"How?"

"His apartment is only a hundred paces that way. You will sense each other as you get near him. Let him think he still controls you. Get close and kill him."

"Can't he tell that I'm not under his influence anymore?"

"Not if you pretend to obey him; you must keep that lethargic look on your face, or he will know you are faking."

"That's not going to be easy. All I want to do is rip him apart."

"Keep that feeling hidden long enough to get close to him, release it, and end him."

"Where will you be?"

"I will cloak my powers and wait outside; if you get into trouble, I will rush in and help."

"You better, or else he'll drug me again."

"Do not worry. I do not want to go through that a second time," she held her stomach.

As they approached, Julie sensed his presence. She knew Nayrah was out in the shadows yet could not find her because she had cloaked her powers. Standing in front of the door, Julie did her best to look lethargic. Wearing the mask of Zombie-like obedience, she waited for him to answer. He did not take any chances because he held an ignited sword in his hand.

"Did you kill her?"

"Yes. Her body is lying near the fountain. Do you want to see it?"

"It is not necessary," he disengaged his sword, "Come in."

Obediently, Julie walked inside, forcing herself to be agreeable.

He moved to the couch and turned on the information monitor, "Come here, take off my boots and rub my feet."

Suppressing a gag, Julie did as he commanded and rubbed his feet as he watched the monitor; she used her peripheral vision to find the hilt of his sword lying beside him, still attached to his belt.

A brief time later, he stood, "Remove my jacket."

Standing behind him, she pulled the jacket down over his shoulders. Once the collar reached the top of his elbows, she saw an opportunity and stopped because the jacket would keep his arms bound. She grabbed the hilt of her sword. Kraeth sensed danger and spun around. Seeing a sword in her hand, he called for his weapon to leap toward him. Before it reached him, she extended her blade, ignited the sword, and swung it through his neck in one smooth, blinding move. Nayrah sensed Julie using her powers, ran through the front door, and saw Kraeth's body lying on the ground.

"Well done, my dear. Well done."

"Now, what do we do?"

"Now that your fighting skills have progressed, I will use the last Skean child to lure Gecheana into a trap."

"That will make the odds even."

"Yes, it will. Do not worry; while you are dispatching Gecheana, I will take care of Jadell."

"Are you sure you can kill her?"

"Very sure. I am a very skilled fighter. I could kill Gecheana if she had not put that veil between us."

"What I meant to ask you is if you can kill your daughter."

"Interesting. Why do you think Jadell is my daughter?"

"Simple reasoning. You said that Stron was Elzer's heir. We killed your four Skean sisters yesterday. There were five of you, which means each of you ruled a city. Since you can morph into anyone you wish, your original identities were that of the Sovereigns' spouses. It means that you Nayrah are Thea, and Jadell is Yetta."

"You are smart, Julie; perhaps too smart. Yes, Jadell is my daughter, but I can assure you that I will not hesitate to end her life. Although Gecheana assigned me the blame, Jadell is why you are here. Her meddling in my affairs put you on Akil. I plan to teach her one final lesson in betrayal by severing her head; it will be her last lesson."

"It doesn't bother you that I know this information?"

"I am a rogue Skean. My alter ego, Thea, no longer matters in the scheme, so you could tell all of Akil who I am, and it would not change a thing."

"All right. What time do we meet?"

"We will return to Argi and meet on the following Terrestrial Revolution, noon Earthian time. Before you leave, I will put more ointment on your wounds to help them recover because I need you at your best when you face Gecheana."

Chapter 41

Dr. Young begged Yanamai for another rest period because they had walked for three hours. As they sat, Yanamai heard voices, told Dr. Young to wait for her, and climbed the small hill beside the road following up on a hunch. At the top, Yanamai saw a large home with a vast yard and a surrounding metal fence. Moments later, Dr. Young climbed beside her. He retrieved the binoculars from his belt and searched the home for clues about Michael's whereabouts.

"If they have him, he could be anywhere inside. There's a fence with armed guards surrounding the compound. There's no way to sneak in, so we must contact the Regime."

Yanamai contemplated her next move until hearing a vehicle approaching. She grabbed the binoculars out of his hands and zoomed in on a woman driving a covered Jeep on the road they had just traversed.

"I have an idea," she ran down the hill to meet the Jeep.

Dr. Young followed her with a sigh, "Have you lost your mind? These people have weapons and will shoot before asking questions!"

Yanamai stood in the middle of the road until the Jeep arrived, and to Dr. Young's surprise, the woman driving the vehicle stopped to get out and reached into her purse, which Dr. Young assumed hid a gun.

Yanamai smiled, "Can you help us? We are lost."

The woman responded in her native language, so Yanamai did not understand her; Dr. Young did.

"I'm sorry to trouble you, miss, my friend and I have lost our way. Would you be kind enough to direct us to the nearest town?" Dr. Young spoke in Spanish.

The young woman studied the two strangers, decided they were not a threat, and answered, "Go back that way."

Turning, she pointed to where they had just come. Yanamai took advantage of her momentary lapse in judgment and ran toward her. Before Yanamai reached her, the young woman's hand appeared from her purse, holding a gun. Yanamai grabbed her arm before she could shoot. As they struggled, Dr. Young removed a syringe from his bag, ran behind the young woman, and injected it into her neck. She collapsed into Yanamai's arms.

"I recognize her. Her name is Camila; she's the daughter of Eduardo Romero," Dr. Young remarked.

"Should I know them?" Yanamai responded quizzically.

"In these parts, he's very well-known and feared. He's the head of the largest guerrilla faction in Brazil and extremely dangerous, so we must take this Jeep and return to the Regime to get help."

"I am not going back without Michael."

"I will not argue this point with you anymore. What good will it do if they capture us? You're too valuable to the Regime, and I'm too old to be a prisoner, so you must return with me now!" he insisted.

Ignoring him, Yanamai undressed Camila.

"What on Earth are you doing?"

"I will put on her clothes."

"For what purpose?"

"I will pretend to be her so we can get inside."

"Have you lost all sense? You look nothing like her. They'll shoot you before you reach ten feet of the fence."

"Not if you help me. Now please, turn around while I change."

Dr. Young spun around, "I don't see how I can be of any help. I'm no good with a gun, and you'll need an army to get past those sentries."

"I have read that the Regime subscribes to a certain level of physician-patient confidentiality. If I show you something, will you promise never to tell anyone?"

"I cannot agree to those terms unless I know what it is first. If it affects someone else, I'm obligated to notify them."

"This will not affect anyone, but if my people find out I have shown you, my sovereign could execute me."

"Now, you *must* show me."

"Give me an Earthian oath. On Akil, if someone gives an oath, they cannot break it. If so, there are severe consequences. I am hoping that it is the same here."

A moment later, Dr. Young responded, "It's not the same here. Nevertheless, I swear I won't tell anyone. Now, what is it?"

Due to the country's extreme heat, Camila wore a light, summery dress, making it easy for Yanamai to change into Camila's outer garment and shoes.

"All right, you can turn around," she pulled the lower end of the dress to her knees.

Spinning around, Dr. Young examined her from top to bottom, "What is it you want to show me? I see you're wearing her dress and shoes, yet you look nothing like her. Her hair is dark; yours is blonde. The shape of your faces is completely different, and your body types are…."

Stunned by Yanamai's transformation, Dr. Young paused in mid-sentence as she physically morphed into Camila's perfect image. Afterward, he looked at the woman lying unconscious in the Jeep and back to Yanamai.

"Impossible!" he exclaimed.

"It may be impossible for Earthians, not for Akilians."

"You even sound like her!"

"Now, will you help me?"

He paused briefly, "You look exactly like her, but you cannot speak her language."

"I have an idea. What if I pretend to be injured?"

Dr. Young nodded, "That would give me a good reason to be with you."

"Exactly, and you can do all the speaking."

"I could tell them I've given you pain medicine, making you very sleepy. The dose will make you tired yet allow you to walk independently. It should take away any suspicion of your silence."

"Are you going to help me?"

"It's still dangerous. We have no idea where they are holding Michael. We may not get him out alive even if we find him."

"Between the two of us, we will figure it out once we get inside."

"What shall we do with her?" he questioned, pointing to Camila.

"How long will she sleep?"

"Several hours, give or take; I didn't have time to measure the dose."

"We should tie her to one of these trees far from the road and release her once we retrieve Michael."

"I'll put a gag on her just in case she wakes up. We don't want the guards to hear her screaming."

Having secured Camila, Dr. Young put a sling on Yanamai's left arm, and they sat inside the Jeep. Since Yanamai had never driven an Earthian vehicle, Dr. Young drove them to the house. As they neared the sentries, Yanamai closed her eyes, pretending to be groggy. Seeing Dr. Young approaching, the guard raised his weapon until seeing Camila beside him with a sling. Dr. Young stopped the Jeep at the checkpoint and spoke in Spanish.

"She fell and sprained her arm. I drove her home as a courtesy for General Romero."

"Camila," the guard said.

Opening her eyes, Yanamai played her part well and groggily looked at the guard. Satisfied their story was right, the guard waved them through. Dr. Young parked the Jeep at the house's front door and helped Yanamai get out. Before they could get inside, Camila's mother ran out, visibly upset at seeing her daughter wearing a sling. Her presence surprised him until Dr. Young surmised that the sentry had called the house, informing Camila's mother of her condition.

"What happened?" she wondered in her native tongue.

"She'll be fine," Dr. Young assured her. "She only sprained it. I've given her a sedative for the pain. Just point me to her room, and I'll help her to bed."

"And who are you?" she demanded.

"I'm Dr. Young. I was in town to get supplies and saw her take a fall. I'd be happy to stay with her until she recovers."

"Thank you, doctor. I appreciate your help," she answered and showed him Camila's room.

Inside, he helped Yanamai onto the bed and tucked her in; seeing that Camila's mother would not leave, Dr. Young suggested, "Why don't you make her something to eat? She might be hungry when she wakes up."

Hesitantly, Camila's mother nodded and left to prepare some food; Yanamai jumped out of bed.

"What do we do now?"

Moving to the rear window, Dr. Young looked out, "Camila's bedroom faces the rear of the home, giving us an unobstructed view."

"What do you see?" Yanamai asked.

"A barn, fenced animals, crops, and a small shed, with a guard in front. That must be where they're keeping him."

Yanamai moved beside him, "Where?"

Dr. Young pointed to the shed.

"How do we get to him?" she quizzed.

Dr. Young scanned the area. Camila's room had French doors that opened onto a second-floor, wraparound deck and stairs at the corner of the house.

He faced Yanamai and smiled, "I have an idea."

Camila's mother returned, set the food tray down, and sat beside the bed, where Yanamai, continuing to look like Camila, rested. Dr. Young stood beside Camila's mother with his hand nestled inside his medicine bag.

"How long will she sleep?" Camila's mother questioned.

"She should wake up any moment now," Dr. Young replied.

Taking her cue, Yanamai pretended to stir in her bed. Camila's mother took her hand and leaned over the bed to pet her forehead, leaving her back toward Dr. Young. He took the opportunity to inject her with the same sedative he had given Camila earlier. Without making a sound, Camila's mother flinched and collapsed on top of Yanamai. They moved Camila's mother off Yanamai and set her to rest comfortably on Camila's bed. Now that they had her mother subdued, Yanamai removed the sling and picked up the tray of food, as Dr. Young suggested.

"We have to hurry. The sun is beginning to set," Dr. Young urged.

Dr. Young taught her a brief statement in the Spanish language, and Yanamai, still looking like Camila, walked outside toward the shed. She kept rehearsing the words along the way until reaching the sentry on duty.

"I made this for you," she spoke in Spanish and tried to make it sound flirtatious.

Thinking Camila had a crush on him, the guard smiled back, took the food tray, sat, and ate. He spoke to her in between bites; not understanding the language, all she could do was nod and smile. Having invited her out on a date, the sentry thought she was coy by not replying.

"Are you going to answer me?" he asked.

Again, she only smiled and nodded. He ate the last of the food, and his eyes became heavy with sleep. Moments later, he fell off his chair, unconscious. Having completed her goal, Yanamai changed back to her likeness. Knowing time was running out, she grabbed the keys from his belt and tried each one until unlocking the door. Inside, she saw Michael sitting on the floor in the corner. The shed was so hot that sweat drenched his clothes.

"Come with me!" she exclaimed.

"Yanamai? What are you doing here?" he wearily queried.

"I am trying to rescue you; now come on!"

Having been in the shed for most of the day, Michael was exhausted and dehydrated, making it impossible for him to move quickly. However, with Yanamai's help, he stood and rested on her shoulder as she guided him outside. He tried to take some water from the food tray.

"Do not drink it; Dr. Young drugged it. I am sorry, we must go now!"

Michael forced himself to walk fast. Yanamai guided him to the lower wraparound deck of the house. Michael slowed down, so she put more of his weight upon her shoulder to speed his pace. Just as they approached the front corner of the house, they heard a siren. Looking to the front gate, Yanamai saw Camila standing in her undergarments, yelling at the guards. *Oh no, she got free!*

Hearing the Jeep's engine spring to life, Yanamai and Michael ran and jumped into the back seat. Gunfire rang out as Dr. Young sped off to the checkpoint. Two sentries appeared on the top front wraparound deck of the house and shot at Yanamai and Michael. As bullets hit the Jeep, Yanamai pushed Michael down and used her body to protect him. Michael would have done the same for her, except he was too weak.

Ducking below the dashboard, Dr. Young ran through the checkpoint. The guards shot at the Jeep as it sped past. Dr. Young sat up outside the compound and saw two vehicles in pursuit. Bullets continued to hit the automobile from behind, so Dr. Young pushed it to its highest speed. Two more Jeeps joined the pursuit as he got closer to their landing site. Dr. Young reached into his medical bag and triggered an emergency return signal.

Before reaching the end of the road, Dr. Young yelled, "Get ready to jump!"

Yanamai helped Michael sit up, and they positioned themselves near the door, waiting for Dr. Young's cue.

"Go!" he yelled.

Yanamai pulled hard on the handle; they fell out of the Jeep's left side and rolled into the brush. Those in pursuit did not see them jump and kept following the vehicle. Yanamai stood and saw Dr. Young lying under some extensive, leafy vegetation, a few feet away, holding his leg.

"Go without me."

"In case you have not noticed, I do not leave anyone behind. Now come on and stop whining!"

Dr. Young reluctantly stood with her help, "We don't have much time. The Jeep will crash soon, and they'll realize we've jumped out. We must get to the landing site before they find us."

"Just aim me in the right direction."

"This way," he pointed into the forest.

Now she had two disabled men to help. Under one shoulder, she supported Dr. Young and, with the other, Michael. They moved through the brush until hearing voices behind them. Looking back, Dr. Young saw General Romero.

"We must move faster!"

They picked up their pace. Within moments, they saw a Regime event horizon leading them back home. Gunfire rang out behind them as Romero's men came closer, and several Regime soldiers stepped through the portal, returning fire. With bullets flying past them in every direction, the trio pushed forward.

Unexpectedly, Michael tripped, causing the other two to fall as well. One of the Regime soldiers closest to Dr. Young helped him get through the portal. At the same time, another Regime soldier helped Yanamai to the event horizon; looking back, she saw Michael on the ground, alone. Breaking free of his grip, she returned to Michael and helped him stand. By now, the Regime soldier, who helped Yanamai, caught up, and together, they helped Michael get to the portal. Once they passed through the vortex, Yanamai and Michael collapsed. The Regime soldiers came moments later, and they closed the portal. Lying on the floor beside her, Michael stared at Yanamai, bewildered.

"You were at the event horizon. Why did you come back?"

"There was no way I would return without you," she insisted.

Her face relaxed as if she had fallen asleep; her eyes were still open.

"Yanamai…Yanamai!" Michael yelled.

Reaching over, he shook her; she did not respond. He pulled his hand away and saw blood.

"Medic!"

Having prepared for such an emergency, a medical team was already on the scene. Seeing Yanamai had the worst injury, they worked on her first. Michael moved to get out of their way. All he could do was watch in horror as they brought out the paddles, trying to jump-start her heart. They were unsuccessful, so they attached an automated, portable, battery-powered cardiopulmonary resuscitation device to keep her heart pumping on the way to the hospital. Moments later, Michael succumbed to exhaustion, closed his eyes, and blacked out.

Chapter 42

Earth
South America - Brazil - Manaus
May 18, 2452

Sitting outside a small café, Dawn waited for Eduardo Romero to arrive. Knowing the air would be hot and humid, she pinned her hair up to let her neck breathe; it was not enough to cool her. Dawn waved a paper fan toward her face, wiped her brow with a handkerchief, and took another drink from her water bottle. A few minutes later, she recognized the sound of Eduardo's Jeep, stood, and walked over to it. Before she reached the door, the driver stepped out and frisked her for weapons. Satisfied, he allowed her to sit in the back, where Eduardo waited.

"Where's my brother," she demanded.

"What? No greeting. Hi Eduardo, how are you today?"

"Fine, Hello. Now, where's my brother?"

"He's back at my house."

"That wasn't our agreement."

"I had to be sure you came alone. Someone in my position cannot take risks."

"What's your plan. Remember, you won't get the money until I take possession."

"I will take you to him now. Once you've seen him, you will transfer the money into my account. I will even give you this Jeep to return to the city."

"I warn you, Eduardo, no tricks, and no harm better come to him either."

"I am a man of my word."

Several hours later, city buildings gave way to the jungle forest. As they neared his home, the faint sound of gunfire caught Dawn's attention.

"Are those your men firing weapons?" she asked Eduardo.

"Yes. I believe it is."

"Who are they shooting at?"

"I don't know."

The driver slammed on his brakes and yelled a Spanish expletive.

"What the hell's going on?" Dawn demanded.

Eduardo held up his index finger to shush Dawn and made a phone call on his cell phone. Afterward, he spoke to the driver, who drove off in the same direction as the other Jeeps.

"Will you tell me what's happening?" Dawn inquired, again with a hint of agitation.

"Our deal is off," he responded angrily.

"What? Why?"

"Don't play games with me, Dawn. I will kill you and leave your body in the jungle."

"Eduardo, I have no idea what you mean. Why are we chasing this Jeep? I want you to take me to my brother."

"Your brother is in the Jeep. Someone helped him escape. I'm betting you had a hand in this."

"If I sent someone else, why would I have met you in the city? I would have just waited to hear from my team back in Scotland. Besides, he's my brother. I would never risk his life by betraying you."

"You have the reputation as a trickster; it's reasonable to assume you're playing a game with me. Whatever it is, you will not win this one."

The road was full of potholes, and the ride became even bumpier. Dawn and Eduardo continued to argue in the back while the driver followed the Jeep to a dead end, where it crashed. Concerned for her brother's safety, Dawn jumped out first to search for him. Eduardo and his driver followed. Eduardo's men in the Jeeps, whom they had followed, walked through the brush, looking for them. Eduardo's phone rang during the search, so he took the call and unexpectedly ordered his men back.

"What's happening?" Dawn demanded.

"My men saw them running into the woods about a hundred yards back. They must have jumped out of the vehicle as it was moving."

"I'll offer a new contract. Bring him back to me alive, and I'll double your fee."

"No more deals. Now I'm going to kill him, to teach you a lesson," he threatened and faced his driver, "Watch her closely."

Eduardo left in the second Jeep to pursue Michael. Determined to save her brother, Dawn removed the pin that held up her hair, pretended to have a hurt ankle, grabbed it, and sat on a nearby stump. She waved to the driver and asked him to help her to the Jeep; he hesitated, causing her to exhale loudly in frustration.

"You've already frisked me. I'm unarmed. I only need a little help getting to the Jeep."

He rolled his eyes, walked toward her, moved his weapon to hang on his left shoulder, and leaned down to help her stand. Dawn used the pin in her right hand to stab him in the neck. It hit his carotid artery, and blood squirted out with every heartbeat. He pressed his hand against his neck to stop the bleeding; it did not help. Dawn stabbed him repeatedly until he collapsed.

Covered with blood spatter, she took his weapon and keys, ran to the Jeep, and chased Eduardo. Hearing gunfire deep in the forest, she ran toward it until reaching Eduardo and his men. Regime soldiers laid down protective gunfire ahead, forcing Eduardo and his men to take positions behind some trees.

Dawn shot Eduardo in the head with careful aim, instantly killing him. Since his men could not distinguish her shots from their own, they were unaware of her presence, giving her the incredible advantage of being invisible. She took down Eduardo's soldiers one by one, hoping to kill them before they could hurt Michael.

In the distance, she saw a young woman running to him and helping him stand. Not wanting Michael to escape, Dawn took careful aim and shot her, hitting her in the lower back, near the liver; the woman did not flinch or fall. Dawn reloaded her weapon as Michael stepped through the vortex; it closed behind him. It angered her to have missed him again, so she set her weapon to automatic and sprayed fire at the remaining four soldiers.

In only a few seconds, she killed all of Eduardo's men who were with him; it was not enough to soothe her anger. She returned to the Jeep and sped off to his compound. Along the way, she used Eduardo's phone to contact Ethan. Stopping about a mile away from Eduardo's home, she gave Ethan the coordinates of her location, and before disconnecting, she ordered him to assemble her men and bring the tank.

About half an hour later, a portal opened twenty feet behind her on the dirt road. The only noise it made after upgrading the tank was a soft, low rumbling. It moved through the event horizon with twenty of her soldiers marching toward her.

"What happened?" Ethan inquired.

"Somehow, Michael escaped. I saw him step through a Regime portal with a woman and Dr. Young."

"How in the hell did they get him out of the compound?"

"I have no idea; Eduardo thought I double-crossed him, so he tried to kill Michael."

"Where is Eduardo?"

"He's dead."

"If he's dead, why are *we* here?"

"Because nobody double-crosses me! I want everything he owned and loved wiped off the face of the Earth! Get your men ready. We're going to his house."

"Yes, ma'am."

As the sun began to set, they reached the compound. Wanting a better view, Dawn sat atop a nearby hill to watch Ethan carry out her instructions. He sent five men to the south, five to the east, and five to the west, leaving him in the north with five and the tank. Instead of using the armored vehicle, Ethan sent his snipers to take down the sentries watching the outer gate. Each team had one sniper, taking them down on his command, one at a time.

Everything was quiet until a siren rang out from inside the compound, and soldiers poured out of the house onto the grounds. Ethan instructed the tank commander to move forward. A few years ago, Dawn bought a Sherman Tank from her supplier. Watching it move onto the field, she remembered his pitch, trying to sell her the idea of a rocket launcher.

"I can put a T34 Calliope launcher atop the Medium Tank M4. It can fire a barrage of 4.5-inch (114 mm) M8 rockets from 60 launch tubes, so anything you want to take down will go down," he explained.

Although they only made a few T34s, she was glad to have found one because it came in handy when dealing with men like Eduardo. As the tank drew closer to the gate, some of Eduardo's men shot at it; a few ran back into the house. She thought they were cowardly until they returned with rocket launchers, hoping to take down her armored vehicle; before they could fire, the tank commander unleashed hell.

The area lit up with explosions, killing the men holding the rocket launchers inside the compound; one of the tank's rockets hit the home's front and knocked the wall down. Afterward, every weapon on the tank fired simultaneously: the cannon, the rocket launcher, and the side machine gun she had installed. Within fifteen minutes, her soldiers leveled the whole compound, so they brought out the few survivors with their hands raised.

Ethan gathered everyone and called Dawn to find out how to continue. Upon arriving, she saw a short line of Eduardo's soldiers with their hands resting on their heads and two women on their knees, weeping at the end. They cried and pleaded for their lives in their native tongue.

"What do you want me to do with the remaining soldiers?" Ethan questioned.

"Kill them."

"And these two?"

Without saying a word, Dawn retrieved her sidearm and shot them in the head, execution-style.

Surprised, Ethan stepped back, "Why did you do that? They were innocents."

"No one is innocent. Besides, if I let them live, they would try to avenge Eduardo's murder. I won't take that chance," she faced Ethan, "I meant what I said. No one is to be left alive, and nothing is to be left standing."

"Even the animals at the south end of the home?"

"Yes, Ethan. Even them."

Gunfire rang out for a few minutes as Ethan's men killed the remaining survivors; they killed the animals, set the barn on fire, and swept the area to ensure no one escaped. Later, Dawn ordered everyone home to Scotland; before stepping through the event horizon, she looked back at the destruction left behind. Satisfied, she smiled. Now, anyone who did business with her would know the penalty for betrayal.

Chapter 43

Sonya's accusation about his fear of intimacy haunted Jared, so he needed to prove her wrong. If not, he could never move forward with a clear conscience. His association with Sonya was his second meaningful relationship, even though it only lasted a few days. The only person who could help him was Laura, his last girlfriend. It had been at least two years since he saw her, yet it seemed more than a lifetime ago. Unable to find her in the public directory, he decided to dig deeper and search the news sites.

Jared expected to find a flurry of articles naming her the state's best defense attorney; there were none, so he further investigated and discovered that she dropped out of college a year after separating. He found her marriage certificate. Knowing she was married made him feel awkward about visiting her, but Jared needed answers only she could give. As he approached her home, his comfort level dropped. His fingers shook as he rang the doorbell and became short of breath.

Ironically, he often faced death without flinching in the field, yet meeting Laura again made him very apprehensive. *I wonder if it was the adrenaline that kept me calm during missions.* The sound of footsteps brought him out of thought. They stopped and the door opened with a chain latched. Through the crack, she tilted her head into view and recognized him; her eyes widened with surprise.

"Jared, is that you?"

"Yeah, I'm sorry to bother you. I was wondering if we could talk?" he asked sheepishly.

"Sure. Come in," she removed the chain and opened the door.

"Are you going to come in, or are you going to stare at my belly all day?" she queried with a wry grin.

"Oh, sorry. I wasn't expecting you to be…."

"Pregnant," she interrupted, closing the door behind him.

As she led him to the living room, he replied, "I guess you can say it's a surprise."

Arching her back, she sat on a chair, "Gary and I wanted to get started on a family right away."

"I don't remember meeting him."

"You didn't. We met a few months after we broke up."

"What about your career? You were on your way to becoming one of the state's top lawyers. You had all the connections, and the schooling lined up. What happened?"

"Things change, Jared. Gary and I dated for about a year until he proposed; naturally, I accepted. We wanted a big family, so we bought this house, and a few months ago, I got pregnant."

He frowned, processing the direction in which her life took.

"We never talked about you quitting college or having children."

"It never came up; now, what did you want to talk about?"

"I realize it's strange to be here; I don't have anyone else I can ask. We were together for about a year, which was my longest relationship. That means you know me better than anyone."

"Let me guess; you just broke up with someone."

"Yes. Our relationship was complicated, and before I left, she accused me of being afraid of intimacy. I remember you wanted to take a break; you told me it was because you had to focus all your attention on your studies. Was that the real reason, or was it what she said, the lack of intimacy?"

"Wow! That's a loaded question. Are you sure you want me to answer it?"

"I would appreciate an honest reply."

"All right, if it's the truth you want, I would have to agree with her. You were attentive at first and slowly drifted away from me. You spent most of your time preparing for the agency's tests. I wasn't angry with you because I understood that you had to study. Still, you spent less and less time with me during the last three months we were together. Whenever I tried to talk to you about it, you avoided the subject, leaving me with no choice.

"I cared for you deeply; I just didn't want to spend my life with someone emotionally unavailable. You were absent most of the time, and even if we were together, you were always somewhere else. You didn't even put up a fight when I suggested a break. It was as if you were hoping for a way out of our relationship."

"I never realized you felt that way."

"I know. You had other things on your mind; it's all right. It worked out for the best. I found Gary, and I heard you got into the agency."

"I didn't fight for you because I didn't want to stand in your way. I knew you would be successful, and I thought you would hate me if I stopped you."

"I gave a reason I knew you would understand, but I was devastated because you didn't even try to talk me out of it. I cried for three days after you left."

"I'm very sorry."

"Don't be. It's how some relationships end up. I'm curious. Did you ever cry about leaving me?"

"No, I was sad for a long time."

She smiled politely, "It means we made the right choice."

"I'm sorry I failed you, Laura."

"You didn't fail me, Jared. We just wanted different things."

"I did want a relationship with you."

"You didn't want it as much as I did."

"I guess she was right. I am afraid of intimacy."

"What happened? Why did you leave her?"

"She lied to me about something, claiming she did it to protect me."

"Do you believe her?"

"Yes. Still, she should have come to me first."

"What do you plan to do?"

"I'm unsure."

"Do you love her?"

"No. We just met."

"I see. Do you care about her? Do you see yourself with her in five years?"

"I did until she lied."

"The choice is simple, although it may be hard to make, and it truly depends on how much you want her in your life. If you can live without her, walk away; if there is a part of you that still wants her, you should forgive her and try to work it out."

Jared nodded absentmindedly.

"By the way, I'm still practicing law. I'm just doing it in a small town. It's less stressful, and I have more time at home."

"I'm happy for you, Laura. I'm sorry for the imposition. I just had to know."

"It's not an imposition, Jared. On the contrary, it was nice talking to you."

"I should have spoken to you sooner. We might still be together."

"It's hard to say. So tell me, now that you're an agent, is it everything you thought it would be?"

Thinking of all the adventures, he smiled, "Yes. It is. I've done and seen so much in the past two years. You wouldn't believe it."

"You see how happy you got just now? That's how I wanted you to be with me, except you never smiled like that during our relationship."

"I see your point; I may not be relationship material."

"It's up to you, Jared. No one can choose for you."

Jared stood, "Thanks for talking with me. I've learned something about myself today that I didn't know. Before I go, I want to congratulate you on your baby, and I hope you have a healthy boy or girl."

She stood, leaned in, and hugged him, "Thanks, Jared. I hope you find what you need; I hope you find happiness."

She let go and gave him a quick kiss on the cheek.

"Now go before I start to cry."

"Goodbye, Laura."

Chapter 44

Akil
Argi City
The 22,282nd Terrestrial Rotation of the Second Summer

Disguised as a caterer, Otsoa delivered Va'ron's lunch, pushing the food cart along the avenue toward his next stop. Gecheana clarified that if he made too many mistakes, she would replace him with Va'ron. If Nayrah taught him anything, it was that Gecheana would turn on him, just as she did. He looked at his timekeeper and smiled; it would not be long until Va'ron died, which meant Gecheana could no longer replace him with his younger sibling.

Killing Va'ron would buy enough time for him to develop a plan to get rid of her. The method he used to kill Va'ron was born from his intent to eliminate Durnah. Since Zorion quietly hid her away, Otsoa viciously interrogated her family; they did not know her location. Now, he had to contemplate another way to find her. Taking a lesson from Nayrah, he knew Durnah could not survive without sustenance.

"Follow the food trail, and you will find your target," she would say.

Zorion slipped up using the same company that brought all the Sovereign and staff meals to feed her. Earlier, he subdued one of the delivery workers and changed his appearance to look like him, except Otsoa was much larger than his victim and had to hide the extra bulk underneath a baggy, white jacket. The difference between them was noticeable in the mirror, but Otsoa counted on the hungry sentries to only look at their plates of food and ignore his poor impersonation of the caterer.

He walked away from Va'ron's apartment and noticed that the following address on the list was a familiar one. Zorion hid Durnah in one of the guest apartments on the upper level. His journey would take him about halfway to the other side of the city. A few thousand heartbeats later, he arrived to find two sentries on duty. He prepared enough poison moss for everyone and ensured that the guards ate first.

He watched them gorge on toxic food and left to set up Durnah's meal in the dining area. Before stepping outside, he waited to ensure she ingested the poison moss and closed the door behind him to wait for the inevitable. The sentries finished their meals outside, so he gathered their trays and put them back on his cart. It was common for the catering service to wait until everyone finished their meal.

Knowing the routine, the guards talked with him to pass the time, asking if he heard any updates on the move to Earth. Durnah finished her meal and called for him. As he approached the table, she started to gather the plates to help him.

"Leave them," he said.

She looked at him quizzically because it was not proper for someone with his status to speak to her that way. While gazing at him, she saw his features morph into that of Otsoa. Realizing it was him, she panicked; before she could call for the sentries, he put his hand over her mouth to silence her.

"Relax. I am not here to hurt you. If I let you go, do you promise not to scream?"

She nodded, and he removed his hand, "How did you find me?"

"It was easy. Zorion does not have much of an imagination. Since everyone must eat, I checked the caterers and saw this remote location on their schedule. I knew it had to be you."

"It was obvious you did not want me, so I left. Why are you here now?"

"I have come to apologize, and if you could forgive me, perhaps we could resume our ceremonial obligation to each other."

"I did not dare dream of hearing you utter those words."

"I have been going through some changes recently. I am sorry that it coincided with my coming-of-age ceremony; I have given it much thought, and I would like for us to start over."

"I would love to."

Taking her in his arms, they kissed; he picked her up and took her to the bedroom, where they stayed in the throes of passion for several thousand heartbeats. Lying beside her in the soft light of the ceiling lamps, he gazed at her as she lay resting. Although her long, thick, pure, white hair partially covered her body, he could still see her shape.

As she looked at him lovingly, with her beautiful, maroon-colored eyes, he knew it would not be long until the drug took effect.

It started with a light cough. As time progressed, the coughing became more profound and more frequent. Even though he believed she would be a loving and loyal companion, it still was not enough. Only Yanamai could fulfill his desires. The only way he could have her publicly was if Durnah died. As her coughing became violent, blood dripped from her mouth. Taking his cue, Otsoa got out of bed and dressed, leaving Durnah behind to die. Remembering her recent illness, she looked at him.

"Why?" she questioned, struggling to breathe between coughs.

"I want someone else, and if you are alive, I cannot have her. Soon, the Information League will report that you and the sentries died from the sickness, leaving me free to lure Yanamai back home on Akil and make her mine."

His words hurt her more than the poison. The look on her face would stay with him for a long time. *I guess that is the price I will pay for Yanamai, but she is worth it.* He watched Durnah take her last breath before transforming into the caterer again. He left the apartment and barely noticed the two sentries lying on the ground. Soon, they would discover Va'ron's lifeless body, and when Durnah's guards changed shifts, their superiors would relay the news of their deaths; Otsoa returned home to practice his surprise reaction to the news.

Chapter 45

Earth
China - Hong Kong - Black Point Power Station
May 18, 2452

Wu Luli hid outside the power station and gazed through the zoom lens of her camera, watching the traffic going in and out of the parking lot. The sun was already rising. She felt tired because her mind and body were still on 'Regime time,' twelve hours behind. Typically, she would be getting ready for bed about now; missions often put her in time zones that were hours off her schedule. That part of the job made it hard to adjust.

Everything was in place, and she was ready to infiltrate the power station. In preparation for the assignment, she rushed the second phase. Chow Dai's pursuit cost her valuable time, yet she got everything ready. Wu Luli scanned the list Yang Shing retrieved last night and chose to impersonate Ma Meilie, one of the scientists who worked at the power station.

Since their height and weight were similar, she could easily replace Ma Meilie with just a little facial makeup and prosthetics. While Ma Meili slept, Wu Luli broke into her apartment, woke her, and injected her with a truth serum to gain access to all her information. She had everything from passwords to coworker relationships in just a few minutes.

After retrieving all the information, she injected Ma Meili with a narcotic to keep her asleep for the better part of the day. Had she still been working for General Ming-tun Fu, Ma Meili would be dead. Dressed in Ma Meili's work uniform, Wu Luli compared Ma Meili's picture with her reflection in the mirror to ensure her makeup and prosthetics matched. The impersonation was spot on, so she returned to Ma Meili for one last thing, her fingerprints.

Wu Luli used the unique software within her tablet, scanned Ma Meili's hands, put on a pair of thin, transparent, synthetic, skin-like gloves, and placed her hand on the tablet. The application used a laser to etch Ma Meili's fingerprints onto the gloves' exterior. *Perfect.* She strapped the C4 around her waist, put on Ma Meili's white lab coat, grabbed the keys to her car and briefcase, and left.

As each vehicle pulled into the power station, she looked for General Ming-tun Fu, the most critical part of the mission. Blowing up the portal machine would only be a temporary setback if he still had the schematics in his possession. Knowing General Ming-tun Fu all her life, he would not leave valuable information in the cloud or on some hard drive connected to the internet. No, he would always be careful with this information and keep it on his person.

He collaborated with her on large projects and used different scientists for each part of the job. This way, they would not have a complete picture of what he was building. Also, he ensured that only their part of the schematics would be accessible to them. After they finished, he moved them to another project. Again, he would only give them details of a particular phase of that venture. Only those whom he trusted would know the full scope of the plan.

As a large black SUV approached, she saw him sitting in the back. As he went by, she snapped several pictures and reviewed them. Using the enlargement feature, she saw a chain hanging around his neck. Since the bottom of the chain disappeared into his jacket, she could not tell if he was carrying a data stick. Nevertheless, she hoped the information would be there if he continued with old habits.

He passed the last checkpoint, so she got into Ma Meili's car and stopped at the gate. The guard checked her ID and waved her through the station. With the keys to Ma Meili's car in her purse, she walked to the new hall entrance and placed her hand on the scanner. The first attempt failed; Wu Luli did not panic. Instead, she put her hand on the scanner a second time. She watched the scanner light move through the transparent glass, where her hand rested as it again took an image of her fingerprints.

Patiently, she waited for the flashing red light to turn green. It seemed to be taking a long time. If this attempt failed, she would only have one more try until the alarms sounded, and leaving now would only draw attention. If the siren sounded, everyone would look for her; the flashing red light changed to green as she was about to leave, and the door unlocked.

With a silent sigh, she stepped inside and saw two large turbines. Each was suitable to charge a capacitor with enough energy to run a portal machine. As Wu Luli walked to Ma Meili's workstation, she could feel the floor vibrate due to the high output generators producing electricity. She set her briefcase on the desk and logged on using the passwords and ID that Ma Meili had given her earlier. The truth serum repeatedly proved extremely helpful in extracting the information needed.

Within moments, the computer allowed her access, and Wu Luli searched for today's itinerary; Ma Meili had a meeting with General Ming-tun Fu in two hours. She smiled. *It's too easy.* Using Ma Meili's tablet as a checklist, she walked around the turbines pretending to inspect the machinery. She strategically placed the C4 during her round so no one could find it. After examining the turbines, she walked to the capacitor and repeated the process.

She reached the portal machine and could tell they were close to finishing it. The design was different from what the Regime fashioned, yet some distinct similarities existed. Now that all the C4 was in place, she unlocked the detonator giving her a choice to prematurely destroy General Ming-tun Fu's project to aid her escape if something went wrong. If her plan succeeded, he would soon be in the Regime's custody. It was just a matter of time.

The only thing left was meeting with him and securing the schematics she believed he kept hung around his neck. On her way to Ma Meili's workstation, one of her colleagues stopped to ask a question. Unfamiliar with the specifics of their work, Wu Luli did not know the answer. Hoping to evade the other without incident, she pretended to be sick and promised to get back to him.

Ma Meili's colleague looked at her suspiciously. Eventually, he nodded, telling her he hoped she would feel better soon. Although it seemed as if she had fooled him, his dubious look made her feel uneasy. The meeting with General Ming-tun Fu was still thirty minutes away, but her gut was screaming that she had blown her cover. At the workstation, Wu Luli opened her briefcase and removed a gun with a suppressor.

She cocked it, shoved it behind her pants' belt, and slipped a few ammunition clips into her pockets. Keeping the gun well hidden behind her lab coat, Wu Luli put her hand into a small opening on the side; now, she could keep the weapon in her grip without anyone noticing. She briskly walked to his office to wait for him. Wu Luli sat in the reception room and scanned the area. It did not take long for her to spot a camera lens strategically placed in the corner, and the lens focused directly on her.

Everything seemed to be going well until two military soldiers took a position outside the waiting room. Even though they did not draw their weapons, Wu Luli was sure General Ming-tun Fu called them. Using her training Wu Luli stayed calm but worried about completing her mission. Still trying to keep her cover, Wu Luli approached the secretary, pretending to be confused.

"What's going on?"

"I'm uncertain," the secretary replied; Wu Luli could tell something was troubling her.

Whether they were there for her, Wu Luli could not tell. General Ming-tun Fu's office door opened, and he stepped into the reception room; the other scientist she spoke with earlier followed behind him. Seeing Wu Luli, he glared at her with distrust; it was not hard to figure out that he notified General Ming-tun Fu of their earlier discussion. Wu Luli stood, getting ready for the inevitable.

Calmly, she asked, "Is there something wrong, Sir?"

She hoped her voice was close enough to Ma Meili's to fool them because it was always the hardest thing to duplicate.

"Why couldn't you answer his question?"

"I'm sorry, Sir, I haven't been feeling well today, so I drew a blank."

"It's a straightforward question for someone with your background," the other scientist insisted.

"I can assure you; I can answer it."

"Well, do it!" General Ming-tun Fu demanded.

He paused briefly for a response; she could not answer it, so he faced the soldiers.

"Kill her."

Before the soldiers could raise their weapons, Wu Luli brought her gun out of her coat and shot them dead, and without hesitating, she spun around, putting a bullet between the eyes of the secretary and the other scientist, leaving only General Ming-tun Fu alive. Surprised, General Ming-tun Fu raised his hands in surrender.

"The only reason you're still alive is that the Regime wants to talk to you," Wu Luli remarked.

Recognizing her voice, General Ming-tun Fu smiled, "Wu Luli. I should have known."

"Yes. You should have. You're getting sloppy in your old age, General."

"I thought you were dead."

"Assumptions are a spy's worst enemy. Isn't that what you taught us?"

"Indeed, it is. Chow Dai made that assumption for me. He told me he would kill you."

"He almost did, except almost isn't good enough."

"Is Chow Dai dead?"

"Yes."

"Pity. He was a good agent."

"Give me the necklace General."

"If I refuse?"

Wu Luli shot his left kneecap without warning, causing him to fall to the floor and scream in pain.

"You'll pay for that!"

"The Regime wants you alive. The condition you arrive in is up to you. Now hand me the necklace."

General Ming-tun Fu reluctantly ripped the chain from his neck and threw it at her; she caught it in midair using her free hand.

"I sent you to infiltrate the Regime, not to join them!" General Ming-tun Fu yelled.

"You used my dad to control me. Once you released him, your power over me ceased. Now, no one controls me."

The main doors to the power plant flew open. Hundreds of soldiers flooded into the building. General Ming-tun Fu smiled wickedly.

"I pulled the alarm before leaving my office. As you know, I always take precautions. If you surrender now, I promise to put a bullet in your head and end you; if you try to run, I will make your death a work of art in pain."

Wu Luli was out of time and unsuccessfully signaled the Regime for extraction several times until discovering that the General was jamming her signal. General Ming-tun Fu laughed at her failed attempt to leave.

"I installed a disruption field. There's nowhere for you to go. Surrender now, and I'll be merciful."

Without responding, Wu Luli grabbed General Ming-tun Fu, dragged him inside his office, and shut the door. She crawled under the desk, removed the tablet from her coat, and pressed the detonation button. The blast shook the building, tearing and destroying everything in its path. Later, Wu Luli woke under a pile of debris. There was no light, which meant the building collapsed on top of them.

General Ming-tun Fu's oak desk was strong enough to protect her from severe injury. This time, the Regime responded to her call. Moments later, a portal opened nearby, and a Regime crew started moving stones and beams out of the way. When they reached her, she told them that General Ming-tun Fu was in front of the desk, so they cleared the rubble and discovered his dead body. They lifted General Ming-tun Fu onto a stretcher and carried him through the portal as a precaution.

Chapter 46

After Wu Luli stepped through the portal, a medical team performed a quick exam; they cleared her, so she followed Captain Yates to the interrogation room for debriefing and handed him the data stick.

"Is this what I think it is?" he asked.

"I hope so."

He inserted the stick into his computer, and they watched the portal schematics display on the screen.

"It looks authentic. Still, I must verify it. Hopefully, this will compensate for killing General Ming-tun Fu."

"He left me no choice."

"I understand, but Supreme Commander Porter wanted him alive. I'll let you know in a few days whether he's happy or not."

"While I'm waiting, would you mind if I take care of some personal business? It's within the Regime."

"I'm sure that won't be a problem. I'll contact you when it's time for your next mission."

"Is my apartment ready?"

"Yes. Your badge will get you inside."

"Thank you."

Exhausted, Wu Luli walked to her new home, took a quick shower, dressed her wounds, collapsed on the sofa, and fell fast asleep.

Chapter 47

Earth
The Regime - Washington, D.C. - Capitol Building
May 18, 2452

Sitting behind his desk, Assistant of Defense Neil Long reviewed the progress report on the project '*Identify.*' Since Michael began his pursuit to develop communicating bacteria, top Regime Generals discussed its many applications. When Michael finally grew them, agents were already in place to distribute the recently mass-produced serum. Although it was a significant undertaking that had been in the works for years, the goal was to discreetly tag all high-ranking government officials worldwide.

Hundreds of insect drones filled with the serum were on their way to the operatives, working deep undercover as chefs, maids, friends, or whatever role they needed, getting within the officials' inner circle. At the first opportunity, the agents would use the drone to administer the serum, allowing the Regime to tag the official and keep watch on him or her. It would give the Regime leverage in every negotiation with foreign leaders. His phone rang, so he set the tablet down.

"Yes. What is it?"

"Sir, General Bailey is on the line. He says he and his men are under attack and that they need your help right away."

"Put him through."

A video screen on the wall across from his desk came to life with General Bailey's image; a mortar exploded behind him, causing him to duck and cover his head.

"General, what's happening?"

"The gangs are clobbering us with mortar fire, short-range missiles, grenade launchers…awe hell, you name it!"

"How did they get those weapons?"

"I spoke to Tucker earlier today. He said Dawn Pierce delivered them. Originally, I thought she sent the weapons to only one warehouse; now I'm getting reports that we're being hit everywhere around the city."

"Any idea who's leading this raid?"

"Yes. His name is Bruce Forge. Tucker handed over his title to him today."

"Never heard of him."

"I hadn't either. I had Colonel Scott checking into his background; he hasn't found anything yet, and it appears he doesn't like us being here."

Another explosion erupted behind him, and dust from the ceiling fell over General Bailey's head as he ducked.

The General faced the camera, "If you don't give us some air support *right now*, we will lose Texas!"

"Pull your men back, General. Help is on the way."

A quick call to General Green brought him up on the monitor, where General Bailey used to be. When he answered, Assistant of Defense Neil Long saw satellite images in the background, showing the suburban frontline's chaos, which circled Houston.

"I see you're already aware of the situation," Assistant of Defense Neil Long commented.

"Yes, Sir," General Green replied.

"Any ideas?"

"Yes. Even though the attacks are hitting close to General Bailey's encampments around the city, it seems they don't have good aim yet. I'm not picking up any tanks or vehicles on our scans, so I suggest an air assault. Once the dust settles, General Bailey's men can pick off anyone missed. I was just about to contact you for approval."

"You've got it. Get those planes in the air, now!"

"Right away!"

General Green gave the order, and technicians downloaded all their satellite data to the airfield for targeting; on another line, General Green ordered the airstrike and turned to watch it unfold.

Chapter 48

Earth
The Regime - Washington, D.C. - Underground Airfield
May 18, 2452

The loud siren jolted Captain Wheeler from his seat at the lunch table. Knowing it was not a drill, he ran to his locker to put on his flight suit and personalized helmet. He and two hundred other pilots were inside their T-10 Exterminator military jets in less than a minute. With his customized helmet on and fastened, he went through a flight check, using the helmet's displays as the airship's computer downloaded targeting information.

One hundred runways and two planes per airstrip took off or landed simultaneously. It was a feat that kept Captain Wheeler in the simulator for more than two thousand hours before his instructor allowed him in a cockpit. Since the airport was underground, the flight deck was the same length as an Aircraft Carrier to avoid a cave-in, and a portal was the only way in or out.

Having created such a short runway, the builders set the flight decks up like a carrier. They used four catapults to get the supersonics from 0 to 165 mph in two seconds. Captain Wheeler understood every aspect of how the jet took off and landed. Each catapult consists of two pistons inside two parallel cylinders positioned under the deck, each equal to a football field in length.

Each piston has a metal lug on its tip, which protrudes through a narrow gap along each cylinder's top. The two lugs extend through rubber flanges, which seal the cylinders, and through a gap in the flight deck, they attach to a small shuttle. As each pilot prepared his or her engines for takeoff, the flight deck crew moved the airship into position at the rear of the catapult and attached the tow bar on the plane's nose gear (front wheels) to a slot in the shuttle.

The crew positioned another bar, the holdback, between the wheel's back and the shuttle, and instead of using a jet blast deflector, the supersonics took off near the rear wall, giving the aircraft a firm foundation to push off. When Captain Wheeler was ready, he signaled the Catapult Officer, sitting in a small, encased control station with a transparent dome above the flight deck.

Steam rose as the Catapult Officer opened valves to fill the catapult cylinders with high-pressure steam, giving the force to propel the pistons at high speed, slinging the airship forward to generate the lift needed for takeoff. After they charged the cylinders to the proper pressure level, Captain Wheeler blasted the plane's engines. The holdback kept the aircraft on the shuttle while the engines generated enough thrust to keep supersonic in the air once it took off.

The engines screamed as they forced heated compressed air through the nozzle. Captain Wheeler saw the countdown within his helmet for when the Catapult Officer would release. Three, two, one, blast! The force caused the holdbacks to release, and the steam pressure slammed the shuttle and jet forward. At the same time, the G-forces slammed Captain Wheeler hard against the back of his seat.

In less than two seconds, his plane neared the end of the flight deck, heading for the side of the station. Before reaching it, a portal opened, and his aircraft shot through the event horizon. One second later, his wingman followed. On his heads-up display, Captain Wheeler saw every angle of the T-10. The outside cameras enabled him to see 360 degrees. During his test flights, the images were so bright and sharp that it almost seemed like he was flying without an airship.

On the other side of the event horizon, Captain Wheeler and his squad (totaling twenty-four) were only two miles from their target. The portals sparsely delivered each pilot in a circumference over Houston's suburbs, where the gangs attacked. Captain Wheeler saw explosions in the distance, and near his destination, the heads-up display started flashing. The mortar fire led back to the targeted area, which gave him visual confirmation that they had the correct location.

"All right, flight wing, we have our targets. Let's hope General Bailey got his men out of there," Captain Wheeler removed the safety from the fire switch.

Ten rockets shot from just his jet alone by pressing a button, each programmed with a specific destination. His squad sent two hundred and forty ballistic missiles to seek their targets. As they glided through the air, each one left a stream of smoke behind, making it easy to track them visually. When they touched the ground, flames engulfed the entire area. At the same time, a quick scan showed that

General Bailey's area went quiet. Billows of smoke rose from the forest, where some of Bruce's men hid.

As Captain Wheeler approached his next target, the heads-up display warned him. His supersonic picked up two bogeys on its radar, and they were heading right for him. A quick visual check through the rear camera confirmed that two rockets were approaching fast. Two of Bruce's men shot off their rocket launchers before Regime missiles vaporized them.

Captain Wheeler broke formation to protect his squadron and accelerated to the airship's highest speed of Mach 2. However, the rockets moved faster, and his heads-up display showed they were still closing in, so he lowered his altitude using the evasive protocol and steered the plane toward one of the old main highways. Everything outside passed in a blur at fifteen hundred (plus) miles per hour.

In his rear-view display, he could see the rockets were now only five hundred feet behind him. Keeping his aircraft level, he waited until they were about fifty feet from him, pressed the button, and the supersonic computer created a portal in front of him, landing him one hundred feet behind the rockets. His airship opened and closed the event horizon so fast that the missiles did not have time to get through.

Now that he was behind them, the heads-up display encased the two rockets with red triangles, showing enemy targets, and using the plane's twin rotary guns; he sent a continuous fire until they exploded, pulled up on the yoke to avoid any debris, slowed the aircraft, opened a portal, and returned to his squadron's position. Once they removed all their targets, the aircraft's computers started the return protocol.

He slowed the jet to 150 mph so the computers would open a portal back to their flight deck. It was up to Captain Wheeler to ensure that the tailhook grabbed one of the four arresting wires. If successful, the hydraulic cylinder system would absorb the energy and bring the supersonic to a complete stop. On his approach, he did not slow the airship any further. If his hook missed one of the wires, an emergency portal would open on the other side, forcing him to fly through the hangar and back out again for another try.

He passed through the event horizon and felt the tailhook grab the wire. The hydraulics brought his 54,000-pound plane, traveling

150 miles per hour, to a stop in only two seconds. The G-force threw his body forward; his seat belts helped absorb most of the shock. Once his aircraft stopped, he throttled down the engines and left for his debriefing. Later, he met with his squad in the local bar to celebrate their mission's success.

Chapter 49

Akil
Argi City
The 22,282nd Terrestrial Rotation of the Second Summer

About two thousand heartbeats passed since Nayrah spoke to Jadell. The message was quick and straightforward. They were to meet alone outside her old apartment on the lowest level. Jadell still wanted her dead, and her tardiness made Nayrah wonder if she had betrayed her again. It would be like Jadell telling Gecheana of their meeting, to get back into her good graces.

It was strange, Nayrah thought, how everything teetered on convincing Jadell to help her one last time. Everything went as planned until now; only two of her rivals were still alive. Once they joined with the other departed, she would offer Julie training in the ways of darkness. Nayrah would need someone to oversee all the small errands after taking control of Akil. As a novice, it would be easy for Julie to transition from Saiph to Skean; if Julie refused, she would remove her head and go on without her.

Sensing Jadell approaching, she pushed away from her thoughts and focused on the inevitable. She looked down the avenue but did not see her; knowing Jadell would attack from the darkness, she retrieved her sword and held it at the ready.

"I did not call you here to fight," Nayrah yelled.

She could hear her words echoing in the dark abyss of the lowest level. A heartbeat later, Jadell lunged from her right; Nayrah's blade moved to block. Their swords arced in the air while Nayrah tried to reason with her.

"You are alone, a castaway like me."

"I am nothing like you!" Jadell snarled.

"Yes, you are, my dear. I have trained you from your youth."

"No, Gecheana trained me!"

Jadell's betrayal made sense. Nayrah understood that her prowess threatened Gecheana. Feeling threatened, Gecheana secretly taught Jadell how to undermine her authority. Using Otsoa to bring Nayrah down caused her plan to backfire because he gave Yanamai the incorrect sector to search. Now, everything made sense.

Gecheana was to blame for everything that went wrong. Nayrah almost smiled.

"Where has that gotten you?" Nayrah asked.

"It does not matter anymore. The only thing that matters is that I will end your life here and now! You deserve nothing less for what you did to Taen and me!"

"Ah, you must ask yourself why I did it."

"Because you are a halfwit like Gecheana says. You could not obey the simplest instructions."

"No, my dear, I did it because every action has an equal reaction. Think of what Gecheana instructed you to do. It is her advice that led us to this point. She turned us against each other. If you succeed in killing me, Gecheana will still hunt you once she has control of Akil. If I win, she will hunt me instead. The result is the same. Gecheana will rule Akil, and we will be dead; unless we adopt an Earthian philosophy I recently read, we can defeat her."

"What is that?"

"The enemy of my enemy is my friend."

"What does that mean?"

"It means that we three are enemies. Currently, Gecheana has the upper hand, but by working together, we can defeat her and fight each other for control of Akil later."

Jadell stopped fighting, "How can I possibly trust you?"

"You betrayed me first, yet I am willing to trust you."

"I do not know."

"I wonder. Have you sensed the death of the others?"

"Yes, the Saiph must be powerful."

"No, my dear. It is not the Saiph who is killing the other Skeans. It is Gecheana," Nayrah lied.

"Why?"

"Did you think she would share her seat of power with us?"

"Well, yes."

Nayrah chuckled softly, "Oh, my dear. No. Gecheana's plans do not include us. You and I are the only ones left. Now, the choice is yours. We can fight each other, or we can work together to free ourselves of that wretch!"

"How can we defeat her? She is too powerful."

"I have put together a small resistance. With your help, we will end her reign."

"What do you want me to do?"

"Tell her that I plan to sneak through the Interstellar Transport Bay on the following Terrestrial Revolution to Earth."

"She will kill me."

"Not right away. At first, she will pretend to accept you to gain your support; her main goal is to kill me, and once I am dead, she will turn on you."

"How can you be so sure?"

"Because that is what I would do. She will set up a blockade to stop me and allow you to help her; once the fighting begins, you must strike her down during the distraction."

"It sounds too risky."

"Do not worry. If you cannot strike her down on the first blow, I will make my way to you and help. Together, we *can* defeat her even with the veil."

"Fine, I will do it."

"Excellent. Now, after you speak with her, contact me. I will let you know when I plan to be there."

They backed away until they could no longer sense the other, and Nayrah returned to her home on the tenth floor. Sitting in the quiet dark, she took a few heartbeats to meditate, felt something was wrong, turned on the monitor, and listened to the news. A picture of Va'ron, her youngest, appeared on the screen, and she heard the Information Gatherer say that he had died in his bed.

Looking down, she saw her hands shaking because she thought Gecheana had killed him until seeing an image of Otsoa in her mind. *Of course, Otsoa must kill him to secure his place as Sovereign.* Free from Gecheana's tutelage, she allowed herself the emotions associated with such loss and emptiness. Before long, the first of many tears rolled down her cheeks.

Chapter 50

Earth
Scotland - Edinburgh
May 18, 2452

Ethan waited for Deputy Brice to finish his drink at a distant table in 'The Standing Order' pub. His dossier showed that Brice liked to have a pint with his Chief Superintendent after work. They talked for more than an hour, and the waiting began making him anxious. At first, Ethan considered killing him in the pub but changed his mind when several police officers walked in at the end of their shift.

Since Dawn insisted his death be public and bloody, he decided to hit him on his way home. Brice drank the remaining beer in his glass, patted his companion on the back, and stood. Seeing movement, Ethan reached into his pocket, placed his money on the table, and followed Brice to the parking lot. Having stolen a vehicle for his mission, Ethan hopped in and waited for Brice to start his car.

Brice turned on the headlights and pulled away; Ethan followed him onto the street. Although Brice was several cars ahead, Ethan was not worried about losing him because he knew Brice's destination. Brice turned onto his home street, so Ethan sped up, making the tires squeal as they skidded across the pavement. Moments later, he caught up with Brice and slammed into the back of his vehicle.

Ethan got out of his stolen car, briskly walked to Brice's, and removed the automatic weapon hidden under his jacket. Brice exited his vehicle, angered by the collision, and cursed at Ethan for hitting him. Ethan exposed his weapon, and Brice froze.

"I'm sorry, Deputy. Dawn sent me," Ethan remarked grimly.

"I hid the paperwork, and they went over my head; I had to let him into the country."

"I believe you. Sadly, it doesn't matter," Ethan pulled the trigger.

A succession of bullets flew into Brice's body that violently shook as Ethan snuffed out his life; Brice collapsed to the ground full of holes. While staring at the bloody corpse, Ethan's urge to get out from Dawn's control screamed at him. His only other choice: allow the capsule in his head to end his life. One thing was for sure; if she kept him on this path, he would lose himself.

Chapter 51

Earth
The Regime - Washington, D.C. - Capitol Building
May 18, 2452

Having sent Ambassador Morris to the United Nations Embassy in Great Britain, Supreme Commander Porter watched on his closed-circuit monitor as Morris explained the recent bombing of the U.S. Capitol in California. Ambassador Morris played the video of Supreme Commander Porter's discussion with the late President Gonzalez, and there was no dispute about who owned the bomb and who was the aggressor.

Still, the U.S. ambassador demanded restitution, blaming the Regime for inciting the action because Regime agents stole a disc on U.S. soil containing confidential data. Ambassador Morris continued to deny the allegations. Without proof, Supreme Commander Porter knew the U.S. would be hard-pressed to gain much support. During an intense argument between the ambassadors, Supreme Commander Porter's phone rang, so he turned down the sound.

"We scanned Alex," General Green commented.

"What did you find?" Supreme Commander Porter asked.

"We confirmed that he was also compromised, and the technicians removed the programming. As a result, I have cleared him to return to work."

"Any clue as to who did this to him?"

"Yes. Someone named Dawn McFadden."

"I don't recognize that name."

"She's the one who owns the warehouse in Scotland; that's where our lead ends, so we investigated further and discovered she forged her credentials."

"Send what you have to Chief Constable Sinclair and ask him to try to match her voice with calls made within Edinburgh. I know it will take some time to figure out the details with him, but I want her apprehended."

"I'll get on it right away."

"Before you go, how long has Alex been leaking information?"

“Several months.”

“That’s a long time.”

“We suspect it’s how the portal specs were leaked, which would explain how Dragon got inside the Regime and disappeared from Vincent’s grasp.”

“I want our satellites over Scotland looking for portal signatures. Also, have them sweep for high energy sources. As we know, opening a portal takes a great deal of energy, and with the number of times she used it just in the past week, something should show up on our scans.”

“If the portal machine is below ground, it will be hard to locate a signature because the Earth acts as a shield.”

“Do your best, General. Let me know if you find anything.”

“Yes, Sir.”

The call ended, and Supreme Commander Porter’s assistant told him that Special Agent Reed waited to see him, so he turned off the monitor to the U.N. and told her to send him in. Special Agent Reed entered his office with a young officer, wearing her best NYPD dress uniform, walking behind him.

Supreme Commander Porter shook Special Agent Reed’s hand, “Who is your companion, Reed?”

“Officer Ashley Gordon, Sir,” she extended her hand.

“Pleasure to meet you, officer,” he looked to Reed for an explanation.

“I have good news, Sir. Dragon is dead, and we have Officer Gordon here to thank for it.”

“Really? That *is* good news! We’ve been chasing him for some time now,” Supreme Commander Porter responded, pausing to remember Vincent.

He faced Ashley.

“How did you manage to kill a rogue hitman outside of your authority?”

“I was helping a friend who was helping Kenny Barnes.”

“Everything is in my report, Sir,” Special Agent Reed added, sending the report to Supreme Commander Porter’s computer, which explained in detail the events that unfolded earlier that day.

“Now you are saying that Kenny Barnes wasn’t guilty,” Supreme Commander Porter noted, reading the report.

"Correct. Kenny pushed me out of the way, taking a bullet intended for me. He saved my life and gave me the chance to stop Dragon," Ashley offered.

"I'll clear his name and give his family the reward for information leading to his capture."

"That's very kind of you, Sir," Ashley replied, staying at attention.

"You can relax, Gordon. I'm not going to reprimand you. I see here that you have a daughter. I'm curious why you would risk so much for someone you didn't even know."

"It's my job to protect and serve, so once I knew he was innocent, I had to help him."

"Have you considered becoming a detective?"

"Yes, Sir. I will be taking the exam in two years."

"Ah, yes, the rules say you must have at least five years of experience before applying."

"Yes, Sir."

"I think in your case, I'll make an exception. I want you to apply for it this year."

"Sir?"

"A simple thank you will suffice."

"Thank you, Sir."

He faced Special Agent Reed, "Based on your conclusion, my friend Jake is innocent of any wrongdoing."

"Correct. Jim Price was the one who bribed the comptroller, not Jake. Ballistics has also matched the bullet that killed the comptroller to the gun Dragon used. We also know that Dragon's real name is Chen Heng. He used to work for General Min-Tun Fu."

"Did you find any evidence connecting him to his employer?"

"Yes. Her name is Dawn Kirkpatrick; our lead ended there because the bank closed the account after she made the transaction."

"Let me guess, the credentials she used were fake."

"Yes, Sir, I've notified Chief Constable Sinclair of our findings and asked him to consider it; it doesn't look promising."

"I want you to send that information to General Green as well. I believe this is the same person who killed one of our special agents and turned Alex into a spy. She's using her first name and changing her last to hide her identity."

"I'll send it to him right away, Sir."

Before Supreme Commander Porter dismissed them, his phone rang. While speaking, he frowned and disconnected.

"More bad news?" Special Agent Reed inquired.

"Yes. It seems that someone assassinated Deputy Chief Constable Brice. To speed up his landing into Scotland yesterday, Vincent spoke to his boss."

"It sounds very suspicious. Do you think he might have been on the payroll of this Dawn character we keep running into?"

"I never assume anything. Still, I agree; it does look suspicious. For now, we cannot interfere with their investigation because it is one of their own, so I'll mention it to the First Minister when I speak to him."

"There is one thing that still bothers me. I don't know why they bribed the comptroller."

"That answer must wait until we find Dawn."

Chapter 52

Olan walked Julie to their private apartment and asked her to fill him in on parts of her conversation with Nayrah he could not hear from the tunnel's entrance. Now that he knew Nayrah's plan, it was time to meet with Zorion. Olan knocked on the door in a pattern to identify himself, and Zorion allowed him inside.

"What news do you have for me?"

"There are only three Skeans left alive," Olan noted.

"Excellent. When can I return?"

"That is why I am here. It is time we took back your seat."

"You said a Skean is working closely with Otsoa. She will stop us."

"Nayrah plans to attack her tomorrow, at mid-Terrestrial Revolution."

"Just her?"

"No. She convinced another Skean to help her, which means the last three Skeans will be in one place."

"You think we should attack?"

"Yes. An ambush can push the odds in our favor."

"Otsoa has control over my army. Even Broll must openly obey him, or else Otsoa will execute him."

"There are many who would fight for you if they knew you were still alive. I managed to gather a few hundred who were willing to listen. They agreed to meet with me if I bring you."

"Excellent, take me to them."

Leaving his apartment, they took the elevator down to the city's fiftieth level, where Olan told the soldiers they would meet. Outside, they heard soft mumblings; the soldiers went silent, seeing Zorion and Olan step inside.

Zorion faced Olan, "I do not think they believe it is me."

One of the soldiers stepped forward, pulling a screener along with him.

"Tell us who he is," the soldier demanded.

"They have employed the services of a screener," Olan whispered to Zorion.

"Do not worry. I recognize her. She is from the upper level," Zorion replied.

A moment later, the screener's eyes widened, and she turned to the soldier nodding with excitement.

"It is him! He is alive!"

Simultaneously, the soldiers all roared a cheer and greeted him. Zorion took the time to meet with everyone and made his way to the center.

"My friends, I had to use a double because there had been several attempts on my life. My substitute gave his life for me, and I will forever be in his family's debt. Allowing my enemies to think I was dead gave them the courage to show themselves. Now that I know who they are, I plan to reclaim my seat in the Argi House with your help. That is if you are still willing to fight for me."

Again, they all roared a cheer and lifted their swords in the air.

"Thank you for your support! We will attack tomorrow, at mid-Terrestrial Rotation!"

Chapter 53

Having received a phone call from Thomas earlier in the day, Dawn agreed to meet with him. He insisted there was something important to discuss with her. Not having time for the stockholder's meeting, she consented to join him at the Martin Wishart restaurant afterward. It had been a favorite of hers for many years. One reason: it kept with the founder's vision, which helped it continue as one of the UK's most highly acclaimed dining venues for the past few hundred years.

The owners tore the building down and rebuilt it several times since its conception. The latest version sat atop a skyscraper in downtown Edinburgh. She stepped out of the limousine and told the driver to keep his phone on and stay nearby if she had to leave in a hurry. All eyes turned toward her when she walked inside the elegant Martin Wishart hotel lobby, including Thomas's. Knowing the venue demanded formal wear, she bought a new white and gold, one-shoulder twist evening gown.

There was not enough time to have her hair done by a professional with such little notice, so she straightened it and let it flow down her neck and over her shoulders. Seeing Thomas approaching, looking dashing as always, made her heart skip a beat, although she would die before admitting it to him. Moments before he reached her, she took a deep breath and exhaled loudly, preparing herself to resist his charms. He took her hand and kissed it. She felt flush, fighting the urge to embrace him.

"What was so urgent that you needed to see me tonight?" she questioned, smiling softly.

"In time. First, I have a reservation for us upstairs," he extended his elbow for her to take. "Shall we?"

She placed her hand firmly on his arm as they walked into the elevator. On the top floor, they exited the car and stepped onto the restaurant's foyer; the waiter took them to a private room overlooking the city. At night, Edinburgh lit up with all kinds of lights; inside, candles dimly lit the room, giving it a romantic ambiance.

They sat, and the waiter poured white wine into their glasses, leaving the bottle in a small, refrigerated container that kept it precisely at forty-nine degrees Fahrenheit. After the steward took their orders, she was alone with him for the first time in many years. Without thinking, she took her wine glass and emptied it, hoping it would calm her nerves.

"You look breathtaking this evening."

"Thank you," Dawn replied, blushing just a little. "You always look nice too, except you're especially dashing tonight. Is this a special occasion?"

"Yes, it is."

"Have you taken over another corporation?"

"You haven't aged a bit since we first met ten years ago," he ignored her question.

"Please, Thomas, you know our agreement. We are friends, just friends."

"Yes. Our agreement is why I asked that you meet me here."

"I don't understand?"

"It's been eight years since our last date."

"Time goes by so fast."

"Indeed, it does, which is why our relationship must change."

Again, Dawn emptied the contents of her glass and refilled it a third time.

"Why does it have to change? I thought everything was fine."

"Everything is not fine. It never was for me. For the past eight years, I've loved you from a distance, and I *cannot* do it any longer," he knelt on one knee.

"Thomas, please don't do this."

"Dawn, from the moment we met, I knew you were the only one I wanted to share the rest of my life with," he gently took her left hand while removing a box with his other. He retrieved the ring, held it inches from her finger, and continued, "When I think about you, I know that no one else will ever hold my heart the way you do."

She stopped him before he could put the ring on her finger. The painful look on his face was unbearable.

"I'm sorry. I can't marry you."

"Very well; this time, you must tell me why. I insist."

"I can't."

"You leave me no choice; I never want to see you again because I can't live in limbo anymore."

Her eyes flooded with sadness. She fought against oncoming tears; one escaped, rolling down her cheek, and she wiped it away.

"You don't understand. Over the past eight years, I've done horrible things; I'm not worthy of your love."

"I'm aware of some of the things you've done; it doesn't matter to me. It never did. All I've ever wanted was to have you back in my life."

"How could you possibly know what I've done?"

"I'm the CEO of the largest conglomerate in the world. Remember? You're very mistaken if you think I don't keep an eye on my most valuable assets. I know about Dragon, the comptroller, Vincent, and the CEO of Shire Inc. I know of the many other things that have occupied your days since we've parted."

She drank the third glass.

"How could you possibly want to marry me?"

"Believe me. I've tried to get over you and discovered a harsh reality; we don't get to choose whom we love in this world. I wish I could change my feelings about you; I can't. I love you, Dawn. I want you to be my wife."

He kneeled, looked up at her, and watched as tears rolled swiftly down her cheeks. It wasn't the reaction he wanted; things weren't going well for him at all.

"I'm sorry. I can't marry you. Your parents will disown you. You'll never become the Duke of Edinburgh."

"Is that why you continue to refuse me? My title?"

"Yes, Thomas. If you marry me, I'll destroy you, and I don't want that to happen."

"Oh, Dawn. Why didn't you tell me? Had I known this was what kept you from me, I would gladly pass the title on to my younger brother."

"I can't do that to you. I know how much becoming Duke means to you."

"Becoming Duke is important, but you mean more to me than a title, so if I must walk away from it, I will."

"The incident with Vincent set things in motion that I cannot stop. I'll need to leave the country very soon."

"I'll come with you."

"Think about what you are saying. You must leave everything behind: the company, your family, and your friends. I'm not worth one of those things, let alone all of them."

"That is the depth of my love for you. I hope you finally see the lengths I will go to be with you. Now, I want you to carefully rethink your answer, knowing that our future is in your hands."

Staring down at him, she could not believe what he would give up for her, especially knowing what she had done to him. Feelings she had not entertained in years came rushing back to the surface, and without hesitating, she blurted out her answer.

"Yes. I will marry you!"

He slipped the ring onto her finger, and they stood to embrace. He longed to hold her in his arms again; now, she was finally back in his life. Feeling her tears on his neck, he leaned back and used his finger to wipe her salty, moist cheeks.

"I don't mean to talk business after such a lovely moment; as you know, we don't have much time. The Regime has been aggressively looking for you. They want you to pay for Vincent's death, so I suggest you gather your things and move in with me immediately. If they come looking for you, I'll tell them I haven't seen you in days."

"I have some things I must take care of first before we can plan our escape."

"How long will it take?"

"A day or two, at the most. Start gathering as many precious metals as possible; we'll need them where we're going."

"I'll begin when we finish our meal," he picked up his glass and held it up for a toast.

"To new beginnings."

Chapter 54

Earth
The Regime - Washington, D.C. - Federal Courthouse
May 18, 2452

Two sentries walked Sonya and her lawyer to the courtroom; she unsuccessfully searched for Jared. Her lawyer worked on his tablet along the way, trying to find some precedent to help his case; his expressions told her there were none. The courtroom was empty of spectators. The only people present were the twelve jurors, the court stenographer, and a woman sitting at the adjacent table, whom she believed to be the prosecutor. She sat, and the guards took a position behind her.

No spectators or news media were present, indicating Supreme Commander Porter planned to keep the incident a secret. Goosebumps raised on her arms as the chilly air settled around her, giving her an eerie feeling. *So, this is where the Regime will decide my fate.* It was hard enough standing before a judge without any familial support. To do so in the same clothes, she wore when Jared arrested her was insulting. At least it was her best dress suit. She always believed that presentation meant everything. It was better than showing up in the orange jumpsuit, which made her look like a criminal. Her attorney broke the silence.

"I've reviewed your case. The MR came in very favorably. It looks like the prosecution dropped the charge of terrorism against you."

Sonya exhaled loudly, "Phew, that's a relief. That means the death penalty is off the table."

"True, but the treason charge is still pending. She's going for a life sentence on the moon."

"What is my defense?"

"The MR clearly shows that President Martinez did threaten Jared's life, and since you're new to the Regime, I'm hoping to find a sympathetic juror."

"Do you think there's a chance they'll let me go?"

"I don't want to get your hopes up; if we find favor with the judge, you may only get ten years."

"What?"

"All rise. This court is now in session. The honorable Judge Mason is presiding," a court clerk announced.

As Sonya stood, her hands trembled at the thought of spending ten years in prison. The judge walked to his bench, and her breathing became labored; she almost passed out. *I can't do ten years at my age. They may as well kill me.*

"Be seated," the judge scrolled through a tablet.

"Please, take the stand," the judge remarked.

Sonya looked at her attorney wide-eyed, "I didn't think I would have to testify in addition to the MR."

"It's all right. We also require a verbal testimony to coincide with the MR evidence."

As Sonya walked to the stand, the sound of her high heels tapping the floor echoed in the silence; the spectator chairs were still empty.

The bailiff stood before her, "Please state your name for the court."

"My name is Sonya Gonzales."

"That's not the name I have on the docket," the judge noted.

Looking to her lawyer for help, Sonya shrugged, so he checked the records and mouthed, Stewart.

"I'm sorry, your honor. Sonya Stewart."

"Counselor, why doesn't your client know her last name? Has she had a psychiatric evaluation?"

The lawyer stood, "May I approach the bench, your honor?"

"You may."

The prosecutor and the defense attorney stood before the judge.

"Mrs. Stewart's husband is filing for divorce. She signed the agreement this morning. She must have assumed the court has already processed it."

"Very well, counselors, return to your seat."

"Let the record show this is case number TR96035627. The Regime versus Sonya Stewart," the judge announced.

The bailiff began, "Please raise your right hand."

She did as ordered.

"Do you solemnly swear that the testimony you are about to give is the truth, the whole truth, and nothing but the truth?"

"I do."

"Please, be seated."

The prosecutor walked toward her from across the room, eager to interrogate her.

"Mrs. Stewart, will you please tell the jury your occupation before you entered the Regime."

"I was the governor of Texas."

"Is it true that you are the daughter of the late President Martinez Santiago?"

"I'm his stepdaughter."

"Mrs. Stewart, as the governor of Texas, isn't it true that you and President Martinez conspired to place you into the Regime so that you could destroy it?"

"No, absolutely not."

"Do you deny having formed a plot to destroy the Regime?"

"Objection, your Honor, asked and answered," her attorney voiced.

"Sustained."

"Mrs. Stewart, as the daughter of the President…."

"Stepdaughter."

"Very well, stepdaughter. You were privy to many of his internal dealings. Were you not?"

"Not all of them, only the ones that pertained to Texas or those that required my help."

"What about his dealings with General Ming-tun Fu?"

"I know that he occasionally purchased information from him."

"What about his latest purchase?"

"I don't know; he forced me to send him a hefty sum of Texas' revenue for it. I heard someone stole it before he could receive it."

"Indeed, someone did steal it. One of our better Regime agents stole it. Do you know who that agent is?"

"I have no idea."

"Come now, Mrs. Stewart. You targeted Jared for a reason."

"What? What do you mean?"

"The contract you forced him to agree upon was specific. You wanted to live with Jared. *He* was the agent who intercepted the disc, and even though the MR may not have shown that you knew it was Jared, it's obvious that you did know, or else, why would you ask a man half your age to marry?" she chuckled at the idea.

A few of the jury members snickered with her.

"All I can say is that I chose Jared because I liked what I read about him. I had no idea he intercepted the disc. The fact is, I'm glad he did."

"I see. It made you happy, so you deposited a nuclear bomb inside a garbage bin alongside the Market Place."

"Objection, your Honor. The prosecution had already dropped the terrorist charge against my client. Furthermore, the MR proved that she wasn't aware of the contents."

"Sustained. Counselor, stay away from bomb accusations, and the jury will disregard her statement," the judge ordered.

"Very well. You knew Jared was the agent who robbed you and President Martinez of classified Regime information."

"What? No!"

"Isn't it true that you decided to exact revenge on him personally by involving him with the contract to sell Texas, which included a deal that forced him to be your husband?"

"No!"

"Please, Mrs. Stewart. The time for lying is over."

"I'm not lying. I didn't know Jared was involved!"

"You were a Regime citizen during these events. Did you know that helping another country purchase Regime secret information is treasonous?"

Sonya became flushed and whispered, "Yes."

"Louder, please, I couldn't hear you."

"Yes. I knew; I only did it to protect my husband,"

"Your reasons do not interest this court or me. If you leak top-secret information, the damage you would do to this country would far outweigh one person's life."

"I never wanted to hurt anyone. I swear!"

"Really? Are you telling me the truth?"

"Yes. I'm not lying to you. It's too important."

"Interesting. Considering you have an extensive list of people you've betrayed by lying to them."

"What do you mean?"

"Isn't it true that to sign over Texas to the Regime, you had to betray your country and the President of the U.S.?"

Sonya was silent.

"After you arrived in the Regime, you betrayed your husband by drugging him so that you could leave your home without his knowledge. Isn't that true?"

Again, Sonya was silent.

"Also, you lied to the Supreme Commander when you signed the agreement because you planned to break it the following day by smuggling a bomb, or rather, what you thought was money, into our country!"

Sonya did not say anything.

"You seem very quiet for someone so innocent."

"I did betray the U.S., only so the people of Texas would have a chance. I did drug Jared to protect him; it's something I'm not proud of."

"Yes, we know how much you must care for him. I thought of drugging my husband just yesterday to keep him from getting hurt going to work."

This time, her comment brought laughter from all the jurors; the judge banged his gavel, and everyone quieted.

"Mrs. Stewart, isn't it true that you've been lying to people all your life. I mean, you are a Politician."

"I tried to be honest, but I had to lie sometimes. We *are* talking about politics, after all."

"How do I know you're not lying to us right now? You say that you and President Martinez didn't conspire together to get you here; you didn't want to hurt anyone, and you didn't know it was a bomb, so how can we trust you now?"

"The MR showed you...."

"The MR showed the past thirty days; it doesn't give us the full picture. You could have planned this attack years ago, so the memory is buried deep within your past, making it almost impossible to find."

“All I can do is hope that you will believe me. I came here for a fresh start and to escape President Martinez.”

“A fresh start?” She looked at the jury. “Your fresh start nearly got us all killed, so I prefer that you do not have a fresh start in my country.”

“Objection, your Honor.”

“Withdrawn,” she smiled and sat.

“Your witness counselor,” the judge commented.

He stood and questioned, “Mrs. Stewart, the jury knows President Martinez threatened Jared’s life; they may not know that you married once before. Is that true?”

“Yes.”

“Please tell us what happened to him in your own words.”

“He was killed in a car accident. Later, I discovered it wasn’t an accident, so I hired a private detective to investigate. It took a few months to discover President Martinez ordered his death.”

“Why did President Martinez have him killed?”

“He was working on a story that would uncover the corruption in the White House, and it showed that he was behind all of it. We also planned to leave the country and start a family. I tried to keep our plans a secret. Still, President Martinez found out and had him killed.”

The painful memory of her first husband’s death brought tears; she had cried so much the previous day that it surprised her she had any left.

“It seems clear that President Martinez could get to someone close to you. I mean, you were the governor at the time, and you had secret service agents protecting you and your husband at the time. Didn’t you?”

“Yes. These men were highly trained, but I discovered that no one could protect me from him. He was too powerful.”

“This same man threatened Jared. Did he not?”

“Yes. President Martinez threatened to kill Jared, who was waiting for me in my office. I knew he would have sent Alonso to kill us if I didn’t comply. It may not have happened right away; we would have died from a terrible accident in a year or two.”

“Why didn’t you tell Jared? Certainly, he could have done something.”

"I wanted to, except I feared for his life, and I don't know anyone here I can trust. I thought President Martinez would find out if I told someone, and it would be too late; I swear on my life, I had no idea it was a bomb."

"You're not on trial for terrorism, but you know what you did is a crime."

"I do. I risked myself for my husband," she looked at the jury with teary eyes and continued, "Isn't that what we're supposed to do as spouses. I would have come forward at some point. I just needed time to find someone I could trust. Jared's life was in real danger. It isn't a game or some story I've made up. You've seen the memory. What would you have done?" she broke down and cried.

"Do not question the jury, Mrs. Stewart. You are the one on trial, not them," the judge warned. "Any more questions, counselor?"

"No, Your Honor."

"Does the prosecution have any more questions for the defendant?"

"No, Your Honor."

"Proceed with your closing arguments."

The prosecutor stood.

"Ladies and gentlemen of the jury, the prosecution is pursuing a life sentence on the moon. We heard directly from the defendant, and it cannot be any clearer that she committed treason - that's treason, ladies and gentlemen! Her reasons for doing so are irrelevant. The law is clear on this subject. Contrary to what Mrs. Stewart or her lawyer would have you believe, we do not betray our country if our spouse is in danger. The only way was for her to notify the authorities or, at the very least, her husband. I've learned that he had her sign a divorce agreement this morning. If her husband doesn't believe in her, why should you?"

She paused for a moment, faced one of the women on the jury, and her gaze moved to the others as she scanned the panel, "Think about your children or your neighbor's children. Do you want this woman roaming free in this country only to betray us at the first chance? What if our agents fail during her next attempt? How many people will she kill? I say, no! Her connections to high positions in the U.S. government make her a severe threat to our nation's security.

I say the only safe place for her is on the moon. I hope you vote guilty. Thank you.”

Sonya’s lawyer stood, “The prosecution is right on one point. Mrs. Stewart did make a mistake. We have heard her reason for doing so. The prosecutor wants you to believe that all of us would have the strength to risk our loved one’s life; it simply isn’t true. None of us know how we would have managed this situation unless we came face to face with it. I’m sure everyone here has done something in the past that we hoped our loved ones would forgive. She came here looking for a fresh start, except her past, President Martinez, wouldn’t let her go. Well, President Martinez is dead now.

“Blown up by the same bomb he intended for us. Since he no longer controls her, I believe she doesn’t threaten us or this country. I wouldn’t mind if she lived next door to me,” he smiled at the prosecutor and returned his attention to the jury. “All I ask is that as you decide this woman’s fate, remember that she did it to protect a Regime citizen, and she didn’t believe her actions would have such dire consequences. I hope you will vote not guilty. Thank you.”

The judge ordered jury deliberation, so they stood and walked into the adjoining room. Sonya returned to her lawyer’s side as the judge got up and left.

“What happens now?” she inquired.

“You’ll return to your cell until they finish deliberating; I’ll send for you once I hear something.”

“I want to thank you for defending me.”

“Don’t thank me. It’s my job.”

“Thank you anyway.”

“Let me be clear, Mrs. Stewart; I defended you because it’s my job, and I do my job to the best of my ability. Despite that, I hope the jury returns with a guilty verdict, and you never see the light of day again. Now, I’ll call you when they’ve reached a verdict.”

As he walked away, Sonya stood speechless. Knowing that her lawyer wished the jury would send her to prison took away the tiny glimmer of hope she managed to conjure during the trial. Laughing at herself, she thought, *that’s what you get for thinking someone cared.* The sentries put restraints on her wrists and returned her to the cell. The stress of waiting for the jury to decide her fate was very taxing, and she began to sweat.

She paced to help the time pass quicker and took deep breaths to ease the pain in her nervous stomach. The thought of living out the rest of her life on the moon shook her sanity. Without a clock to track the time, she could only guess how long the jury had been deliberating. If they convicted her, she would never step on the Earth again.

It was the end of the road for her. She was alone in a strange country, which planned to condemn her to a life of solitude, and there would be no knight in shining armor to come to her rescue. The soles of boots pounded the concrete, and they were getting louder as the guards approached. She looked at them, and they nodded, which was a clear sign they wanted her hands through the bars so that they could restrain her.

She changed into dress clothes, and guards led her to the courtroom. The chilly air surrounded her, reminding her of the morgue she visited after her first husband died. Knowing her attorney's true feelings for her, she preferred to sit elsewhere but had no choice in the matter and sat beside him. She stared blankly at the wooden table before her, and her heart pounded as she waited for the inevitable.

It seemed as if the entire world finally turned against her. A deep melancholy hit her. She almost felt eager to go to the moon because at least she would be away from everyone that hated her. She had an idea. If the jury found her guilty, she would find a way to end her life before returning to her cell. *I could grab the gun from one of the sentries. That would be a quick and painless death.*

"All rise. This court is now in session. The Honorable Judge Mason is presiding," a clerk announced.

The judge walked to his seat and faced the bailiff, "Bring the jury in."

In her peripheral vision, she watched them enter the courtroom, one by one. None looked in her direction, which gave her an overwhelming sense of dread; she turned her head and saw that the guard's gun was within reach.

"Will the jurors please answer as the clerk calls your name?" the judge queried.

As the court clerk called their names, Sonya could only hear them distantly in the background because she focused on getting the guard's gun into her hands long enough to end her life.

"Mr. Foreman, have you agreed upon a verdict?" the judge asked.

"Yes, Your Honor, we have," the foreman replied.

"How say you?"

"We, the jury, find Sonya Stewart...."

"Your Honor!" the prosecutor yelled.

His gavel hammered the desk and yelled, "Order, counselor!"

"Your Honor, may I approach the bench?"

"We were just about to have the verdict."

"I'm sorry, Your Honor; you will understand once you see what I have here."

Confused, Sonya watched as the attorneys approached the bench. The prosecutor handed the judge her tablet, which he read for several minutes. Carefully, Sonya looked back. The prosecutor's outburst distracted the guard. His eyes were on her, not Sonya. Being free of the restraints, she decided to make her move. Sonya stood, faking a coughing spell; her attorney stood in her way before she could move toward the sentry.

"Sit down," he whispered angrily.

"Why? What are they going to do? Hang me?"

"You've been given a deal. I suggest you shut up and take it."

"I don't understand. I thought they were about to give the verdict, which you and I know was guilty, so why would the prosecutor stop it, only to offer me a deal?"

"I don't know; I suggest you read it carefully and sign it so we can all go home."

Sonya read the information written on the tablet. The more she read, the more relieved she felt. Later, she signed the deal and handed it back to her lawyer.

"Ladies and gentlemen of the jury, I want to thank you for your time. The prosecution and the defendant have made a deal. You may all go home now."

He slammed the gavel, and everyone left, except for Sonya and the two guards. Again, they restrained her and brought her back to her cell, where she anxiously awaited her next visitor. The technician came within the hour and injected a serum into her spine. He made a few checks and nodded to someone she recognized right away.

"Sharon? What are you doing here?"

"The name is Christine," she responded flatly.

Sonya nodded, "Ah, you're an agent too, makes sense."

"Come with me."

Sonya walked beside her, "Um, I'm sorry I drugged you."

"Save your apologies. You wouldn't have had a trial if it were up to me. I would have shot you between the eyes."

Sonya swallowed hard, "I'm glad it isn't up to you."

Christine took Sonya back to the house on the beach, where Sonya and Jared spent their first night together, took off her restraints, and showed her all the cameras in the house.

"Just so you know, we've installed extra lenses; there are no more blind spots. Also, technicians moved the camera board to another location; if you try to circumvent our monitoring of you again, there won't be another trial. I'll kill you myself."

"I understand," Sonya answered apologetically.

Christine started to leave until Sonya stopped her, "Wait. I know you don't owe me an explanation, but please tell me who did this for me?"

"Who do you think?"

"Jared?"

"Although I'll never understand why," she added, slamming the door behind her.

Knowing Jared saved her life made Sonya so happy that her eyes flooded with joy.

Chapter 55

Akil
Argi City
The 22,282nd Terrestrial Rotation of the Second Summer

Jadell paced, waiting for Gecheana to arrive. Just a few hundred heartbeats earlier, she contacted her and set up a meeting at the lowest level, hoping not to divulge her secret plan in her presence. Standing outside, protected by the darkness, Jadell watched Gecheana enter the apartment, discover Jadell was not there, and return to the avenue.

"Jadell, show yourself!"

"Not before I have a chance to speak with you," she replied.

"There is nothing you can say that will save you from my wrath."

"I did not betray you; as I prepared for my coming-of-age ceremony, Nayrah captured me and took my place."

"I saw Nayrah on the dais."

"That was me. I escaped, and knowing she was impersonating me, I arrived as Nayrah, so I could try to stop her."

"Obviously, you failed because she did not join houses with Noka as I ordered."

"She knew you told me to choose Noka and chose some random Akilian instead to anger you."

"You are lying. My informants have seen you with this Taen many times."

"I swear it was not me. Ever since you turned Argi over to me, Nayrah has been plotting against me. She must have pretended to be me to secure my downfall."

"Your alibi does not excuse you."

"That is why I am here. I know she intends to leave Akil on the next mid-Terrestrial Revolution."

"That little beast will not escape me."

"If you allow me, I would be honored to assist you in capturing her."

"I do not need your help. I have an army at my command."

"I know you are strong enough to stop her yourself, yet I was hoping you would allow me to do it for you. This way, you risk nothing."

"I see you are trying to get back into my good graces."

"Yes. I dearly wish to stand by your side once again."

"Very well, I will temporarily give you back control of Argi. If you do not kill Nayrah, my only mission will be to hunt you down."

"I understand. I will not fail you again."

"Now, show yourself."

Appearing from the darkness with her head lowered, Jadell cautiously moved to put her forehead on top of Gecheana's feet. It was a sign of submission.

"Thank you for giving me another chance."

"Do not make me regret it. Now stand and come with me because we must make plans for a blockade."

They returned to the Capital, and Gecheana changed her appearance to the young female she uses whenever meeting with Otsoa. Instead of using Yetta, Jadell used a different alter ego so that Otsoa would not know it was her. Otsoa opened the door to the private entrance and saw Gecheana enter his office with a companion.

"Who is she?" he inquired.

"This is Jadell. She will be helping us."

"Another Skean?"

"Do not concern yourself with my matters. Now fill me in on what has been happening."

"Some sentries missed their shift, so I sent others to look for them. They discovered their bodies along with Durnah's on the first level, nearly halfway to the other side of the city."

"I hope no one saw you," Gecheana remarked.

"No. I was careful."

"I have fulfilled my first promise to you; now explain to me this business about Va'ron dying," Gecheana asked flatly.

Hearing of her brother's death, Jadell almost gasped, which would have revealed her identity.

"I killed him as well," Otsoa responded as if discussing casual business.

"I did not approve it," she snapped.

"I know how you Skeans work. The first mistake I make, you will kill me and put Va'ron in my place."

"I should strike you down for your insolence!" Gecheana yelled.

"You still need me."

"Do not tempt me, Otsoa. I am too close to my goal to stop now. I will not let anyone stand in my way, even you."

"I am not standing in your way. I am only ensuring that I remain an asset."

"You are, but the next time you disobey me, it will be your last."

"What do we do now?" he questioned, ignoring her threat.

"Jadell told me that Nayrah plans to sneak off Akil on the following mid-Terrestrial Rotation. We need a plan to stop her. I have given Jadell permission to kill her. Once you have her head, I will only have one more promise to fulfill for you."

"Yanamai."

"Yes. I have coerced her parents into sending an official request to the Regime for Yanamai's return. Soro recorded a message telling Yanamai that Lilzah was ill. I erased his memory of the request, so they would not even know they helped us. I am sure that once Yanamai receives it, she will come back to Akil, and you can do with her what you will."

"I will send guards to put her parents in prison and use their freedom as leverage in case she refuses to take her place by my side. She will grow to love me."

"That is between you and her. Now, we must make plans to stop Nayrah."

Chapter 56

Earth
The Regime - Washington, D.C. - Mercy Hospital
May 19, 2452

Michael found himself in a hospital bed with an I.V. attached to his arm. Despite dehydration, he was feeling stronger. He stood and walked to the door. A nurse saw him and ran toward him.

"Sir! Please return to your bed!"

Michael ignored her order and instead asked, "Where's Yanamai?"

The nurse gently and firmly grabbed his arm, trying to guide him back to his room. Michael pushed her away in a sudden rush of anger.

"Where *is* Yanamai?"

"It's all right, nurse. I'll take it from here," Dr. Young said.

Having injured his leg, Dr. Young used a cane to help him walk.

"Is she…." Michael tried to ask, unable to finish the question.

"Don't worry. She's alive and well. She recovered very quickly, I might add."

"I saw her die."

"I believe the medics brought her back because it was touch and go until her heart started beating again. From what I've heard, she is close to full recovery."

"There was blood everywhere."

"Yes, I know. I was there. Remember? They revived her and examined her injury. Based on their report, it was only a flesh wound."

"No. I saw it. She had a hole in her back near her liver, which is why there was a large puddle of blood. The bullet must have nicked an artery."

"I didn't see her wound, so I can only tell you what the surgeon told me."

"If it was only a flesh wound, why did she die?"

"The only answer I can give you, the only one that makes sense, is that she's an alien. Therefore, we must assume that her species reacts differently to trauma than we do," Dr. Young replied, remembering how Yanamai transformed into Camila; it was something he still struggled to accept.

"Do you think they can recover that fast?"

"I honestly don't know; it would make sense based on the amount of blood we saw."

"Their recovery rate must be accelerated exponentially."

"She's been asking for you."

"She has?"

"I'd be happy to take you to her room."

Michael nodded, "Yes. I'd like that very much."

Due to his injured leg, Dr. Young moved slower than before, grabbing Michael's I.V. stand for support; he pulled it along with them along the way.

"I guess we're a sight, huh, Doc. Me with this stand and you with the cane."

Dr. Young chuckled, "I guess we are."

"How long will you need it?"

"Oh, not too long. I just landed on my knee a little too hard, is all. I should be good as new in a week or so."

"I'm glad to hear it."

At Yanamai's room, Dr. Young pulled him aside, "Michael, there's something you need to know about that young woman in there."

"What's that, Doc?"

"If it wasn't for her, I'm not sure we would have found you."

"What do you mean? You were right there with her during the escape."

"I think it's obvious I'm in no shape to be traipsing around the jungle, trying to save a colleague. Nor do I have the skills needed to save a hostage. I planned to contact the Regime and have them send a professional team; she wouldn't have it and insisted that if I didn't help, she would go on without me."

"I don't understand. When we first met, she wouldn't give me the time of day. Now, she took a bullet for me. It doesn't make any sense."

"Love seldom does."

"Come on, Doc; you must be kidding. She doesn't love me; she doesn't even know me."

"My dear boy, I'm older than I'd like to admit, and in all that time, I've never seen a civilian do what she did yesterday. It may not be love, but she was willing to risk her life, whatever her feelings for you are. That must mean something."

"I had no idea she would go to such lengths. I'll be sure to thank her."

"Maybe you should forgive her too. I think she's earned it."

"I don't know, Doc. What she did was awful."

"You have two choices, Michael. Thank her for saving your life, forgive her, and give her another chance, or you can thank her and walk away. If you walk, I'm unsure you'll ever find someone like her again. She is *unique*."

"Thanks, Doc. You've given me a lot to think about."

"You're welcome, my boy. Now, get in there and thank your rescuer properly."

They shook hands, and Michael watched Dr. Young walk down the hall. He turned into Yanamai's room.

"Michael, there you are! I've been so worried about you. No one will tell me anything!"

Seeing her sitting up in bed and appearing spry surprised him. Even more shocking was that she did not have an I.V. hooked to her arm. Also, she moved as if nothing had happened to her.

"You look well," he said, still baffled at her state of good health.

"You do too," she smiled at him.

"I hope you don't mind me asking about your wound. You had a severe injury and lost a great deal of blood. Also, I saw you die just before I blacked out, so how can you be doing so well?"

"I think you are not giving your medical staff enough credit. They are good at their jobs."

"May I see the wound?"

"Sure," she separated her gown in the back, just enough for him to see her lower spine.

Reaching out with his hand, he touched her skin, "It's completely healed. You don't even have a scar."

"As I said, your medical team is the best. I believe they used something called accelerant."

She covered herself, and he marveled at how her body had recovered overnight. Even with the help of the Regime's advanced medicine, an injured person would still be recovering. Apparently, her alien DNA is vastly different; it was the only explanation. He hoped to gain more insight into this unique ability, except to do so, he had to request a blood sample; for now, he had other business with her.

"Dr. Young told me what you did for me."

"He did?" Yanamai inquired cautiously.

She worried that the good doctor might have revealed her secret.

"Yes. He told me you wouldn't turn back. Instead, you insisted on rescuing me. Although I appreciate what you did, I can't imagine why you would risk your life for me. You barely know me."

"After what my sister and I did to you, it was the least I could do."

For a moment, they were silent, and in the quiet, they stared into each other's eyes. The look on her face made him remember how he felt during their breakfast date. He was upset with her for lying but desperately wanted to feel that euphoria again. Before he could reply, she broke the silence.

"Look, if you give me one more chance, I swear to spend the rest of my life making it up to you."

"I think we're even now."

"Does this mean you will see me again?"

"Yes. It does."

"That is wonderful! Now, how long do we have to stay here? I want to get out, so we can do something together right away!"

"Don't you have work to do?"

She sighed deeply, "Yes." She paused to think and offered, "Can we meet for lunch? The Regime gives me a whole hour."

"Sure. Let me see if I can find someone to get us checked out of here first."

Chapter 57

Earth
The Regime - Washington, D.C. - Fort McNair
May 19, 2452

Unable to meet Yanamai for lunch, Michael rescheduled their date for later in the afternoon. He stood outside her apartment smiling because of the surprise he had in store for her. She opened the door, wearing a casual green dress that clung to her body, and it surprised him to see that her eyes were green, not blue. Accrediting the change to her alien heritage, he dismissed his curiosity and focused on his plans. Before he could say a word, she embraced him in a surprisingly affectionate kiss. He had to pull away a few minutes later, or they would be late.

"It feels so good to kiss you again," she licked her lips and inhaled deeply.

Not understanding her reaction, he raised an eyebrow, "It's good to see you too."

"Are you going to tell me where you are taking me?"

"No. Don't worry; you'll enjoy it."

"I am uncertain," she replied playfully, "It will be hard to top the atrium and the restaurant."

"It'll be right up there with them."

She closed the door to her apartment, took his hand, and they headed for the Interstate Transportation Station. It still amazed him how easily she moved around with no sign that someone had shot her the day before; the portal technician loaded the coordinates.

"At least tell me why we are going for lunch when it is almost dinner time?" Yanamai asked.

"Because I told you we would go for lunch, and I don't break my promises. Plus, where we're going, it's lunchtime."

Chapter 58

Earth
The Regime - Hawaii - Maui
May 19, 2452

When Yanamai exited the Maui Interstate Transportation Station, warm air engulfed her, and a cool breeze caressed her skin, pushing away the warmth. Looking out over the balcony, she squinted because of the bright sunlight; white, puffy clouds dotted the brilliant blue sky, and to her right, she saw water instead of land. As she took in the scenery, the wind blew her hair in every direction and sometimes into her face.

With her right hand, she corralled the rebel strands and held them together beside her neck. Michael tapped her left shoulder and pointed to a large turquoise lagoon surrounded by mountains covered with tropical, green plants and trees. Also, at the top of one of the hills, a waterfall poured into it.

"It is beautiful, Michael."

"Welcome to Maui. Come on. I made reservations at a nearby restaurant."

While waiting for the server, Michael asked, "Are your parents here yet?"

"No. Zorion could only allow certain personnel to leave Akil. My parents, Soro and Lilzah, own a small business, a few hundred levels below my office, so they were not considered essential."

"That's harsh."

"It was a necessary choice our Sovereigns made. The survival of our culture depends on the few thousand we sent over first."

"We'll get them over here before too long. I promise, and as I said before, I don't break my promises."

The gesture made her smile, yet she knew the odds of everyone surviving were slim to none. Simply put, their numbers were too high for the time they had left.

"What about your parents?" she inquired, wanting to change the subject.

"I haven't seen them in over a year."

"Why?"

"My dad and I have a strained relationship. Even though I miss my mother, I hate being around him, so since I can't see one without the other, I don't go."

"If possible, I would like to meet your mother."

"I don't know, Yanamai."

"Oh, please," she pouted.

"Don't give me those sad, puppy-dog eyes."

"I have never seen a puppy dog; why do they look sad?"

Michael chuckled, "I'll have to show you later."

Seeing how important it was for her to meet his mother, he put aside his rule of avoiding her and exaggerated a sigh, "All right, I'll contact her and set something up for tomorrow. She's been trying to get me over there anyway."

"Oh, that is wonderful! Thank you, Michael!"

"Why is it so important?"

"Families are important in my world. Are they not important to you?"

"Sure. I just don't want you to see how dysfunctional mine is."

"Trust me. Every family has some issues, even on Akil."

They compared their likes, dislikes, hopes, and dreams as they ate; he discovered she wanted children. She wanted a lot, not just one or two, which made him wonder if she would have time for them with her busy schedule. After their meal, he took her to the beach, where she explored the sands and the waves as she waded into the ocean barefoot.

Yanamai ran back toward the shore as a surprising massive wave came at her. He laughed at her girlish screams as the tide rushed toward her, getting the lower part of her dress wet. Farther out, surfers caught her attention, and with a child-like fascination, she watched them glide across the water's surface; she faced Michael with a gleam in her eye.

"Will you show me how to do that?"

"I've never surfed before, so I can't teach you; I will sign us up for lessons and let you know when I find an instructor."

"It looks like fun!"

"It is until a wave takes you underwater, and you're struggling to reach the surface for air."

"I am sure the lessons will help us prevent that from happening."

Taking her hand, he led her to the waterfall promenade, and she watched the water cascade down the mountainside.

“This reminds me of Akil.”

“I thought your homes were underground?”

“They are, but there are waterfalls everywhere. I love the sound of falling water. It is soothing.”

She closed her eyes and imagined the Argian courtyards where she grew up. It was as if she were back home again until her phone rang, bringing her out of her thoughts. She put the device to her ear.

“Hello…yes…All right, I will be there shortly.”

“What’s wrong?” he queried after she disconnected.

“General Saunders summoned me to his office.”

“Is everything all right?”

“I do not know. His secretary would not say.”

“I better get you there now.”

“Wait! Just give me one more moment here with you,” she begged and, with a sly grin, pulled him close and stared deep into his eyes, “I wish I could save this moment somehow. I would relive this perfect day often.”

“Yes. It was a perfect day, and we can come back and visit as often as you like.”

“That sounds wonderful,” she replied and kissed him.

He returned her affection and felt himself falling for her. It was not a surprise because she was easy to love. What amazed him was that she chose him out of everyone on Akil and Earth. He did not know the odds of them meeting and falling in love, so he made a mental note to do the calculations later to show how happy he was to have met her. Still, there was one thing he had to be sure of before going any further.

“Are you a spy?”

Chuckling, Yanamai responded, “Why would you think that?”

“My last girlfriend turned out to be one.”

“Oh, you poor dear.”

“It was painful to discover her identity.”

“I can assure you, Michael. I have never been a spy. I have worked as a portal technician for my entire career. If you like, I can show you documents to prove it.”

“No. You don’t have to do that. I just wanted to hear you say it. Now, let’s get you back to the base.”

Chapter 59

Earth
The Regime - Washington, D.C. - Fort McNair
May 19, 2452

Michael and Yanamai went to General Saunders' office, where his assistant told Yanamai to enter. Standing in the doorway, Yanamai asked if Michael could join the conversation. Knowing she went to Brazil with Michael, it was easy for General Saunders to surmise that they were now a couple, primarily because Yanamai fiercely pursued him.

"I'll allow it since this will most likely affect both of you," General Saunders agreed.

Michael shut the door behind him.

"Yanamai, I'm afraid I have some sad news. We received an official request from Soro, asking for your return to Akil. I'm sorry; Lilzah is ill."

"Does she have the sickness?"

"There were no other details."

"If she has the sickness, it will be fatal. May I return home to see her?"

"Yes, we expected your request. You may leave whenever you're ready. Feel free to take all the time you need."

"Thank you, General. I will return soon. The sickness moves swiftly. I do not expect that she will survive the night," Yanamai replied grimly.

"Maybe you can request to bring them here so our doctors can examine her; I could test her blood and produce immediate results," Michael offered, hoping he could take part in saving Lilzah's life.

"I think we could make an exception in this case," General Saunders agreed.

"Thank you; I will ask Zorion if she could leave Akil with me," Yanamai remarked.

"I'm afraid I have some more sad news. Someone killed Zorion. His eldest son is now in charge," General Saunders reported.

"Oh, no!" Yanamai exclaimed, shaking her head, weeping.

"You must have been close," consoled Michael.

“We were. I saw him every day. He was like a parent to me,” Yanamai cried.

“You should see Lilzah and attend Zorion’s funeral,” Michael suggested.

“There is one problem. His son, Otsoa is obsessed with me,” Yanamai informed.

“I don’t like the sound of that,” Michael countered.

“You don’t have to go. I can try to do some maneuvering from my office. For example, I can put in a request to have your parents sent here due to a medical emergency,” General Saunders suggested.

“No, thank you. It would take too long. As I said, the sickness is quick. I want to be there before it consumes her. Besides, I know Otsoa would prevent her from coming here, just out of spite,” Yanamai responded.

“What if this is a trap?” Michael surmised.

Pausing to think, Yanamai shook her, “No. I do not believe he would keep me on Akil. My job here is too important. The lives of every Akilian are at stake. After I arrive, I will speak with the Interstellar Transfer Officer myself. He should give my parents special permission to return with me. That way, Otsoa will not know until it is too late.”

“How obsessed is he?” Michael wondered with a raised eyebrow.

Yanamai sighed, “He thinks we were in love.”

“Oh,” Michael frowned.

“We were not. He imagined everything. Even Zorion knew of his delusions,” Yanamai added defensively.

“I’m concerned about your safety. General, is there any way we could send an escort? If Jared went with her as a favor to me, it would make me feel better. I would go with you, but I’m useless in a fight,” Michael furrowed his eyebrows.

“I’m sorry; they will not allow our military personnel on Akilian soil,” General Saunders explained.

“Even though it is dangerous, I must take a chance. If Lilzah is ill….” Yanamai was saying until Michael interrupted her.

“You don’t need to defend going. I would go. How long do you think it’ll take you?” Michael inquired.

"It should only take a few hours. I will go to the Transfer Office first; if they do not allow her to leave, I will visit until the end and return," Yanamai remarked.

"I'll be waiting at the Fort Levan Interstellar Transportation Station until you get back," Michael smiled to comfort her.

"All right, it's settled. Get going and let me know if there's anything else I can do," General Saunders ended abruptly, having a great deal of work ahead of him.

On the way to the Interstellar Transportation Station, Michael asked, "You haven't mentioned Otsoa before. Should I be worried? Are you sure there isn't something between you?"

"Yes. I am very sure, Michael. I have *never* wanted to be with him. I did not mention him earlier because Zorion kept him away from me. Since I came to Earth, I did not think it possible for him to bother me again."

"Let's hope he doesn't notice your return."

At the Fort Levan Interstellar Transportation Station, Yanamai checked in at the desk. After security cleared her, she hugged him tightly and whispered to him.

"I will miss you terribly."

"I'll miss you too. Please, be careful. I'll be waiting right here until you return."

They had a long and sorrowful kiss goodbye until she let him go and stepped through the event horizon, back to Akil.

Chapter 60

Akil
Argi City
The 22,283rd Terrestrial Rotation of the Second Summer

Yanamai stepped through the Interstellar Transport Bay's emergency door and saw two sentries stationed at the exit. Tadra, her colleague, frowned.

"What are you doing here?"

Yanamai walked next to her, so the guards could not hear, and whispered, "Soro sent an official request for me to return. Lilzah is ill."

"Oh no, that is terrible! Is there anything I can do?"

"Do you have some free heartbeats?"

"Sure, why?"

"On Earth, they have physicians who may be able to save Lilzah. I would appreciate it if you would speak with the Earth Transfer Official on my behalf. See if you can get him to start the process for my parents' emergency leave request."

"Consider it done. I will get someone to cover for me and go right away."

"Thank you, Tadra. I will contact you soon."

Yanamai left the Interstellar Transport Bay and stepped onto the avenue, finding it eerily quiet. She walked toward the elevator and heard her shoes hitting the pavement, echoing throughout the courtyard. Before she could reach the elevator, two other sentries stopped her.

"You are to come with us," one of the guards commented in a deep, throaty voice.

"Why? What is wrong?"

"Do not question us! Either come willingly, or we will restrain you," the other threatened.

"Fine. I will come willingly. There is no need for violence."

They escorted her to a holding area on level one. When they opened the door to a cell, she realized they intended to incarcerate her. Panicking, she turned and tried to run; they stopped her.

"No! Why are you doing this?" she pleaded, struggling against their unyielding grip.

Without replying, they pushed her inside, slammed the door shut, and locked it.

"You have falsely imprisoned an Akilian citizen! You will lose your job and face incarceration yourselves!" Yanamai yelled.

Laughing, the sentries took a position nearby. Having watched an Earthian movie where a prisoner picked the lock with a hairpin and escaped, Yanamai removed one from her hair and tried for a few hundred heartbeats until the clasp broke. She swore under her breath and sat to wait for her jailor; a few moments later, the steel door creaked open.

Otsoa stood on the other side, wearing the formal apparel that Zorion once donned. The change in his body mass surprised her. Every muscle increased five times its original proportion, making him an intimidating sight. Still, seeing his smug grin angered her, so she confronted him.

"Welcome home, Yanamai," his wicked smile grew.

"Why have you arrested me?"

"It is all part of the plan."

"Lilzah is sick," she started to say until understanding what he had done to her. "She is not sick. Is she?"

"No. A colleague coerced Soro into sending you the formal request."

"I can see that you have not changed. You are still delusional."

Otsoa snickered, "I think you will find that not only have I changed, but many other things have also changed. For instance, I am now Argi's sovereign."

"I heard someone killed Zorion, and I am sure you had your hand in it. Although, I must say, even I did not think you would stoop that low."

"I was nowhere near him when it happened. There are many witnesses to the fact. In any case, Argi is now under my control."

"I am sure your colleague did it," she replied defiantly and waited for a reply; when none came, she continued, "You will not get away with this. When the Information League hears about what you have done, the other Sovereigns will remove you from office."

"Instead of focusing all that energy on removing me, I think you should be more concerned about your predicament. The city is accusing you of treason. I am the only one who can keep you from spending the rest of your life behind bars."

"You have truly sunk to depths even I did not think possible."

"That is why you are here. You continually underestimate my resolve."

"What do you want from me?"

"It should be obvious."

"You already have Durnah. You cannot have both of us."

"Durnah died of the sickness. She is no longer an obstacle."

"You *putok*! Everyone knew she genuinely cared for you. How could you do that to her?"

"Sometimes, one must make sacrifices to obtain one's goal."

"Do you really expect me to join houses with you?"

"You belong by my side, Yanamai. The sooner you accept that fact, the sooner we can move forward with our lives. I am thinking; ten offspring should make me look fruitful."

Holding down a gag, she asked, "If I refuse?"

"Argi City will convict you of treason and sentence you to life in prison, and you will not be the only one who suffers. Currently, your parents are in a cell at the central prison. If they stay there too long, they will lose everything. Soro will be unable to work, which means he cannot pay his tribute, so the Argi government will confiscate everything he owns, including his business and home," he paused to emphasize his next point. "They will remain in separate cells and alone for the rest of their lives."

"I will see you burn in Abadose for this!" she spat.

"I did not think you were religious."

"Somehow, I know the universe will curse you for this."

"All I am trying to do is help you remember. Now that I am Argi's Sovereign, I have access to all its knowledge and power. I *will* find a cure for your memory loss. I have my best lab technicians working on it right now."

"Whatever formula they create, it will never work. I have never cared for you in any measure."

He loved her deeply and hated her resistance toward him. Pushing away his anger so as not to harm her, he stepped closer and growled through gritted teeth.

"You will be mine, Yanamai, one way or another, with or without your memories intact. I will give you time to consider your answer. If you give me the wrong one, I can assure you; the consequences will be swift and devastating."

Spinning abruptly, he left, slamming the door behind him. Alone in her cell, Yanamai paced, trying to understand why he was so adamant about her. Even though he had pursued her before, she did not expect this level of cruelty. Now, her parents' life and freedom were in jeopardy; she would have to accept his repulsive offer if there were any chance of escaping.

Doing so would get her out of the cell, and she could contact her parents warning them to hide until she could secure safe passage to Earth; that would only work if he kept his word and released them. If he did, she would be free to plan their escape. If she could somehow return to Earth with her parents, it would finally free her of Otsoa forever.

Chapter 61

Akil
Argi City
The 22,283rd Terrestrial Rotation of the Second Summer

Julie woke from a troubled sleep and reflected on the dream. In it, she desperately tried to clear a path for someone named Yanamai. Julie thought about her and remembered seeing her in Akil's Interstellar Transport Bay. *That's right; she's the one who sounded the alarm, so why does she need to go to Earth?* Julie changed and found Olan in the kitchen, eating his breakfast. She sat beside him and told him about her dream.

"I sent a message to Yanamai yesterday, warning her that Otsoa planned to trick her into returning," Olan informed.

"Based on my dream, I don't think she got it," Julie answered.

Olan groaned, "Do not worry. I can get her back to Earth. You have enough on your agenda."

"No. I think I'm the one who needs to help her. I felt a deep sense of urgency. Plus, there were Skeans present."

"I may not be able to fight them, but there are other ways of taking them down," he stood and shoved one last morsel into his mouth.

"Where are you going?" Julie asked.

"To get some help. Now, eat something; it is getting late. You must meet with Nayrah soon."

Julie closed her eyes and tried to see the future as Urki taught her. She sensed something pivotal was about to happen yet could not see it. It was elusive. She pushed the images out of her mind and contacted Nayrah.

"I'm ready."

"Good; we must do something first."

"What?"

"We must rescue a prisoner named Yanamai."

"Did you dream about her too?"

"Hmm."

"What's wrong?"

“Nothing, I will tell you later. We do not have much time. Meet me at the prison level courtyard.”
“I’ll see you soon.”

Chapter 62

Akil

Argi City

The 22,283rd Terrestrial Rotation of the Second Summer

Nayrah received an encrypted message from Jadell, saying that Gecheana temporarily reinstated her, which meant she regained her trust. As Nayrah predicted, Gecheana planned to stop her on the level one courtyard near the Interstellar Transport Bay at mid-Terrestrial Revolution. The second part of her message was disturbing.

Otsoa tricked Yanamai into returning to Akil. Upon her arrival, he imprisoned Soro, Lilzah, and Yanamai until she agreed to join houses. *I told him she would be the death of him, stupid putok.* Yanamai had only been a minor distraction. Initially, Nayrah planned to kill her until Gecheana tried to end Yanamai, so Nayrah defended her simply because Gecheana wanted her dead. She wondered if that had been the right move, especially now that Gecheana had given Yanamai to him.

If Yanamai knew how many times her life was in danger, she would never sleep again, Nayrah mused. She felt a ripple from the shadows. It was the signal her dark puppet master sent to get her attention. Closing her eyes, she opened herself to it and saw an image of Yanamai and her parents in prison. *Are you serious? I am facing Gecheana soon. I do not have time for a rescue.*

Even though it was an imposition, she trusted her instincts, and just as she was about to contact Julie for help, her communicator signaled. Julie answered. Nayrah thought it strange that Julie's dream directed her toward the same path. It almost made her reconsider helping Yanamai and her parents, but she recommitted herself to her original plan after careful thought. It was always best to allow the darkness to guide her, even though she did not always understand its logic.

She would need to call in a favor from a local business owner to successfully rescue Otsoa's prisoners. After giving him instructions on what to bring and where to meet, she thought about the rest of her plan and sighed at her timekeeper, knowing it was only four thousand heartbeats until mid-Terrestrial Rotation. There was not enough time to get everyone out safely. Knowing Gecheana, she would have her blockade set up at least two thousand heartbeats before the mid-Terrestrial Revolution.

That left her with only half the time to execute her rescue from now to mid-Terrestrial Rotation. To make matters worse, Jadell mentioned that Otsoa ordered ten soldiers to guard Yanamai's parents and another ten to guard Yanamai. Soldiers were stronger and faster than guards, making it harder to take them down. *At least there is no pressure.*

Since Yanamai would not leave without her parents, Nayrah decided to rescue them first. Once they were safe, she would hurry to Yanamai's cell and release her. If everything went smoothly, Nayrah could get her through customs before Gecheana set her trap; if not, her mission to get Yanamai on Earth would fail. Walking toward the door, she instinctively checked her sword to ensure it was secure.

The prison-level trip cost five hundred heartbeats, a quarter of the time needed to complete her mission. When she arrived, Julie and the business owner were already there. *Okay, one less thing to worry over.* Julie did not wear her headpiece and kept it covered with a hood to conceal her identity.

Standing five hand widths from her, Nayrah spoke softly, "Ten soldiers are guarding her parents, and another ten are guarding Yanamai. You and I must be quick, so they do not sound the alarm. If they do, our rescue will be over before it even begins."

Julie nodded, "Don't worry about me. I'll do my part."

Facing the business owner, Nayrah handed him a data stick, "The moment we return with the prisoners, give them the change of clothes you brought and the data stick, which contains their passports. I am also giving you two vials that will disguise their pheromones. Make sure they change their likeness to match the Akilians on their passports. Once they are ready, you may leave and return home."

The business owner nodded, took the items, and hid them, so Nayrah signaled to Julie, and they headed for the prison entrance.

"I will need your help getting past the screener," Julie remarked.

"You can do it. Just push the thought into her mind; I will be right behind you if you get into trouble."

When it was Julie's turn for the screener to evaluate her pheromones, she concentrated and pushed the thought of recognition into her mind. The screener's eyes blinked rapidly for a few moments and spoke in the Akilian language.

"Welcome back."

Having passed her test, Julie walked toward the corridor that led to the prison. Looking back, she saw Nayrah's face morph into someone else's moments before reaching the screener. Julie watched the screener blink rapidly and knew Nayrah would be through shortly. Once inside the prison, Nayrah stopped to look at a directory. Julie kept her distance because they did not want the guards to know they were together.

Nayrah found their location and gave Julie a covert signal. At separate times, they headed down the passageway toward the cells. Julie disappeared from the guards' line of sight and walked to catch up with Nayrah. Moments later, they arrived near the rooms that held Lilzah and Soro. Raising her hand, Nayrah signaled Julie to stop.

"It is time to put your headpiece on. I will be the first distraction," Nayrah whispered.

Before pulling her headpiece down, Julie watched with amazement as Nayrah's appearance changed again. This time, she looked like an unfamiliar, beautiful young woman.

"I will pretend to be lost and do my best to get them to encircle me, and if they do, I want you to attack at that moment because your suit will blind them, causing a second distraction, which is when I will join the assault," Nayrah explained; Julie noticed that her voice changed too.

"How do you do that?"

"What?"

"Change your appearance and your voice. I mean, you look and sound completely different."

"I cannot explain how I do it; I just do. Do the people of your planet do the same?"

"Nope."

"Pity," Nayrah replied smugly.

She made a mental note of her enemy's weakness for safekeeping, and as with all the information, she would somehow use it to her advantage.

"All right, it is time," Nayrah advised.

She walked over to where the soldiers stood, leaving Julie behind. Moving forward, Julie peaked around the corner and saw the soldiers standing at their assigned posts. *Damn, they're standing far apart. I hope she can get them to gather closer together.* Julie saw two soldiers at one cell door from her hiding place, two more at the neighboring cell door, and two on the corridor's opposite side. Two stood on either side of the passageway, preventing Nayrah from getting through. However, Julie also sensed two farther down the corridor out of her line of sight.

"Stop," Julie heard one of the soldiers say in the Akilian language, with a deep throaty voice.

"Oh dear, I must be lost again," Nayrah pretended confusion.

Initially, the soldiers were rough with her until Nayrah brought her hood down, exposing her beautiful features (as she was in her youth), and their attitudes changed drastically. Leaving their posts, all the soldiers moved closer to their new visitor, each hoping for the opportunity to get her attention. In no time at all, Nayrah drew them to her, and the last soldier moved into place; Julie felt an invisible nudge urging her to move forward. *I guess it's time.*

As she ran toward them, her suit caught the attention of the five soldiers facing her. Encircled by ten trained killers, Nayrah watched and waited for Julie to attack; the five warriors squinted, indicating that Julie was on her way. The soldier's hands move toward their swords. Simultaneously, Nayrah allowed her hidden Skean sword to slide down her sleeve and into her hand; the blade extended to its full length, displaying the glowing crimson metal. Not allowing a wasted heartbeat, Nayrah spun her sword.

At first, Julie thought it moved wildly to distract, which it did. That was part of the plan. The sword always seemed to land in a vulnerable spot on a soldier's body. After she subdued three, two unsheathed their swords; they were no match for a Skean's sword. With the flick of her wrist, she cut the other blades to the hilt, taking away their only means of defense. Before Nayrah landed her first strike, Julie reached the five soldiers facing away from her.

Seeing their fellow soldiers squinting, they turned, and the bright reflective light from her suit blinded them. It was just enough distraction for Julie to take down two before they knew what had happened. The other three realized they were under attack and unsheathed their swords. Julie's white glowing blade cut through them with no resistance; she pierced their hearts, causing their legs to go limp, and they collapsed. Having taken down four, Julie watched the last one run toward the alarm; Nayrah flung her sword at him.

As it spun toward him, it moved end to end and from top to bottom. Once it left her hand, it stopped glowing because Nayrah was its power source. As the sword cut through the air, Julie heard it whistling in a low, threatening manner. Before the soldier reached the alarm button, the blade landed, penetrating his back. The blade's impact forced him into the wall headfirst, knocking him unconscious. Before his body fell, Nayrah extended her hand. Her power ripped the sword from his back and returned it to its master.

She faced Julie and smiled, "No one is *permanently* damaged."

"Thank you."

Nayrah extended her hand toward the cells and used her power to unlock the doors and pull them open. Lilzah and Soro stepped out, unsure of what had happened; they covered their eyes, seeing Julie's reflective suit.

Julie removed her headpiece and approached them, "We're here to rescue you."

"What do you want us to do?" Soro asked.

"Select a soldier and put on his uniform," Nayrah instructed as she began to change her clothes.

"What are you doing?" Julie inquired.

"The only way to get them out of here is to pretend to be soldiers," she answered, removing some of the body armor.

Soro and Lilzah did as Nayrah instructed. They put on the soldier's attire and morphed into their likeness, whose clothes he or she wore.

"I'll never get used to seeing your image change," Julie shook her head.

"The breastplates will hide our bodies' inability to duplicate their mass," Nayrah explained, with the deep throaty voice of the soldier she impersonated.

"How do *I* get out?" Soro queried.

"The same way you got in," Nayrah chided.

"Can you tell us why Otsoa put us in prison?" Soro questioned.

"Yes, but there is no time. We must get out of here before the next shift arrives. Now go!" Nayrah urged.

Nayrah used her power at the prison exit, forcing the screener to believe they were the soldiers they had just defeated. They passed through, walked out of sight, and Nayrah led them into the shadows where the business owner waited.

"Change out of the soldier's uniforms," Nayrah commanded.

She morphed her likeness back to that of her Skean identity. All three of them changed while Julie watched for any trouble until they were ready.

Nayrah led them to the elevator, selected the top level, and looked at her timekeeper, "We will not make it in time."

"What do you mean?" Julie wondered.

"We still must free Yanamai."

"Yanamai is here on Akil?" Soro asked.

"Yes. We are trying to get all of you to Earth; now be quiet and do as you are told," Nayrah snapped.

"Calm down, Nayrah; we're trying to help them. Remember?"

"I do not have time to be polite. I must get them through the Interstellar Transport Bay, free Yanamai, and send her through before Gecheana sets her trap."

"I thought they had passports."

"They do, and they drank the potion to hide their identity; those things are not full proof on their own, so I must go with them to ensure the screener accepts the deception."

"Tell me where they are holding Yanamai, and I'll bring her to the Interstellar Transport Bay once I free her."

Nayrah laughed, "Did you forget the ten soldiers Otsoa put there to watch over her? You cannot subdue them before one of them sounds the alarm."

"Do you have a better idea?"

Nayrah thought for a moment and exhaled loudly, "No."

"What do you want to do?" Julie inquired just as the elevator came to a stop.

As the doors opened, Nayrah pointed in the direction of her cell, "He is keeping Yanamai in the upper-level prison, about one thousand paces that way. If you can subdue the soldiers before they sound the alarm, return here and meet me at this elevator. That should give us enough time to get her through."

"I'll see you here shortly."

Julie left to complete her mission, so Nayrah went with Soro and Lilzah to the Interstellar Transport Bay. Nayrah morphed her likeness into one of the departure coordinators that was not due to arrive for another thousand heartbeats. She handed the screener a small chip (having their passports) at the checkpoint.

"I have two Earth-bound Akilians Otsoa wants expedited."

It took only a couple hundred heartbeats to disembark until they received their approval. Before they entered the Interstellar Transport Bay, Nayrah faced Yanamai's parents.

"When you get to Earth, tell whoever is in charge to have soldiers ready. If things go as planned, I will send Yanamai through shortly. If Otsoa finds out, they must be there to protect her. I believe he will follow her to Earth to bring her back."

"We understand," Soro remarked.

Watching on the monitor, Nayrah saw them step through the event horizon and onto Earth's soil. *Two down, one to go.* Having completed her mission, she returned to meet Julie at the elevator.

Chapter 63

Earth
The Regime - Africa - Sahara Desert - Fort Levan
May 19, 2452

Standing in the Interstellar Transportation Station's waiting room, Michael stared at the open vortex behind a protective glass wall surrounding the lounge. The longer Yanamai delayed her return, the more worried he became. Unexpectedly, two Akilians stepped through the event horizon, briskly walked away from Akil, and stopped at the checkpoint. Michael stood near the clerk to see if they said anything about Yanamai. It surprised him how well they spoke English.

"My name is Soro, and this is Lilzah. Otsoa imprisoned our daughter and us until someone came to our rescue. She said to have armed guards ready when they send our daughter through."

"Who is your daughter?" the clerk asked.

"Her name is Yanamai. She was on Earth but returned to Akil," Soro replied.

Hearing her name, Michael asked, "Is her life in danger?"

"Our rescuers said they might not make it in time."

"In time for what?"

"On the elevator ride up, we heard them discuss Otsoa's plan to trap them."

"If they have Yanamai with them, he'll recapture her!" Michael exclaimed.

"We are worried about her safety, too," Soro added.

Michael contacted General Saunders, who sent orders to beef up their security team at the vortex; he brought food and something to drink to Yanamai's parents and led them to the lounge to wait for Yanamai's return.

Michael introduced himself as Yanamai's friend, "She received a message that you were ill."

Soro shook his head, "She should have known it was a trap. I would have never sent her a message while Otsoa was in charge. That *putok* harassed her since she was young."

"Although there was a risk, she wanted to be by Lilzah's side."

Hearing that her daughter wanted to be with her during her last moments made Lilzah cry. Soro held her, trying to comfort her. Michael had never felt this helpless. Feeling the urge to do something, he excused himself, stepped out of the lounge, and waited in the landing area near the vortex, where twenty heavily armed soldiers took positions around the room. The General ordered his staff to set the alert at its highest level. Michael could not do anything except wait for her return. He hated waiting.

Chapter 64

Akil
Argi City
The 22,283rd Terrestrial Rotation of the Second Summer

Ten soldiers arrived at the prison, passed the screener, and walked to the corridor where their supervisor had assigned them. Upon reaching the appointed cells, they discovered their colleagues were down, and three were missing their uniforms. Even worse, they found that the prisoners had escaped. Nine stayed behind to care for the injured, and one ran to notify the warden, who informed Otsoa.

"Shilda, get Dolas in my office right now!" Otsoa yelled from behind his desk, not bothering to use the communicator.

"Yes, Sir! Right away," she replied.

Moments later, Furin (Dolas's second in command) stood at the doorway, and Otsoa waved him in right away.

"Where is Dolas?" Otsoa inquired.

"He is not answering his communicator, so I came in his place. How may I be of service?"

"There has been a prison break."

"Yanamai's parents?"

"Exactly. I want you to find them. Close the Intercity Stations if you must. I do not want anyone leaving Argi until we have apprehended them."

"Understood."

"Dismissed."

Furin returned to his desk, stopped intercity traffic, and sent out an all-points lookout for the two escaped prisoners. Meanwhile, he reviewed the video logs from the Central Prison and saw three soldiers leave the Central Prison; he slowed the recording for a closer look. The mannerism in which one of the soldiers communicated with the screener caught his attention.

The examiner questioned their early departure until the soldier asked again, and the screener nodded with an absentminded stare allowing them to pass. Knowing that all ten original soldiers were still in the prison area, the three he saw leaving were the captives and rescuers. Now he needed to know if the analyst was involved. A few hundred heartbeats later, she was sitting in front of Furin, trembling.

"You seem nervous," he noted indifferently.

"Of course, I am. Two prisoners escaped during my shift. The blame will fall on me. It *must* fall on me."

"I want to know what happened in your own words."

"As they approached, I thought it was strange because their shift was not over, so I verified their schedule, showing they were early. One requested I check again, and I felt strange for a moment, looked down, and saw a different departure time. I could not believe I had made such a mistake, so I let them through. I even apologized for my error. Later, I learned the prisoners had escaped; I rechecked the schedule and discovered I was right the first time, except it does not matter because I unwittingly allowed them to pass."

"This strange feeling you had; can you explain it?"

"I have only felt it twice before. The first was earlier in the Work Cycle."

"Can you give me an approximate time?"

"Yes. Just a few hundred heartbeats before the three left."

Furin played the video and told the screener to point out the exact moment she felt the sensation. He noticed it happened when she allowed two females into the facility; he did not recognize either. Based on her testimony and the circumstances surrounding the escape, Furin did not believe she collaborated with the vigilantes. To be sure, he did a quick financial check on all her accounts; nothing unusual showed up.

"You may go," he stated.

"I am free?" puzzled the screener.

"For now. I suggest you stay in Argi near your home during leisure. I want you to be available if I have any further questions."

She bowed nervously, "I will go home now."

He reviewed all intercity departures videos before the lockdown but did not see anyone who resembled the two females the screener spotted. *Think Furin. Where could they be?* The idea came to him, and his eyes widened. *No, they could not have been so bold!* He accessed the Interstellar Transport Bay video and saw two unscheduled Akilians rushing through the checkpoint. With his discovery, he ran to Otsoa's office to give him the news.

"What do you have for me?" Otsoa questioned gruffly.

"I believe the Saiph you mentioned earlier released the prisoners."

"What?" Otsoa queried in disbelief.

"I interviewed the screener and watched the video. Her testimony convinced me that the Saiph manipulated her mind to pass through the checkpoint. My research shows that only a Skean or a Saiph can control someone's mind this way. Even more troubling is that two were exhibiting that kind of power."

"Two?"

"Yes. Based on their body mass, they were female."

Nayrah, Otsoa thought. *Why would she be working with a Saiph?* "Where did the Saiph take them?"

"They are on Earth, Sir."

Enraged, Otsoa stood, slamming his fists on the desk, and yelled, "How did they get past the checkpoint?"

"I verified that the information given to the security team was valid. Somehow, the Saiph must have accessed our database and produced legal documents for them."

"I want them back here at once!" he yelled.

"Sir, you must contact Earth. They are out of our authority."

"Shilda! Contact Supreme Commander Porter now!"

"Yes, Sir!" she answered.

Moments later, Supreme Commander Porter's face was on Otsoa's office monitor. During his wait, Otsoa tried to get his anger under control because Supreme Commander Porter was in control of their survival.

"Yes, Otsoa, how may I be of help?" Supreme Commander Porter inquired politely.

"Two of our prisoners have escaped. They used forged documents to illegally leave our planet. I would like you to return them, please. I will have my assistant send their identities to you at once."

Supreme Commander Porter advised, "As per our contract, I have agreed not to interfere with your social issues."

"Good, I will expect them back within the hour."

"No."

"Excuse me?" Otsoa challenged, standing.

"The contract in which the five Sovereigns of your world agreed also included a clause, where I may add or take away any part of the agreement, I see fit. My General told me that you falsely imprisoned them. Therefore, I'm introducing a new section of our contract. I'm protecting them under our new 'right of asylum' agreement. It means that if an Akilian makes it to our soil and asks for asylum, I will give them haven. I'm sorry, Otsoa; they are now under my protection."

Rage turned Otsoa's face blood red, making it impossible to contain himself, so he yelled, "You will return them to me, or I'll close the vortex and keep anyone else from leaving Akil!"

With a raised eyebrow, Supreme Commander Porter smiled, "Really? Go right ahead."

"You would let trillions die just to save two?" Otsoa wondered, surprised at how insensitive the Earthian seemed.

"You're the one who will let trillions die, including yourself. You forget that I have everything I need from your civilization. I have your technology, a complete copy of your database, and everything your culture recorded from its birth. We already have about a thousand of your best and brightest building new portal machines.

"If you decide to stay behind and die, it will not affect the Regime. Although it would be sad if the citizens of Akil perished, their blood would be on your hands, not mine. Don't worry; I'll ensure every surviving Akilian here on Earth knows that you were the idiot responsible for the deaths of their loved ones. Every Akilian generation to follow will despise the name, Otsoa."

Supreme Commander Porter disconnected their communication without another word. Otsoa stared at the dark screen in disbelief and, in a fit of rage, threw every piece of furniture in his office.

Chapter 65

Akil
Argi City
The 22,283rd Terrestrial Rotation of the Second Summer

Having left Nayrah to her task, Julie headed to the level one prison area. Unlike the last time, Julie visited the upper level, it was vacant. Keeping her hood over her head, she faced the floor, hoping to remain hidden. Upon reaching the small prison section, Julie did not waste time gaining entry. She realized the problem with accessing this new and strange power was that her body could only manage so much. She remembered Urki's warning during one of her training sessions: *Do not allow all of it to pass through you at once, or else.* The rest he left to her imagination.

It dramatically heightened her senses as she drew the High Lord's power into her body. It was her second time going through a checkpoint, and she found it easier to confuse the Screener this time around. She entered the upper prison section without incident. Once inside, she searched for Yanamai's cell, which did not take long. Peering down a nearby corridor, she spotted the ten soldiers Nayrah mentioned. It was not farfetched to think that Yanamai was in the cell nearby.

Using Nayrah's example, Julie decided to distract them similarly. Since she could not morph into someone more voluptuous, her appearance would have to suffice. Julie approached the soldiers, wondering if her beauty was enough to entice them. It was the first time since her teens that she felt apprehensive about her looks. As she approached the first soldier in the passageway, he put out his hand.

"Stop! You cannot enter this area!"

Taking a cue from Nayrah's earlier distraction, Julie removed her hood, exposing her face. *I hope it didn't mess up my hair.* Smiling, she flirted with him without speaking, knowing her language would give her away; the soldier noticed she was female and spoke in a gentler tone.

"I am sorry. You must turn around."

Still wearing the earpiece, Julie understood him but did not reply. Instead, she continued to flirt with him with facial expressions until another soldier yelled and pointed.

"Hey! That is the alien Otsoa is trying to find!"

Oh crap! That distraction allowed the nearest soldier to grab her wrists with both hands and pin her against the wall until the others could help him. Even though the soldier's weight and strength had her outmatched, she had access to the High Lord's power, so again, she allowed the surrounding energy to flow through her body and, with little effort, spun out of his grip.

Using the power that flowed through her, she blasted him so hard he hit the other wall and collapsed. As the other soldiers moved to capture her, she ran to the other side of the corridor. Upon reaching the wall, she used her momentum to run upward. Nearing the top, she pushed off the ceiling. Her feet circled over her head, and she landed behind the three closest soldiers that pursued her. It was the perfect backflip.

Faster than the eye could see, she unsheathed her sword and took down the three combatants before they could turn around to search for her. *That's four down and only six to go.* She turned and saw one of the soldiers running to sound the alarm. Reaching out with her power, she lassoed his feet like a calf back home, which caused him to fall face forward, and instinctively, she pulled him toward her.

She yanked too hard because he flew fast in her direction. Ducking, she watched him soar overhead, careening into a soldier who had snuck up behind her. They landed hard on the concrete floor. The four remaining soldiers surrounded her. They each held a crossbow-like weapon, which they pointed at her. Her Saiph powers enabled her to sense where each soldier stood around her. One was in front; one was behind; the other two were to her left and right.

"If we shoot at the same time, one of us will hit her," one of the soldiers suggested.

She closed her eyes until feeling the nudge, and just as they pulled the trigger, she jumped high in the air, allowing the projectiles to pass underneath as each soldier shot his opposite. They fell to the ground with foam oozing out of their mouths, and she realized they had coated the tips with a drug, causing them to convulse briefly and stop moving. She used her powers to unlock the steel cell door, mimicking what Nayrah had done earlier. In the corner, she found Yanamai curled up, trembling.

"Don't be afraid. I'm here to help you," consoled Julie.

Julie brought her outside, where Yanamai saw ten soldiers lying unconscious.

"Did you do this yourself?" puzzled Yanamai.

"Come on, there's no time for explanations," Julie replied, grabbing her hand.

They reached the checkpoint and the Screener, seeing Yanamai, moved to sound the alarm. Instinctively, Julie used her power to stop her. Two guards noticed that the Screener became motionless outside the station with a wide-eyed frightened look. As Julie and Yanamai walked out, the guards recognized Yanamai and rushed to apprehend her. With a wave of her hand, Julie made them crash headfirst into each other, knocking them out. Turning back to the Screener, Julie put her to sleep and gently let her body fall to the ground. With no one else to stop them, Julie led Yanamai back to the elevator, where Nayrah waited for them.

"What took you so long?" Nayrah snapped.

Tired of her rude comments, Julie suppressed the urge to send a wall of energy in her direction.

"Hey, I did this on my own. Remember?"

"Come on. We must send her back to Earth, now! There is no more time," Nayrah urged.

Realizing their plan, Yanamai refused to move.

"I cannot leave. Otsoa has my parents. If I go, he will kill them."

"I have already sent them to Earth. Now come on, before it is too late!" Nayrah spat.

As they approached the courtyard in front of the Interstellar Transport Bay, Julie and Nayrah stopped simultaneously.

"What is wrong?" Yanamai inquired.

"It's too late. They're here," Julie explained.

"Yes, because you took too long, you idiot!" Nayrah hissed.

"Hey, drop the attitude, or you can do this alone," Julie snapped.

Nayrah ignored her comment, "We have no choice. We must move forward."

"Yeah, I figured you were going to say that," Julie remarked.

"Do either of you have an extra sword?" Yanamai queried.

"Do not worry. Once the fighting starts, there will be plenty of swords on the ground for you to pick up and use," Nayrah remarked.

"What do we do now?" Julie questioned.

"I will walk out first because Gecheana is expecting me. She will show herself to ensure I know it was her who stopped me, and the moment she sends her soldiers to attack, you cut a path to the Interstellar Transport Bay and get Yanamai to the vortex. I will try to keep the others busy. Gecheana can only control them for a few hundred heartbeats," Nayrah responded.

"How many are there?" Julie wondered.

"Twenty acolytes are linked to Gecheana's mind. Otsoa planned to send two hundred Argi soldiers here too until Jadell sent a message. He sent them to the Argi House not long ago because someone saw Zorion leading a rebellion."

"Is he alive?" Julie asked excitedly.

"Perhaps. It could be a dupe, someone pretending to be him to dethrone Otsoa. In any case, the distraction is a welcome one. The odds of us surviving have just increased. Just make sure to hide your powers until I need you."

Nayrah held the hilt of her sword and moved out into the courtyard. As expected, Gecheana moved out of the shadows with her band of twenty soldiers, all mentally linked to her mind with swords drawn; they were not glowing yet. Jadell stood beside her, glaring back, which Nayrah hoped was for Gecheana's benefit. Behind them, Otsoa stood more than several hand widths taller than the rest.

"Otsoa, the betrayer!" Nayrah spat.

Otsoa laughed, "I have looked forward to this Terrestrial Revolution for a long time, Nayrah."

"Once I finish these, I promise your punishment will be more severe than you can imagine. I do not think you will survive this one."

"Your rule over me has ended. You do not stand a chance with Gecheana and Jadell by my side."

As he finished speaking, the soldiers' swords began to glow, and they moved to encircle Nayrah. Before Gecheana attacked, Otsoa whispered a question in her ear. Even from her distance, Nayrah could hear Gecheana's response.

"Do not worry. Yanamai is here, somewhere. I can sense her cowering nearby. Now do your job, and do not bother me with stupid questions again!"

"Only twenty soldiers? I expected more from you," Nayrah chided sarcastically.

"These are enough to defeat the likes of you," Gecheana growled.

"If you surrender now, I promise to go easy on you," Nayrah smiled smugly.

"There will be no surrender this Terrestrial Rotation. Your life is at an end, Nayrah. It is time for your final lesson," Gecheana responded with an equal amount of smugness.

"Enough talk. I have things to do," Nayrah spoke dismissively.

Julie faced Yanamai and spoke through her headpiece, "Stay here until I call you."

Yanamai nodded, and Julie moved closer to Nayrah's position and stayed hidden with her powers cloaked. Julie watched tensions build and assessed the battlefield. Standing beside Gecheana was another Skean, whom she believed was Jadell; she was the one Nayrah told her about earlier.

It was still hard to tell them apart since they all had the same appearance. Already surrounded by Gecheana's soldiers, Nayrah stood in the center, mocking Gecheana. As the hairs on her neck stood, Julie knew it was only a matter of moments before the battle started. She saw Jadell unsheathe her sword; faster than the eye could see, she swung at Gecheana. The move caught Julie entirely off guard because most of her focus was on hiding her powers. However, Jadell's bold attack did not fool Gecheana, who blocked it before the blade contacted her neck. *Ok, here we go.*

"Do you think me a fool? I knew you would betray me," Gecheana spat.

At that moment, everyone began swinging their swords. Otsoa stood near the Interstellar Transport Bay entrance with his sword still sheathed, as Gecheana instructed him. Although it took more effort and slowed her down, Gecheana directed her soldiers to attack Nayrah and defended against Jadell's strikes. Even though twenty soldiers surrounded Nayrah, they could not charge her simultaneously, so they struck two and three at a time. Nayrah moved faster than the eye could see, blocking and striking each one as they moved to kill her.

Seeing how well the acolytes fought under Gecheana's control, Nayrah knew they had been practicing. The volunteers fought faster and better than soldiers, except with Jadell fighting Gecheana; they were no match for Nayrah's speed and prowess. Nayrah noticed that Gecheana would rotate her subordinates in and out of the fight to keep them from tiring during the fight. Every other attack came from a different fighter. Nayrah planned to wear her down and had a surprise waiting.

Julie lunged from her hiding place as if on cue, allowing everyone to feel the High Lord's power and see her glaring suit. The distraction caught Gecheana's attention, allowing Jadell to cut her midsection. Biting back the pain, Gecheana winced and kept fighting. The attack had disrupted her connection with her soldiers, and for a moment, they were defenseless, so Nayrah and Julie took advantage of the situation. Out of twenty soldiers, they took down six before Gecheana could refocus. Enraged at having lost so many at once, Gecheana used her anger to increase her power.

Nayrah and Julie continued to fight off Gecheana's rhythmic attacks while Julie planned a way to cut a path for Yanamai. Julie spun, punched, kicked, and instinctively drew more and more power from the light until turning once more to release a powerful blast of energy, dispersing most soldiers on her side of the circle. It created an open path to the Interstellar Transport Bay. Instinctively, Julie called for Yanamai telepathically. Hearing Julie's voice inside her mind, Yanamai gasped and obeyed her command, running to the Interstellar Transport Bay.

Seeing a sword lying on the ground, she bent down to pick it up along the way and headed straight for the exit. Before reaching it, she engaged a few soldiers who returned from Julie's push. Their speed and strength put her at a significant disadvantage. She would have lost her head a few times if Julie had not saved her. With Yanamai beside her, Julie used another power push to clear a path; Yanamai dashed to the doorway. Seeing her from his position, Otsoa reached the exit simultaneously. Grabbing her by the arm, he threw her down.

"Where do you think you are going?" he menacingly questioned.

Yanamai stood, holding her sword in front of her, ready to defend or attack. Julie sensed that Otsoa was about to strike at Yanamai. She leaped from the courtyard to the doorway using her power and blocked Otsoa's blade as he brought it down, landing between them.

"Step aside," Julie commanded.

Instead of moving, Otsoa snarled and raised his sword to strike. *Ok, so we do this the hard way.* As he brought his sword down, she blocked it; before he could raise it again, she attacked with several blindingly fast strikes. He stopped them all; she could tell it was not easy for him to keep up. *That's ok; I'm just warming up.*

Julie used the High Lord's power to enhance her attack; she spun and swung at him with extra force, knocking him backward. Now that he was out of the way, Julie faced Yanamai.

"Run!"

This time, the words came from her voice and through the headpiece interpreter; it sounded deep and strange. Yanamai obeyed by dropping her sword and sprinting toward the event horizon. Julie turned her attention to Otsoa, who stood. Julie ran toward him with her sword raised to end his life; before she could strike, Gecheana sent an invisible wall of energy that knocked her back into the courtyard, exposing the Interstellar Transport Bay doorway.

Yanamai had a head start but turned back to ensure no one had followed her. She frowned, seeing that Otsoa had just run through the doorway at full speed. In a panic, she fumbled, opening the emergency door to the vortex with Otsoa right behind her, and after unlocking the door, she ran toward the portal with a frightful scream; the vortex was only several paces away. Otsoa kicked her right ankle, tripping her, and she landed only a few finger widths from the event horizon.

"Yanamai!" she heard Michael yell from the other side.

Looking up, she called for him. Reaching out with her hand, she hoped he would pull her to the other side; as he ran to get her, Earthian soldiers restrained him.

"I'm sorry, Sir. You can't go onto Akilian soil!" she heard the soldier say just before an unyielding hand grabbed Yanamai by the hair.

Otsoa lifted her until she rested on her knees. Yanamai screamed in pain. On the other side of the event horizon, she saw Michael struggling to break free from the soldiers. She knew he was trying to help her, but the Earthian warriors outnumbered and overpowered him. Yanamai continued to reach for him with tears streaming down her cheeks.

Otsoa held onto Yanamai's hair with a firm grip and glared defiantly at the Earthian troops, who had their weapons pointed at him. If he stayed on Akilian soil, they would not attack. It left him free to do whatever he pleased with Yanamai. Before dragging her back to her prison cell, he noticed someone on the other side, screaming and struggling against Earthian soldiers. Otsoa studied him and wondered why he was fighting so frantically until realizing that Yanamai had found someone on the alien planet. He leaned down to whisper in her ear.

"You chose that scrawny alien instead of *me*?"

In that heartbeat, Otsoa finally understood that Yanamai would never love him. This revelation angered him. *If I cannot have you, no one will.* He snarled, ran his sword into her back, and pushed it through until the blade protruded from the center of her chest. As she gasped for air, Michael's eyes widened with fear.

"Shoot him!" Michael yelled.

Struggling even harder, Michael tried to wrestle the weapon away from the soldier. The man hit Michael on the forehead with the butt of his gun, stunning him. With blood dripping down his face, Michael could only watch as Otsoa yanked his sword out of Yanamai's back, causing her head to fall forward, exposing her neck. Using both hands, Otsoa raised his sword high in the air.

As tears streamed from his eyes, Michael screamed again, "Shoot him!"

To his horror, no one moved to help her. Instead, Michael watched Otsoa bring his sword down and through her neck with teary eyes and outstretched arms.

Julie finally stopped sliding on Akil in the courtyard; the push had sent her at least thirty yards in the opposite direction. She ran back to the door, realizing that Gecheana had been the one who attacked her. Knowing that Otsoa pursued Yanamai, Julie followed until several of Gecheana's fighters blocked her path before reaching the door. Meanwhile, Nayrah killed four more of Gecheana's warriors; her progress came with a price.

With fewer soldiers to control, Gecheana could put more of her energy into the remaining acolytes. It allowed them to fight faster and longer, even though she continued to engage Jadell. As Julie struggled to get past the fighters, she heard a cry from the Interstellar Transport Bay. Simultaneously, she sensed a drastic power shift. It was as if the universe had become darker. She continued to fight three of Gecheana's acolytes, who blocked her path and saw Otsoa appear from the Interstellar Transport Bay covered in blood. There was no doubt that it was Yanamai's.

"I have failed my mission. Yanamai is dead," Julie whispered to herself.

Knowing she may never get another chance at Gecheana, Julie pushed the soldiers aside and ran to join Jadell. Now that she was battling two, Gecheana could no longer put all her energy into her acolytes. Taking advantage of her weakness, Nayrah killed her soldiers and joined Jadell and Julie in their fight. From the Interstellar Transport Bay doorway, Otsoa watched with great interest.

Nayrah suspected that fighting Gecheana would be tricky, even with the three attacking her at once. Gecheana moved faster than expected, especially for her age. Gecheana's blade moved toward her neck. Nayrah ducked; Jadell did not. In an instant, Gecheana succeeded in removing her head. Now it was up to her and Julie. The fight continued for a few hundred heartbeats, and Nayrah noticed that Julie was tired. *Hold on*!

As the fight continued, Nayrah felt a familiar presence, *Zorion*! His appearance distracted Julie. Just when Nayrah thought she had her, Gecheana jumped over Julie's head, slicing her belly open along the way, nearly cutting her in two. Julie fell, and Gecheana faced Nayrah.

"Now, *Putok*, I will destroy you!" Gecheana venomously spat.

Just as she went to strike at her, Zorion's army rushed into the courtyard. Nayrah and Gecheana fought hard against Zorion's soldiers, who drastically outnumbered them. Zorion's army overwhelmed them, taking their heads. After they secured the area, Zorion entered the courtyard. His soldiers brought Otsoa before him. Without hesitating or saying a word, Zorion removed his head and spat on his corpse as it fell to the ground.

"Sir, this one is still alive," Broll stood over the Saiph.

Zorion rushed to examine the Saiph's wounds after recognizing the outfit.

"You will recover by the following Terrestrial Revolution."

Julie shook her head, "No. I won't."

Her headpiece distorted her voice, so Zorion did not know it was her. He hesitated until curiosity won him over, and he removed her headpiece and saw her face.

"Julie!" he exclaimed.

She struggled to breathe and chuckled, "Surprise."

"How?"

"Remember the black and white moss I mentioned earlier?"

"Oh, no."

A tear rolled down her cheek, "I'm sorry. I failed you. I failed all of you."

"Do not say that."

"Sir, you will want to see this," a soldier yelled, appearing from the Interstellar Transport Bay.

"Not now," Zorion grumbled.

"Sir, it is Yanamai."

"Is she hurt?"

"Someone killed her."

Turning his attention back to Julie, he looked at her with tears, "I will send you back to Earth. I am sure they can help you recover."

She shook her head, "It's too late. I can feel myself slipping away."

She struggled to raise her right hand, touched his cheek with her finger, gently stroked it, and whispered, "I thought you were dead."

"I am sorry. I did not want to deceive you; I had no choice."

“I understand. I only wish we had more time together.”

He swallowed hard, “Me too.”

Julie’s hand fell to her side, her body relaxed, and she exhaled for the last time. Zorion pulled her to his chest, hugged her tightly, and wept. He set her down, and her eyes were still open as if staring into the great abyss that took her from him. Gently, he closed her eyelids, stood, and faced Broll.

“I want her to have a hero’s burial and rest with the other Saiphs in the catacombs.”

“She deserves nothing less.”

He forced himself to his office, contacted Supreme Commander Porter, and filled him in on all the events. Lastly, he told him about Julie’s death.

Chapter 66

Earth
The Regime - Africa - Sahara Desert - Fort Levan
May 19, 2452

Michael glared at the blood, freckled face of Yanamai's killer. Trapped beneath the weight of two soldiers, who had him pinned to the ground, he could not move, let alone avenge her death; if possible, Michael would empty an entire clip into him. A few moments later, the killer looked at Michael, smiled, and exited the Interstellar Transport Bay, leaving Yanamai's lifeless body behind on Akilian soil.

Once the Akilian Sovereign disappeared from their sight, the officer ordered the soldiers to allow Michael to stand. Michael could not take his eyes off the gruesome sight because blood spatter covered the walls and floor where he slew her. Some landed on Earth's side of the event horizon. Now that she was dead, he wanted to give her a proper burial.

"Will someone help me carry her to the morgue?" he yelled with a shaky voice.

"I'm sorry, Sir; we cannot step onto Akilian soil, even to retrieve the dead."

Michael felt a flash of rage yet held his tongue. It was not the officer's fault; it was politics. Something he grew to hate over the years. The officer escorted Michael out of the Interstellar Transportation Station. Along the way, he kept looking back at Yanamai. The image of her reaching for him and struggling to get free would haunt him for the rest of his life. Michael returned to the lounge where General Saunders waited, and together, they approached Yanamai's parents. Even though they tried to comfort them, there was nothing they could do or say to relieve their pain.

"I'd like to extend my deepest sympathy for your loss. Please let me know if there's anything I can do," General Saunders solemnly offered.

He meant every word, yet they still seemed empty, even to him. Nodding absentmindedly, her parents could only sob as they mourned the loss of their daughter.

Michael got General Saunders' attention and took him aside, "They won't let me take her body. I can't even bury her."

"I don't like it either, but it's out of my hands. We could start a war if we put one foot on their planet. Countries are very territorial, not to mention planets."

Jared opened the door unexpectedly, and Michael looked at him quizzically, "What are you doing here?"

"I came as soon as I heard the news."

"Thanks for coming, Jared. It means a lot to me."

"What can I do?"

"If you could find a way to retrieve her body, I'd appreciate it."

"I'll do what I can."

"I need to find Garbi and tell her what happened," Michael walked toward the lab.

Not willing to leave his brother during such a dark time, Jared followed him. Michael took Garbi aside and explained everything that happened. As expected, she broke down and wept; Garbi surprised him with an embrace and held onto him tightly to the point that he found it hard to breathe. An hour later, Michael, Jared, and Garbi went to her apartment, where her parents joined them. Michael stayed until losing control over his emotions, so he left. On his way out, Jared stopped him.

"Let's go visit mom."

With everything that happened, Michael forgot to visit them today and decided not to go. Jared gently encouraged him to reconsider.

"I know you're hurting, but your family is here for you."

"I don't think I could deal with dad today."

"I'll ensure he's on his best behavior."

"Well…"

"Come on, Michael. You haven't seen mom in a year."

"I don't want to see her while I'm like this."

"I've already told her what happened. She wants to see you."

"This isn't going to be a fun visit."

"You're grieving. It's not supposed to be fun."

With a sigh, Michael conceded and returned with him. As they pulled up to the front of their childhood home in the rented hovercar,

Michael saw his mother waiting on the porch. Initially, Michael imagined this trip much differently. He thought it would be a joyful day with Yanamai by his side; instead, he hugged his mother, walked past his dad, ignoring him, went straight to his old bedroom, and shut the door behind him.

Lying on the bed, he stared at the ceiling where he had put homemade twinkling stars to help him fall asleep during his teenage years. The thought that one of the stars symbolized Yanamai's solar system caused tears to well up and stream down his face. Memories of their brief time together weighed heavily on his mind, and exhaustion made him drift off to sleep. Later, there was a knock on the door. Half asleep, he opened it and thought he was looking at a ghost.

"Yanamai?"

"No. It is me, Garbi."

"Why are you wearing the same dress she wore on our first date?"

"I am sorry. It is mine. I gave it to her to wear. I can leave and change if it bothers you."

"Why are you here? Shouldn't you be with your parents?"

"I was until I realized that you had lost someone too. For a moment, I forgot that you two were dating. I know you must be hurting."

"I appreciate your concern; I'll be fine. I just need some time."

Garbi's presence did not make it easier for him to mourn Yanamai, especially since she looked exactly like her.

"Yanamai cared for you, and I want you to know that I care for you too."

"I appreciate it."

"I hope that one day you will forgive me too."

"Let's not talk about that now."

"What would you like to talk about?"

"Nothing," he paused and continued, "Do you know who killed her?"

"It was Otsoa. My parents recognized him right away."

"I thought so. We spoke about him before she left."

"He was obsessed with her."

"You look just like her. Did he ever pursue you?"

"No. It was always her."

"If he wanted her so much, why did he kill her?"

"I can only guess that he finally realized she would never accept him."

"Or he figured out that we were dating."

"How? She would never reveal that to him. Besides, it would not stop his advances."

"She called out and looked at me; he knew something was between us."

"I think, at that moment, he decided that if he could not have her, he would destroy her instead," Garbi noted.

"I guess," he replied as more tears rolled down his cheek.

Seeing his pain, Garbi embraced him, and they cried until Jared knocked on the open door behind them, "You have another visitor. She's on the back patio."

"I'll be right back," Michael spoke to Garbi.

Stepping outside, he saw Wu Luli staring out into the forest, waiting for him. He stepped outside, and she turned to face him.

"What happened to you?" he asked.

"Oh, I found my employer with the Regime's help."

"Did you capture him?"

"I tried; he gave me no choice. He died in an explosion."

"I'm guessing by the bruises and scrapes; you were in the explosion too."

"Yeah, it was close."

"What about your colleagues? Are they still looking for you?"

"If I'm in the Regime, I should be safe. I have a new identity. Captain Yates is developing a plan to get the word out on the street of what happened."

"I'm glad to hear it. I'd hate to think of you looking over your shoulder for the rest of your life."

"It's too early to know, but it's a start."

"Why are you here?"

"I heard what happened to your friend. I just wanted to let you know that I'm here for you. That is if you can stand to be around me," she smiled slightly.

She desperately hoped he would give some sign of forgiveness.

"A lot has happened since we broke up; I'm not mad at you anymore."

"You don't know how happy that makes me. One of the reasons I wanted to speak to you is to let you know I'll be working right here in the Inner Circle. If you ever want to talk, ring me. I'll give you all my contact information once I get settled."

*****

Inside the house, Garbi watched Michael speaking to an unknown female. She found it unnerving, especially the way he looked at her. Feelings of jealousy flooded her mind. Although she had no claim on him, it was still hard to fight back her Akilian urge to attack. Jared stood beside her and noticed she balled up her fists, and her expression screamed that something was about to happen.

"Is everything all right?" he inquired, hoping to distract her.

"I have been better," she mumbled through gritted teeth.

Just as he was about to say something, her expression changed to that of confusion, "What is that red dot on Michael's shoulder?"

Jared saw the red laser dot; his eyes widened, and he sprinted toward Michael. Jared pushed through the screen door, ripping it to shreds, and stretched his arms, hoping to catch Michael and Wu Luli, who instinctively moved aside, not knowing Jared was trying to help her. Jared and Michael landed on the patio floor and heard the whisper of a projectile going overhead. Jared looked up and saw a dart firmly planted in Wu Luli's shoulder. Moments later, she fell, unconscious.

"What the hell happened?" puzzled Michael.

"Someone was trying to shoot her, except you were in the way, so I tried to take the two of you down; she moved."

"We were talking about her colleagues still chasing her. You think someone got through Regime security?"

"It's hard to say. Take her inside, remove the dart, and stay down. I'll see if I can find the shooter."

Michael dragged Wu Luli inside, and Jared released the subcutaneous chemical into his body, raised his head, and scanned the area. In the distance, he heard the release of compressed air; a dart hit him on the forehead and bounced off. Now that he had a general location of the shooter, Jared ran off to find him. Michael removed

269

the dart from Wu Luli. Garbi arrived and helped him move her to the couch in the living room.

"Oh my, what happened?" his mother queried.

"Someone shot her with a tranquilizing dart! Call for help!" Michael yelled.

Just as the words left his mouth, someone kicked in the front door. Several men entered the house with weapons aimed at each person sitting in the living room. Once the place was secure, Michael saw Mai Li walk inside.

"Mai? What the hell is going on?" puzzled Michael.

Mai pointed to Michael and Garbi, "You two, outside."

With their hands raised, they left as ordered. Mai waited until they were alone.

"We can do this the hard way or the easy way. It's up to you."

"What do you want?" Michael questioned.

"If you come peaceably, no one gets hurt."

"What about Garbi?"

"I just want you."

"Fine, let's go."

Mai Li made a call, and a vortex opened nearby. She motioned with her gun to ensure Michael walked through the event horizon without resisting; before stepping through, Mai faced Garbi and handed her a phone.

"Don't tell anyone you have it. When it rings, answer it. Do what I've told you, and you'll see Michael again."

Slipping the phone into her purse, Garbi nodded her understanding, so Mai called her team, and they returned through the portal. A minute later, Jared appeared from the woods.

"I couldn't find the shooter."

"He was a decoy to keep you busy. Mai Li knocked down the front door and pointed weapons at everyone. She forced Michael and me outside and took Michael with her."

"I'll call for a portal team. Maybe we can track them."

"It is not necessary. She gave me a communicator. I think she wants me to do something for them in exchange for Michael."

"Good, I'll assemble a team; if we can't track them, maybe we can find another way to catch them."

Chapter 67

Mai Li's assistant exited the vortex with Michael restrained by his side and waited until Mai Li landed. She arrived, the portal closed, and another opened, which Michael presumed was his destination. He landed in a make-shift Transportation Station with similar Regime equipment. Upon his arrival, a butler met him and escorted him to an extensive, old library.

The butler cut off his restraints and asked if he wanted any refreshments. Michael refused and demanded to know why Mai Li kidnapped him. The butler politely smiled and left him alone, locking the door behind him. Moving to one of the windows, Michael looked out. Below, he saw a cliff that led to an ocean. Without any recognizable landmarks, he had no idea of his location. Several minutes later, someone opened the door and stepped inside. She approached with a warm smile; it did little to ease his concerns.

Standing before him, she extended her hand, "Welcome, Michael; my name is Dawn. I'm your sister."

"I don't have a sister," he replied, taking a step back.

"I thought you might have been too young to remember me; we *are* family. You used to call me Darn," she chuckled softly. "You were adorable."

"My parents never mentioned you to me."

"Our mother sent me away after the Regime arrested dad."

"That's not true. I just saw him moments before you abducted me."

"First, please accept my most sincere apology for the way I had to bring you here. I'm running out of time, and I've been trying to contact you for months. Second, the man you think is your dad isn't. He's Jared's. The Regime arrested Jack a year before our mother sent me away. He's on the moon now, serving a life sentence."

"Why didn't you just send me an email?"

"You think I haven't tried? The Regime blocked every attempt I've made to contact you."

"Why?"

"Because our mother is ashamed of our dad. Following his arrest, I wouldn't stop asking for him, so she sent me to London."

"Is that where we are?"

"No. We're in Scotland. This castle is my home."

"You've done well for yourself."

"Everything I've done has been to reunite my family."

"Why didn't you have our mother brought over with me?"

"She abandoned me; I don't consider us related anymore."

"Why was Jack arrested?"

"Do you want a drink? I need a drink."

"No, thanks."

She walked to a table with several half-full liquor bottles and poured some into a glass.

"You were almost two years old, and I just turned nine. We were in the shopping mall when they took him," she paused to take a sip. "As they arrested him, my former mother didn't act surprised or plea for them to release him. I know now she had a part to play in his capture. I remember crying and trying to fight off the police until she held my arms. I'll never forget how helpless I felt. Later, I discovered that he was on the brink of discovering the ultimate power."

"Ultimate power? You make him sound like a mad scientist."

"He isn't mad; he's brilliant. For example, during an expedition, he discovered scrolls that spoke of plants linked to great power."

"Scrolls? It sounds like you're talking about Jack Mason."

"I am; *he's* our dad."

"No. It can't be. I'm Michael Stewart. The Regime convicted Jack Mason of treason and sentenced him to life on the moon. Every news article reported that he was insane."

"You *are* a Mason, Michael, not a Stewart. Even though I was only nine, I remember Jack always being good to us. I don't care what those reporters said, he was a good man. I plan to get him off the moon and back here."

"You can't be serious? He's a level-one criminal."

"He isn't dangerous, Michael. The Regime forbade him to continue his research, even though he tried to explain the benefits.

The scrolls stated that we could live longer, healthier lives and have supernatural abilities."

"What is this plant you keep referring to?"

"It's a particular species of moss. Although I've never seen it, I'm convinced it exists."

"Black moss?"

"According to the ancient text, it's a mixture of black and white moss; time damaged some of the scrolls, so we know little about the moss, except that you must ingest it to gain extraordinary abilities. I obtained some of Jack's digital notes on the project. Based on my botanist's review, Jack discovered that the moss was poisonous and tried to breed a version we could safely ingest. The Regime arrested him before he succeeded and thought they destroyed all his work but missed his backups. Here, I have all his research on this data stick; you can see for yourself," she handed it to him.

"That means the black and white moss are poisonous," he frowned, taking the stick from her.

Remembering the moss in his lab and how someone destroyed it with an herbicide made him think twice before doubting her claim. The tests he ran on the black moss, which multiplied overnight, confirmed it *was* poisonous. Since the scrolls indicated that the two grew together, he thought it odd that only the black moss sprouted in his lab. There could only be two reasons this happened. The conditions were unsuitable for the white moss to grow, or none of their spores made the transfer.

"You've found some. Haven't you?" she inquired and finished her drink.

"It's classified."

"Who am I going to tell? Besides, it's obvious you haven't told Porter about it, or he would have arrested you for growing it."

"Fine, the Regime arrested someone who had moss in his bag. The police sent it to my lab for analysis; the black moss didn't grow until later."

"If they arrested him for carrying moss, you should believe that Porter will not tolerate it if you are experimenting with it, so you better be careful, or he'll arrest you too."

"I believe they arrested him for trespassing, not growing or carrying it. In any event, I'll be careful."

"Tell me, what did you find?"

"Not much. Someone destroyed most of it before I had a chance to analyze it thoroughly."

"Porter did the same thing to Jack's experiments."

"I can't believe Supreme Commander Porter would do that."

"Wake up, Michael! You've worked for the Regime your whole life. I know Porter visits you from time to time. He must have seen the moss in your lab, or someone told him about it. What about Lisa, your assistant?"

"No. I trust her, but you're right. He did see it during a visit."

"He's been watching you this whole time."

"I have to admit; he *has* been a hands-on Supreme Commander."

Dawn laughed, "Supreme Commanders don't visit lab technicians, even with your brilliant discoveries. They deal with their chief of staff and dignitaries. He's keeping a close watch on you to ensure you don't follow in Jack's footsteps. Think about it, Michael. You know what I'm telling you is the truth."

"How do I know anything you're telling me is the truth? You say you're my sister without proof."

"Here," she handed him a strand of her hair, "test it against your DNA once you return home; it will prove I'm telling the truth."

Looking at his life through her eyes, answers to questions he often wondered about became apparent. For example, why his dad was so distant from him, why Jared was more athletic than him, and the strange destruction of the moss in his lab.

"Why do you need me to break him out of prison?"

"I don't need you for that. I only wanted to meet and talk to you and let you know that you have a family who loves you. My only hope and desire are for us to be together again without mom."

"Are you saying that I can leave at any time?"

"Yes, but Jack will be here soon. I want you to meet him before you go. Talk to him yourself. You can go home if you don't want to come with us. We'll find some way to stay connected."

"Where will you go?"

"I can't tell you because if Porter scans your mind, he'll find us, but if you decide to come with us, I'll reveal our destination following our landing. In the meantime, would you join me for dinner?"

"I'm not hungry."

"Please, I only have a little time left. At least allow me the memory of one meal with my brother."

"Sure," he answered absentmindedly.

"Good, Alfred will help you get ready. I need to take care of some business first. I'll join you in a few minutes."

She summoned her butler and left Michael in Alfred's care.

Chapter 68

Earth
Scotland - Dunnottar Castle
May 19, 2452

Dawn stood in front of her communications screen in a private room, selected the contact number, and Garbi's image appeared.

"Who are you?" Garbi demanded.

"Who I am is none of your concern. If you wish to see Michael again, follow my instructions to the letter."

"What do you want me to do?" Garbi questioned.

"Within the communicator, my associate left you; there's a Supreme Command Summons for Jack Mason. You will pose as a guard, go to the Moon Penal Facility, and bring him to the location shown in the communicator. Upon your return, use the signal app I installed on your communicator, and I'll pick you up, but remember this, if you don't have Jack Mason within two hours, you'll never see Michael again."

Without another word, Dawn disconnected, knowing everything rested on whether Garbi could fulfill her tall order. Her alien DNA allowed her to take on any image, including a correctional officer, assuming her source was correct. She, Jack, and Michael would be together again in two hours. Dawn allowed herself a smile because she would finally reunite with her family after ten years of arduous work.

Chapter 69

Earth
The Regime - Texas - Houston - George Bush Park
May 19, 2452

Larkin loaded his Jeep with food, guns, and ammunition and double-checked his sidearm to ensure he had loaded it. A few minutes later, Larkin saw his pilot approaching and extended his hand to greet him.

"The name's Aiden."

"Larkin. Thanks for comin'."

"Sorry, I'm late. Before leaving, I researched private jets to prepare myself."

"Do you think you can fly one?"

"If I can figure out how to get the engines started, I can keep her level. My only question is: where do you plan on landing her?"

"General Bailey gave me the coordinates before I left. Here, you can study them on the way," he answered, handing him the device.

They jumped into the Jeep; Larkin started the engine and headed for Houston. Along the way, Larkin made a detour to visit his brother at the warehouse, handed Aiden an automatic weapon, and told him to watch the Jeep.

Aiden gulped, taking the gun, "Don't take long. I'm a civilian, not a soldier."

Sensing his brother inside the warehouse, Larkin approached the door. Before opening it, Larkin removed his sidearm and stepped inside. Tucker paced in the Pit with his back facing him, kicking sand around with his hands buried deep in his pants pockets. A quick scan of the building confirmed that he was alone; Larkin put his gun back in its holster and stepped into the Pit. Tucker turned to face him, and Larkin punched him with a right hook.

Tucker could sense it coming yet did not try to dodge the attack. Larkin's fist landed, sending him back several steps. Tucker spat blood and wiped his mouth with his shirtsleeve; guilt prevented him from fighting back.

"I want you to know I'm sorry for what happened to your woman and child," Tucker apologized.

"You take sorry and shove it up your ass! You tried to kill 'em!"

"I told Bailey that weren't true. I'd never hurt your family. Hell, I'd never even fight you in the Pit. What I did to you was just funnin' is all. I was gettin' you back for leavin'," Tucker explained.

Using his reflexes, faster than the human eye could see, Larkin had his sidearm in his hand and pressed it against Tucker's forehead with his finger on the trigger before he could blink.

"I almost didn't make it in time to save 'em!" Larkin yelled.

"Rico lied to me. I brought his head to General Bailey as proof that I didn't plan that attack. I only told him to say those things to scare you, is all. I didn't know he'd do it."

"That's what you get for dealin' with lowlifes like yourself," Larkin responded, pressing the barrel harder against his forehead.

"Fine, if you believe I'd knowingly do anything to hurt your family, pull the trigger, brother. I ain't never been afraid of dying," Tucker challenged.

Larkin wanted to put a hole in Tucker's head, just on principle but did not sense that he meant him any serious harm, so instead of pulling the trigger, Larkin struck him with the butt of his gun, knocking Tucker down on his ass. As Larkin turned to leave, Tucker jumped to his feet.

"Take me with you! I want to help find the bitch that killed your family."

Larkin turned to face him and saw blood dripping down Tucker's forehead from where he hit him.

"I don't need your damn help," he snarled.

"You don't know what she's capable of doing. Hell, I don't even know what she's capable of doing, but you'll stand a better chance of finding her with my help; I figure it's the least I can do. Besides, you're my brother, and brothers stick together, even us."

Larkin hated it when Tucker was right. There was not much to go on except the two names the General gave him: Ethan Brun and Dawn Pierce. Even their location was not specific: someplace in Scotland he had never heard of before, Edinburgh. With Tucker's help, he could cover more ground, assuming he could trust him.

"If you step out of line, even once, I'll kill you on the spot," he threatened.

Tucker wiped the blood out of his eyes, "Don't worry about me. I want this bitch just as much as you do."

Chapter 70

Earth
Regime - Texas - Houston
May 19, 2452

Having parked near the airport, Larkin stood outside the Jeep. Before making his move to steal a jet, he waited for the sun to set. In the backseat, Aiden fell asleep following their arrival. Knowing that a tired pilot could get them killed, Larkin insisted he rest, especially since they would be flying for about ten hours. They would be in Scotland by tomorrow, assuming nobody shot them down before they left Texas.

"What are our chances?" Tucker wondered.

"Slim. General Bailey said the new U. S. president isn't giving Texas up without a fight. The intel showed that U.S. jets are patrolling Texas' airspace, looking for a fight; for now, the Regime is standing down, trying to avoid further confrontation."

"That leaves us vulnerable. I guess we're not important enough for air support?"

"Nope, we never are."

They watched the airport, saw several private jets land, and noted that the vehicles towed them into a nearby hangar. At sundown, Larkin woke Aiden; they jumped the metal fence and snuck into the garage. Once inside, they spotted a captain getting ready to board a small jet. Hoping the pilot had already fueled it, Larkin signaled Tucker to go left as he moved right.

Before the captain could get inside the plane, Larkin pressed his gun firmly against his back and forced him inside. Outside the plane, Tucker knocked out a mechanic who was nearby. Once the area was clear, Tucker waved Aiden inside and followed. Inside, Aiden walked to the cockpit and found the captain sitting with Larkin beside him.

"It looks like you didn't need me after all," Aiden remarked.

"Not true. I don't trust 'em to get us where we're going but havin' 'em with us is a bonus. At least he'll make sure you press all the right buttons," Larkin commented before facing the captain, "Do we have enough fuel to make it to Scotland?"

"Yes, more than enough; I was on my way to Hawaii."

"Sorry for the detour; this is important," Larkin commented and faced Aiden, "Here, you take my seat."

Aiden sat, and the captain started the engines. Larkin confirmed Tucker was on board, closed the door, and ensured everyone had buckled up.

"We're ready," Larkin yelled to Aiden,

The captain obtained permission to take off, and the plane started moving toward the runway. They were in the air a few minutes later, so Larkin walked to the cockpit.

"Is everything all right up here?"

Aiden nodded, "Yep, we're heading straight for Regime territory."

Satisfied that there were no problems, Larkin returned to his seat and saw Tucker with a drink in his hand.

"Don't get too drunk. You never know what's going to happen," Larkin warned.

For a time, everything was quiet until about forty minutes into their journey.

"Larkin! Get up here now!" Aiden yelled.

Larkin jumped out of his seat, ran to the cockpit, and demanded, "What's wrong?"

"There are two US F-16E fighter jets behind us, ordering me to land. They say that if we don't, they're going to shoot us down," the captain warned and pushed forward on the flight control yoke.

As the plane descended, Larkin closed his eyes, hoping for an idea to safely get them out of this situation, and saw an image of flying geese. He instinctively reached over Aiden and took control of the plane, not knowing how his hands knew to steer the jet in the right direction; they just did.

His arm pushed the flight yoke forward, causing the plane to descend rapidly. Above them, Larkin sensed the fighter pilots carefully following them. Fearing for his life, the captain struggled against Larkin's hold on the yoke, unable to overpower him. Over the radio, Larkin could hear the pilots of the fighter jets warning that they would fire if the pilot did not level out their flight; Larkin ignored them.

When they reached 20,000 feet, Larkin pulled back on the flight yoke, and the plane leveled out. Moments later, a gaggle of geese flew overhead, and as the pursuing fighter jets descended, they dove into their midst. The thrust of their engines sucked some geese into the cold section of the chamber, and their bodies locked the turbine, causing it to stall.

Larkin turned the jet just enough to see the pursuing aircraft plunging to the ground with their engines on fire. He saw the pilots eject, open their parachutes, and float safely to the ground. The two planes exploded in a great fire on impact. Satisfied they were safe, Larkin released the flight yoke and turned control of the jet back over to the captain.

"Get us back on course."

Astonished, the captain nodded.

"How did you know them geese were out there?" Aiden asked.

Larkin shook his head, "I don't know how; I just *knew* they were."

"It's a good thing, or we'd be in the hands of the U.S. right now."

"How far to Regime territory?" Larkin queried.

"Just a few more minutes, and we'll be safe," Aiden reassured.

Chapter 71

Earth
Great Britain - Wimbledon Common
May 19, 2452

Dawn stepped through the event horizon and sat on a bench behind a small Wimbledon home. Back at the castle, Michael waited for her in the library. Like most of her properties, she bought or rented them under an assumed name; the Wimbledon residence was no different. Dawn waited for Garbi to call. Although the area was lush with green plants of every kind and displayed many of her favorite flowers, she barely noticed because the thought of seeing Jack again occupied her mind.

Her communicator beeped, showing that Garbi was ready for transport, so Dawn sent the coordinates to her technician at the castle, stood, and waited for their arrival. A vortex opened within moments, and Garbi pushed a man sitting in a wheelchair through the event horizon. Dawn could not see his face since his head bent forward as Garbi pushed him toward her. After the portal closed, Dawn moved to his side to unfasten his restraints.

"Jack, can you walk?"

When he was free, the man sprung out of his seat, grabbing Dawn by the forearms. Using a sweeping move, he put her hands behind her back and fastened restraints around her wrists. Dawn struggled but could not break free. As he spun her around to question her, she immediately recognized him.

"Jared," she noted indifferently.

"Where's Michael?"

"He's safe. Let me go, and I'll tell you where he is."

"Not going to happen," he replied, rifling through her purse, where he found a mobile device with all the information.

He signaled the Regime, a portal opened, and he escorted Dawn to an interrogation room in Fort McNair.

"Sit tight. We will use your communicator to find Michael, and I'll return to deal with you."

Chapter 72

Earth
Scotland - Dunnottar Castle
May 19, 2452

Michael stared out the window as his thoughts drifted back to Yanamai. He missed her and was having a tough time coping with the loss. While contemplating how to deal with his grief, someone kicked in the doors down the hallway. As footsteps approached, it was only a matter of time until his door flew open. On the other side, Jared stood, relieved to find him alive.

"Phew, you had me worried."

"Sorry, it wasn't my choice."

"Are you hurt?"

"Not at all."

"Good, now let's get you back home."

"How did you find me?"

"Your captor, Dawn, tried to blackmail Garbi into breaking a prisoner free. Garbi told me what happened, so I set a trap for her. Now she's back in Fort McNair, where technicians are prepping her for an MR."

"Thanks, Jared."

"Hey, you're my brother. I wasn't going to let a psychopath take you away from us."

Staring at the strand of hair, Michael wondered if Dawn was crazy or just desperate to find her family again. Finally, he faced Jared, "I'd like to go home now. I had enough excitement for one day."

Chapter 73

Earth
The Regime - Washington, D.C. - Mercy Hospital
May 19, 2452

Wu Luli woke from a drug-induced sleep and found herself in a hospital. She performed a quick body assessment; her shoulder hurt, and she had a slight headache. Thinking back, the last thing she remembered was talking to Michael on his back porch. Reaching over, she pressed the button, summoning a nurse. A few minutes later, someone came to see her.

"Welcome back."

"What happened?"

"Someone hit you with a tranquilizer dart, having a strong dose. Don't worry; your baby is all right."

"Baby?"

"Yes. We do a pregnancy test on all young women, just in case. That way, we don't give you something that might hurt the fetus."

"I can't be pregnant. I haven't been with anyone since…."

"Think hard, sweetie. It'll come to you. The tranquilizer will make remembering a little difficult for a while."

"Oh no, Michael."

"There you go. See, I told you. Now, let me get your vitals."

Wu Luli was happy to be pregnant with Michael's child but was uncertain of his reaction to such news. The unknown made her fearful, causing tears to run down her cheeks. *Will he come back to me? Of course, he will. Once he finds out I'm carrying his child, he'll do the right thing. Eventually, he'll forgive me for what I've done.* Even though she was lying down, her head started spinning at the possibility of having Michael back in her life. When her doctor released her, she planned to rush over and tell him. The thought of being in his arms again made her smile.

Chapter 74

Earth
The Regime - Washington, D.C. - Fort McNair
May 20, 2452

Michael tossed and turned violently in his bed, unable to stop dreaming of Yanamai's death. In his nightmare, he struggled to reach her. Just before Otsoa struck her neck, Yanamai looked at him, "You broke your promise." Startled out of his sleep by a loud clap of thunder, he gasped, covered in sweat. As the rain pounded against the windowpanes, he stared blankly at the wall as yesterday's tragedy continued to replay in his mind.

Yanamai's death repeatedly played in his mind until his thoughts drifted toward Dawn. Upon his return, he went to his lab and compared her DNA to his. She is his sister, which means that his mother lied to him. At least, it explained why the man, whom he thought was his dad, kept him at a distance. He found even more curious information on the data stick she gave him.

Along with Jack's old news stories and photos, Michael found the scrolls that fueled his research; everything was as Dawn told him. Still, it was not enough to keep his thoughts from drifting to Yanamai. Later, he found a teary-eyed Alex waiting for him at his apartment door because news that someone had murdered Julie came late last night.

Michael fell to his knees, wept, and only slept because of the sedative. Michael had offered to help; Alex insisted on preparing her memorial, leaving him to grieve her loss alone. All his life, Michael fixed things; sadly, death was way beyond his ability, and the helpless feeling frustrated him. The rain finally stopped, and the silence caught his attention, bringing him out of his brooding.

Sluggishly, he got out of bed. With a zombie-like walk, he went to his living room. Turning on the news, he hoped it would distract him, if only for a brief time. He sat on the couch and rested his feet on the coffee table beside a tray of black moss. Last night, he smuggled some home from the lab with the intent of examining them later. He surfed through the channels, unable to find anything to divert his attention.

The raw images of Yanamai's lifeless body, lying on the platform in the Akilian Interstellar Transport Bay, dominated his thoughts. He also imagined Julie lying in a pool of blood on the alien planet. For a long time, he sat, staring blankly at the television until his stomach growled, bringing him out of another stupor, and he resumed surfing the channels.

His stomach growled a second time, so he stopped at a news station. Moments before getting something to eat, he smelled freshly cooked pastries. Knowing there were none in his home, he searched for the source. It did not take long to discover that the black moss on the table had somehow imitated the scent of one of his favorite foods. *How and why?* As a botanist, he theorized that it was an act of propagation.

Somehow, the plant can mimic scents to attract nearby animals. The beasts eat the moss and spread its spores when it defecates. He thought about other possibilities and absentmindedly moved closer to the moss. As he came near, the more enticing it became. He knew the moss was poisonous, yet he grabbed some from the tray and put it in his mouth. Its taste was as sweet as the pastry it pretended to imitate.

It was good enough that he ate more until there was nothing left. After swallowing the last bite, he noticed a reporter interviewing a retired portal technician. They discussed a rumored accident in a local Regime prison a few days before. His attention focused solely on the TV show, causing him to forget the tray of black moss he had just consumed.

"Some people have nothing better to do than to watch daily portal activity," Michael whispered to himself.

"My scanners indicate that a time loop occurred," the retired technician explained, pointing to a table showing a spike in portal activity. "This jump is off the charts. We don't even use that much energy in our attempts to reach Mars."

"There are rumors that someone discharged a disrupter near an open vortex. If that is true, how could it spike so high with such little power?" the reporter queried.

"I've held to the quantum foam hypothesis for many years. I believe that microscopic wormholes appear and disappear spontaneously at the Planck scale. If one of these tiny wormholes opened near a vortex while someone released a certain amount of energy, say a disrupter, I believe it could create a stabilized, traversable portal to the past. Even though the portal would initially be tiny, it could absorb enough negative power lingering in the atmosphere to expand once it opened and grow large enough for a human to step through, thus, connecting the present to the past."

Those were the last words Michael heard before collapsing to the floor. As his body shook from the toxin in his veins, foam oozed from his mouth until he blacked out. Michael lay dead to the world, allowing his subconscious to drift to unimagined places. A point he somehow knew was between worlds. In this region, he woke, staring into a large mirror; darkness dominated the eerie haven, making it dim and difficult to see.

In the mirror, he could make out his reflection and felt shivers run down his spine as his eyes turned black to the rim of their sockets and his reflection unexpectedly morphed into someone else who wore a hooded cloak. Michael could not see his face, only darkness.

"Do you know who I am?" he inquired.

"I have no idea," Michael replied.

"Some know me as the Angel of Darkness, and others call me the Prince of Darkness. I prefer Night Lord. I rule the Shadow Universe."

"What do you want?"

"I need your help, Michael. Through you, I will reclaim what is rightfully mine."

"Which is?"

"This universe; I will start with this galaxy."

"How can I possibly help you?"

"Swear allegiance to me, and I will give you access to all my power. With it, you will conquer this region."

The thought horrified him, and he backed away from the mirror.

"I understand your hesitation. What if I could give you something you desperately want?"

"The only thing I want is dead."

"Ah, you speak of Yanamai."

"How do you know her?"

"I make it a point to know everything, and I can help you bring her back only if you pledge yourself to me."

"No. I will never join you."

"Take some time to think it over. We will meet again soon."

Michael woke, lying on the floor of his apartment, coughing violently. Once the choking stopped, he looked at the time and discovered it had only been a few minutes, even though it felt like hours. Michael lay still until regaining his composure, stood, and went to the bathroom to clean up; standing in front of the sink, he stared into the mirror, remembering the vision. The retired technician on the television had said something that gave Michael an idea to save Yanamai and Julie; he could not do it without Alex's help.

*****

"I'm sorry, Michael. I want Julie back just as much as you want Yanamai, but time travel isn't possible."

"There must be a way, Alex. I know there is. It's already happened. It was on the news. They interviewed some guy…."

"I know what you saw. I did too. He's retired, and everyone in the science community has discredited his theories."

"I can't believe you would give up on them so easily."

"Hey man, that isn't fair! Just because I won't entertain your time travel theory doesn't mean I don't want them back!"

"I'm asking you as a friend! Please, help me!"

"Even if possible, messing with the timeline doesn't seem like a good idea. We would never know what we changed or if we made things better or worse; I'm sorry, as your friend, I won't do it, and I strongly suggest you don't pursue it any further."

"You're right. I'm sorry, Alex."

"You don't have to be sorry. You're grieving, only you always try to fix things, except you can't fix this, Michael," Alex hugged and patted him on the back.

Michael let go, "You're right. I do try to fix things; I can't help myself."

"Before you go, here's the time for Julie's memorial service. The Argi's Sovereign contacted me and asked if he could bury her on Akil. I said no until he told me about what she did there and how they

288

would remember her. After that, I changed my mind and would like you to be there."

"Sure, I wouldn't miss it, except I thought Otsoa was Argi's Sovereign."

"Not anymore. I've learned that Zorion faked his death and retook the city. You should contact him about Yanamai. I'm sure he would let you see her one last time."

"I will. Thanks for telling me," Michael answered.

On his way home, Michael thought: *I can't let this go. I know there must be a way to open a portal to the past.* Just as he was about to turn a corner, a prickly sensation flowed down his neck. He stopped as another person, who was in a hurry, came rushing around the corner. He was moving so fast that they would have collided if Michael continued.

Distracted by his dream, he had not noticed the subtle change in his perception of things around him. Everything had depth and detail that went beyond the five senses. It was as if he had a sixth sense that allowed him to see further than his body's natural ability; it excited him. Still, he did not let it distract him from his mission to save Yanamai. He sat in front of his computer and searched the Regime's database for anything related to time travel.

A few hours later, he still had not found anything to help him and was about to give up until he remembered that his access level gave him the authority to browse the Akilian database, so he searched through tiers of portal technology data that the Akilians translated into English; most were beyond his comprehension. He continued to open folders until finding pages of diagrams labeled accessories to the portal machine.

The attachments in the diagrams looked like they did something special. Michael hoped they related to time travel. To ensure they did, he studied them carefully, thinking of Garbi. *Yes, she would know what this is.* A few minutes later, he knocked on her door. She opened it, and he absentmindedly stepped inside.

"I think there's a way we can save Yanamai."

She closed the door behind her, "How? She is dead."

"I know this might sound crazy," he stopped talking, seeing the same diagrams displayed on her monitor.

"What, Michael?"

"You have the same idea," he turned to face her.

Realizing he understood the schematics on her screen, she moved to shut it down; he blocked her path.

"You know how to build a portal machine that will open a vortex to the past."

"That is silly," she tried to hide the truth from him.

"Stop lying to me, Garbi!" he yelled.

"Fine, earlier today, I saw one of your scientists interviewed. He said that someone accidentally opened a portal to the past."

"I saw it too. That's where I got the idea. I'm guessing by the diagrams you have on the monitor that you already know how to build a machine that can do the same."

"I must do this alone."

"Why?"

"Because, Michael, it is a one-way trip."

"You can't build a machine to bring you back?"

"I could, but there is no time. The power needed to open a portal to the past is enormous. The Regime only has enough energy to send me back just a few minutes before Otsoa killed Yanamai, assuming I can get all the needed parts. Even if I am successful, I still do not know how I will stop him."

"You'll have to be on Akilian soil because we can't attack him from Earth."

"Based on the reports I have downloaded from our Information League on Akil, there was an all-out battle going on in the courtyard when Otsoa killed her, so I do not even know if I can get to her in time."

"I'm going with you."

"No. I will not let you do this."

"You will, or I'll tell General Saunders what you plan to do."

"What will happen if we go back and save Yanamai and Julie? Do you expect to live happily ever after with Yanamai?"

"Well, yeah, isn't that the point?"

"Wrong. Once we go back, we cannot return. There will be two of you when we arrive in the past. There will be the Michael from the original timeline on Earth and you, who traveled back in time on Akil. What happens if you succeed and save her life? Do you plan to take her from yourself in the original timeline? If you do, the other

Michael will try to figure out a way to return in time to take her away from you. It will never end unless you kill him, you. That is why I must go alone. At least I could live on the lower levels of Akil and survive in secret."

"If we go, you'll have a better chance of success," Michael insisted.

"I cannot condemn you to that life. We will not have our identities because our original selves will have them. We cannot work, so we must live on handouts."

"The choice is mine to make. Tell me what it will take for you to let me go with you?"

For an uncomfortable time, Garbi was silent, "I agree that there is a better chance of success if we go. Still, we will end up as outsiders. Since we will be together for the rest of our lives, I will not allow you to go with me unless you take me to be; oh, how do you Earthians put it, ah yes, your wife."

"Whoa, I wasn't expecting that."

"Why not? I found you attractive first, not Yanamai."

"You pushed me aside for some other guy."

"I was indecisive because we just met. All I needed was a little time. Yanamai agreed to pretend to be me until I could decide whom I should choose. Once I made my decision, I chose you, but she stole you by forcing me to abide by an Akilian Oath I made beforehand."

"Are you telling me that if Yanamai didn't like me, you would have dropped the other guy?"

"Yes. That is what I am saying. You and I should be together; Yanamai interfered with my pursuit."

"I don't know, Garbi. It's too bizarre."

"You leave me no choice, I will go by myself, and if you tell General Saunders, I will tell him that you are the one who plans to build the machine."

"You wouldn't."

She pretended to speak with General Saunders on the communicator, "Yes, General. He came to my home begging for help and threatened to do it alone if I refused. Michael's accusation that I plan to build the machine is a distraction because he wants you to focus on me while he charges the capacitors and sends himself back in time."

Michael thought of his options and realized that Garbi left him with only two choices. The first was to back down and let her go independently, which he could not allow. The second was to go with her as husband and wife. Since he agreed with her summation of what would happen after stepping through the time portal, he accepted her offer.

"All right, I agree to your terms. I'll call General Saunders tomorrow and have him set a day to…," Michael started to say.

Before he could finish, Garbi unhooked her dress from behind her neck. Since the fabric clung to her figure, she had to pull it down with her hands. In a matter of seconds, she was naked.

"What the hell are you doing?" Michael questioned.

"You have agreed to take me as your wife, so take me."

"Now? Don't you want General Saunders to perform a ceremony first?"

"We do not have time for formalities, Michael. Besides, the ceremony will not have happened once we move back in time. Remember, we are outsiders. Soon, we will not be in any society," she walked toward him.

She ripped his shirt open without warning, and Michael's buttons flew everywhere. She gently touched his cheeks with both hands, turned his head to face her, and kissed him. A few moments later, she unexpectedly pulled away.

"Are you wearing cologne?"

"No, why?"

"You are different from before. You smell and taste different."

"Not bad, I hope," he sniffed his shoulder.

"No. It is not bad; it is different. You remind me of an Akilian soldier, strong and virile."

He laughed, "I'm no soldier. Nor am I strong or virile."

"Something about you has changed. Whatever it is, I like it," she smiled flirtatiously, took his hand, and led him to the bedroom.

Chapter 75

Earth
The Regime - Washington, D.C. - Fort McNair
May 20, 2452

Later that afternoon, Garbi and Michael met in her office to bring up the schematics on the time machine. Knowing that he could gather the items needed, she gave him a shopping list and started the calculations. An hour later, he returned to find her unhooking some wires in the unfinished Interstellar Transportation Station.

"How many of these portal machines did the Regime build?" he queried.

"Several. Yanamai had one, I have one, Alex has one, and a few other members of the Regime Portal division have their own."

"Wow! Supreme Commander Porter is serious about off-world travel!"

"I agree. With so many machines, you can explore the universe much quicker than we ever could."

"How will you power our time machine?"

"I am currently diverting power from the grid in tiny amounts. That way, it does not raise suspicion because opening a portal to Akil will require fifteen gigawatts."

"Phew, that's a lot! I mean, one large power plant has one gigawatt; how are you hiding that much energy?"

"You forget it is normal for what we do here, so moving enough to run a small town will not even show up on the screens. Once I have the portal open, I will use a laser to find a wormhole that links the present to the past and send a five hundred megawatt burst into it."

"Wait. That means that what the guy on television said was true; tiny wormholes are opening at the Planck scale."

"I do not know the Planck scale, but a network of tiny wormholes that appear and disappear as time moves forward connect the time continuum. The idea is to energize one of the tiny wormholes at the right moment and near an open portal, in our case, one that opens on Akil. It will create a bridge through time that we can walk through."

"I'm amazed. Is there anything I can do to help?" Michael inquired, looking over her shoulder.

"Yes. You must figure out how to stop Otsoa. Remember that there will be a battle raging in the courtyard. We will need something powerful to stop the fighting and to stop Otsoa."

"Right. I'll go to my apartment and see what I can find."

Sitting in front of his computer, Michael searched for weapons to take down someone as big as Otsoa. Also, it had to be something he could buy without raising eyebrows. The only thing that made sense was a twelve-gauge shotgun. Although a permit would allow him to buy and carry any weapon of choice, he never had the time to get one, and the current circumstances did not allow for a background check.

Having no other choice, he searched the seedy side of the internet and connected to several different servers worldwide to hide his IP address. He found a black-market site and set up a meeting. Since the seller only gave him an hour, Michael rushed to the agreed location; his map led him to a back alley in the heart of New York City's Immigration District.

It was not the best of circumstances; neither was traveling back in time. *In for a penny, in for a pound.* He withdrew two thousand Regime Talons from his account to pay for the gun and ammunition and arrived at sunset. Shadows of the tall city buildings blocked out most of the light, plunging the city into early twilight. Standing at the alley entrance, he noticed that his eyes adapted to the night.

The alley led to a dead end, where he saw a small table with the gun and ammunition waiting for him. He was sure the supplier was watching nearby. His instructions were clear: *leave the Talons on the table before taking the merchandise.* He walked toward the weapon and sensed several eyes upon him, yet he was not nervous. *Strange, I should be terrified.* The farther he walked, the darker the alley became; his vision stayed clear. It felt strange.

He set the money beside the weapon on the table and picked up the gun to ensure it worked correctly. While examining it, he felt two beefy hands grab him from behind, throw him into the wall, rip the gun from his grip, and spin him around, forcing Michael to come face to face with an old enemy.

"Max," Michael said flatly.

"Well now, fellas. Look at who we got here," Max spoke to his friends, who were standing behind him, each wearing devilish grins.

"I must admit, Max, I'm surprised to see you here in New York City," Michael commented.

"Thanks to you, I almost got kicked out of the Regime. It took a lot of begging and a lot of Regime Talons to convince the judge to let me stay. Now, since no one will hire me, I'm forced to sell on the black market 'cause of you."

"I didn't start the fight."

"But I'm gonna finish it," he pressed his thick forearm against Michael's throat, cutting off his airway, "The way I look at it, you owe me a thousand Regime Talons for the fine and another thousand for my trouble. I think what you brought makes us even. Don't you fellas?" Max asked his friends, who grunted their agreements.

Max's brute force was too much for him because of his small frame. As Michael slipped into unconsciousness, it seemed as if the shadows moved around him. In seconds, Michael blacked out and again woke in that same place between worlds. Standing in front of him, he saw the Night Lord.

"What do you want?" Michael questioned.

"The same as when we last spoke," the Night Lord answered.

"I don't need your help to save Yanamai. Garbi and I have it covered."

"What about Max? He's choking the life out of you. If you die, Garbi cannot save Yanamai alone."

"This is a trick."

"I don't need to use tricks, Michael. Your choice is simple. Swear your allegiance to me now, and I will help you defeat Max and his merry band of idiots, or you can stay here until he smothers the life out of you, forcing you to move on to the next realm."

"I would rather die than help you," Michael replied defiantly.

"Then you will die."

"It doesn't matter because I will find Yanamai and spend eternity with her in the world to come."

The Night Lord laughed.

"What's so funny?"

"How do you know you are going to the same place?"

"I've been a decent person."

"You think that decides your fate?" the Night Lord laughed. "I cannot tell you how many times I've heard that excuse."

Michael frowned. The subject of philosophy was out of his scope. He always thought there would be more time to consider the afterlife; now, death was approaching him head-on, and he was unsure if the Night Lord was right.

"You have only a few more seconds, Michael. If you want my help, you must act now. Say yes, and you will have your life back and the ability to save Yanamai and Julie. Say nothing and take your chances with the good life you lived."

Michael panicked, unable to contemplate all the ramifications of his choice. He did not want to face the hereafter without Yanamai by his side.

"Yes."

Michael woke from his near-death experience, feeling a surge of power flowing through his body, and as it grew, every cell in him burned. Max's forearm was still on his throat, and he could hear Max's friends urging him on and laughing in the background. Enraged by their taunt, Michael used his newfound strength and pushed Max backward, sending him flying into an adjacent wall. Max landed hard; the wall knocked the wind out of him. Michael inhaled deeply to refresh himself and moved toward Max's friends, who were not laughing anymore. Along the way, he saw his reflection in some broken glass.

His eyes and sockets were dark, making him look hollow. Seeing Michael's gruesome appearance, the others took a step back, merely out of surprise. They shook off their fear and ran toward him, hoping to rush him. Before they took three steps, Michael sensed their plan and was ready for them. One threw a punch; Michael's reflexes allowed him to dodge the attack.

The other attacker punched Michael's face; Michael grabbed his wrist out of the air and brought it to a dead stop. Michael used his newfound strength to twist the attacker's arm until it broke in several places, causing the man to scream from the pain. Michael punched him hard in the face, and the force of the blow was so powerful that Michael felt the life leave his body before he hit the ground.

The other moved in as Michael finished with his first attacker, hoping to catch Michael off guard. One punch to his ribs stopped further attacks because he held his stomach from the pain. Michael took advantage of the opportunity and used his new speed and strength to hit the other's ribs until he spat blood. Michael stopped punching, and the man fell dead.

Now that they were no longer a threat, Michael turned his full attention to Max, standing a few feet from him. Max took a swing, and Michael saw his movement in slow motion. Stepping out of its path, Michael easily dodged his fist and unleashed a barrage of power-backed punches to Max's torso and face. Max's body could not take anymore and fell backward, landing on his butt against the same wall. He gasped through his injured lungs as blood trickled out of his mouth.

Satisfied that Max was no longer a threat, Michael moved toward the table to retrieve the gun and money. Before leaving, something urged him to hit Max one more time. Instinctively, Michael struck Max's throat with the butt of the gun, breaking his trachea. Max gurgled until he stopped breathing. Through darkened eyes, Michael watched Max take his last breath. For reasons unknown to him, it brought Michael immense pleasure.

Before exiting the alleyway, Michael looked down at the shotgun in his hands and realized he did not need it to stop Otsoa because now *he* was the weapon. Michael wiped the gun clean of his fingerprints and set it on the table. On his way out, he glanced at Max's friends. Their lifeless bodies lay motionless on the concrete. He would have felt regret, sorrow, or sympathy in the past; instead, he felt great satisfaction.

Chapter 76

Earth
The Regime - Washington, D.C. - Fort McNair
May 20, 2452

Michael's eyes became normal again before returning to Garbi's Interstellar Transportation Station, where he found her sitting in front of a computer, punching keys. He saw several new accessories, pointing to where the event horizon would be once it opened.

"It is almost ready," she greeted distractedly.

"You have already built a time machine?"

"Engineers had constructed the portal machine days ago. I just added the accessories needed to open a vortex to the past. Once I finish the calculations, all I need is power."

"I'm surprised your people didn't do this to save yourselves. You could have traveled to the past, before your civilization existed, allowing you plenty of time to search for another planet."

"Believe me; I tried to convince Zorion many times to build one; he kept saying, *you cannot cheat time.*"

"Is that a warning?"

"Yes. The inventor claimed that he returned in time to save his wife, but others close to them died in her place. Although he went back several times to try and save everyone, it never ended. Finally, he allowed his wife to die as she did in the original timeline, and everything returned to the way it was originally."

"Are you saying that people close to us will die?"

"All I know is that someone has already opened a portal to the past. That means whoever did it has already altered the timeline. For all we know, we could be fixing it."

"How much time will we have once we go back?"

"Only ten minutes. There is not enough power to send us back any farther. At least, not with the amount of electricity the Regime has available."

"It'll have to do. Just ensure we land close to the Interstellar Transport Bay."

"This is not my first portal, Michael; I know what I am doing," she replied, with just a hint of agitation.

"Take it easy; we're on the same team," he reminded her.

"I am sorry. I need to focus on these calculations. Once I am sure they are correct, I will create a macro to run it, and we can leave. What weapon did you find to take down Otsoa?"

"Don't worry. I found something; just get us there."

Taking a moment, she scanned his clothes for some sign of a gun. She did not see any bulges protruding from his jacket.

"I hope you are right, or else this was all for nothing."

Just as she finished speaking, the computer beeped, alerting her that it had completed its calculation. It was her third attempt, and each result came out the same, which made her feel confident enough to use it.

"Tell me how this thing works," he remarked.

"When I start the application, the computer will open a portal to the exact location in space that Akil was ten minutes before Otsoa killed Yanamai. My calculations must account for the planet's orbit and stellular drift. Once the portal opens, a second application will run. Using the lasers, it will search for a small wormhole linked to the past.

"The moment it finds one, the software will send a five hundred megawatt burst of electricity into it. In that instant, the wormhole will open slightly, and being close to an open vortex will allow it to absorb its energy and merge with it. The result will be an open vortex to the past on Akilian soil. I set the system to self-destruct after we step through the event horizon, so no one will know what we have done."

"It sounds like you have everything covered."

"I hope. Altering the past is dangerous."

Michael felt a warning.

He faced Garbi, "Are we ready yet?"

"Yes. Once I hit the enter button, we can leave. Why?"

"I sense someone coming. They must have noticed that you diverted the electricity to this Interstellar Transportation Station."

"How can you possibly know someone is coming?"

"Just trust me. Soldiers are on their way."

Garbi started the application, and a portal opened in space on the other side of the Milky Way galaxy. The protective shield she installed prevented the Earth's atmosphere from forcing its way out into the void of space, and the eight lasers flashed at a breakneck speed, searching for the wormhole. Once it found it, the computer sent a second blast of energy. Michael and Garbi watched as the vortex grew until it merged with the portal already opened, just as Garbi had said. They saw Akil on the other side of the event horizon when the theatrics were over.

"You did it!" he exclaimed.

"I told you I could."

"Hurry, they're here."

"Freeze!" General Saunders yelled.

Standing only ten feet from the event horizon, Garbi and Michael stopped, turned, and faced General Saunders. Behind him, several armed soldiers pointed their weapons at them.

"What the hell are you two doing?" General Saunders asked.

"It's all right, Sir. It's just an experiment; it will benefit the Regime greatly."

General Saunders shook his head, "I didn't approve any experiment that would require fifteen gigawatts of electricity. Now, what the hell is going on here?"

"It's Akil, General," Michael explained.

"If you wanted to go there, all you had to do was ask."

Looking at her watch, Garbi nudged Michael, "The clock is ticking, Michael. We are down to nine minutes."

"Sorry, General. I don't have time to explain. All I ask is that you trust me," Michael remarked.

"I'm sorry, son. I can't do that," General Saunders apologized.

"I understand," Michael responded and turned to Garbi, "Go; I'll be right behind you."

"Don't do it! You'll force me to shoot!" General Saunders yelled.

"Do what you must, General."

As Garbi ran through the vortex, Michael instinctively put his hand toward General Saunders and his men. They fired their weapons; the bullets froze in midair. Seeing they could not stop

Michael, General Saunders held up his hand, ordering the soldiers to stop firing.

"Don't do it, son. Whatever it is, I'll help you get through it."

"I know you would, General. You've been a good friend and a mentor, but you can't help with this."

Without another word, Michael backed through the event horizon, landing on the other side, triggering the application to fry every electronic device they used, including the computer.

Chapter 77

Akil

Argi City

The 22,283rd Terrestrial Rotation of the Second Summer

The prior Terrestrial Rotation: eight minutes before Otsoa kills Yanamai.

"How did you do that?" Garbi asked.

"Do what?"

"Stop those bullets?"

"I'll tell you on the way because we're running out of time."

As they walked toward the courtyard, Garbi questioned him, "Explain."

"Something happened to me, and I don't know exactly what."

"I knew it! I could tell there was something different about you at my apartment. What happened?"

"I'll tell you later. Right now, we need to focus on saving Yanamai and Julie."

They arrived near the Interstellar Transport Bay and heard swords clashing; they poked their heads around the corner to see what faced them.

"Who are the three women that look like gothic sisters?" Michael inquired.

"I do not know who they are, but I think I know what they are."

"What do you mean?"

"Akilian legend says that Skeans take on the same likeness to hide their numbers and identities."

"What about the one dressed in white?"

"I have never seen the outfit before; based on the sword, I would guess he or she is a Saiph."

"What are Skeans and Saiphs?"

"I thought they were just fables; now that I have seen them, I believe they are real. Our legends say they have supernatural abilities," she paused to face him. "Something like what you just did back on Earth."

"Interesting."

"Michael, there is Otsoa!" she yelled in a whisper.

"I'll never forget that face."

"We must stop him."

"I'll go. You stay behind."

"We agreed to do this together."

"You've seen what I can do. I'll have a better chance of succeeding if I go alone. If you get into trouble, I'll have to save you, and that could cost Yanamai her life again."

"Before you go, put this on," Garbi removed a cloak and mask from her bag.

"What is it?"

"It will hide your identity. If anyone sees your face and clothes, they will figure out who you are and what you have done and may try to undo it. I chose the mask of Gau for you, hoping it would intimidate Otsoa. Now change!"

As Michael put on the costume, Garbi said, "There is one more thing you must know about Akilians. To kill one of us, you must remove the head. His body will recover if you leave Otsoa with any lesser injury."

"How can I do that? I don't have any weapons?"

"There are plenty of swords lying around. Just pick one up along the way."

Michael finished changing his clothes, put the mask on that completely covered his face, and pulled the hood down. Now that he was ready, Garbi pointed him toward the Interstellar Transport Bay. Michael moved forward, trying to stay hidden from prying eyes. Nearing the door, he saw the Saiph attack Otsoa. Seeing that Otsoa outweighed the Saiph by more than a hundred pounds, he was uncertain if the Saiph could stop him. The Saiph knocked Otsoa backward into the wall, and he heard an unrecognizable voice yell, "Run!"

Out of the crowded courtyard, he saw Yanamai sprint straight to the Interstellar Transport Bay. Simultaneously, the Saiph flew backward as if some unseen force yanked him or her off the ground. The Saiph landed about forty feet from his position. Yanamai ran through the door, and Michael saw Otsoa follow her, so Michael chased him and unsuccessfully scanned the area for a sword. *I guess I'll have to do this the hard way.*

His cloak flowed in the air behind him in a grand fashion as he darted along the avenue. At the Interstellar Transport Bay, he saw Otsoa trip Yanamai, causing her to skid across the floor. For a second, Michael froze, remembering the pain as he watched the scene play out as it did the day before. *This hasn't happened yet.* From the other side of the event horizon, he heard his doppelganger yell, "Yanamai!"

She reached out to his counterpart on Earth, and it was as if someone flipped a switch inside him, unleashing his rage. Otsoa grabbed her hair and wrestled her into a sitting position; Michael allowed the dark energy to course through his body and, within moments, became keenly aware of everything around him. As the scene unfolded, Michael saw Otsoa draw his sword to pierce Yanamai through her back.

Not this time, you son of a bitch! Reaching out with his hand, Michael instinctively called for the sword Otsoa held. The handle ripped itself from Otsoa's grip, flew to Michael's grasp, and the blade ignited with a menacing, scarlet glow. *Well, that's new!* Turning to see where the sword went, Otsoa saw a cloaked figure wearing Gau's mask. Seeing the glowing blade, he thought Nayrah got past Gecheana and planned to take her revenge. As expected, the cloaked body reached out with its left hand, and Otsoa felt himself spring into the air.

It was not the first time Nayrah had done this to him, and he knew nothing could stop her. Otsoa flew into the Interstellar Transport Bay Emergency Section and heard the door slam behind him as he landed against the wall. Otsoa stood to confront his attacker.

"Nayrah, you have no right to interfere in my business! I am the Argi's Sovereign!"

His words did nothing to prompt a reply from the attacker hidden behind the mask, and for about thirty heartbeats, the other was silent, except for the soft humming of the glowing blade heating the air around it.

"If you plan to punish me for betraying you, get it over with, so I can get back to work," Otsoa spat, still thinking Michael was Nayrah.

Instead of a reply, Michael removed his hood with his free hand and took off the mask, revealing his face. Seeing him, Otsoa panicked, recognizing his attacker as Yanamai's Earthian companion.

The difference between them was that the one standing before him had darkened eyes that seemed to look through him.

"How? I just saw you on Earth," puzzled Otsoa, unable to hide his surprise.

When a response was not forthcoming, he craned his head to look past the small glass pane. Through the emergency door window, into Akil's Interstellar Transport Bay, Otsoa saw his attacker's doppelganger hugging Yanamai in Earth's Interstellar Transportation Station. Michael dropped the mask onto the floor, catching Otsoa's attention. Turning, Otsoa faced him as he approached.

"Do you plan to strike down an unarmed Akilian?"

With his translator still in his ear, Michael understood him and laughed, "You tried to kill Yanamai, who was an unarmed Akilian."

Michael spoke English, and Otsoa did not understand him without a translator. Otsoa recognized his expression, and his laugh taunted him. Having no choice, Otsoa charged at Michael, who stepped aside to avoid the rush. As Otsoa went past, Michael sliced through his thighs, and without legs, Otsoa fell to the floor, screaming in pain and pulling himself aside with his arms.

"Please, do not kill me!"

Hearing Otsoa beg made Michael feel powerful. Even though there was no time to draw out his kill, the darkness convinced him to indulge in one little pleasure. With an experienced swordsman's skill, Michael moved his blade through Otsoa's shoulders, removing his arms. Again, Otsoa screamed out from the pain. Someone tried to open the door to the room; Michael locked it and, knowing he was out of time, positioned himself for one last strike.

Otsoa frantically shook his head, pleading, "No, do not do this. I do not want to die!"

"Then, you should not have tried to kill Yanamai."

Those were the last words Otsoa heard, except Yanamai was the only word he understood. He remembered Nayrah's warning that pursuing Yanamai would kill him; now, it was too late. The last sound he heard was the humming of a Skean's blade as it passed through his neck. As Otsoa's head rolled off his shoulders, Michael watched with great satisfaction as he picked up the mask and gently pulled it down over his face. Someone continued to pry open the door, so he turned for one last look at what his life should have been; on Earth's side of the vortex, he saw Yanamai hugging his doppelganger.

She would never know he had saved her. Even worse, he would never be with her again. He only hoped it would be enough to know that she was still alive in the universe. Turning, he opened the door to find an Akilian soldier with a pry bar in his hand. The soldier swung at Michael, who blocked it and, using his new fast reflexes, spun, removed the soldier's head, and started for the courtyard to find Julie.

Chapter 78

Akil
Argi City
The 22,283rd Terrestrial Rotation of the Second Summer
The prior Terrestrial Rotation

Standing outside the Interstellar Transport Bay, Michael searched for Julie among the soldiers in the courtyard. Based on Garbi's account, Julie fought for Zorion, which meant she had to be here somewhere, yet he could not see her. Behind the mask, he closed his eyes and searched for her. As power flowed through him, it heightened all his senses. Now, he could hear the Skeans breathing heavily from a distance. *Julie, where are you?* Before finding her, he sensed one of the Skeans moving toward him and opened his eyes to see her with a raised sword.

"You killed Otsoa!" she growled.

A second Skean near her followed close behind. He planned to run until he remembered Garbi. They would find and kill her if he ran in her direction; running in the other direction would lead him to unfamiliar territory. His only choice was to fight, so he moved to meet his attacker, and their swords clashed loudly.

He found it very odd allowing something to take control of his body, moving his limbs without his command. He assumed it was the Night Lord. Within moments, the second Skean joined the attack. Michael defended himself against them and found the whole ordeal amusing. It was like being a spectator from within his own body, watching someone else do the fighting. Michael continued his search for Julie as their blades arched back and forth with blinding speed.

He frowned, seeing the image of the Saiph come to mind. Thinking his newly discovered abilities had misled him, he gave up searching for now. As their fight continued, his opponents maneuvered him closer to the guardrail. Nearby, he saw the Saiph fighting the third Skean. All the other soldiers were down, leaving five.

The Saiph flew backward from an attack, leaving him to fight the three Skeans alone. When the third Skean joined the fight, he felt more power surge through his body, enhancing his defensive capabilities. It seemed like an endless supply of power was within reach, and it was all just for him. As he spun to block and parry each attack, his cloak flowed through the air behind him grandly, making it look more like a dance than a fight.

He got close to one of the fighters and used her body as a shield against the other two; it did not last long. One of the Skeans jumped high above him with an open flip. She landed directly behind him and attacked. Now, there was one Skean behind him and two in front. Although his newfound power kept him alive, he knew it was only a matter of time before his body would tire, so he had to start thinning the horde of attackers.

Instinctively, he gathered power, spun to meet one of the Skeans, and pushed out instead of blocking the strike, sending her over the guardrail. He turned to confront the blade of one of the two Skeans left and saw the other run away. The Skean left behind spat a curse at her. It was clear that the other's cowardly retreat upset her.

Now it was one-on-one, and he was unsure which Skean stayed behind. Feeling invigorated, Michael sped up his attack to deal with the one remaining. As the fight continued, he could not tell if he was the stronger fighter or if his opponent was tired. Whatever the case, Michael was starting to gain the advantage and unexpectedly broke through her defense. Remembering Garbi's warning, he brought his blade through the Skean's neck, removing her head.

As he watched it roll to the guardrail, the power dissipated from his body, and his sword stopped glowing. Once the energy left, exhaustion overcame him, so he moved to the guardrail to rest and looked out over the busy alien city, taking deep breaths to replenish his body of oxygen. He felt the Night Lord's warning and turned too late to stop the Saiph from running toward him.

There was no time to raise his sword. He felt an invisible wall of energy slam into him. It was powerful and lifted his body off the avenue, sending him over the guardrail. He tried to grab the bar; it was too far away. With nothing to stop him, he descended to the lower depths of the underground city. Along the way, he cried out for Garbi.

Chapter 79

Akil
Argi City
The 22,283rd Terrestrial Rotation of the Second Summer
The prior Terrestrial Rotation

Garbi saw Michael return from the Interstellar Transport Bay in a secluded place near the courtyard, holding an ignited Skean weapon. Having seen one of the Skeans attack him, she almost left her concealed spot to help, but he took control of the fight. At one point, she saw him defend against three Skeans.

His newfound abilities only reassured her that choosing him to help on this mission was the right decision. Seeing the Saiph send him over the guardrail made her gasp and run to the railing a few hundred paces from where he fell. Looking down, she searched to find him; it was too late because he was no longer within eyesight. She ran to the elevator and selected the lowest level.

Gradually, her descent increased in speed; it was not fast enough for her. At the bottom, she ran out and searched the grounds. The area was thick with fog and dark, making it impossible to see more than thirty paces in any direction. She called out to him occasionally, but he did not respond. She searched for more than two thousand heartbeats, returned to the higher levels to buy a portable lamp, and resumed her search for him.

On her way down, the express elevator stopped three times, which was unusual; it landed on the six hundredth level, where she saw hundreds, if not thousands of Argians, moving toward Gau's temple. Stepping out onto the avenue, she blended in with the crowd. Along the way, she got the attention of one of the pedestrians.

"What is happening?"

"I am not exactly sure," he excitedly replied. "The rumor is that the one true Gau returned to slay Otsoa, who dared claim his sword. Although the story varies depending on who tells it, one version says Gau ripped his sword from Otsoa's grip and used it to dismember him. Witnesses have testified that they saw Gau fall from above and land in front of the temple gate, just as the ancient scrolls prophesied!"

As the Akilian briskly walked away, she contemplated the meaning. *Somehow, Michael must have landed on this avenue. Since he was wearing Gau's mask, they must have assumed he was Gau. I must find him before they realize he is an Earthian!*

Moving with purpose, Garbi pushed through the crowd until reaching the temple's outer court. A line had formed at the gate and extended so far down the avenue that Garbi could not see the end. She moved ahead to the gold bars and ignored those murmuring against her. At the front gate, she got the attention of one of the sentries.

"I must speak to High Priest Elazar!"

"He is not seeing anyone right now. Come back later."

"He will see me. I work in the tribute department on Level One. If you do not want a horde of soldiers down here going through your treasury, you better let me speak to him now."

Fearing that the government planned to audit the temple, the guard nodded to Garbi, "Wait here."

He returned a couple hundred heartbeats later and opened the gate, "Come inside."

Those in line jeered at her until the guards opened the gate. Seeing an opportunity to enter the temple, the crowd pushed forward, trying to get inside; the sentries pushed back until Garbi entered. As the guards pulled the gate shut, the mob rushed them, trying to get in before they secured it; the pack's sheer force pushed it closed, preventing them from getting inside. Simultaneously, the momentum of the gate closing knocked Garbi down. She stood and came face to face with one of the acolytes from the temple.

"Please, follow me."

As they walked down the corridor, Garbi noticed tapestries embroidered with images of Gau and his mate, Izar. Supporters draped scarlet-colored cloth from one section to another, reaching the end of the hallway. The assistant opened the door at High Priest Elazar's office, and she stepped inside. High Priest Elazar sat behind a large desk, wearing his black robe with gold embroidering. His hand appeared within one of the sleeves, pointing toward a chair for Garbi to sit.

"Why are you here?" he cautiously asked.

Using her best gambling face, she glared at him, "I am here to substantiate the claim made by representatives of your temple. My superiors tell me that the Akilian you have inside these walls is Gau reborn."

"We have not made that claim. These are rumors. Besides, I have already officially stated that Otsoa is Gau reborn."

"You should have contradicted the rumors."

"Due to his injuries, he will not speak to us. Once he recoups, we will send him to Otsoa for judgment."

"How bad are his injuries?" she inquired, trying to keep calm.

"They are minor, but he has not recovered yet. We believe something is wrong with him because he has been resting in a private Recovery Station for a few thousand heartbeats, and our best assistants have examined him. They do not know the reason his body will not heal."

"I want to see him now."

"I am afraid that is impossible. I will not allow anyone to see him until he is well enough to leave alone."

"You will let me see him, or I will contact my superiors and tell them you refused to cooperate with me."

With a sigh, Elazar stood and extended his hand, "Come with me."

Along the way, Garbi queried, "What other rumors have you heard?"

"Only the one that some are claiming, he is Gau reborn; as I said before, it is impossible because I have already confirmed that Otsoa is Gau."

Since one of the Skeans spat at Michael for killing Otsoa, Garbi decided to use that knowledge to her advantage.

"You might want to consider hiring a defender. I know that Otsoa is dead. The Akilian you have in the Recovery Station took Gau's sword from him and slew him with it."

"Impossible," Elazar remarked dubiously.

"Are you saying he did not have Gau's sword in his hand when you found him?"

Elazar hesitated, "Yes. He did; it was off. Only Gau can spark his sword."

"I suggest you send someone to bring it. My superior wants absolute proof as to whether he is the one, true Gau."

Turning, Elazar looked at one of the acolytes following them and snapped his fingers. He ran off to fetch it. They reached the room, and Elazar opened the door for Garbi, where Michael rested on an elaborate bed in the center. Black covers reached his shoulders, and his head rested on scarlet-colored pillows. Near the bed, trays of untouched food and water sat waiting for him to eat and drink. Relieved to find him, she walked to his side and sat beside him on the bed. Michael opened his eyes, feeling her touch, which widened with excitement at her presence. Before he could say anything, she gave him a warning look to hold his tongue and leaned close to his ear.

"Are you hurt?" she whispered.

"I'm a little bruised. Don't worry; I haven't spoken a word to anyone."

"Good, they would know that you are an Earthian by your speech."

"How am I going to get out of here?"

"You are not."

"What?"

"I have an idea, just follow my lead, and everything will work out fine."

Standing at the door, Elazar held Gau's sword and cleared his throat to get their attention.

"Let everyone standing in the corridor, inside. I do not want there to be any doubt," Garbi shouted in the Akilian language.

As they walked inside, Michael whispered a question, "What's going on?"

"Do you remember the sword you used during the battle with the Skeans in the courtyard?"

"Yeah, why?"

"Where did you get it?"

"I took it from Otsoa," he smiled slightly. "It flew out of his grip to my hand."

"That is just what I thought. Do you think you can do it again?"

"Right now, in front of them?"

"Yes. It is important for our future."

"All right, if you say so."

Michael extended his right hand, and Elazar stepped forward to hand him the sword. Before Elazar reached him, it flew out of his grip into Michael's hand. Within his grasp, the blade extended and ignited before all the acolytes. They gasped and bowed before Michael, including Elazar, who shook from fear. While their foreheads pressed against the floor, Garbi faced Michael.

"I will tell you what to say; you must rehearse it back to me until you get it right and say it to the High Priest," she whispered.

Michael nodded, and she taught him the phrase in the Akilian language. Once he perfected the phrases, he spoke the Akilian words with a loud, threatening voice.

"Elazar!"

"Yes, my Lord!" he responded, trembling.

"This is Izar, my beloved mate. Whatever she commands, you will do!"

"Yes, my Lord! Anything you say!"

"Leave us and remain outside the door until I call," Garbi commanded.

As everyone moved to leave, Garbi yelled, "Elazar, the betrayer!"

The accusation made him shake even more in fear, but he gathered enough courage to face her and inquire, "Yes, my goddess?"

"You will wait outside, and I will plead to Gau for your life; once he decides your fate, I will call for you; do not go far."

He bowed as he left, "Thank you, my goddess. I will stay outside with the others."

Once they were alone, Michael questioned, "What's going on?"

"They believe you are Gau reborn."

"Who?"

"Gau is a deity some Akilians worship."

"Garbi, that isn't right. I'm not a god."

"Look, if they think you are Gau, we are safe for now. Just go along until we figure out what to do next."

"Fine, just be nice to them."

"Akilian gods are not nice," she advised with a wry grin; before he could reply, she quizzed, "How bad are the bruises?"

Moving the covers down, he showed her. She examined his naked body and saw black and blue wounds on his stomach and side. She frowned.

"This is more than a little bruising, my love. How long will it take you to recover?"

"I don't know. Without accelerant, it will take a few days, maybe more."

"You Earthians heal slowly; it will not be quick enough."

"Excuse me?"

"Akilian bodies heal much faster than Earthians, meaning we would recover in no less than an Earthian hour."

"There's nothing I can do about it."

"Are you in pain?"

"Yes. It hurts to move."

"You must pretend to have recovered. Your clothing will cover your bruises, and I will ensure no one gets close enough to see them."

"I'll do my best."

"Tell me, *how* did you survive the fall?"

"I'm not completely sure. During my descent, all I could think about was grabbing onto something. I concentrated on the rails during the fall; they went by so fast I couldn't grasp one. Somehow, I managed to focus on one far below me, and as it came closer, I grabbed onto it with my mind and tried to pull myself toward it. I passed it and somehow held onto it with an invisible grip, slowing my descent, and unexpectedly, I swung toward the avenue, landing harder than I would have liked."

"That is amazing, Michael! Do you know how you got these powers?"

"Yes, except I am ashamed to say it."

"You must tell me. I need to know everything if we are to survive."

"I ate the black moss I had in my room and met the Night Lord. I had to swear allegiance to him for his help to save Yanamai."

"This is perfect!"

"How can you say that? The Night Lord is evil, Garbi. He tricked me into joining him."

"The traditions of Gau and the Night Lord are the basis of our whole society, which we can use to our advantage."

"How?"

"Elazar is the High Priest for Gau's temple. They believe you are Gau, meaning they will serve us, so we can live here rather than at the lowest level as planned."

"One day, they will discover the truth."

"It will give us time to make a new plan."

"What do you have in mind?"

"By going back in time, we have saved Yanamai. Now, I want us to save Akil."

"How?"

"We can stop Gau from destroying our sun by time traveling again."

"Excuse me?"

"It is a legend; Gau tried to destroy our sun."

"How? Why?"

"No one knows why; how is a different matter. History credits him for building the pyramid, which he somehow used to destroy the sun. I saw how you defeated those Skeans who attacked you, which means we have a chance to stop him; you can stop him."

"I thought you destroyed the time machine."

"I still have access to the schematics here, so all we need to do is build another one and go back to the year of Gau."

How far back in time do we have to go?"

"Forty Akilian revolutions around our sun."

"Oh, forty years isn't that long."

"No, Michael. We are going back about ten thousand Earthian years, give or take. I would aim for about ten Earthian years before the year of Gau, just in case."

"Are you insane? I'm not traveling back in time ten thousand years! We'll never come back!"

"If we stay here, they will discover our identities. You have already drawn attention to yourself by claiming to be Gau."

"Wait. I haven't claimed to be anyone."

"Yes, you have, just by being here. They found you, wearing his mask and carrying his sword, so you got the attention of every believer in Akil. Everyone here thinks you are Gau simply because you ignited his sword.”

“Everyone thinks I’m Gau just because I ignited a sword?”

“Most, especially the acolytes in this temple. If those who found you did not believe you are Gau, they would have left you on the avenue to die because they would have thought you to be an Akilian, who would naturally recover swiftly.”

“Messing with the timeline once was dangerous enough, and we only went back a day. Now, you want to go back ten thousand years. We could wipe out entire generations. If we screw up, you and Yanamai may never be born.”

“I do not believe that will happen. Our only goal is to find Gau and kill him. Once he is dead, we can live away from society. No one will ever see or know we exist, and we would have stopped Gau from destroying our sun.”

“You’re forgetting that you would not have any reason to search for a new home, and we would never meet.”

“We will be living before the timeline changes, allowing us to live our lives together the moment we complete our mission. We will still have each other, and our counterparts in the new timeline will not know what they missed. Also, my people will not have to worry about the destruction of our sun.”

“I’ll need some time to think about it.”

“Do not take too long. For now, they believe we are Gau and Izar reborn. You do not speak our language, and it will take too long for me to teach you; someone is likely to figure it out before long. Remember, we still do not know if our sun will explode before everyone is off the planet. We could save billions of lives, including our own, because if we are still here when it destroys Akil, we will die with everyone else!”

“We knew that was possible before we decided to time travel.”

“Now we have another choice! We can live on Akil under a beautiful, yellow sun, and we might stop a tyrant from destroying it as well; oh, please, Michael, please….”

“Fine, I’ll do it for you.”

Excited, she kissed him lovingly, and Michael pushed her back.

“How will you get the funds to build another machine?”

"That is the easy part. Now that you have ordered Elazar to do what I say, I will list things needed to build a portal machine and order him to retrieve them. The temple is wealthy, so he will not have trouble getting the items; just make sure you do not talk around anyone, and we will be fine."

"I'll do my best."

"Elazar!" Garbi yelled.

Her sudden shout made Michael jump, causing his injuries to inflame. Simultaneously, Elazar ran into the room and fell to his knees before them.

"I have pleaded to Gau for your life. He made you my responsibility. If you do not complete even one task I set before you, there will be no more mercy for you. He *will* end your life."

"Thank you, my goddess. I will do anything you ask."

Looking around the room, Garbi saw that it was large enough to support the machine and all its accessories.

"I want the best Information Terminal available brought to this room and set up. After feeding our lord, I will give you a list of things I need. You must get them at any cost."

"Yes, my goddess. Will there be anything else?"

"Be sure to collect an offering. Gau has a mission he must complete. We need large sums of Sovereign Cubes to accomplish it."

"Yes, my goddess. As you command, I will do. I will send word to all the temples to hold a collection gathering. But…"

"What is it?"

"We could get even larger amounts if my lord would be willing to meet some of the wealthier believers."

"I will allow it, except I must be by his side during their visit, and it is only by appointment. Tell them he will not speak with them; he will only ignite his sword in their presence if they bring an offering of one million Sovereign Cubes or more."

"Yes, my goddess. I will spread the word at once!" he exclaimed, leaving with the others to start their work.

Garbi told Michael what she ordered Elazar to do, grabbed some moss from the platter, and fed him.

"You surprise me. I never expected you to be so devious," Michael raised an eyebrow.

"I am not devious. I know what I want and how to get it."

Michael finished eating what turned out to be the blandest meal of his life and started to roll over, hoping to get some sleep; Garbi stopped him.

"You can rest after we finish."

"Garbi, I'm bruised and sore."

"Do not worry. I know how to be gentle; just do not get used to it."

Chapter 80

Earth
The Regime - Africa - Sahara Desert - Fort Levan
May 19, 2452 - The prior day and new timeline

From his position, Michael watched Yanamai fall inches away from the event horizon. Out of concern, he yelled for her. Hearing his voice, she looked up. Seeing him, she reached out with her hands, hoping someone would pull her to the other side. Instinctively, Michael ran toward her until a soldier grabbed him, destroying any hope of rescuing her.

"What the hell are you doing?" Michael exclaimed.

"I'm sorry, Sir. You can't go on their soil!" the soldier advised.

"Let go of me! I swear I'll have you court-martialed!"

Although Michael struggled with all his might, he could not get free. Behind her, he saw a sizeable Akilian grab her hair. Seeing her treated so horribly, he struggled even more against the soldier's grip until another joined, pinning him to the ground, leaving him helpless.

"Get your damn hands off her!" Michael yelled.

The other looked at him defiantly and drew back his sword, ready to plunge it into Yanamai's back. Just as he was about to run her through, the sword unexpectedly flew out of his hand. It was enough of a surprise that Michael stopped struggling and everyone else in the room looked on in amazement. Michael and the other soldiers looked at each other, hoping for an explanation.

Turning his gaze to Yanamai, Michael saw her would-be killer look off to the side. No one on Earth's side of the event horizon could see. The large Akilian, who would have killed Yanamai, lifted off the ground and flew into the adjoining room as if invisible cords pulled him. Seeing she was free, Yanamai crawled to the safety of Regime territory, and the soldiers released Michael, who ran to help her.

"Are you all right?"

Yanamai nodded, "That was too close."

For a long time, they held each other, knowing that she had almost lost her life. Later, they heard a man screaming from the Akilian side of the vortex.

"That sounds like Otsoa, the one who tried to kill me," Yanamai guessed.

"Good, whoever is doing that to him, I hope they kill him."

"I never wanted anyone to die before, but after what he planned to do to me, I will not feel safe until I know he is either dead or in prison."

Another scream came from Akil.

"Let's go; your parents are waiting for you in the lounge."

Before they could leave, one of the soldiers stopped them, "I'm sorry, an officer must debrief her first. Please, follow me."

In a small room on the Regime base, Yanamai explained, in detail, the things that happened during her visit to Akil. She spoke of how Otsoa imprisoned her and threatened to kill her family unless she agreed to join houses with him. Michael could not believe his ears.

"We must do something. We can't let him get away with this!" Michael exclaimed.

"We'll investigate it further and get back to you; right now, I have a report to write up," the officer explained.

Michael walked Yanamai to the lounge, where her parents waited; it was a tearful reunion. Still, Yanamai made it a point to introduce Michael.

"Michael, these are my parents, Soro and Lilzah."

Michael started to shake their hands until he remembered the Akilian greeting and changed the position to palm forward.

"He is not Akilian?" Lilzah queried.

"No, ma'am, I was born here on Earth."

"I see," Lilzah smiled politely.

Michael saw disapproval behind the mask of a pleasant greeting. At least Soro took a liking to him.

"Tell me, Michael. What is it that you do here?" Soro inquired.

He did his best to explain his work and was uncertain if they fully understood it, even though he kept it simple. While Soro spoke with Michael, Lilzah took Yanamai aside.

"Please tell me you did not join houses with him."

Yanamai smiled bashfully, "No, not yet. I hope…."

Lilzah interrupted her, "I do not understand you. There are more than six billion Akilians you can choose from on our home planet; instead, you plan to mingle with an Earthian?"

"I did not do it on purpose."

"We are disappointed in you."

"Oh, are you speaking for Soro now?"

"I know him well enough. At least we got here before the ceremony."

"The customs are different here. We are currently dating."

"What is that?"

To the best of her ability, Yanamai explained the concept to her. It was not easy, especially since she struggled to understand it herself. It would have made things more comfortable if she had already asked Michael to join houses, which would have prevented her parents from interfering, but it was not the Earthian custom.

"Michael promised to take me to his childhood home and meet his parents. I would like you two to come along."

"No, I am not interested…."

Yanamai interrupted her by saying, "Michael, I believe your mother is expecting us today. Right?"

"I'm sure we could postpone."

"No!" she replied. "I want to meet them today. Since my parents are here, it only makes sense that we all go together," she said, with wide eyes, hoping he could see her cry for help.

"I don't know, Yanamai. They'll need translators, and I don't know how I can explain that to my parents. Remember, your presence here is top secret."

"We do not need translators. Soro and I learned the simple Earthian language in a short time."

"Lilzah, be nice. We are guests on his world," Soro countered.

Lilzah gave him a dirty look; he did not reply.

"I'll need approval from General Saunders before they can leave the base, and we'll have to create a background for them. I don't know if we can pull this off in time."

"Please, Michael," Yanamai begged.

"Sure, I'll make a few calls."

"I know what you are doing, Yanamai, and it will not work. He is not Akilian, so I disapprove of any union with him," Lilzah insisted.

"I hate to admit it, Yanamai. Your mother does have a point. He is from a completely different culture. It seems you will be making all the concessions in the relationship," Soro added.

"It is my decision. I have already chosen him."

"Has he chosen you?" Lilzah wondered.

"I believe he will. It just takes them a little longer to commit, is all."

"How long?" quizzed Lilzah.

"I do not know. A month, maybe a year."

Lilzah gasped, "You would wait an entire year for him to commit?"

"I hope it will not take that long, but I will wait."

Lilzah faced Soro, "She gets this stubbornness from you!"

She abruptly turned and moved to a different part of the waiting room.

Soro smiled, "Good, I am glad I am in there somewhere."

Seeing Soro was finally coming over to her side, Yanamai smiled and hugged him.

"Where is your sister?" Soro questioned.

"She is probably still working. I would be too if it were not for my trip to Akil. They have given me a Terrestrial Revolution to recoup."

"Please contact her and see if she would meet us there; we have not seen her in a few Terrestrial Rotations."

"Sure," she answered and walked beside Michael. As he spoke to the other person on his phone, she tapped him on the shoulder and whispered into his ear.

"Uh, yeah, there is one more person, sorry. Garbi, her sister," Michael added as Yanamai gave him the latest information.

Over the small phone speakers, Yanamai recognized her voice as one of General Saunders' assistants.

"These passes are only good for two hours. You must return on time, Michael. If not, I will not be sticking my neck out for you again," General Saunders' assistant warned.

"I promise, Maggie, and thank you," he disconnected and faced Yanamai, "Are you sure Garbi will want to come?"

"I believe she will. When she hears that our parents are here, she will want to see them."

"All right. Contact her and tell her to meet us at the 105th Interstate Transportation Station."

*****

At the 105th, Michael retrieved several small preordered personal phones, confirmed each one had their pass, walked over to the group, and handed them their phone.

"I obtained a two-hour pass for everyone. We must return in time, or else they will not give us anymore in the future."

It was Lilzah and Soro's turn to receive their phone, so Michael held them out.

"I had your back story loaded. You are originally from a country called Basque. You currently live in the Maryland Immigration District and put Garbi and Yanamai in the Inner Circle school at age five."

Lilzah grabbed the phone from his hand in a huff, "I told you, we can read and speak your language just fine."

"I just thought I'd give you the highlights. Now, if you will excuse me, I'll contact my mother," Michael conceded, leaving to speak to her in private and later returned.

"She's looking forward to meeting all of you. Don't worry; there'll be enough food for everyone."

"Excellent; I was looking forward to tasting the local cuisine," Soro remarked.

Chapter 81

Earth
Regime Territory - Maryland - Eastern Shore
May 19, 2452 - The prior day and new timeline

On the other side of the event horizon, they arrived at the hovercar rental agency near his parent's home on the Eastern Shore. Having already paid for a vehicle, Michael found the hovercar and unlocked the doors. Everyone stepped outside and stopped to look at their surroundings. The planet's sights, sounds, and smells were new. Even Yanamai and Garbi were excited about being outside.

Michael urged them to leave a few minutes later, or their passes would expire before they even arrived. As he approached his home, his mother heard him approaching and waited for him on the front porch. Seeing his dad dressed in more formal attire than his usual jeans and T-shirt surprised him. Jared stood beside him and waved, and as everyone got out of the vehicle, his mother walked up to Yanamai's parents to greet them.

"Welcome to our home. I'm so pleased to meet you," she greeted them with genuine warmth.

Before he and Yanamai stepped inside, Michael whispered, "I'm surprised to learn that you and Garbi don't need to use translators. Why do you still wear them?"

"We use them to ensure we have not misinterpreted anything. Lilzah was right; it did not take us long to learn your language's basics. I am sorry. I hope it does not upset you."

With a raised eyebrow, he responded, "I'm not angry. Your ability to learn speedily is impressive. Akilians must be highly intelligent."

"I do not want to mislead you, Michael. Not everyone on our planet can learn as fast as my family; we have, how do you say it; oh yes, the knack for it."

Everyone stepped inside, and Michael introduced Yanamai's family, saving her for last. His mother hugged her and stepped back to admire her appearance.

"Oh, Michael. You found real beauty in this one."

Although Yanamai blushed, Michael could tell Lilzah was unhappy with the comment.

"Is the food ready?" Michael hoped for a distraction.

"Sure, everything is set up buffet style. Lilzah, please come in with me; you can make a plate for Soro. I'm sure you know what he likes."

To her credit, Lilzah played along and kept her opinions in check. As they walked into the kitchen, he heard his mother ask what it was like in Basque. *I hope she took the time to read up on the culture, or my mother will suspect something is wrong.* After dinner, everyone moved to the living room. Michael's mother talked without taking a breath for several minutes; it seemed like hours. It always amazed him how some people had the knack for gabbing.

She steered the conversation to his achievements during his earliest years. He listened to the embarrassing list of small and inconsequential awards won over the years and prayed for an interruption. As if on cue, the doorbell rang. Jared was already halfway there and answered. In the hallway, Jared waved for him to come into the other room.

"What's wrong?" Michael inquired.

"Wu Luli is here. She asked to speak to you, so I sent her to the back patio."

"Now?"

"I told her we had company; she has something important to tell you."

"Fine. Do me a favor and keep Yanamai out of sight. I don't want them meeting."

"Will do."

Stepping outside, he saw Wu Luli staring out into the forest, waiting for him. She turned to face him when the door closed. He saw scratches and bruises scattered over her body.

"What happened to you?"

"Oh, I found my employer with the Regime's help."

"Did you capture him?"

"I tried; he died in an explosion."

"It looks like you were in the explosion too."

"Yeah, it was close."

"What about your colleagues? Are they still looking for you?"

"If I stay in the Regime, I should be safe. I'll have a new identity soon. Captain Yates is developing a plan to get the word out about what happened."

"I'm glad to hear it. I hate to think of you looking over your shoulder for the rest of your life."

"It's too early to know for sure."

"Why are you here?"

Before speaking, Wu Luli rehearsed the words in her mind one more time. *I want us to try again.* She paused briefly and decided against it at the last moment.

"I heard you almost lost your friend at the Sahara Base today. I just wanted to let you know that if there's anything I can do to help, please let me know. Assuming you don't hate me."

She smiled, hoping he would give some sign of forgiveness.

"I appreciate the offer, but everyone is safe, so there's nothing to do, and I'm not mad at you anymore."

"That makes me very happy, and just so you know, I'll be collaborating with Captain Yates right here in the Inner Circle. If you ever want to talk, ring me. I'll give you all my contact information once I get settled."

*****

Inside the house, Yanamai left the living room to find Michael. Jared tried unsuccessfully to stop her; she froze, seeing Michael talking with another woman on the back patio.

"Don't worry. They're just talking. She's an old friend," Jared consoled in a soothing tone.

"Do not lie to me, Jared," she insisted in a quiet, firm voice. "That is Lian, correct?"

"That was her alias. Her real name is Wu Luli, and as I said, they're just talking, so if you go out there, you'll only make things worse."

"I am not going anywhere," she mumbled through gritted teeth.

Seeing how Wu Luli looked at Michael made Yanamai insanely jealous. Although she had no claim on him, she found it very difficult to suppress her Akilian urge to attack. Jared stood beside her

326

and noticed her fists; her expression screamed something was about to happen.

"Tell me about Akil," he inquired, hoping to distract her.

"There is nothing to tell. It is a huge ball of ice in the middle of nowhere."

Just as he was about to try again, her expression changed to that of confusion.

"What is that red dot on Michael's shoulder?"

Jared saw the red laser dot, and his eyes widened as he sprinted toward Michael. Jared pushed through the screen door, ripping it to shreds, and stretched his arms, hoping to catch Michael and Wu Luli, who instinctively moved aside, not knowing Jared was trying to help her. Jared and Michael landed on the patio floor and heard the whisper of a projectile going overhead. Jared looked up and saw a dart firmly planted in Wu Luli's shoulder. Moments later, she fell, unconscious.

"What the hell happened?" puzzled Michael.

"Someone was trying to shoot her. You were in the way, so I tried to take both of you down; she moved."

"We were talking about her colleagues still chasing her. You think someone got through Regime security?"

"It's hard to say. Take her inside and remove the dart. Stay down, and I'll see if I can find the shooter."

Michael dragged Wu Luli inside, and Jared released the subcutaneous chemical into his body, raised his head, and scanned the area. In the distance, he heard the release of compressed air; a dart hit him on the forehead and bounced off. Now that he had a general location of the shooter, Jared ran off to find him. Meanwhile, Michael removed the dart from Wu Luli. Yanamai arrived and helped him carry her to the couch in the living room.

"Oh my, what happened?" his mother wondered.

"Someone shot her with a tranquilizing dart! Call for help!" Michael exclaimed.

Just as the words left his mouth, someone kicked in the front door. Several men entered the house with weapons aimed at each person sitting in the living room. Once the place was secure, Michael saw Mai Li walk inside.

"Mai? What the hell is going on?" Michael asked.

Mai pointed to Michael and Yanamai, "You two, outside."

With their hands raised, they left the house as ordered.

Mai waited until they were alone, "We can do this the hard way or the easy way; it's up to you."

"What do you want?" Michael challenged.

"If you come peaceably, no one gets hurt."

"What about Yanamai?"

"I just want you."

"Fine, let's go."

Mai Li made a call, and a vortex opened nearby. She motioned with her gun to ensure Michael walked through the event horizon without resisting. Before stepping through, Mai faced Yanamai and handed her a phone.

"Don't tell anyone you have it. When it rings, answer it, and follow the caller's instructions. If you do, you'll see Michael again."

Slipping the phone into her purse, Yanamai nodded her understanding, so Mai called her team, and they returned through the portal. A minute later, Jared appeared from the woods.

"I couldn't find the shooter."

"He was a decoy to keep you busy. Mai Li knocked down the front door and pointed weapons at everyone. She forced Michael and me outside and took Michael with her."

"I'll call for a portal team. Maybe we can track them."

"I hope you find him soon."

Since their passes were about to expire, Yanamai and her family had to return to the Regime Base without Michael.

Chapter 82

Sitting alone in her room, Yanamai contemplated telling Jared that Mai had given her a phone until it rang, causing her to jump; on the tiny display, she saw a stranger.

"My name is Dawn. If you wish to see Michael again, follow my instructions to the letter," she threatened in a calm, firm voice.

"What do you want me to do?" Yanamai asked.

"Within the device, there's a Supreme Command Summons for Jack Mason. Go to the Moon Penal Facility and bring him to the location shown in the device you have in your hand."

"I do not have the authority to go there. How do you expect me to free him?"

"You'll find credentials in the phone's memory. Use them to gain access to the facility. You have two hours."

Without another word, Dawn ended the connection. Yanamai set her watch for two hours and searched the phone for the Summons and credentials but only found the Summons form. She could not reconnect with Dawn and, not having much time, decided to improvise. On her way, she told her parents and Garbi that she had to leave on urgent business.

In front of the computer inside her Interstellar Transportation Station, Yanamai searched the Regime database about the Moon Penal Facility. The only Transportation Station on the moon was inside a Regime prison, so she memorized the directions and hurried to the mall, where a large crowd gathered. Yanamai spotted a woman close to her height and weight, bumped into her, and stole her transport pass clipped to her belt.

Yanamai's appearance matched the woman who owned the pass as she left the bathroom. Yanamai used Regime Talons to buy a roll of duct tape and a duffle bag, using the other woman's identity, and headed straight for the prison. Since she did not know anyone who worked there, her only choice was to find an employee and take her place. Standing in the lobby, she frantically searched the crowd for a guard close to her size.

Fifteen minutes later, she saw a woman entering the complex, perfect for her plan. A sentry entered the lobby; Yanamai approached, pulled her aside, and looked at her badge to get her name.

"Samantha, there is someone unconscious in the women's bathroom. I think she needs medical attention."

"Show me," Samantha replied, eager to help.

They walked into the bathroom, and Yanamai pointed to the furthest stall. Seeing no one there, Samantha realized something was wrong and reached for her gun; Yanamai attacked and applied a chokehold she learned in her youth. Using the rehearsed technique, Yanamai constricted her arm so tightly that Samantha could not scream for help.

Samantha went unconscious, and Yanamai changed her likeness to match hers exactly. Without wasting a heartbeat, she undressed Samantha and put on her uniform. Yanamai posed Samantha's unconscious body in the stall to make it appear like someone was using it and put tape over her mouth. With her left hand, she held Samantha's wrists and taped them together to the metal handicap bar in the stall.

Yanamai did not bind her legs because if someone were to see tape on them, they would call for help. Before leaving, she balled up her original clothes, shoved them into the duffle bag, shut the stall door, and slid underneath it to get out. Outside the stall, she looked underneath the door. Even if Samantha woke before Yanamai had a chance to retrieve Jack, she could not cry for help or leave the booth.

If Samantha made enough noise, it might get someone's attention. If so, they would not look for Yanamai; they would search for the woman at the mall she mimicked for a temporary identity. Before leaving the bathroom, Yanamai fixed her hair and headed for the checkpoint. Using Samantha's identification card, she entered the prison without incident.

Yanamai put the duffle bag into Samantha's locker and used a hallway computer to find the Moon Transportation Station directions; as instructed, she put on the weighted boots that would keep her grounded on the moon's surface and walked to the technician that ran the vortex machine. She showed him the Supreme Command Summons on her phone.

"I must bring a prisoner back for questioning," Yanamai informed, speaking in Samantha's voice.

"Wow! That's the first Supreme Command Summons I've ever seen," the technician marveled.

"Me too," Yanamai agreed.

"Just make sure he's secure before you bring him back."

"I promise."

He selected the macro on the computer screen, and the portal to the Moon Prison Facility opened. Yanamai walked through the event horizon, and it closed behind her. Again, she had to show the Summons to another sentry.

"Welcome to the moon, Samantha."

"Thanks," Yanamai smiled politely.

The guard verified the request and said, "I'll have him here in a couple of minutes."

While Yanamai waited, the portal technician on duty started flirting with her, or instead, Samantha. Although she tried to ignore him, he would not take the hint, so she gave him false contact information to shut him up. A few heartbeats later, the guard returned, pushing a wheelchair carrying a man dressed in a bright orange jumpsuit. She stopped and handed Yanamai a loaded syringe.

"Be careful with this one; we sedated him because the government considers him a level one criminal, and they're the most dangerous. He'll wake on his own in a few hours; if you need him alert sooner, use the drug inside the syringe."

"Thanks; I'll be sure to keep a close eye on him," Yanamai reassured.

Before leaving, Yanamai checked the prisoner's restraints to ensure they correctly secured him. The tension on the leather straps holding his arms and legs was very snug, and the chest band held him firmly against the wheelchair back support; the drug made him limp, causing his face to hang down. She lifted his chin to compare his face with the image on the form and, being close to him, noticed that his features and his pheromones were familiar.

Pushing her curiosity aside, she signaled for the Portal Technician (who commented about calling her tonight) to open the vortex. *It is not going to happen, idiot.* She landed on Earth, and the portal specialist smiled.

"Welcome back. Do you want me to call other guards to help you?"

"No. I will be fine. He is sleeping, and there is no way he can get out of these restraints."

She retrieved her duffle bag, pushed Jack to the Prison Transportation Station, and typed in the address listed on the phone Dawn gave her. The portal machine rejected the coordinates because it did not connect to another station, so she used the override code within her instructions. Once the machine accepted the cipher, a vortex opened to a grassy field surrounded by small, wooded areas. She stepped through, and the portal closed behind her. As expected, the site was vacant.

Yanamai took advantage of the opportunity, ducked behind a tree, changed into her original clothing, and returned to her likeness. She left the duffle bag near the tree, checked her phone on the way back to Jack, and found the last item on the list, which was the easiest. She had to press an app on the screen to signal Dawn. Afterward, a vortex opened, and she pushed the prisoner through the event horizon onto a stone patio, where she found Dawn waiting for them with another wheelchair.

"Why is he unconscious?" Dawn queried.

"He is a level-one criminal, so they always sedate them before moving them," Yanamai explained and handed Dawn the syringe. "This will wake him."

Dawn injected the serum into Jack's arm, and as he woke from his drug-induced slumber, she ordered Yanamai to remove his restraints; his legs were too weak to stand on his own.

"Don't worry. You'll get your strength back soon enough. In the meantime, we need to get you into a different chair. I'm sure there's a tracking device on that one."

Dawn motioned for Yanamai to help her move him into the new wheelchair.

"Are you ready for one more transport?" Dawn inquired.

"Yeah, take me as far away from the Regime as possible," Jack confirmed.

Dawn faced Yanamai, "Come with us."

"You said you would let Michael go!"

"I told you no such thing. I said, if you wanted to see him again, you'd do what I say, so if you want to see him, come with us."

A vortex opened behind Yanamai. On the other side, she saw a sizeable make-shift Transportation Bay, crowded with boxes and equipment of all kinds. The vortex closed behind them, and Dawn waved to a worker.

"Ethan, let Thomas know it's time and have everything ready to go in fifteen minutes."

"Yes, ma'am," Ethan answered.

She faced the technician, "Are the capacitors ready?"

"Yes. They're fully charged and ready to go."

"Load the coordinates and wait for my signal. We'll leave shortly."

"Yes, ma'am."

"Follow me," she spoke to Yanamai, pushing Jack forward onto a small elevator.

Before leaving the room, Yanamai noticed that the accessories surrounding the portal machine looked familiar. *Where have I seen that before?* She followed Dawn into a small elevator. As it climbed, Jack extended his hand toward Yanamai.

"Thank you for getting me out of there."

She turned her head and pointed her nose upward, disapprovingly, "I did not have a choice."

"Well, thank you anyway," he smiled and faced the other, "Do you mind telling me who you are?"

"I'm your daughter, Dawn."

Jack marveled, "Look, I'm grateful for what you've done, but why would you risk everything to break me out of prison? I didn't even think you would remember me."

"I remember everything, and I know that you didn't deserve to be imprisoned and forgotten."

"You took a big risk; the Regime will find us."

"No, they won't. I have a plan for our escape; before we go, there's someone I want you to meet."

As the elevator doors opened, Yanamai gasped, "You are Michael's dad too!"

"She didn't know who I am?" puzzled Jack, looking at Dawn.

"I'll explain later," Dawn assured.

The elevator doors opened, and Yanamai saw Michael sitting on a sofa in a large room with walls of books surrounding it. Unable to hold her excitement, she ran to hug him.

"Michael! You are alive!" she exclaimed.

Yanamai hugged him tightly; he looked to Dawn for an answer.

"I used her to break Jack out of prison; I didn't tell her you were dead."

"Damn it, Dawn! How could you use her like that? They could have arrested her or even worse!" he yelled, breaking free of Yanamai's grip.

"Calm down, Michael. Everything worked out for the best. Jack is finally free, and Yanamai has a solid alibi; no one will get into trouble."

Looking down at the feeble man smiling back at him from the wheelchair, Michael was speechless.

"This is a wonderful surprise, Dawn. I never thought I'd see my family again, and yet, here you all are," Jack wept.

"I didn't know you existed until Dawn told me what happened. She said you were on the brink of discovering the ultimate power."

"She must have shown you the court records. The prosecutor said it that way, hoping to convince the jury I was criminally insane, and as you can see, he was successful."

"Why didn't you stop? Why did you risk everything for this power?" challenged Michael.

"Dawn was about nine years old when I discovered scrolls during one of my expeditions. I deciphered them and found something pivotal for humanity. It spoke of a plant that could potentially give someone supernatural abilities. I brought my discovery to General Bracken and requested the Regime's support.

"He reviewed my documentation and forbade me to pursue it. At first, I backed away from my studies. I had another ten years on my contract with the Regime and couldn't pursue it, but it kept gnawing at me. I couldn't understand why they would suppress my research. I mean, the rewards were too great to ignore."

"There's no question that they thought this kind of power would be dangerous," Michael noted.

"Any kind of power in the wrong hands is always dangerous, yet the scrolls said that this power could cure any disease," Jack explained.

"Dawn told me that the source of this power is a rare black and white moss mixture."

"Yes. I found some in a cave in a South American jungle, along with the scrolls. I brought everything back with me, studied its properties, and made a complete report; they destroyed it," Jack lamented.

"I have heard legends of this moss. We were never to go near it," Yanamai added.

"We?" quizzed Jack.

"She's from Basque," Michael chimed in.

Jack raised an eyebrow, "What does this legend tell you?"

"It is dangerous and will kill anyone who eats it," Yanamai warned.

"I was trying to work around that problem; I didn't have enough time," Jack frowned.

"The legend says that those who survive will revive, having great power; we call them Skeans or Saiphs, depending upon which side they fight for," Yanamai added.

"I'm unsure what you mean by 'side,'" Jack responded.

"The Night Lord or the High Lord," Yanamai answered.

"Interesting, perhaps there was another scroll that I missed," Jack guessed.

"This explains a lot," Michael interjected.

"What do you mean?" wondered Jack.

"A few days ago, a perpetrator's bag ended up in my lab for analysis."

"Let me guess, black and white moss," Jack concluded.

"No, it was a mixture of everything except black and white. I took samples of each and grew them in a small room inside my lab. I didn't tell anyone, except for my assistant, and the next day, someone destroyed all the moss."

"The same thing happened to me," Jack furrowed his eyebrows.

"They didn't know I removed some samples and grew them in the back of my lab. Then, a strange thing happened; black moss started growing from within the other color mosses."

"Destroy it, Michael," Jack urged.

"If it's what you've been looking for…." Michael started to say; Jack interrupted him.

"You must destroy everything. If the Regime catches you with it, you'll end up on the moon too."

"No one has ever told me not to search out this stuff," Michael protested.

"I believe that they're watching you closely. They think you're just like your old man, power-hungry and crazy. Now that I've escaped, if they find it in your possession, you'll pay the price for being the son of Jack Mason."

"I guess you're right; your name *is* synonymous with level-one criminals," Michael agreed.

"I only sought the power to benefit humanity. I hoped to figure out a way to develop healing abilities. Imagine the sicknesses we could cure!" Jack exclaimed.

"I'm sorry. We must leave," Dawn interrupted.

"Is there any way they can come with us?" Jack inquired.

"Yes," she faced Michael, "except you can never return to the Regime."

"Never?" Michael asked.

"I know it's a lot to give up, but I promise, you'll never worry about money or anyone stopping you from researching anything your heart desires. The Regime will never find us where we're going," Dawn explained.

"Where are you going?" Michael queried.

"I'm sorry. I can't tell you. You'll have to trust me," Dawn insisted.

"After what you did to Yanamai, I can't trust you, Dawn," chided Michael.

"I know you're mad at me, Michael; just remember that I did it to bring our family back together. If I tell you where we're going, and you decide not to go, they could use your MR machine to find out where we went. I can't take that chance."

"I wish I'd never invented that stupid machine," fumed Michael.

"What is it?" Jack questioned.

"It can read a person's memory for all to see," Dawn smiled. "I think it's brilliant."

"That's amazing, Michael!" Jack exclaimed.

"Jack, we must leave now," Dawn insisted.

"Are you coming, son?" wondered Jack.

"I can't," Michael stated.

Jack smiled, "It's all right. I understand. Perhaps we'll meet again someday."

Dawn approached Michael, "Once we leave, you can use your phone to contact the Regime. They will find your signal and pick you up; I'm sure they'll arrive shortly."

She looked at him with teary eyes, hugged him tightly, and handed him a data stick.

"This is a website where we can communicate. You can either leave a message or check to see if we have left any for you." Again, she paused briefly, "I will miss you."

She returned to Jack and pushed him into the elevator. As the doors closed, Jack waved goodbye. Michael waved, sat on the couch, and retrieved his phone.

"What do we do now?" puzzled Yanamai.

"We wait for a tower signal, and I'll contact the Regime. Unless they get here before they leave."

Twenty minutes later, Michael's phone beeped, letting him know it had contacted the nearest tower. Before he could dial General Saunders' number, an alarm sounded.

"I think they're here," Michael noted.

"What do we tell them?"

"The truth. We couldn't have stopped them. Dawn wouldn't have let us."

"She wouldn't hurt you."

"That wouldn't stop her from tranquilizing us. Trust me. You don't want the headache the drug leaves behind when you wake up."

Moments later, Regime soldiers entered the building from all sides. Michael and Yanamai patiently waited for them on the sofa. As they approached their room, Michael raised his hands, and

Yanamai mimicked him. Someone kicked in the door, and it flew open. It did not surprise Michael to see Jared enter first.

"Are you hurt?"

"We're fine," Michael responded.

"What happened?"

"A lot; let's go home, and I'll explain everything."

Chapter 83

Earth
The Regime - Washington, D.C. - Fort McNair
May 19, 2452 - The prior day and new timeline

Michael left the debriefing and walked Yanamai back to her apartment. Exhausted from the day's events, they decided to end their evening. Michael kissed her goodbye; as he turned to leave, Yanamai stopped him.

"Wait! I just remembered what the accessories to her portal machine are for!"

"I don't remember seeing any attachments."

"They must not have assembled them when you walked through the vortex.

"What are they for?"

"Time travel."

"Is that possible?"

"I know it is because Garbi and I are the only two Akilians who know how to build one."

Michael thought a moment and realized what must have happened, "Someone must have sold the schematics to Dawn."

"You must have a spy. We should tell General Saunders."

"There's no need; we already found them."

"Them?"

"Yes, and it's my fault."

"How?"

"My ex-girlfriend stole the MR machine's schematics from my computer and sent them to her boss. She didn't know what it was because I put it in a Parlor Games folder. It's obvious that Dawn bought the schematics, built one, used it to turn General Saunders and Alex into spies, and ordered Alex to send her the portal schematics. It's the only thing that makes sense."

"I've read about the MR machine, and until you spoke to Dawn about it earlier, I had no idea you were the one who invented it."

"I wish I never did."

"Michael, if Dawn and Jack traveled back in time…."

"I know, they've already changed history, but how will we know?"

"Without setting up a protective time shield and watching it, we will never know the changes."

"Since we're aware of what they did, doesn't that mean they didn't change the timeline?"

"Perhaps. They may have lived in a remote area and kept themselves away from the population. If that is the case, I am sure the timeline is still intact, except we still do not know how far back they went."

"At least we still know each other," he smiled.

"Yes. For that, I am grateful."

"We'll investigate it more tomorrow; right now, I need sleep. It's been a stressful day."

"I agree. Rest well," she kissed him again before he left.

Upon returning to his apartment, he threw his keys in a bowl. Before going to bed, he noticed the data stick Dawn gave him. Although tired, curiosity got the best of him, so he inserted the stick into his computer, which connected to the covert website she mentioned. There was a message with a video attached. He clicked the play icon, and the screen displayed an image of a young-looking Jack Mason. When Michael last saw Jack, he looked in his late forties; the man on the monitor appeared twenty or younger.

"Hello, Michael. It's been a while, at least for me. I was hoping we could talk. There's something I need to show you. I've sent another message with the coordinates of where to meet. I'll be there at 6 AM tomorrow, your time. Tell no one, come alone, and be careful. There are spies everywhere."

The message faded from the screen; Michael turned off the computer and went to bed. *What has he done now?*

Chapter 84

Earth
The Regime - Florida - Miami
May 20, 2452 - New Timeline

Having risen early, Michael typed in the address to the nearest coordinates Jack left in the message and landed in Miami, Florida, where he drove to a deserted beach in a rented hovercar. Michael shut down the vehicle, walked to the shore, and found a motorboat tied to a dock. Onboard, he found a tablet, hit the play icon, and an image of Jack appeared.

"You must take this boat the rest of the way. Just follow the directions on the tablet, and I'll see you soon."

Once the two onboard engines started, Michael pushed the throttle forward. It was a quiet morning, so the ocean was calm, enabling him to move at a quick pace. About an hour later, he found Jack's ship anchored in international waters. He noticed an array of cannons and automatic weapons positioned around the deck, with a few rockets for good measure.

"Pull up to the side, Michael. Someone will be there to assist you," Jack said over the radio.

He stopped the boat alongside the ship, where two crewmembers helped him tie it to the platform and climbed the ladder leading to the deck. At the top, Jack waited for him and shook his hand.

"I'm so glad you made it."

"Jack? Is that really you?"

"Yep, in the flesh."

"How? You look younger than me."

"Let's go into my cabin, and I'll tell you everything."

As Jack led Michael through a series of stairs and hallways within the ship, men would stop and salute. Their respectful greeting left no doubt in Michael's mind that Jack was in charge. Jack's private quarters surprised Michael because the size and extravagant furnishings would shame most luxury hotel rooms.

"Would you like some water?" Jack offered.

"Yes, thanks."

Michael sat on a soft, cushioned chair, took a drink, and asked, "Last time we met, you were much older, so tell me, how did you do it?"

"Yes, well, that might be hard to explain."

"Let me guess, part of whatever happened included going back in time."

Jack smiled, "I can see your sister was right. You are very intuitive. How did you figure it out?"

"I recognized the portal's accessories from the Regime database," he lied to protect Yanamai. "Knowing that Dawn could have only obtained them from someone within the Regime, it wasn't hard to figure out that she bought the stolen Mind Reader schematics, built the machine to imprint commands and memories, and used General Saunders and Alex to get classified documents. I guess Alex sent her the schematics just before we discovered him. I'm surprised she had enough time to build it."

"Dawn liberated one of General Ming Tun-Fu's top portal scientists, Wang Hai, a few years ago. All it took was a few bars of gold, and he was eager to help her out."

"How far back in time did you go? A year? Two years?"

"Try five hundred."

"What?" Michael shouted, jumping out of his chair.

"Five hundred years, Michael, so it's been a long time since I've seen you."

"How are you still alive, let alone look younger than me?"

"Do you remember our conversation concerning the moss before we left the castle?"

"Yeah, why?"

"I returned to the cave, where I first found it, and brought it back to my lab. My research yielded so much, Michael. I can't wait to share it with you."

"I'm anxious to see it, but why did Dawn travel to 1952?"

"The Regime didn't exist, so it left us free to do the things we needed to get done, without anyone being the wiser."

"I'm surprised you didn't take steps to prevent the Regime from forming."

"That would have been suicidal. I wouldn't have been born without the Regime, and neither would you. Since Dawn brought back a fortune in gold, we had enough funds to buy a small island in the Caribbean, where I built a lab and performed all my research without interference."

"After you found the moss, did you eat it? Is that how you stayed alive for so long?"

"No, neither of us ate any, except for Ethan."

"Who's Ethan?"

"You saw him briefly at the castle yesterday in the Transportation Station. He was one of Dawn's employees who came with us to help with our work. She said he had the reputation of getting things done. He collaborated closely with us, found a copy of the scrolls, discovered that the moss had the potential to endow the person who eats it with power, and ate some in my absence."

"What happened to him? Did it make him powerful? Could he heal?"

"He did become powerful, except instead of healing, he had other abilities that made him deadly. I tried working with him; he was beyond reason and claimed the Night Lord compelled him to leave this solar system to complete a mission and did not elaborate further. I tried to talk him out of it; he still left."

"Where did he go?"

"Dawn still had the schematics of Interstellar Portal Machines. Ethan stole the blueprints and threatened to kill Wang Hai unless he built one secretly for him. We found it too late because Ethan had traveled to another world in this galaxy. He destroyed the machine and any clue to his destination. I'm sorry he took a copy of the Mind Reader schematics too."

"I can't believe this! Dawn steals highly classified technology from me and lets someone else steal it from her! How could you allow this to happen?"

"Believe me; the theft upsets us. Although Dawn stole the technology from you, it was in my possession when Ethan took it, so the fault lies with me. Dawn and Thomas were living in Britain at the time."

"Who's Thomas?"

"He is, or rather, he was her husband."

"What happened to him?"

"I'd rather let her tell you that story."

“You still haven’t explained how you survived so many years.”

“Right, I’m getting to that. After Ethan left, I tried to track him, and with Wang Hai’s help, we found the planet within our galaxy where he landed, except he had already left.”

“That means you’ve been off-world too.”

“Yes, we have. We discovered that he works for someone called Imperial Majesty Abaddon. To make matters worse, Lord Abaddon, or Emperor Abaddon (as some call him), has claimed millions of planets in the Milky Way, planets with billions of people living on them. In response, Dawn and I began uniting civilizations to fight him. We call ourselves, Intransigent.”

“Are you saying a war rages in the galaxy that we’re completely oblivious to?”

“I’m afraid so, and to avoid disrupting the original timeline, I had to wait until this day to see you again; I’ve come to ask you to join us in the fight.”

“I wouldn’t know how to help you.”

“Why don’t you come with me to see our headquarters before you make your decision?”

“I thought this ship was your headquarters.”

“This is just a temporary base during my visits to Earth. My home is thousands of light-years away.”

“How are we going to get there?”

“You’ll see; follow me.”

Jack left his private room and led him into the lower area of the ship. All the rooms Michael passed were small, except for one. Inside, it expanded to the vessel’s width and almost fifty feet in length. In the center were eight spheres (precisely like the Akilians used) hovering in midair by an electrical field, making a circle near a ramp leading to the spheres’ center.

“Is that what I think it is?” wondered Michael.

“Yes, it’s a portal machine to another world,” Jack replied and nodded to the tech on duty.

Seconds later, a vortex opened before them.

“Now it’s time for you to expand your horizons, Michael. Come with me, and I’ll show you things you’ve never imagined.”

Michael took a deep breath and followed Jack through the event horizon.

Chapter 85

Mar Nova
Northwest Hemisphere - Intransigent Headquarters
May 20, 2452

Michael landed on the other side of the vortex and saw a technician wearing a gray uniform with strange symbols on the jacket's lapel. The specialist recognized Jack and bowed.

"Welcome home, Regent."

"Thank you, Jaylic; it's good to be home," Jack replied and led Michael toward his war room.

Along the way, Michael stopped at a window. Everything outside was alien to him. There was an assortment of purple, orange, and green vegetation everywhere and some of the strangest animals imaginable. Michael's eyes moved toward the sky, which was lavender and opened up to a gas giant with rings that stretched from one horizon to the other.

Feeling overwhelmed, he exclaimed, "Wow!"

"Wow, indeed. Welcome to Mar Nova, Michael."

"Is this a moon?"

"Yes, and, at one time, it was a planet circling a sun."

"How did it get here?"

"We moved it."

"You did what?"

"We moved it. It's not that difficult for the Mar Novians," Jack commented and started walking.

Keeping with his pace, Michael stayed beside him, and Jack continued, "The Mar Novians are an intelligent species of humanoids. They can do almost anything if they have someone to lead them."

"Are you leading them? Is that why he called you, Regent?" Michael asked.

"Yes. When I first arrived, they were living in huts. They used bows and arrows to hunt and were very primitive. Without a Regent, they become disorganized. I brought technology to their world, and they absorbed it like a sponge. I find them intriguing because they would return to their old way of life if left alone. If you give them a problem, they'll diligently work until they solve it. They can only thrive with leadership. Take that away, and their whole society crumbles."

"Can't you train one of them to be a Regent?"

"I've tried; they tend to question themselves too much, and nothing gets done."

"That's odd."

"I've never met any other humanoids like them," Jack held the door open for him.

The inside amazed Michael. On their way to Jack's seat, hundreds, if not thousands, of Mar Novians were sitting at computers. Each one worked diligently on whatever task their superiors gave them. Jack took his seat, which oversaw the entire area; Michael stood beside him and noticed a large monitor on the opposite wall. The screen displayed red, blue, and white dots. The red dots caught his attention because they outnumbered the blue and white about a hundred to one, if not more.

"What does that monitor show?" Michael queried.

"The dots represent solar systems in our galaxy. The blue dots stand for our allies, and the red dots stand for Imperial Majesty Abaddon's territory. However, we have yet to explore the systems represented by the white dots."

"Have you ever met Abaddon?"

"No, and to my knowledge, no one has ever seen his face. He distorts his voice during speeches and wears a black hooded cloak at every public appearance."

"Someone should have seen past the hood at some point."

"He wears a black cloth over his head that covers his whole face. Until now, he has successfully hidden his identity."

"How will you know you've caught him if you don't know what he looks like?"

"That's one of the many problems we face in this war. Our main goal has been rallying systems to our cause, yet he has the advantage, as you can see. We ask our allies for their help; he conquers and enslaves."

Michael stared at the board in awe, "Are there that many systems with humanoid life on it?"

Jack sighed, "Yes, humans dominate the galaxy, perhaps even the whole universe. They control every world they inhabit; it shouldn't impress you because I've been to hundreds of planets and have interacted with more civilizations than I care to remember. They all have one thing in common."

"What's that?"

"They are corrupt and destructive, even our allies."

"I assume they all speak different languages, so how did you communicate with them?"

"As you so keenly figured out earlier, Dawn bought the Mind Reader schematics. Later, I gave the schematics to the Mar Novians, who created an application that can imprint multiple languages without overwriting any memories or influencing thought. It's quite remarkable. I've downloaded it into my mind, and it works great. It's enabled me to speak to delegates on alien planets and establish alliances in days rather than the years it would take to learn their language."

"I'm glad you used it for something good, but if Ethan took a copy of the schematics with him, there's no doubt Abaddon has put it to use also."

"Again, you're right. He has."

"What has he done with it?"

"He's used it to build a vast army."

Michael sighed loudly and bent his head in shame, "I should have never built that thing. That way, Dawn or anyone else could not have bought it on the black market."

"Easy, Son. Don't be so hard on yourself. Humanoids can use anything for good or bad. For example, we use vehicles to travel from one place to another, saving lives in some cases, except some have used them to kill, yet we don't stop making them. Your discovery is no different."

"Except that the MR has possibly destroyed millions of lives."

"If you feel that bad about it, you have a chance to fix it. Join your sister and me in our fight against the emperor."

"Where is Dawn?"

"She's on a planet called Eblion."

"Eblion?"

"It's near the core of the Milky Way. I'm due to arrive within the hour and scheduled to give a speech to rally support for our cause. You're welcome to join me if you'd like."

Looking at his watch, he saw that it was nearing 9 AM, "I don't know. I'll be late for work."

"This could be your job if you want it. At least come with me to see her. I know she misses you."

"All right. I'll go, but I need to get back soon."

"We'll need to stop by the doctor's office before we leave."

"Why?"

"You're going off-world, and there are always alien strains of bacteria or viruses our bodies have never met. Some are benign; many are deadly."

"Are you telling me he can immunize me?"

"Not in the traditional sense. This physician is unique. We call them, Quels."

"What do you mean, unique?"

"You wanted to know how I stay young. Stav Barin is a Quel and can heal the human body just like the scrolls said."

"Can he cure any sickness?"

As Jack led him to Stav's office, he answered, "Yes. During our exploration of the galaxy, we learned many things. The war I told you about has been going on for millions, if not billions, of years. I also found out that your girlfriend was right. The universal names for the humanoids with these powers are Saiphs and Skeans. Some have multiple abilities, including a limited ability to heal; others may only have a few or even just one ability. It depends upon the individual."

"How many different abilities does Ethan have?"

"Quite a few. He can move things with his mind, fight with blinding speed, and back it with exceptional strength."

"That's scary to know someone like him would have that power."

"Someone like Stav can do many extraordinary things with the human body. Quels are unique in the sense that all they can do is heal. They can rid your body of disease or injury if you are still alive. The downside is that a Quel cannot help another Quel, even for a simple finger cut."

"That seems harsh."

"The universe is a cruel place. Some Quels consider it a curse, yet most live to be eighty or even a hundred Earth years unless they injure themselves."

"Do their bodies recover like ours?"

"Yes. Stav is the tenth Quel during my five hundred and some years."

"That is how you've stayed alive all this time?"

"Exactly. Once a month, Stav sets aside a day just for me. Using his gift, he goes through every cell in my body, forcing them to regenerate just like they did in my early twenties. The process is exhausting for him, so he doesn't do it for everyone, nor could he. I have a contract with him. I take good care of him, and he takes good care of me."

As they approached the office, a receptionist waved them through. Jack opened the door.

"Hey Stav, how are you?"

"I am well, thank you. Are you going off-world again?"

"Yes, we will need our immune systems boosted for Eblion, and if you don't mind, I'd like you to give Michael a level ten cellular regeneration."

"Ah, welcome, Michael. Jack has told me so much about you. It is a pleasure to meet you," Stav extended his hand.

Michael returned his greeting, "It's a pleasure to meet you too, Stav. What's a level ten cellular regeneration?"

"You will love the way you feel afterward. I will go through your vital organs and rejuvenate key areas until they are at their best. Even at your young age, you will notice a difference. All you need to do is sit back in the reclining chair and relax. It will not hurt, and I will finish in only a few minutes."

Seeing Michael hesitate, Jack offered to go first. Michael sat and watched Stav take his hand. Although Jack closed his eyes, there was no outward evidence that the Quel did anything during the process, making Michael think it was all a hoax. However, when it was his turn, Stav took his hand, and Michael felt a warm, soothing sensation go through his body until falling asleep. He woke feeling energetic, the kind of vitality he had as a teenager.

"Wow! I could get used to that!"

"It is addictive. Now, we better leave if we're going to see your sister."

Before exiting the Interstellar Transportation Station, the technician handed Jack a device.

"What is it?" Michael inquired.

"It's our way back. Inside this little tablet is a Galactic GPS device. It lets Jaylic know where I am, so if I need to leave in a hurry, I press a button, and a portal will open."

"Why would we need to leave in a hurry?"

"The galaxy is a dangerous place, Michael. You never know what will happen. Even in a peaceful world."

"I thought your treatments would keep you alive if something bad happened," Michael remarked.

"It doesn't work like that. If I die in the field, it's over for me. That's why I always take precautions. Dawn is securing the area where I will give my speech. You can't be too careful these days."

"At least you're cautious."

"Are you ready?"

"Yep."

"All right, let's go see your sister."

Chapter 86

Eblion
Central Continent - The Contender's Coliseum
May 20, 2452

Jack and Michael stepped through the event horizon and landed on a platform at the top of a skyscraper. Michael saw buildings of assorted sizes in every direction; they were all tall like the Immigration Districts back home on Earth. Below, the buildings' foundations disappeared into the shadows of the other superstructures.

At the very bottom, Michael saw the faint glow of streetlights. Also, hovercars flew in every direction between the buildings. As they passed, their engines grew so loud that it was hard to hear anything else. Above, a dim sun hung in the sky. Although its orb was twice the size of Earth's sun, it did little to brighten the planet.

"Why is it so dark here?" Michael yelled over the rumbling traffic.

"The planet has a strong magnetic field, allowing the atmosphere to hold enormous amounts of ozone and preventing most sunlight from getting through. It traps what little does get through, which keeps Eblion hot."

"Why did we land on a platform instead of another Interstellar Transportation Station?"

"It's just a precaution. I never land on a planet in the usual places. The emperor has many acolytes who would kill me if given the opportunity. Eblionians have known of the emperor's existence for many years. In fact, with our help, they withstood an attack by the Emperor's Galactic Warships. Instead of wasting more men and equipment trying to take the planet, he chose to wage a propaganda war against Intransigent. Currently, he has a small, strong cult following here on Eblion. I must give speeches sometimes because it has been difficult convincing them that we're the ones who will keep them free."

"Why? Don't they know he'll enslave them?"

"His propaganda machine has been going nonstop. He continually shows them images of worlds he has modernized: bringing food to hungry worlds and technology to failing cultures. We do the same thing, except those we help get to keep their liberty if they join us. It's one thing he does not include in his promotions."

"It seems you have your work cut out for you."

"You have no idea," Jack replied.

A hovercar stopped by the platform, and the rear door opened. "This is our ride."

They stepped inside, and the vehicle sped off. Along the way, Michael saw large video screens everywhere, and just like Jack said, the displays showed various propaganda images. The most disturbing was a hooded being, whom Jack confirmed was the emperor. As troops marched on the big screen, the emperor stood with his face hidden from view while inspecting his military. He armed each soldier with many weapons.

There were even interviews with teenagers; Jack interpreted it for him since Michael did not understand their language. They promoted how wonderful it was to be a part of the emperor's army. It was a strange sight to see. He would never have imagined a modern civilization torn apart by two outside forces it did not need to survive or continue its growth, yet there it was, in living color, on most buildings as they drove by. They arrived at the Contender's Coliseum, so their vehicle pulled up to a platform attached to a private room; Jack opened the door.

"When you see Dawn, don't mention the tattoo on her cheek; she's a little sensitive about it."

"Why?"

"It covers a scar."

"How did she get a scar?"

"I think it's best if you let her tell you."

"All right. I won't mention it."

Michael left the hovercar and made the mistake of looking down because there was nothing to stop him from falling hundreds of floors between the vehicle's floorboard and the platform. Michael had never been afraid of heights before, but this altitude made him dizzy until he was safely on the platform. They stepped inside the room out of the dim sunlight and saw Dawn waiting as they crossed the threshold.

Unlike the last time, she wore an all-black dress suit with her hair pulled back into a ponytail. Underneath her jacket, Michael saw the grip of a weapon and a bulge protruding from her coat, which showed she was carrying something powerful. She also had a communication device lodged in her left ear, with a small mic protruding to the tattoo's tip on her left cheek.

"Jack is here. Everyone, stay alert," she ordered into the mic and tapped the device, muting it.

She smiled warmly, approached Michael, and hugged him tightly, "I've missed you so much!"

"Jack told me how far back in time you traveled. You need to remember, for me, we just met yesterday. I'm still trying to process that I have a sister and a different dad," Michael gently patted her on the back.

They separated, and he looked at her closely, "You look younger than before too. Do you share Jack's Quel, or do you have one of your own?"

"Oh, we share, Stav. He's been a good friend for twenty years now."

"You throw twenty years around like it's nothing."

"Trust me, every year seems to go by faster and faster," she paused to face Jack.

"My team has already arrested fifty armed protesters, so you should give the speech behind the shield."

"That will make me look weak."

"If someone kills you, appearances won't matter."

"I thought you said you were cautious, Jack?" Michael challenged, siding with his sister's discretion.

"Even Michael agrees with me," Dawn smiled.

"Just ensure it's not noticeable because the emperor's propaganda machine will use it against me," exasperated Jack, surrendering to their logic.

"Michael, did Jack convince you to join us?" Dawn inquired.

"Now, don't pressure him, Dawn. He needs time to assimilate everything," Jack interjected.

"It's a lot to take in, Dawn. I don't see what good I could do. I think I've already done enough damage, don't you?"

"I see Jack told you what happened with Ethan and the Mind Reader schematics. Don't blame yourself for that, Michael. That was my fault. I should have done a better job guarding the diagrams. My failure is part of what drives me to fight so hard against the emperor."

"Are you in charge of Jack's security?" Michael questioned, hoping to change the subject.

"Yeah, and it's not an easy job, especially because Jack doesn't always listen to me," she glared at Jack.

"Look, I deal with the public, and sometimes you must put yourself out there," defended Jack.

"Not without protection. Jack, sometimes I think you're trying to get yourself killed," Dawn grumbled with an edge of frustration.

There was a high-pitched sound, and Dawn's eyes widened, having recognized it.

"Get down!" she yelled.

They hit the floor, and there was an explosion. The door leading to the hallway flew apart into thousands of tiny pieces. Some hit Michael and Jack. Dawn landed on the floor, removed her weapon, and fired through the bomb's smoky opening; the intruders returned fire.

"Get to the car, now!" Dawn yelled.

As bullets passed by him, Michael crouched to make himself a smaller target, and with Jack by his side, they ran back to their vehicle. Behind them, Dawn followed, giving cover fire until they reached the car, where Michael frantically opened the door; a bullet caught him in the shoulder before entering. Jack placed himself between Michael and the shooters and pushed him inside; Michael turned to help, and as Jack leaned to enter the vehicle, Michael heard him gasp.

Knowing he must have taken a bullet, Michael rushed to pull him inside; it was too late. The look in Jack's eyes showed unconsciousness or death, and his body went limp. Michael reached out to grab him and caught his forearm; Jack's sleeve ripped. Looking down between the platform and the floorboard, Michael watched in horror as Jack's limp body tumbled into the shadows below. Dawn ran toward Michael from the platform, dived into the vehicle's back seat, pushed him to the other side, and shut the door behind her.

"Go!" she yelled to the driver, who sped off into traffic.

"We have to find Jack!" Michael exclaimed.

"I will, after I get you home, safe."

"What if he's still alive?"

"There's no way he could have survived that fall. Besides, I saw his back before he fell. He was hit several times and probably died before falling from the platform."

Once they returned to the building where Michael and Jack landed, Dawn sent Mar Nova a signal. A few seconds later, a portal opened before them.

"Will I see you again?" Michael queried.

"I'll return to Mar Nova after I retrieve Jack's body and figure out who betrayed us."

"Please be careful. I don't want anything to happen to you before I get to know you," Michael hugged her goodbye.

"Don't worry. I'll be fine, and I'll be back on Mar Nova before you know it."

Michael walked through the event horizon, turned around, and watched Dawn return to the vehicle. As it sped off, the vortex closed.

Chapter 87

Mar Nova
Northwest Hemisphere - Intransigent Headquarters
May 20, 2452

The portal closed; Jaylic saw Michael's injuries and called for Stav. To Michael's surprise, his body recovered rapidly with Stav's help. He even removed the bullet lodged in his shoulder. As Stav worked on him, he faced Jaylic.

"I'm sorry; some protesters shot Jack, and he fell off a platform. Dawn is trying to find him now."

"Is he dead?" Jaylic asked.

"It is possible."

Jaylic spoke into a communicator, and a woman walked into the transmitter room as Stav finished with Michael.

"I am Stova, the Regent's assistant. Please, tell me what happened."

"As I said, some protesters shot Jack, and he fell from the platform. I'm uncertain if he is still alive. Dawn will return soon to confirm everything."

For a moment, she bowed her head out of respect, "Please, follow me."

Stova entered a nearby room and recorded the events as Michael recalled them for their records. Afterward, he looked at his watch.

"I must return to Earth. I'm already late for work."

"Please, you cannot go. You are to take Jack's place as Regent."

"I haven't agreed to that. Besides, we still don't know for sure if he's dead. I'm hoping he's still alive."

Seeing Michael's hesitation to claim Jack's position, Stova became nervous.

"Regent Jack Mason told me that you would take his place if something happened to him. If you do not become Regent, we will not have a leader. We must have a Regent!"

"What if he's still alive?"

"Upon his return, he will relieve you of your command; until then, we must have a Regent!"

"I'm sorry, Stova. Right now, I must return home."

She fidgeted nervously, "Very well, I will send you back."

Out of curiosity, Michael inquired, "What will you do now?"

"I will try to become Regent for our people, or I might appoint someone else, or I will search the galaxy for a replacement. I am unsure. What do you think I should do?"

Seeing the fear in her eyes and remembering how Jack said they were very peculiar people, he felt sorry for her and planned to help her as long as he did not have to take Jack's place as Regent.

"Don't do anything yet. Continue with your current projects. I'll contact you in a few hours and help you find someone to replace Jack."

"Thank you, Michael Mason. I eagerly await your communication."

"Don't worry, Stova. We'll find someone to replace Jack."

Chapter 88

Michael returned to Jack's ship, boarded the boat, drove back to the shore, retrieved his hovercar, and returned home at 10:09 AM. While changing clothes, everything that happened in the past few hours replayed in his mind. He shook his head. In such a brief time, so many things had happened. Shortly after arriving on Jack's ship, he landed on two alien planets, met his sister, watched Jack fall (possibly to his death), and Stova offered him a job to fight an evil empire destroying worlds in the galaxy.

If that was not enough, he was late for work. He ran to his lab and scanned his itinerary. *Naturally, they scheduled a last-minute meeting for 10:30 AM.* He checked his watch and rolled his eyes; it was 10:39 AM. *Great, General Saunders will be furious.* Turning from the computer, he ran off to the meeting. Before entering, Michael paused to catch his breath and opened the door without a sound. Every eye in the room focused on him as he sat in the open seat beside Yanamai.

"Where the hell have you been?" General Saunders barked.

"I'm sorry, General; it'll take too long to explain. I'll tell you after the meeting."

Seeing tears on Yanamai's face, he leaned close to her and whispered, "What's wrong?"

"As I was saying," General Saunders roared, looking at Michael for silence. "Akil is in crisis. The sun unexpectedly ejected a plasma fountain right into the planet's path. Even though they're evacuating their cities, we have less than six hours before Akil moves into the plasma path. Currently, thousands of Akilians are landing at our Sahara Base. As you're all aware, we cannot support that many people, so I called this meeting to brainstorm. We must figure out a way to get them water, food, and shelter, as soon as possible, or they'll die in the desert. I want ideas, people. I don't care how crazy they sound."

One by one, different people spoke up, giving various ideas, some logical and some farfetched. One person thought of directing a large river into the Sahara; the General shot down the proposal because there was no time to dig a trench or reservoir to hold the water. Michael held Yanamai's hand, trying to comfort her as they listened to everyone's thoughts. The more they talked, the clearer the situation became hopeless.

Looking into Yanamai's teary eyes, Michael had to do something. Remembering that Jack told him about how the Mar Novians moved their planet, he knew they could save Akil from destruction. By now, the noise level in the room had escalated as everyone started arguing over their suggestions. Since Michael knew there was not much time, he stood.

"What if we could move Akil to our solar system?" he shouted over the noise.

The room went silent, and General Saunders looked at him as if he had lost his mind.

"The Akilians don't have that kind of technology," Alex said cautiously and faced Yanamai for reassurance, "do you?"

"No," Yanamai replied, shaking her head and looking at Michael quizzically.

"I know someone who does," Michael commented.

"Who?" General Saunders asked.

"The Mar Novians."

"Who?" General Saunders queried again, but more quizzically.

"I'll give you the details later, General; I just need you to trust me," Michael faced Yanamai, "I need you to get some information."

"Where are you going?" General Saunders demanded.

"To see if they'll help us," Michael answered.

"What do you need, Michael?" Yanamai questioned, walking beside him.

"I need Akil's current coordinates and trajectory. Furthermore, I need the corresponding coordinates and trajectory for an orbit in our solar system."

"Come with me."

Yanamai ran to her station, calculated the coordinates, downloaded the information into a data stick, and gave it to him.

Michael touched the icon on the communicator Jaylic gave him and sent Mar Nova a signal for his return. Seconds later, a vortex opened a few feet before him inside Yanamai's station.

"Michael, where you are going?" she wondered.

"To Mar Nova," he gave her a quick hug. "Don't worry. I'll do everything I can to save Akil."

He kissed her, and he disappeared through the vortex.

Chapter 89

Mar Nova
Northwest Hemisphere - Intransigent Headquarters
May 20, 2452

Michael landed on Mar Nova and found Stova waiting for him in the Interstellar Transportation Bay. She smiled with anticipation.

"You have returned!"

"Yes, and I need your help."

"We will do what we can."

"Jack mentioned that you moved Mar Nova from its orbit to where you are now?"

"Yes, we were in danger of the emperor. It was our only choice."

"Can you move a planet other than Mar Nova?"

"Yes."

"Great."

Michael handed her the data stick Yanamai gave him. Stova put it into her tablet, and a few seconds later, Yanamai's calculations scrolled down the transparent screen.

"I need you to move a planet from the solar system indicated in the data stick to my home system," Michael explained.

Stova sighed, "I am afraid we cannot help you."

"Why not? You just said it was possible."

"Only if we have a Regent."

"Are you telling me that you have the technology to do this, but unless you have a Regent, you can't do it?"

"You are correct. It is the way of my people. We must have a Regent."

"What if I agree to be your temporary Regent until I can find a replacement?"

"I am sorry; that will not do."

Of course, not. He looked at his watch and sighed.

"If you had a permanent Regent, how long would it take you to move the planet?"

Stova calculated the figures in her head.

"I estimate we could move it in five hours, thirty-six minutes, and twenty-two seconds from the time we have a Regent."

Michael felt frustrated yet resisted the urge to roll his eyes because to save Akil, he had to give in to Stova's subtle demand.

"Fine, I'll take over for Jack. Now get started."

"You must take the blood oath first."

Why is there always blood involved? "What do I have to do?"

Stova retrieved a pin, took Michael's hand, pricked his index finger, held it over her tablet screen, and squeezed it until a drop of blood fell onto the surface, where it absorbed it.

"Now that we have your DNA in our database, you are the official Regent of Mar Nova."

There was a moment of silence because she did not follow up with any more information.

"Is there anything else I need to do?" he asked.

"No, Regent. I await your command."

"Take the information I brought and move Akil into Earth's solar system, now!"

"Yes, Regent! Right away!"

She bowed and led Michael into the operations room, where he took Jack's old seat. Stova delegated the work, and one by one, the Mar Novians began the task of moving Akil.

Michael faced Stova, "Will the Akilians feel anything as you move their planet?"

"No, Regent. The move is seamless."

"Explain to me how it works."

"It is simple, Regent. First, we must verify the information you gave us. Once we are certain of the planet's current and future trajectory, we will program our Planetary Vortex Transport System to open a portal in Akil's path, and the planet will pass through the event horizon in a matter of seconds to its new destination. Based on the information I have seen, Akil will circle the sun just inside of Earth's orbit because of its slower speed."

"That's impressive. What about its two moons?"

"Our initial scans show a plasma fountain in Akil's direct path. The planet moves at 66,000 miles per hour, almost matching Earth's velocity. I am sorry, Regent. With Akil's current speed and path, there is not enough time to save the moons too."

"I understand. In the meantime, I need to speak to the Regime's Supreme Commander and Argi's Sovereign. I must tell them what we're planning to do. Can you connect me to them?"

"Yes, Regent. Just a moment."

Michael scanned the room, waiting for Stova to connect him. Every Mar Novian was working diligently to complete the task set before them. It gave him a power he had never felt before, bringing a chill to his spine.

"Here, Regent. Just tap the screen when you are ready," Stova remarked.

Afterward, two nearby monitors lit up with the faces of Supreme Commander Porter and Zorion.

"Thank you for speaking with me on such short notice. I know Supreme Commander Porter; I'm not familiar with Akil's current Sovereign," Michael began.

"I am Zorion."

"Forgive me, Zorion. I wasn't expecting to see you; I heard someone had killed you," Michael replied.

"All I can say is that they missed, again," he grinned; it faded, "It does not look like any of us will survive the plasma stream."

"You may have a chance," Michael offered.

Supreme Commander Porter and Zorion perked up.

"I've met a people called the Mar Novians. They have graciously offered to help. We plan to move Akil to Earth's solar system shortly."

"Do you actually plan to move a whole planet? I didn't think that was possible," Supreme Commander Porter marveled.

"I didn't either, until recently. Stova said that Akil would not feel any disturbance as it passed through the vortex. Since you're underground, you won't even see the portal, so I'll notify you once the mission is complete."

"Tell the Mar Novians that Akil owes them a great debt," Zorion offered.

"Don't worry. They've received payment."

Michael disconnected the communication before Zorion and Supreme Commander Porter could ask him how because there was no time for elaboration. For now, he had to wait but not alone.

"Stova," he called.

"Yes, Regent."

"Would it interfere with your mission if Yanamai joined us?"

"Not at all, Regent."

"Very good. Please contact her and ask if she would like to join me here on Mar Nova."

"Right away, Regent."

*****

Yanamai arrived, so he explained everything that happened to him during the day, from meeting Jack and Dawn to watching him fall and the Mar Novians. She tried to console him because of Jack's death; Michael did not feel mournful. He conducted a self-analysis and believed his lack of empathy was due to his unfamiliarity with him. Since Michael could not get to know him better, it still left a void. It was a shame for him to have lived for so long, only to die moments after their second encounter.

"We are ready to begin, Regent," Stova brought him out of his thoughts.

"Please, continue," Michael ordered.

The large monitor near Michael and Yanamai displayed where the Planetary Vortex Transport System hung in space. The first thing to catch Michael's eye was its similarity to the Akilian's transport machine; only it was on a larger scale. Eight spheres hovered in fixed positions, evenly spaced in a circle large enough to engulf a planet. Earlier, Stova told him the orbs were the same size as a large city; in the distance, Michael saw the frozen planet approaching.

Although it was moving at 66,000 miles per hour, it seemed like it was not moving in the vastness of space. At the top right of the monitor, Michael saw a vortex open near one of the spheres. That portal, Stova said, would feed power to the orbs, and in turn, the globes would open the planetary vortex. Moments later, there was a brilliant white flash that touched the spheres. Its arc reminded Michael of a spark plug. Moments later, the largest portal he had ever seen opened in Akil's path. Nails digging into his left hand made him turn his head. Fear made Yanamai grip him tightly.

He could not blame her for being afraid. It was her people trapped in the dying world. The closer the world got to the vortex, the

364

tighter she squeezed his hand. Precious moments passed until Akil was near the event horizon. Moments before the atmosphere touched it; another brilliant light lit up the screen. The light faded, and the vortex collapsed; Akil passed through the spheres continuing its current path straight for the plasma fountain.

"No!" Yanamai yelled, pressing her nails deeper into Michael's skin. "What happened?"

"Stova, what's wrong?" Michael inquired, prying Yanamai's nails off his skin.

"It is too soon to tell; something on the planet stole the energy used to keep the vortex open. I am sorry, Regent. The mission failed."

Chapter 90

Akil
Argi City
The 22,284[th] Terrestrial Rotation of the Second Summer

Michael tossed and turned in his sleep, dreaming of Akil's imminent destruction. The sun shot forth a plasma fountain directly into Akil's orbit. As his inward eye hung in space, watching Akil move toward it, he saw eight spheres appear, a bright flash of light, and a vortex opened in Akil's path. The power, which kept the portal open, went to Akil's surface. He woke in a cold sweat.

"What is wrong?" Garbi asked, startled by his abrupt movement.

"I had a bad dream."

"What was it about?"

"I saw a plasma fountain shoot from the sun's surface into Akil's orbit."

"Hmm."

"What?"

"Let me check something.

She ran to her computer, verified the latest news report, and her face turned pale.

"The Information League reports that Akil will collide with a plasma stream in less than six hours."

"What can we do?"

"Did you see anything else in your dream?"

"Yes. It looked like someone opened a vortex right in Akil's path."

"A portal that large would require an enormous amount of power."

"What are you thinking?"

"Six hours is not enough time to build up sufficient power to travel back in time."

"It sounds like we're stuck here with everyone else."

"Not unless I can divert the power from the planetary vortex you saw."

"It was only a dream, Garbi. You can't be sure it will happen."

"Why not? You have strange new abilities and were right about the plasma stream. What if seeing the future is one of them?"

"What will you do?"

"I will get the machine ready before Akil reaches the plasma stream."

"How will you get it done so fast?"

"Leave that to me," she called for High Priest Elazar.

A few heartbeats later, he arrived groveling, "Yes, my goddess. How may I serve you?"

"Did you get the items I requested?"

"Yes. Everything is in the corridor. We were waiting for you to call us."

"Excellent. Bring everything in now. We must complete this task right away and bring something to eat."

"As you command, my goddess."

A few heartbeats later, the door opened again, and hundreds of acolytes entered, carrying equipment. Garbi instructed the movers to put the twelve supercapacitors against the wall to be closer to the city's power grid's main cable; other acolytes assembled the portal machine while she focused on connecting the supercapacitors. Once their food and water arrived, Garbi took a short break from her work, brought the tray to Michael, and fed him.

"How much do you know about the year of Gau?" Michael inquired between bites.

"Only that he descended from Mount Gaurette."

"How do we stop him from destroying your sun?"

"You have his sword and the power to wield it. It is you, my love, who must strike him down."

"I don't know if I'm strong enough."

"You must try. It is the only way we can save our sun and world."

"How will we even find him?"

"We must hunt for him on Mount Gaurette before he descends. Since no one found anything about him before that time, I believe he must be a hermit. Based on what we know about Saiphs and Skeans, he must have stumbled into a cave where the black and white moss grew, ate some, and woke with the same kind of abilities that you have now."

"If we travel far enough in time, maybe we can get to him before he enters the cave," Michael suggested.

"I agree. He would not have powers like yours, and you could easily defeat him, allowing us to live out our days in seclusion, in the peaceful Akilian forests."

"What if we find him after he has eaten the moss?"

"It will be more difficult. Still, we must try to stop him."

"I must be honest. I'm not looking forward to fighting this guy. I mean, he's a legend."

"I would eat the moss and fight him if I knew where it grew."

"No, don't even think about it. If something happened to you, it would devastate me."

She smiled and kissed him, "I certainly hope so."

Kneeling at the foot of the bed, Elazar cleared his throat, "Forgive the intrusion, my goddess; I must give you some unwelcome news."

"What is wrong?" she queried.

"There has been a report that our sun ejected a plasma fountain into Akil's direct path. We only have one-fourth of a Terrestrial Rotation before it burns us alive. All work in the cities shut down. Everyone has gathered on level one to flee through the portal to Earth."

"Yes. I am aware of the dilemma."

"Will we leave as well?"

"No! You and your acolytes will stay with us. Gau has a way for our escape, so you must do what I say."

"Anything, my goddess."

"Are there any true believers who work for Argi electric?"

"Yes, my goddess. There are many true believers there."

"Excellent. We will connect the capacitors to the grid shortly because I will need an enormous amount of power from the grid to charge the number one capacitor, so tell Gau's followers, who work in Argi electric, to hide the diverted power from the authorities."

"As you wish, my goddess. Anything else?"

"Yes," she replied, bringing up two images on her computer. "Do you know what they are?"

"It is a power receiver and a power relay module."

"Find them, set up the relay on the planet's surface, connect it to the power grid, and ensure you deliver the power receiver to me at once."

"I will oversee the mission myself."

"Gau may yet find you worthy, Elazar. He will allow those most loyal to leave Akil with us when it is time. If you are successful, I will request he allow you to come with us as his High Priest."

With a smile, Elazar bowed, stood, and left in a hurry.

"What was that all about?" Michael questioned.

"I do not have time to accumulate enough power to travel ten thousand Earthian years, but I can open a portal in space just outside Akil's atmosphere."

"What good will that do?"

"Elazar will set up a relay module on the planet's surface and connect it to the power grid. Once I have enough energy to open the portal, I will send a power receiver into space. When they open the planet portal, I will divert the power to the relay and use it to open a vortex to the past."

"Are you sure it will work?"

"I am the one building it," she smiled.

"Is there anything I can do?"

"Just rest. You will need your strength to fight Gau."

Chapter 91

Akil

Argi City

The 22,284[th] Terrestrial Rotation of the Second Summer

Noka (Argi Electric's owner) finished packing, heard a knock at his door, opened it, and found High Priest Elazar waiting for him.

"High Priest Elazar, what are you doing here? Have you not heard?"

"Yes. Everyone on Akil is aware, but true followers of Gau must stay behind to serve him."

"Who are we serving? I thought you pronounced Otsoa to be Gau reborn, and now he is dead."

"He died because of his betrayal to the one true Gau, who currently rests in my temple."

"What is it that you want?" Noka inquired.

"I will divert a large amount of energy to the temple soon, so you must ensure the authorities do not know about it."

"Zorion has a direct link to Argi Electric distribution, so there is nothing I can do. Besides, I will never get through the portal to Earth if I delay any longer."

He tried to get past Elazar, who held his arm to stop him.

"Gau will greatly reward those who serve him now by allowing them to go with him."

"Where is he going?"

"To a new and prosperous world. All you need to do is ensure Zorion does not know where we are transferring the power."

Elazar, seeing Noka wavering, paused briefly.

"Imagine the wealth and honor Gau will give you in return for your help when you join him in the other world."

"I do not know. I can imagine quite a bit."

"You will have it. He has already granted me the position of High Priest. I promise you will never want for anything."

"Very well, I will disable Zorion's connection to the monitoring system. There will be nothing he can do since most everyone in my company has left."

"Remain at Argi Electric until exactly two thousand one hundred heartbeats before Akil merges with the plasma stream. Then, make haste and meet me at the temple on the six hundredth level. I will let the guards know you are coming."

"Thank you, Elazar."

"There is one more thing. I need a small team to install a power relay module on the surface and connect it to the grid."

"A few workers can do it; they might have left by now."

"Find them and tell them that Gau will grant them life."

"I will."

"Have them meet me here so that we can leave together."

"As you wish," he stepped back inside to contact them.

Four supporters later arrived around a thousand heartbeats; Noka gave them the work details, and Elazar brought them back to the temple. They retrieved the power relay module, and one large guard left to help get through the crowd. However, on level one, it was still tricky moving through the hoard of panicking Akilians because everyone on the planet was trying to get through the portal to Earth. Elazar ordered the guard to move ahead to speed their journey, and the crowd stepped aside to let them pass.

There were no complaints since they moved in the opposite direction, yet they did receive some strange looks. Elazar was not surprised that Zorion's security was tight; it made sense since someone had tried to kill him twice. Noka got the screener's approval by saying Zorion's office needed emergency repairs; they stood near Zorion's private entrance, where Elazar knocked. A few heartbeats later, Shilda, Zorion's secretary, opened the door and let them inside.

"Hurry, I do not know how long he will be away."

The guard waited for them at the private entrance while Elazar and his team followed Shilda to the tower's elevator. As promised, the door was already open, with three protective suits waiting for them inside. Elazar faced Shilda.

"You have done well; now, go to the temple on the sixth-hundredth floor before it is too late."

"I will, and thank you."

Upon entering the elevator, one of the assistants selected the ground level, taking them down to the tower's base. Two helpers exited the car and connected the bottom of the tower to the grid. On the way up, the rest of the team put on protective suits, and at the top, the two remaining laborers installed the relay module. Elazar stepped out of the elevator, looked on the horizon, and watched the plasma stream; it was so bright that it lit up the night sky as if Akil were facing the sun at mid-Terrestrial Revolution. The installation took about nine thousand heartbeats to complete. Afterward, they contacted their counterparts below; the workers finished connecting everything, and one of the acolytes faced Elazar.

"We have grounded the relay to the tower, which is metal. Our colleagues have connected the base of the tower to the grid. The power receiver module will capture the electricity Noka described and send it directly to the relays. They will, in turn, convey it through the tower and into the grid at the base. If anyone is standing in the tower during that time, it will kill them."

"I understand. Now we must leave."

Chapter 92

While sleeping, Julie had the nightmare again. Standing midway on one of the many pyramid steps, she looked down at its base and saw hordes of people fighting each other. In every dream before, the person wearing the white cloak had always been someone else; this time, it was her. Experiencing the vision as if it were real, she felt the unction to move upward and stop the one on the summit. *Who is he?*

She reached the top, and the other turned to face her. *Michael!* She gasped. Although she did not want to fight him, he left her no choice, and they battled. Every block and attack felt real; when he pierced her stomach, she fell to her knees in pain, which also was tangible. She looked up at him and saw his eyes were as dark as space; it was like looking at a madman.

He raised his sword, and she knew from earlier dreams what would happen. Concentrating, she pulled in more power than imaginable, and the energy burned as it coursed through her body. She willed herself to teleport as he brought his sword down, and she reappeared behind him. The move surprised him because he continued to slice through the air where she had once been.

Without hesitating, she swung her sword with all her might through his neck, killing him. As she watched his body tumble forward, her power drained away, and her body collapsed; she followed him in a free fall down the pyramid's steps and blacked out before landing. At that moment, she woke, gasping for air. She calmed herself, dressed, and asked Olan to take her to see Urki. As she entered the domed room, he materialized in front of her.

"Welcome back, Julie."

"I had the dream again; this time, I was the one wearing the white cloak."

"Interesting."

"Why do you say that?"

"Your dream confirms that you are Lehoi, the Saiph who defeated Gau."

"Impossible. Gau lived thousands of years ago, and my dream is on an Akilian pyramid, which the snow has buried."

"That is true, except many reports indicate that he returned."

"Again, that is impossible. I saw his face," she paused to face Olan. "It was Michael."

"Your friend, from Earth?" puzzled Olan.

"Yes, so my dream can't be real."

"It can if you travel back in time," Urki explained.

"Are you telling me I can move through time now?"

"No, not with your powers. Many Earthian years ago, our scientists built a machine that used portal technology to open the door to the past; they destroyed it, and we do not have enough time to build one," Urki replied.

"Why?"

"I planned to tell you, but you insisted on seeing Urki immediately, so I waited. The Information League says that our sun released a plasma stream right in Akil's path, and it will destroy us in a matter of Earth hours," Olan interrupted.

"Great, everything I've done since I've been here: learning to fight, killing the Skeans, has all been for nothing," Julie lamented.

She stared at Urki, waiting for a response that did not come; since he stayed motionless, she knew his electronic brain was searching through the city's database again. Eventually, Urki blinked.

"I have just discovered that someone in the sixth hundredth level temple purchased the items needed for building a portal machine."

"Someone plans to move back in time," Olan concluded.

"Who? It can't be Michael; he's on Earth," Julie countered.

"It might be an Akilian who looks like him," Olan offered.

"I guess it's possible, but it *felt* like Michael."

"I have discovered something interesting," Urki interjected. "Yesterday, our sensors detected a vortex on level one. Due to the battle in the courtyard, its signature faded before anyone could investigate."

"What are you saying?" Julie inquired.

"The only other civilization we know of with portal capability is yours, and since we gave you our technology, an Earthian could have opened a vortex on Akil."

"Why?"

"That remains to be seen."

"I think you will find the answers you are looking for on the sixth hundredth level," Olan suggested.

"We better go before the plasma stream destroys Akil," Julie agreed.

Chapter 93

Outside their door, hundreds of acolytes waited for Garbi, whom they believed to be Izar (Gau's mate), to tell them when to leave Akil. They gathered food, water, equipment, and supplies to take with them on their journey, just as Izar commanded. She instructed them to set up a small community far from civilization upon their arrival. Once they settled, Izar (Garbi) would give them further guidance.

For now, they waited anxiously for her command. Garbi tasked her Information Terminal with several complex calculations. Once it finished, she executed one of her macros, and a portal opened in space, just outside Akil's atmosphere; she used the mechanical arm, pushed the power receiver through the force field out into space, closed the portal, and started another application.

"What now?" Michael asked.

"Everything is ready. Once the planetary vortex opens, the power receiver will function as a grounding wire. The energy will travel through the tower and the grid to these supercapacitors, taking only a few seconds to charge them. Once there is enough power, my portal application, which is watching the capacitors, will engage. Moments later, it will open a portal to Akil's past. At that point, I will call Elazar and have him send everyone through. After that, we will go last to ensure the portal machine does not fail. After our departure, another application will engage and cause the capacitors to self-destruct, leaving no evidence of where we went," Garbi explained.

"It seems like you have all the bases covered. However, we have many Akilians traveling with us. Won't that increase the risk of disrupting the timeline?" Michael wondered.

"Not if we keep a good distance from the cities. I have set our destination far enough away so that our ancestors will not find us. Besides, we will need their help to establish a safe dwelling," Garbi answered.

"I hope you're right, or else we'll mess things up."

"Do not worry, my love. I have taken every precaution. Since the acolytes fear you, they will obey our commands, without question."

Her Information Terminal beeped.

"What's that?" Michael queried.

"It is time. I told you the dream you had would happen."

From his vantage point, Michael saw the supercapacitor gauges flip from orange to blue in a matter of seconds. Even though they were at total capacity, more power was still racing through the grid. Michael felt the ground shake as the energy transferred to the eight spheres. The event horizon appeared accompanied by a loud clap of thunder. On the other side, they saw a waterfall, surrounded by a lush forest. Garbi ran for the door and ordered Elazar to send his people through the event horizon.

*****

Olan and Julie reached the temple gate and found it locked. Although Olan tried to call for a guard, no one answered. Using her sword, Julie cut through the lock in seconds, and they walked inside. To their right, they heard a loud commotion. Olan signaled Julie to stay back and left to investigate. He returned a few heartbeats later.

"Urki was right. Someone has built a portal machine."

"Does it open the door to the past?"

"I am uncertain; the only way you will find out is to follow them," he replied, pointing to the last few acolytes.

"Aren't you coming with me?" puzzled Julie.

"No, I must tell Zorion what they are doing."

"Wait, what did you say?"

"Zorion."

"Are you saying he's alive?"

"Yes. I discovered later that his body double was the one Gecheana killed. Zorion and I agreed that you should not know until the danger was over."

"Will he get off Akil before it's too late?"

"I am afraid he is stubborn about these things. He swore to be the last Akilian to leave."

"I must see him!"

"No! You must stop whoever has built that portal machine. If they go back in time, they could destroy us."

Begrudgingly, she pulled her hood up, covering her face, and moved to the end of the line. At the doorway, Julie felt darkness emanating from inside, retrieved her sword, and entered. She saw an open portal near a wall, just as Olan had said, and several workers were sending boxes of supplies through the event horizon. She removed her hood, scanned the room, and saw him.

"Michael?"

"Julie? Is that you?"

"Yes. What the hell are you doing here?"

"It's a little hard to explain," he started to say.

Garbi stood and interrupted, "We are traveling back in time to save our planet."

"You can't do it, Michael. You'll disrupt the timeline. There's no telling how many people you'll kill just by setting your foot there."

"Michael will stop Gau. He has the power," Garbi interjected.

"You're the one I sense?" surprised Julie.

"I don't know what you mean," Michael lied.

"I feel the darkness in you, Michael. Please, stop this madness now, before it's too late."

"Saving a planet isn't madness, Julie; we're doing the right thing. Garbi and I ensured we wouldn't interfere with Akil's ancient society. All we need to do is find Gau and kill him, and we'll live the rest of our lives in seclusion."

"You don't understand, Michael. I dreamed about the last battle of Gau, where he died, and I saw his face."

"Wonderful! Describe him so that I can identify him," Michael answered excitedly.

"He's you, Michael. If you go back in time, you become Gau."

"Impossible; how can I become Gau? He was an Akilian."

"I don't know the specifics, Michael. I only know that I saw you atop the pyramid. You were the one who destroyed their sun."

"Do not listen to her, Michael. I know your heart. You will save my people from destruction. Remember, you promised me," Garbi insisted.

"I'm sorry, Julie. She's right. I made a promise, and I mean to keep it. I will find this Gau person, stop him, and we'll disappear from history."

"I made a promise too, Michael."

Julie leaped toward one of the capacitors and used her sword to cut its cable to the portal machine, causing the event horizon to appear and disappear.

"Stop her, Michael!" Garbi yelled, running to her Information Terminal.

Michael ignited his sword and stood between Julie and another capacitor.

"The lack of power caused the portal to jump through time, so now we are years behind them! We must go now, Michael!" Garbi yelled, running toward the event horizon.

As he backed up to join Garbi, Julie jumped over him and landed in his path. Their white and crimson swords hummed in the quiet as they faced each other. He tried to figure out a way around her that did not involve injury, yet at the same time, the darkness within him wanted to kill her.

"I will not let you pass," Julie said defiantly.

"Then you leave me no choice," Michael threatened.

His eyes turned black as the night, and he swung at her. Their swords clashed, creating a thunder-like rumble. As their blades arced from side to side at blinding speed, Michael focused on getting Julie out of his way; she would not move.

"Come on, Michael! We are losing time!" Garbi yelled.

Her call distracted him enough that Julie knocked his sword out of his hand. As it clanged across the room, her blade approached his neck. Anger swelled within him, and instinctively, he released a wall of energy in her direction, knocking her out of the way.

"Now, Michael!" Garbi yelled.

Reaching out with his hand, Michael called his sword toward him; Julie grabbed it with her powers too. The handle hung in mid-air for several seconds until Garbi grabbed his arm and pulled him through the event horizon, leaving Gau's sword behind.

Chapter 94

Akil

Argi City

The 22,284th Terrestrial Rotation of the Second Summer

Having searched for Olan and Julie for the past few thousand heartbeats, Zorion returned to his office, worried that he would not find them before Akil reached the plasma stream. On his way in, he dismissed all the sentries and urged them to get off-planet. Everyone, including Shilda, vacated, except for Broll. Shilda had left a video message informing him that the elevator broke down, so he could not watch the event from the tower. Although Michael had given him a glimmer of hope, moving a whole planet did not seem realistic to him, and even crazier was to think it possible to move a world from one solar system to another,

Nevertheless, he did not take chances with Julie's safety and had to find her soon, or her fate would be the same. Looking at the surface monitor, he saw that Akil was close to its doom. If Michael planned to move the planet, he better do it soon. As Zorion and Broll watched the monitor, there was a sudden flash of light. It was so bright that the monitor screens whited out for a few heartbeats; they saw a gigantic vortex in Akil's path as the lens returned to focus.

"He did it!" Zorion and Broll yelled simultaneously.

As Akil moved closer to the event horizon, another bright light appeared. Beneath them, they felt the ground shake; all the lights went out, and his office's emergency power returned, allowing him to see that someone had diverted all energy to the city without a clear destination. Again, the surface monitor came back on; the vortex had disappeared.

"The portal to Earth!" Zorion exclaimed.

He ran to his communicator and contacted the operator at the Interstellar Transport Bay. "Is the vortex still open?"

"No, Sir. The loss of power shut it down. I am trying to get it back open, but the capacitors do not have any energy," Tadra replied.

In the background, Zorion heard the screams of those trying to leave.

"What is happening?"

"A few were passing through the event horizon; without power, it closed and cut them in half. The rest are panicking since there is no way out," Tadra explained.

"What could have drained so much power?" Zorion wondered.

"Another portal machine," Olan had entered his office unexpectedly.

Seeing Olan, Broll moved to strike him down until Zorion stopped him.

"Olan, where is it?"

"It is in one of Gau's temples, on the six hundredth level. We should go now. Julie is there trying to stop them."

"Why is Julie there?"

"I will explain on the way; we must go now."

They followed Olan to the temple, and he told him what Julie had become along the way. When they arrived, he saw Julie lying down, several paces from the event horizon. Nearby, sparks shot from the capacitors, and the lights in the room flickered. What got his attention was a countdown coming from an Information Terminal. There were only a few heartbeats left before it reached zero. It was clear that whoever built it set it to self-destruct.

"Julie!" he yelled.

Hearing his voice, Julie woke. Seeing him, she smiled. At that moment, the self-destruct engaged. Electric fingers danced from one capacitor to another, and the event horizon phased in and out rapidly. Zorion moved to help her until there was an explosion, and Broll pulled him back into the hallway. Zorion struggled against him, unable to break free. Left with no choice, he could only watch as the room collapsed on top of her.

He saw her stand and jump into the vortex between the falling debris. Even though it continued to phase in and out, she entered it while it was engaged and just before the machine exploded. The force shook the ground, causing concrete and dust to fill the air. Moments later, Zorion looked inside; it was full of debris. He swore, using every foul Akilian word in their language.

"There was no time," Broll apologized,

"It is all right. I think she made it out safely."

"You would have died trying to save her."

"I will die anyway," he looked at his timekeeper. "Akil's surface will touch the plasma stream in twenty heartbeats."

"Before it happens, let me say it has been an honor."

"Thank you for always being there, Broll. You have always been more than a friend to me. You are family."

As they waited for the inevitable, Zorion stared at his timekeeper, counting the heartbeats until the plasma stream cut through Akil's surface to their underground cities.

Chapter 95

Mar Nova
Northwest Hemisphere - Intransigent Headquarters
May 20, 2452

"What do you mean the mission failed?" Michael asked, nearly yelling at her.

"Forgive me, Regent; something took power from the spheres and closed the vortex."

"Reopen it, now!"

"The planet has passed by them!"

"Then move them!"

"Regent, they will be too close to the plasma stream. It could destroy the spheres!"

"If so, you'll make new ones! Now move!" he yelled.

"Right away, Regent!"

Stova relayed his order. Michael watched the monitors and saw that Akil was dangerously close to the plasma stream. One by one, the spheres disappeared from one monitor and reappeared on another. Although Stova was right, the orbs were dangerously close to the fountain; it did not matter to him. They could replace the globes; they could not replace Akil and the people on it. As the planet approached, he saw plasma raining down on the surface of the frozen world and melting multiple layers of snow and ice before freezing itself. Now, Akil was seconds away from the spheres, and the vortex still was not open.

"What's wrong, Stova? Why isn't the portal activated yet?"

"The amount of energy required to open that size vortex takes time to generate, Regent."

"How much time?"

"That is what I have been trying to tell you, Regent. When we have power, it will be too late."

"You must improvise."

"Regent?"

"Get the power from another source."

"The only other source is for our cities."

"Divert it, Stova! It is life or death for the Akilians!"

"Right away, Regent!"

Michael and Yanamai intently watched as the planet came closer to the spheres. As precious seconds passed, Yanamai squeezed Michael's hand harder, drawing blood this time.

"Come on, Stova! Where's my portal?"

"Engage!" Stova yelled.

On the monitor, they saw another bright flash of light exit a nearby portal as before. Plasma passed between it and the spheres, absorbing the energy and preventing the portal from opening.

"I am sorry; we have failed again, Regent."

"Try again."

"But Regent!"

"Try again!" Michael yelled angrily this time.

Not expecting his tone, Stova jumped and, with a girlish squeak, yelled, "Engage!"

Nothing happened, and she planned to tell Michael they failed again until seeing his glare.

"Engage!" she yelled.

One after another, the Mar Novians fired multiple ignition shots, trying to open the planetary vortex. The upper atmosphere reached the would-be event horizon, yet Stova did not give up, knowing how Michael would react. There was an explosion, and the vortex opened. Anxiously, Michael and Yanamai watched as Akil passed through the event horizon in a matter of seconds, just as Stova had said it would, and on another monitor in Earth's solar system, they saw it reappear in one piece. Once the planet was safe, everyone in the room cheered. Yanamai hugged Michael tightly for a long time; she released him, allowing him to take a deep breath and order Stova to retrieve the spheres before the plasma destroyed them.

"You saved us!" Yanamai exclaimed to Michael.

"No, Yanamai. The Mar Novians saved your people."

Chapter 96

Akil
Argi City
The 22,284[th] Terrestrial Rotation of the Second Summer

Having decided to take a final walk, Zorion and Broll headed out of the temple and strolled aimlessly down the avenue, waiting for the plasma stream to carve its way to them. A few hundred heartbeats later, Zorion looked at his timekeeper and frowned.

"What is wrong?" Broll queried.

"We should be dead by now," Zorion answered.

"How did we survive?" Broll questioned.

"Somehow, Michael must have succeeded."

"Who is Michael?"

"I will explain later; now, I must return to my office and confirm what I think happened!"

His office was still running on backup electricity. He turned on the surface monitor; the camera only returned static. Not used to making the calls himself, it took several hundred heartbeats before he opened a channel, and although the signal was slightly fuzzy, he could see and hear Michael well enough to communicate.

"I am still alive," Zorion remarked.

"It was close. We almost lost you because something strange happened after we opened the vortex. Someone diverted the power to the planet," Michael explained.

"Yes, I saw it too. I am afraid someone in my city decided to build a portal machine of their own," Zorion left out that they believed it was a connection to the past.

"Whoever they are, they almost destroyed your planet," Michael replied.

"Believe me; they will pay for their crime. Did we make it to Earth's solar system?"

"Yes, but because your planet moves a little slower than Earth, Stova placed Akil in a closer orbit, and you're about three months ahead of Earth in its cycle around the sun, so only those with telescopes can see you. To others, you'll be another star in the sky. It will be up to Supreme Commander Porter to explain your presence to Earth's national leaders."

"I do not envy him. If Earthian leaders are like ours, they will argue for years."

"You're probably right, except it won't just be your planet. Soon, I'll have Mar Nova in Earth's solar system, along with others, as time goes on. Having the planets in one solar system will make them easier to defend."

"Defend against whom?"

"Someone who calls himself Imperial Majesty Abaddon or Lord Abaddon or Emperor."

"I do not like the sound of that."

"You shouldn't. For now, worry about getting your cities back up and running. Once you're fully operational, let me know. We'll meet with Supreme Commander Porter and begin working on a strategy. Until then, if you need any help, don't hesitate."

"I think we will be fine now that the planet is safe. I will contact you the moment we are of any help. And Michael, before you disconnect, there are no words to express my gratitude."

"It was my pleasure."

They ended the call, and Zorion started the long, arduous task of getting Akil up and running again.

Chapter 97

Mar Nova
Northwest Hemisphere - Intransigent Headquarters
May 20, 2452

Sitting in his private quarters, Michael reviewed details about the war Jack and Dawn mentioned earlier. Based on the information Stova provided, it was clear that Imperial Majesty Abaddon was a severe threat. Jack had fallen from a great height, and it was unlikely he survived; even so, Michael hoped he was still alive.

Since the Mar Novians saved Akil, he felt obligated to continue as their Regent, even if Jack did not survive, so until Dawn returned with news of Jack's fate, he decided to investigate the language software. The computer completed the diagnostic and showed a report saying the algorithm it used was like Michael's, which he created in the hopes of speaking to Chu Lian in her native tongue before she had left him. Satisfied it was safe to use, he ordered Stova to run the MR language application on him.

The idea of having a machine imprint data into his brain did not thrill him, yet he had to meet alien leaders if Jack did not return. Knowing their language, as Jack had said, would make things much easier for him. As he continued to read the material Stova gave him, Yanamai appeared in his peripheral vision, going through the data he asked her to review. Even though he was a speed reader, there was too much information to analyze in one sitting.

There were thousands of details, including photos, videos, and written accounts of agents who had been to thousands of planets across the galaxy. Some joined Intransigent; most aligned with the emperor. He read a section describing the Education Facilities and became interested in knowing how they ran. Surprisingly, no one had ever tried to break into one to see what the education process entailed. He gave it thoughtful consideration and wanted to see what happens inside before diving headfirst into this war.

"I need to get inside one of these Education Facilities to see how they operate," Michael commented.

"It is too dangerous, Michael. What if they catch you?" Yanamai worried.

"I need to know how and what they're training these recruits."

"Why is it so important to know? Would it not be best to destroy them so they cannot educate more volunteers?"

"No matter how many buildings we destroy, it won't help me understand the kind of techniques they're using to train them and how long it takes. Besides, I have a gut feeling I know what they're doing, so I must confirm it."

"Fine, I will go with you."

"No. You will go back to Earth. I will contact you the moment I return."

"You cannot stop me from going."

"Yes, I can," he smiled slightly. "I'm their Regent, remember? If I don't want you to go, you're not going. I'm already risking my life. I will not risk yours too."

Yanamai explained in detail why he was wrong to leave her behind, yet it still did not change his mind; she stood, frustrated with him, but before leaving, she stopped.

"Promise me that you will not go alone?"

"I plan to ask for an escort. I've learned that Mar Nova houses thousands of Saiphs, so I'll ask one of them to guide me."

"That makes me feel better. When do you plan on leaving?"

"Once you land on Earth."

They arrived at the Mar Novian Interstellar Transportation Bay, and he kissed her goodbye. She stepped through the portal, and he ordered Stova to escort him to the garrison, where she spoke to a clerk on duty.

"Please, summon Areus. Tell him the *Regent* needs his help."

Whenever she referred to him as *Regent*, it made him cringe because she said it was the highest title her people could give someone. Since he was their leader, it would be impossible for the Mar Novians not to call him Regent; it did not help ease his conscience. Michael waited until seeing a large, humanoid male walking beside the clerk sent to fetch him.

Although Areus wore Earth-like army fatigues, Michael saw the hilt of a sword fastened to his belt and thigh. Seeing a sword rather than a gun did not surprise him. Earlier, Yanamai told him stories from her youth about the Saiphs and Skeans. Being close to someone with that power made him a little nervous. Areus did not bow, as the Mar Novians often did. Instead, he looked Michael in the eyes.

"I am Areus. You called for me."

Michael recognized and understood his dialect right away. It made him glad that he opted to download the languages into his mind; it was still bizarre being able to understand an alien dialect.

"I can tell you're not Mar Novian," Michael spoke in Areus' native tongue.

"No, my world and my people no longer exist. I am the last of the Odians."

"I'm sorry to hear that, Areus," Michael replied.

"Our Regent desires to visit one of the Emperor's Education Facilities," informed Stova.

"Do you plan to blow one up?" Areus queried.

"Not yet. I'm not much of a General, but the more you know your enemy, the better your chance of defeating him."

"I like your way of thinking. We should have done something like this long ago.

"Will you take me?"

"Yes, if you are aware of the risks involved. If they capture us, we could become one of the emperor's faithful citizens."

"Do not fear, Regent. Areus is one of our most gifted Saiphs. I trust he will bring you back safely," Stova interrupted.

"I understand the risks, Areus."

"When do you want to leave?" quizzed Areus.

"Right away, if you're available," Michael answered.

"I was waiting for my next assignment, and it sounds like I just got it."

At the Mar Novian Interstellar Transportation Bay, Stova handed the technician the coordinates, and as he worked on their destination, another assistant gave Michael and Areus a small backpack with food, water, and communication devices.

"What planet are we landing on?" Michael questioned.

"It does not matter. Every one of the emperor's worlds has hundreds of Education Facilities, which means it will be dangerous no matter where we go," Areus explained.

"The planet is called Hunnus," Stova offered.

The vortex opened, and Areus faced Michael, "Last chance to back out?"

"Nope, I'm moving forward."

"All right, here we go."

Chapter 98

Hunnus
Southeastern Hemisphere - Education Facility
May 20, 2452

Michael and Areus landed in a wooded area, which helped to hide them from the enemy. On the horizon, Michael saw the sun rising. Above, four distinct-sized moons reflected the sun's light to Hunnus in separate phases. Around him, the vegetation was like Earth, except with unusual color variations.

The trees had dark green bark and orange leaves. It was hot and humid, giving the local area abundant life. Sounds of insects and animals filled the air; it felt like summertime. As a precaution, Areus scanned the area for humanoids. Satisfied they were safe, he motioned for Michael to follow him.

"What happened to your people?" Michael asked.

At first, Areus hesitated, "Abaddon demanded we join his empire. We resisted. Realizing that he could not buy or scare us, the emperor sent General Hades to our world."

"General Hades?"

"Yes. He is in charge of the emperor's space war vessels."

"What did he do to your people?"

"Odians were peaceful, yet we had weapons. Still, nothing could have prepared us for what the emperor had planned. General Hades surrounded our planet with his space warships, and our military attacked at once. There were too many of them, and their defenses were too strong. We saw them descending from the sky like rain from a cloud. They destroyed our military bases until we were defenseless, landed, and sent troops to harvest everyone."

"Harvest?"

"That is what they called it."

"How did you escape?"

"One of their pilots shot my plane down early in the battle. I crashed into a building. The debris kept me buried alive for days. The reaping was over when news of the attack reached Intransigent. A few days later, Intransigent arrived and performed a search and rescue operation. A Saiph found me a day later and brought me to Intransigent Headquarters; a Quel repaired my injuries.”

“Is that why you decided to become a Saiph because one found you?”

“No, you do not decide to become one. You either have the potential, or you do not. Gril, the Mar Novian’s liaison to the Saiphs, told me about their powers and abilities shortly after healing my wounds. He claimed to see a blue haze around my aura, which meant I had the potential to become one. Having lost everything, I saw a chance to fight the emperor on a different level than before, so I went through the trial, and here I am.”

“The trial?”

“You must eat some weird species of black and white moss, and if you survive, you go through some trials to figure out which side chose you. Had the Night Lord chosen me, Gril would have killed me on the spot.”

“Yikes! That sounds insane!”

“It is not for the faint of heart.”

“What did the emperor do with your people?”

“I learned he sent them to several Education Facilities, like the one we are about to visit.”

“Did it change them?”

“You could say that,” he paused and continued, “Once I became a Saiph, Gril helped me find my wife, Nilah; it took a few years to find her on Hadrian, in the Nerva System.”

“Where is that?”

“It is located near the core of the galaxy.”

“Oh.”

“Gril, a Quel, came with me, hoping to help. We broke into Nilah’s home and waited for her to return. As I stood in her living room, staring at her, I waited for some hint of recognition, except none ever came. She reached for her communication device and tried to alert the authorities. I knocked it from her hand and restrained her while Gril tried to bring her back to me.”

“Could he undo her conditioning?”

“No. Gril could not detect anything wrong with her. As far as he could tell, she was in her right mind, so at that moment, the rage I had been holding back over the years boiled to the top. The emperor took Nilah from me and replaced her with someone else. Using my powers, I looked deep into her eyes one last time, hoping for some glimpse of the woman I used to know; I could not find her, and there was nothing I could do to save her."

"What happened next?"

"I knew my wife very well. She would not have wanted someone controlling her this way."

"Did you kill her?"

"I could not bring myself to do it; instead, I made her forget I was there and left with Gril."

"Maybe I can figure out a way to reverse this."

"If Gril could not do it, I do not see how you can. She did not recognize me, and it will haunt me for the rest of my life."

They reached a road, so Areus stopped to scan the area.

"What's wrong?" Michael queried.

"Nothing. I will set up an ambush here."

"Who will you ambush?"

"Every day, hundreds of trucks travel roads like this, bringing the emperor's product to the Education Facilities."

"His product?"

"Yes. Humanoids, from all over the galaxy," Areus replied.

He closed his eyes and focused on a nearby tree that had fallen from an earlier storm. Michael watched in awe as the tree lifted off the ground. It floated in the air until it was over the road and fell, blocking the path.

"That's quite a neat trick," Michael observed.

"It is no trick. The High Lord's power moved it. I am just a vessel it flows through."

"Sounds like a bunch of hokeypokey to me. You're probably just more evolved than the rest of us."

"It is not evolution or magic or trickery, Michael. Two powerful forces fight to control this universe; we are their champions."

Michael heard a truck approaching, and the brakes squealed as it stopped a few feet from the tree; the driver and his companion got out to look at the obstacle. Areus moved toward them surprisingly fast and quietly. Even the leaves did not crackle under his weight. Areus stopped about ten feet from them, took the hilt of his sword from its holster, and ignited it. The humming sound got their attention, and they reached for their weapons; they were too slow. As they pulled their firearms out, he cut their guns in two and knocked them out with the butt of the sword.

"Come on, that one's yours."

Areus undressed one of the drivers.

"Mine?"

"Yeah, remove his clothes and badge and put them on; if we go into the facility looking like we do, they will spot us before we even get through the gate."

Michael put the uniform on, which was too big for him, and hoped it would not distract the guard at the facility. Michael finished, faced Areus, and smiled, seeing him struggling with his uniform buttons.

"Won't they question how badly our clothes fit us?" Michael wondered.

"Do not worry about it. I can manipulate a weak mind for a brief time."

He secured the drivers to a nearby tree, put gags on them, and took the driver's seat. Michael sat on the passenger side.

"Are we going to free those people in the back of the truck?"

"If we go in without product, they will stop us."

"We can't just hand them over. These are humanoids!"

"Do you want the intel or not?"

"Of course, I do."

"Then you must make a choice. We either take them back to Mar Nova or bring them to the factory. If we take them back, there will not be another chance like this again because they will be alerted to our method."

Michael thought about what to do and felt a cold chill run down his spine. The price of this fact-finding mission just went way beyond what he expected to pay. He never imagined that humanoid lives would be in his hands so soon.

"I don't know what to do," Michael exhaled loudly.

"Look, we do not know what we will find there; if there is even a small chance that what we discover will save more lives, we must sacrifice them."

"How many do you think there are in the back?"

"About a hundred. Abaddon has them fitted with electric, metal wrist bands that magnetize to a bar above their heads to pack them tightly into five rows to maximize space."

Disgusted by Areus's description, Michael desperately wanted to free them, but Areus was right; they had to find out what was happening inside the factories.

"Fine, let's get going."

Concentrating, Areus motioned for the tree to move out of the way, placed the truck in gear, and moved forward.

"For what it is worth, I think you are making the right decision because no one has ever bothered to find out what they do in these facilities," Areus commented.

"I can't believe Jack didn't try this."

"I do not know his reasons why, yet he did destroy many of them over the years."

"Maybe he hoped it would slow the emperor's ability to build such a large army."

"Perhaps, except something like that is hard to measure, especially if you do not know how many lives are going through it daily."

As they approached the gate, Areus slowed the truck, rolled down his window, stopped where the guard signaled and faced Michael.

"Let me do all the talking."

The sentry took the tablet from Areus and gave him a disapproving look seeing his uniform.

"The cleaners shrunk it, so I have ordered a new one," Areus said, using the High Lord's power.

Accepting the lame excuse, the guard forgot about his uniform and focused on the inventory.

"Everything is in order."

He handed the tablet back to Areus and waved them through.

"Did you use mind manipulation to get him to believe your excuse?" quizzed Michael along the way.

"Yes. Once I gave him an excuse to explain my uniform, I made his rational mind accept it. By removing the distraction, he focused on the list."

"I can see how that can come in handy out here."

"It saved me more than a few times."

Areus backed the truck up to a loading dock, and workers opened the trailer's loading door from inside the facility. Areus and Michael watched the workers connect the metal rails to a machine that pulled them out and into the facility. The procedure was callus, and he wondered how anyone could participate in such a vile act; the machine led one hundred primitive-looking humanoids from the truck into the facility.

"Come on. I will ask the manager to sign the manifest and persuade him to give us a quick tour," Areus urged.

Inside, Areus used his ability to coerce the facility's manager to show them around. Michael thought the manager seemed too excited about telling them how the facility functioned. They reached the observation hallway beside the education corridor, and the manager began explaining.

"As you can see, the product you have just delivered has been secured and is ready for processing."

Earlier, Michael could not see the prisoners' faces as the machine unloaded them from the truck. Here, the look of panic and fear through the transparent glass partition was impossible to ignore, and he regretted bringing them here. He wanted to kill the manager and break through the glass to save them, but the machine left the captives magnetically handcuffed to a bar above them, which kept their hands uncomfortably raised for the reeducation process duration, making a successful rescue impossible.

"The entire operation is automated," the manager continued, bringing Michael out of his brooding. "The machine handles everything from beginning to end. The first step is cleansing; each product must be cleaned and sanitized before going any farther," he nodded toward the prisoners through the glass.

The machines stripped them of what little clothing they wore, water shot out from the machine's arm-like extremities, soapy bubbles appeared from another mechanical arm covering everyone, another set of arms scrubbed them from head to foot thoroughly, and lastly, it gave them a final rinse. The process reminded Michael of a car wash; instead of cars, it cleaned humanoids.

"As you will see during the next step, the machine will secure them to a chair and draw blood to determine if any has an incurable disease or serious flaws in their DNA."

As if on cue, mechanical arms grabbed them by their bonds and moved them into chairs where they kept their head, hands, and feet magnetically secured to the metal bars on the seat. Michael wanted to turn away yet forced himself to watch. One hundred robotic arms holding syringes plunged the needle into their arms simultaneously, drawing blood. The blood moved through the siphons to a small container.

"Where does the blood go?" Michael queried.

"It is sent directly to a lab, where it is examined and diagnosed in seconds by a supercomputer. The process saves us countless hours of waiting for results," the manager explained.

Red lights flashed behind two of the prisoners.

"What does that mean?" Michael inquired.

"Oh dear, there must be something wrong with them. There is no need to worry; we will not introduce them into the population."

"What will happen to them?"

"The machine will kill them. Do not worry; I assure you it will be quick and painless. We take compressed air and release it into the temples. With one quick blast, it is over."

As if on cue, Michael heard a sound that was like a gunshot. Turning, he saw two prisoners with a hole in their temples. Their eyes stared blankly at the ground.

"You son of a bitch!" Michael yelled.

Unable to control his anger, he rushed the manager and choked him. Areus intervened to separate them. Using his powers, Areus made the manager forget Michael's outburst and angrily faced Michael.

"Are you trying to get us killed?"

"How can you stand there and do nothing! He's killing these people!"

Grabbing Michael by the collar, he pushed him up against the glass and spoke through gritted teeth, "Do you think these are the first to die at the emperor's hand? They are only a fraction of what he takes daily! I lost my wife to this system, but I refrain because this information will help us somehow!"

Ashamed, Michael lowered his head, "I'm sorry. You're right."

Areus released him, "I cannot keep him in this trance forever, so either watch in silence or else we leave now, and if you do something like that again, I will throw you into the system myself!"

"I understand. Again, I'm sorry."

Turning back to the manager, Areus brought him out of the daze.

"Uh, where was I?"

"You were telling us about the two that died."

"Ah yes, the machine will take them aside and burn their bodies. Oh, look over there," he pointed to the prisoners. "The machine is inscribing bar codes onto their necks with a laser. All of us have them," he bent his head forward, exposing his code.

"He's proud of it," Michael whispered to Areus.

Having overheard Michael, the manager pleasantly offered, "It is an honor to serve the emperor."

The prisoners screamed from the pain as the lasers burned into their skin; the procedure did not last long.

"Now, if you will walk along with me. You will see the chairs moving to where they will receive a basic trim based on gender. Later, they can choose whatever style they want. With one exception, those designated for the military will receive crew cuts."

Michael, Areus, and the manager followed along in the observatory hallway as mechanical arms trimmed their hair.

"Now, the machine will give each one an injection of MR-12."

"What is that?" Michael asked.

"The serum prepares their minds to receive their education," the manager replied pleasantly.

Again, mechanical arms injected each prisoner with the MR-12 serum, and a glazed look came over each one. Nevertheless, the fear Michael saw on their faces before the injection would stay with him forever.

"As you can see, once they have received the MR-12, the Education Domes are lowered onto their heads. Before educating them, we scan their minds and download their memories into our computers. After that, the information is sent to our technicians for review, just in case they have seen something that would benefit the war effort."

Michael saw the domes, went pale, and started hyperventilating because it was what he feared. The emperor was using his Mind Reader design, the one Ethan stole from Jack, to overwrite the personalities and memories of anyone he chose. Seeing Michael in distress, Areus walked over to help. Michael leaned against Areus for support and watched in horror as the light on the dome flashed blue, showing it was scanning their memories. It turned red, and the manager told them it was now writing someone else's thoughts and memories into their brains.

"What is wrong," Areus whispered.

"This is my fault. I designed these domes."

"Please, keep up," the manager insisted, ignoring Michael's dilemma.

"Can you walk?" Areus questioned.

Nodding, Michael stood and followed the manager as the chairs moved forward. With every step, Michael knew that they were dying. The application he wrote was overwriting their thoughts with someone else's intellect. Although it was not a traditional death, it was still death, and Michael felt solely responsible for it. In due course, the chairs stopped moving at the end of the line, the domes raised, and their restraints popped open. Michael looked at them and noticed that determination had replaced fear. Behind their eyes, an alien intellect took control. They each stood with purpose in unison, walked to a locker, put on a brown jumpsuit, and waited in line.

"What are they waiting for?" wondered Michael.

"Their assignments. Everyone has an ability suited for various kinds of labor. The computer determines what each body is best suited for and imprints their brain with the correct personality and appropriate experiences."

"Where do the personalities come from?" quizzed Michael.

"The emperor, himself, chose each personality for every occupation, so for example, the computer downloaded my personality from a man named Vul, who is best suited to my job. He was from a planet called Fideon V. I (or rather he) was a high-ranking official who diligently worked with the emperor to conquer his homeworld.

His reward was to be imprinted onto thousands of minds, making him immortal."

"That means more than one human mind will have the same personality," Michael spoke matter-of-factly.

"Yes. For example, education facilities everywhere have implanted Vul's personality onto tens of thousands of humanoids, giving the region stability. There is no need for police or social programs. Everyone pulls their weight and has a job to do. They do it without the desire for promotion or material gain because the emperor has already rewarded us."

"That means you send the humanoids that you just educated to work a job somewhere in the galaxy."

"Exactly! It all depends on the age of the product and the need at the time. That decides their education. For example, if the military needs soldiers, any male or female fit to fight will go to a garrison. If our breeding communities need them, we send them there for reproduction. The computer will also pair up individuals based on genetics to produce the best product possible. As the population of our communities increases, so do our food, supplies, and everyday necessities. They are essential to our progress."

"What happens to the children?" Michael inquired.

"They work alongside everyone else until the age of education when we send them to a facility like this."

"And the process starts all over again," Michael frowned.

"Exactly!" the manager exclaimed.

"Are we finished here? Areus queried.

"Almost," Michael answered and faced the manager, "Would it be possible to have a copy of the computer's software?"

"I would be glad to give it to you, except it takes several large servers to store it."

"You can download it to this," Michael handed him a small data stick.

The manager raised an eyebrow, "I will try, but I cannot make any promises."

"Where did you get that?" Areus questioned.

"Stova made it for me before I left, just in case I gained access to their computers. She said it would store millions of Terabytes of data."

"I hope it does not take all day for it to transfer," Areus warned, paused briefly, and continued, "You said you created the domes."

"Yeah."

"How is that possible? I thought Abaddon designed it."

"No. I did a few years ago. I originally made it to read memories. I considered it a parlor game. Supreme Commander Porter discovered what I created, took the schematics, and built thousands."

"How could he do that?"

"I am under contract with the Regime, which owns everything I develop. At first, Supreme Commander Porter used it in the courts to ensure justice prevailed, even though it brought much controversy."

"If you only designed the machine to read memories, how did they make it overwrite them?"

"They didn't. I did. A brief time later, I met a girl, Chu Lian. It was funny. I saw her many times in the cafeteria over the years until she started talking to me one day. I should have known something was off; I just wanted to believe she cared about me. As time went on, we grew closer. At least, I believed it. Knowing she and her mother were from China, I wanted to impress her by learning to speak Mandarin.

"At first, I tried the traditional route, using tapes and books; it took too long, so I figured out a way to imprint thoughts and memories into the brain. However, she left just as I finished developing a language application. A year passed until she returned, and I discovered she was a spy. If that wasn't bad enough, she confessed to inadvertently copying the schematics to the machine and sending it to her employer. I had no idea it had been on the black market for an entire year."

"Abaddon has been using these factories for hundreds of years; it cannot be the same machine you created," Areus concluded.

"It can if the person who ended up buying it from Chu Lian's employer traveled back in time."

"Is that even possible?"

"Yes. It happened."

"If what you are saying is true, had you not invented it, someone else would have. Even if it did not exist, the emperor would have chosen another control method."

"It doesn't matter. I'm responsible for this!"

"Your intentions were good. How someone else uses what you have created is on them. Look, I lost my wife to that machine, and until now, I believed the emperor made it, so if anyone has the right to hate you, it is me, yet I do not. Now, stop feeling sorry for yourself and use the information we get to figure out a way to stop the emperor."

"I promise. I'll do everything in my power to end this war."

"Ah, there you are, my friends," the manager had returned with the data stick. "I must say that this technology is impressive. Will Imperial Majesty Abaddon release it to the public soon?"

"Yes, do not worry. Everyone will have access to it shortly," Areus lied. "Now, go back to your office and forget you ever saw us."

The manager turned and walked away in a trance with glazed eyes, allowing Michael and Areus to escape in the truck without incident. Upon returning to the site, where they accosted the drivers, Areus set them free, and before leaving, he made them believe that they had dropped off their cargo and were on their way home. He also made them forget ever seeing him and Michael. On their way back to Mar Nova, Michael held up the data stick.

"All right, you son of a bitch, let's see if I can figure out a way to stop you."

Chapter 99

Michael and Areus returned to Mar Nova, where Stova waited for them; Michael thanked Areus before he left. Stova escorted Michael to his office, where she obtained his approval for several projects and operations that needed his review. Afterward, she told him that Dawn had returned; Michael was excited to speak with her again. He raced to her office with Stova and found her sitting behind a desk, frowning.

"I'm sorry; I've confirmed Jack's death," she sniffled, holding back tears.

"Did you find his body?"

"Yes. I returned to the hotel and ordered my team to search the area. We found him on the street, hundreds of floors below. I had him cremated. I hope you don't mind; I'm not one for funerals."

"I understand. Neither am I. Did you find out who attacked us?"

"A group calling themselves *Eblions for the emperor* claimed responsibility. I have my team reviewing evidence and video; they wore masks, so it's unlikely we'll find Jack's killer."

"That's too bad. I'm sorry this happened, but don't blame yourself. You did your best to protect him."

"My best wasn't good enough; now Eblion will fall to the emperor because the attack made Intransigent look weak."

"What if I give a speech on Eblion? Will that help?"

"No. It's much too dangerous, especially now. It's just another world we'll have to count as lost."

"We'll figure out something."

"Is what Stova tells me true? Have you taken control of Mar Nova?"

"Yes. I agreed to be Regent until we could find Jack; now that you have confirmed his death, it looks like I'm here permanently. Besides, I have much to atone for."

"What do you mean?"

"I asked Areus to take me inside one of the emperor's Education Facilities. Dawn, he's using the mind reader to create his army."

"That was a foolish thing to do, Michael! They could have caught you, and the emperor would also control you!"

"It had to be done. I need intel."

"Did you get any?"

"Yes. I have a copy of his software and all the data stored on his servers. I'll have the Mar Novians sift through it later."

"I can see you'll be just as reckless as Jack."

"I'm not worried. I have you to protect me," he grinned, trying to lighten the mood.

"Knowing what happened to Jack, I would prefer if you put someone else in charge of your security; I can use my ships for other things, like making the first contact with other worlds or something."

"I thought you would want to protect me. Besides, it would allow us to get to know each other."

"There'll be plenty of time for us to meet during vacations; in any case, you're too reckless, Michael. I'm having a tough time dealing with the guilt of Jack's death. I don't know what I would do if something happened to you during my watch."

"I understand. Don't worry about it; I'll find someone else. Where will you go?"

"I'll go wherever you tell me. You're the one in charge now."

"You've been here longer than me, Dawn. I don't know what I'm doing. Why don't you take the position as Regent?"

"No. Jack wanted you in charge of Mar Nova; don't worry, you'll figure out what to do. Besides, you have Stova to help you. She knows everything that goes on around here."

"Yes, she does, and she's waiting outside the door to give me more forms to review."

"Call her inside. We can find out what she needs me to do, and I'll get started," Dawn remarked.

"Stova," he called through a crack in the door.

"Yes, Regent."

"Dawn declined to take charge of my security, so what else do we have for her to do?"

"There are still thousands of worlds that we have not contacted yet. A few hundred planets have requested our help defending against the emperor's attack. There are a few thousand battles already underway that she could support. There are…" she started to say until Michael interrupted her to speak to Dawn.

"What if you map all the factories that produce the mind reader?"

"Ah, you want a search and destroy mission."

"No. Just search for now. I want to know their location on every planet."

"To what end, Michael?"

"Once we know where they are, we can make a coordinated attack, taking out as many as possible. That way, the emperor won't have time to move them before we get a chance to destroy them."

"That's a good idea, Regent," Stova replied, amazed.

"She's right, Michael. A coordinated attack would slow him down, but it would stretch our forces too thin. He controls millions of worlds."

"I have a plan for that, too; for now, I need you to start mapping each world with its locations."

"I think it's doable. The emperor usually doesn't leave starships behind on a conquered world."

"Really? That sounds arrogant."

"Oh, they're fully protected from air assault by ground-to-space missiles. Also, he leaves a regiment behind. Attacking would be foolish; sending in a two-person team to scout the area would work."

"Good, keep me informed of your progress."

He faced Stova, "Would you give us some privacy?"

"Yes, Regent," she answered and stepped back outside to wait in the hallway.

"Before you leave, I was hoping you would tell me what happened to you after you traveled back in time."

"I don't know, Michael. It was so long ago. I would prefer not to dredge up the past right now."

"At least tell me what happened to Thomas?"

She sighed, "All right, I planned to tell you at some point. We landed in an unpopulated area in 1952. I brought enough supplies and equipment to keep us going until we could buy an island for Jack in the Caribbean Sea, where he set up his lab, and Thomas and I got married."

"Wow! That's wonderful, Dawn!"

"It was, for a while. I brought back enough gold with me to get whatever we wanted. Thomas decided to buy a yacht, and we traveled the world. It was the best time of my life."

"What happened next?"

"We traveled for a few years and decided to settle down. We planned to have children and raise them in London."

"I guess by the look on your face, something went wrong."

"At first, everything was fine. We bought our home; I called Jack, asked him to visit us, and told him about our plan. He seemed genuinely excited about having grandchildren; a few months later, Thomas began to change."

"How?"

"He became paranoid and accused me of having an affair, which I wasn't. Every day we argued, and each one was more violent until one day, I returned from seeing the doctor, and for reasons unknown, he completely lost control and attacked me. That was the first and last time a man ever hit me. Let me tell you; it hurt like hell. I'll never forget the fierce look on his face as he repeatedly punched me in the stomach. I begged him to stop.

"I fell backward, and he hit my face, breaking my nose and fracturing my eye socket. As I lay on the floor, holding my injury and moaning, he grabbed a sharp knife, sat on my stomach, and pinned me to the floor. I couldn't get up, so I tried slapping and punching him; it didn't help. He took the knife and cut my cheek, leaving the scar on my face."

"That's horrible, Dawn. Why did he do that?"

"He continued cutting me, marking me with his family crest so that everyone would know I belonged to him. This area here is as far as he got before I could stop him," she turned her cheek and pointed to the scar.

"What did you do?"

"I knocked over a coffee table with a heavy ashtray on it. With my left hand, I picked it up and hit him once on the head. He stopped moving. For the longest time, I stood in shock, staring at his body, until I came to my senses and called for help. They told me Thomas was dead. Thankfully, they didn't charge me for his murder. The police took my testimony, studied the crime scene, and agreed that he had attacked me. I returned from the hospital, sold our home, and went to help Jack with his experiments."

"I guess you must hate Thomas now."

"I did hate him for a long time. He did not get the chance to learn that the doctor told me I was pregnant; his attack caused me to have a miscarriage in the hospital. I would have had a baby girl: I named her Tabitha. I lost my husband and unborn baby in one week; it left me devastated."

"I can't imagine what that must have been like."

"It hasn't been easy. I put a tattoo over my scar as a constant reminder of what happened, so I will never make the same mistake. I should have never allowed myself to care about him."

"Loving someone isn't a mistake, Dawn. Even though it didn't work out with Thomas, it doesn't mean you can't find someone else who can make you happy."

"The memory is too painful. I cannot get over it, even in five hundred years."

"There are no words to convey my sympathy."

"That's sweet of you to say," she paused, looking past Michael for a moment. "I still visit their graves on Tabitha's anniversary. I had them buried beside each other at the Highgate Cemetery in London. I usually sit there for hours, crying."

"I can understand why you were reluctant to talk about it. Now I feel bad for insisting that you tell me what happened."

"It's all right. As I said, I would have told you; at least you won't have to wonder why I kept the scar with a tattoo over it."

"True, it was something I thought of every time we met. I hate that you had it so hard. I wish I could have been there for you, but I'm here for you now. If you ever need me for anything, let me know."

Dawn smiled, "Thank you. I want you to know that I will always love and trust you. You are my brother. Everything I've done and will do is for our family, what's left of it," she stood to leave.

"Before you go, I'm planning something special tonight, and I was hoping you would be there."

"Sure, what is it?"

"It's a surprise; I think it will lighten your mood."

"Is Stova having a party in your honor?"

"It won't be here. It'll be on Earth, within the Regime territory."

"I'd love to be there, Michael, except I can't attend. Porter would arrest me on the spot for my role in freeing Jack."

"I understand."

"Thank you. Before I begin the mission, I'll give my crew a few days of rest; they've been going nonstop for months. We'll land on Minaria IV; its equator has thousands of tropical islands for vacationing. By the end of the week, I'll begin searching for those factories and give you an update in a month."

"I look forward to hearing from you. Be safe."

Chapter 100

Earth
The Regime - Washington, D.C. - Capitol Building
May 20, 2452

Later that evening, Michael sat in silence in front of Supreme Commander Porter, waiting for his reply. His new position on Mar Nova would affect his contract with the Regime, so he had to speak with Supreme Commander Porter face to face rather than through a computer display. Supreme Commander Porter became silent when he heard the news, making Michael worry. The Regime rarely ended a contract before its fulfillment, and if Supreme Commander Porter decided to force him to finish his obligation, Michael had to leave and never return.

He hoped that would not be the case. It was odd meeting with Supreme Commander Porter as an equal. Now that Michael accepted the Mar Novians' Regent's position, he did not just rule a country; he governed a world. It was a lot to take in. The long silence gave Michael time to contemplate everything that had happened over the past day. It was hard to believe that so much had changed in so little time.

"I can't believe you're leaving us," Supreme Commander Porter said, bringing Michael out of his thoughts.

"I don't want to go. I want nothing more than to return to my old life, but I've seen what the emperor is capable of, and I must do something to stop him. He's using my invention to kill trillions of people and using their bodies to conquer the galaxy."

"These factories you mentioned will cause me to lose sleep at night."

"Believe me; I know how you feel."

"Will you be living on Mar Nova?"

"Yes, I plan to have the Mar Novians move the planet into this system. That way, we can more easily coordinate our efforts against the emperor. I also plan to set up a Space Navy with as many starships as we can build to help guard our planets. The Mar Novians know how to build battleships designed for space travel."

Supreme Commander Porter shook his head, "I thought teleporting across the galaxy was the ultimate technology. Now I hear you can move whole planets from one system to another and build starships; it's quite a change from your normal routine."

"I'm still pinching myself because it feels like a dream."

Supreme Commander Porter stood, extended his hand, and asked, "What should I call you, now that you rule an entire planet?"

"Michael is fine."

"From now on, I want you to call me Jay since we're on a first-name basis."

Standing, Michael shook his hand and replied, "Thank you, Supreme - I mean, Jay - boy, that will take some getting used to."

"Since we'll be working together, I recommend daily briefings, say, 9 AM Regime time?"

"Agreed. I'll speak to Zorion later and update him. I'm sure he'll want to help us fight this war."

"I agree. Well, until tomorrow."

"Before I go, I have a couple of requests, if you don't mind...."

Chapter 101

Earth
The Regime - Washington, D.C. - Fort McNair
May 20, 2452

Standing under a Willow tree in the atrium, Michael fidgeted with his tie. Beside him, Alex whistled a familiar tune that only made him even more nervous. Jay authorized him to brief his mother and stepdad at his request on a few top-secret events. Among those, he told her he met Dawn, and they were working together. The rest of what he had to say to her should have been easy, except it was not.

He told her about Jack's escape and eventual death, the Mar Novians and their successful attempt at saving the planet, Akil, and, the most difficult, Yanamai is an alien. She did not believe him until he showed her proof of everything, and given the circumstances, he thought she took the news very well. She was in a daze during their journey to the atrium and started feeling better after they arrived.

Earlier, he entered the atrium with his mother and stepdad and watched the guests make small talk with one another. Everyone accepted his invitation, except for Zorion and Dawn. It was understandable because Zorion had to put his society back together, and Dawn was a wanted criminal. He looked at his watch again. Only thirty seconds had passed since the last check. Michael faced Alex.

"Where are they?"

"Relax, Michael; they'll be here soon," Alex replied.

*****

Rushing toward the atrium, where Michael took her on their first date, Yanamai fidgeted with her dress. Lisa walked beside her, pulling on the material to help straighten it.

"Really," Yanamai huffed, "I do not understand why I must wear this white dress to a meeting. Do you know how hard it is to keep white material clean? There is nothing on the shoulders to hold it up, and it keeps moving."

She fidgeted with it again.

"And why is General Saunders holding it in the atrium? Something is not right. There are hundreds of other venues he could have chosen."

"General Saunders classified the meeting details; I can't tell you. Now stop complaining and practice your smile," barked Lisa.

"Lisa, I do not know much about the Earthian culture, yet even I know it is unusual for the General to insist that I fix my hair in this fancy manner, just for a simple meeting. Furthermore, why did the hairdresser put (what did she call it), oh yes, baby's breath in my hair?"

"You look pretty. That's all you should care about right now. Besides, we're here, so start smiling and shut up!" Lisa opened the door for her.

Yanamai stepped inside, pulling up the lower part of her dress because it dragged the floor. Inside, she heard a group of people talking nearby, moved closer to their voices, and saw General Saunders standing under a Willow tree with its branches dangling overhead. Hundreds of white lights hung in patterns on the trees and walkway.

Seeing the bridge again brought back memories of discovering her feelings for Michael on their first date. She smiled, remembering how fast everything changed with him. Had it not been for Garbi's plan to trick him, she may have never discovered her desire for him. The closer she came to General Saunders, the more people appeared. At least they were all wearing something formal, which made her feel slightly more at ease.

She saw the faces of those attending the meeting and became confused. It made sense that General Saunders, Garbi, and Lisa would be at a Regime meeting; it did not make sense that Michael's parents, her parents, and Jared were there. Also, Supreme Commander Porter's presence made her nervous. *What kind of meeting is this?* In her bewilderment, she absentmindedly allowed Lisa to guide her in front of General Saunders.

They stopped walking, and Yanamai whispered to Lisa, "What is going on?"

"Shhh, you'll see," Lisa smiled.

From behind the Willow Tree, Yanamai saw Michael approaching with a bright, nervous smile. She barely noticed Alex walking beside him because Michael had her full attention. The situation became more confusing as he came toward her wearing an Earthian Tuxedo with his hair combed in a fashion Yanamai had not seen before. Pushing aside the distractions, she focused on Michael and smiled.

It was the first time she had heard from him since he left to investigate the education facilities. She was happy to see him safe. *Ah, now I know why we are here. Michael will tell us about what happened off-world.* She expected him to hug her as he drew close, but Michael stopped a few paces away. She frowned as he knelt on one knee until realizing what was happening.

His actions reminded her of a similar ritual she saw in an Earthian romantic movie. Turning to Lisa for an answer, she gasped, seeing Lisa nod, confirming her suspicion. She looked back to Michael, who held a box with a ring inside and looked up at her.

"I'll never forget our first date," he paused, seeing her blush.

"I learned you were loyal because you did something for your sister that made you uncomfortable. You also proved persistent because you followed me into the jungle, even though I told you to stay away. Strangers kidnapped me, and you showed courage by risking your life to rescue me; the time I thought you died, you showed me the true meaning of loss.

"Now, every time I see you smile at me, I know what it feels like to have someone as incredible as you love me. You're beautiful, stubborn, smart, kind, and gentle. Although we only met a few days ago, it seems like I've known you all my life. In that brief time, I've grown to respect and love you very much. So, Yanamai, daughter of Soro and Lilzah, would you do me the honor of becoming my wife?"

As she listened, her breaths became shallow and fast. The moment felt as if it were a dream. *Is this real? How did I win him so quickly?* At first, she questioned her success, yet there was no mistaking the scene playing out before her. Michael was down on one knee, performing the Earthian custom she so dearly desired. The moment the words left his mouth, she responded.

"Yes, Michael. I will marry you!"

The guests applauded and cheered as Michael slid the engagement ring onto Yanamai's trembling finger.

"I asked General Saunders to perform the ceremony. That is if you don't mind getting married right now?" Michael smiled sheepishly.

"I do not mind at all," she answered happily.

As General Saunders continued to speak, Yanamai carefully listened to every word. Unfamiliar with the Earthian vows; she wanted to understand their meaning to avoid breaking them. The ceremony only lasted a few hundred heartbeats until it was time for Michael to slip the wedding ring on her finger; her hand still trembled.

"You may kiss the bride," General Saunders said.

They embraced in a kiss. At one point, Alex yelled out for them to get a room, everyone laughed, and the guests cheered as they walked over to congratulate the newlyweds. Even Yanamai's mother gave a practiced smile, approaching the couple.

"Where do you plan on living, Akil or Earth?" Lilzah questioned.

"I am sure we will live on Earth," Yanamai guessed, looking to Michael for confirmation.

"I was hoping Yanamai would live with me on Mar Nova," Michael offered.

"Mar Nova? Where is Mar Nova? I do not remember seeing it on Earthian maps," Lilzah huffed.

"It's not on Earth. It's a planet now orbiting a gas giant on the outer rim of the Milky Way; very soon, it will be in our solar system," Michael looked at Yanamai for an answer.

"Are you sure you want to lead the Mar Novians?" inquired Yanamai.

"Yes. I'll explain the details later; the abridged version is, they need me."

"Very well, that is where we will live," Yanamai responded.

"No!" Lilzah snapped. "Your offspring should be raised on Akil!"

"Excuse me, what makes you think that? The Regime has an excellent education system," Michael's mother chimed in.

"That's enough!" Michael exclaimed sharply.

With a raised eyebrow, Yanamai looked at Michael with surprise. His take-charge reaction reminded her of how he spoke to Stova on Mar Nova. Seeing it again excited her.

"All our parents have done an excellent job raising us. Now it's time for us to make our own decisions. I will move Mar Nova into this solar system so everyone can be part of our lives; you will not dictate where we can and cannot live. Is that understood?" Michael glared.

His boldness shocked Lilzah. She knew by the look in his eyes that he would not back down, and there was a good reason. As Mar Nova's Regent, he must have respect, especially if someone did not give it to him. The last thing he needed was Yanamai's mother thinking she could manipulate him. She would end up undermining his authority, and he could not allow it. Plus, if he could not stand up to Yanamai's mother, he had no business leading the Mar Novians and others to battle the emperor. Instead of arguing with him, Lilzah, embarrassed by his sharp admonishment, sheepishly smiled.

"I apologize. You are right."

Smiling, Soro looked at Michael and nodded his approval; Michael's mother approached.

"Michael, this is all new to me. You've been distant for a long time, and now you're moving to another planet. How do you expect me to react?"

"Don't worry. I won't be distant anymore. I know who I am now and want my family close."

"I'm glad to hear you say that," Jared approached the group smiling.

"Why?" Michael asked suspiciously.

"I want to join you on Mar Nova."

"Don't you have a contract with the Regime?" Michael queried.

"Supreme Commander Porter suggested I go with you. He said you need all the help you can get," Jared explained.

"Yes, except it will be dangerous. Are you sure you want to go?"

"I think it's about time the Stewart brothers worked together. Don't you?"

Michael smiled, "There's a position that just opened. I'll put you in charge of my security. Welcome aboard."

"Great. After the reception, I'll pack my things and meet you. Uh, by the way, how do we get to Mar Nova?"

"Just meet me at the Interstellar Transportation Station."

Jared gave him a brotherly hug, and everyone sat to eat. The celebration ended; Michael said his goodbyes to his guests and assured them they would see each other often. Facing Alex was hard because they had been friends for such a long time. They had a teary goodbye until Michael and Yanamai went to their Regime apartments to pack.

Chapter 102

Earth
The Regime - Washington, D.C. - Fort McNair
May 20, 2452

On her way home, Wu Luli ran into Alex in the hallway. Seeing him in a Tuxedo, she asked him the occasion. When he was not forthcoming, she pressed him; his answer shook her. In her apartment, she sat in front of her monitor. Alex told her that Michael was recording the ceremony, so she hacked into the server. As her finger hovered over the execution key, she paused. *Do I want to watch this?* The answer was no. *How could anyone want to see the person they love married to another?* Without thinking, her finger landed on the keyboard and an image of General Saunders, wearing his military uniform dress, came into view.

As the camera's eye moved, she saw Michael's family and recognized two others as Yanamai's parents. Soon after, Yanamai entered and stood before General Saunders, wearing a beautiful white gown. *That should be me in that dress.* Michael approached her behind the Willow tree and got down on one knee. The pain became too much to bear, and tears flowed down Wu Luli's cheeks. Although Michael had forgiven her, seeing him with Yanamai destroyed any future dreams of reuniting with him. As General Saunders began the ceremony, she watched, undiscerning, as her thoughts drifted defiantly.

Michael had been her lover and best friend. They grew to trust each other entirely until she broke that confidence. He came to mean so much to her that she never dreamed someone else could become so dear to him. Her thoughts were far away, yet her eyes returned to the ceremony ripping her heart out. Finally, she conceded. *She is a good fit for him; he can count on her. Not like me.* Their eyes met adoringly, and they kissed. She closed her eyes against the burning pain rising inside. *He will be happy. It is what I want for him. I guess that will have to be enough.* The ceremony was brief; for Wu Luli, it lasted a lifetime.

Wu Luli took a moment to collect herself as the guests moved toward the newlyweds to congratulate them. *It's over now. There is no hope of a future together.* Her hand moved to shut down the connection until stopping because she heard that they planned to move to another planet. *How is this possible*? Before contemplating the whole meaning of their conversation, she hears that they must pack before they leave. *Do I dare?*

*****

Standing behind the cracked door of the building's emergency exit, Wu Luli waited for Michael to arrive; he walked the hall alone and opened his door. Knowing it was her last chance to speak with him privately, she walked up behind him. Before the door closed, she put her hand up to stop it.

"Michael, it's me," she whispered through a tightly clenched throat.

"Chu L…I mean, Wu Luli," he paused, "What are you doing here?"

"I'm going away for a little while. I just wanted to say goodbye. May I come in?" As Michael hesitates, she continues, "Please, it's only for a moment. Don't worry. I won't try to seduce you. I know you're married." She forced a smile.

He let her in and closed the door. Just being alone with him again made her heart leap to her mouth. She brutally swallowed it. *It's too late to think like that.*

"I won't take much of your time; I just wanted to congratulate you on your marriage to Yanamai. She's beautiful," she forced the words out of her mouth.

"Thank you. I know it's sudden, and I barely know her, but I feel…."

"Like you can trust her. I can understand. She did risk her life for you. She makes you feel secure." *The feeling I once gave you.*

"Exactly."

"I hear you're moving to another planet?" she asks, ferociously pushing away thoughts of their wedding night.

"I shouldn't be surprised you know that information. You are a spy," he replied, smiling.

"Some habits are hard to break, I guess."

417

"It's called Mar Nova. It's in a distant part of the galaxy right now, and, as I'm sure you're aware, it'll be in our solar system soon, so I won't be far from home."

"How is that even possible?"

"Their technology is advanced; I wouldn't believe it myself, except I've seen them do it."

"What will you do on Mar Nova?"

He smiled in disbelief, "I'm going to be their ruler."

"Really? How wonderful! I would love to hear how you managed it."

"It's a long story; the condensed version is that the only way to save an alien world called Akil from imminent destruction was to accept the position of Regent."

"It sounds to me like you saved many lives."

"I can't take credit for it. It was the Mar Novians who did all the work. I just encouraged them."

"I've always admired your honesty."

A gleam of disappointment was visible on his face, "I want you to know I tried to find a way back to you."

"I made too many mistakes and was too late to rectify them." *A lesson I will never forget.*

"I wish you would have returned to me sooner."

"Trust me; no one wishes that more than me."

Staring into his eyes, she pushed away the strong impulse to blurt out that she was pregnant with his child. If Wu Luli had given him that information, he might change his mind about staying with Yanamai. She knew he would hate her for it. *No, I'll raise our child on my own.* With her last bit of strength, she forced another smile.

"I should leave. I don't want to upset your new bride before your marriage is barely an hour old."

As she started to leave, Michael moved his hand to her arm. Stopping, she turned to face him. *No, don't do this. You're happy now. I will only destroy it for you.*

"I want you to know that I'm still your friend. I will always care about what happens to you."

"Thank you; I needed to hear that. At least you don't hate me."

"I could never hate you."

But you can never love me again, either. "Friends then?" She extended her hand.

Michael leaned in, hugged her, and whispered in her ear, "If you need me for anything, I'll be there. General Saunders knows how to contact me."

Abruptly, he kissed her on the cheek; without another word, he walked to his bedroom to pack his things. Standing motionless, she listened to his footsteps until he disappeared. She left his apartment and blinked as tears rushed down her cheeks. Knowing there was no chance of sharing her life with him would haunt her until the day she died. Looking down, she touched her belly. *At least you gave me this wonderful gift before we parted.*

Chapter 103

Akil
Argi City
The 22,284[th] Terrestrial Rotation of the Second Summer

Standing in the shadows, Olan watched the apartment where his Skean compass led him. He looked at his timekeeper. Olan had been waiting for about a quarter of a Terrestrial Revolution for the opportunity to get inside. Earlier, he saw someone enter with a large plate of moss. It was not hard to surmise that the Akilian elite he had been spying on helped one of the surviving Skeans from the earlier battle.

The Akilian left the apartment, so Olan appeared from his dark hiding place and blended into the crowd. Level ten was home to some of the wealthiest Argians in the city. Their attire was so cumbersome that it made it difficult for Olan to move, let alone mimic their swagger. He looked left at the door, then right, to ensure no one was watching him; satisfied, he removed a small set of tools.

With a practiced hand, he picked the lock, stepped inside, shut the door behind him, and quietly stood in the darkness. Using a small handheld light, he searched the first room; it was empty, so he passed through the kitchen and saw a plate of uneaten moss sitting on the table. *Someone is here*. Looking at his Skean compass, he saw it flash a warning and unsheathed his sword. *I am getting close.*

Standing in the hallway, he saw a dim light through a space underneath a bedroom door. He approached cautiously, opened the door with his left hand, and brought it back, joining the other to hold the handle of his sword. Inside, he saw someone with horrific wounds on blood-soaked bedsheets. Her clothes showed the seriousness of her injuries.

Earlier, he watched as someone wearing Gau's mask sent a fighter over the guardrail like a child's toy during the fight. *It must be her*. It was a long way down to the bottom from that point. She must have used her powers to slow her descent. If not, regaining consciousness so soon would be very unlikely. *The other brought her here*. Standing in the doorway, he saw her eyes turn toward him; she recognized him immediately.

"Olan," she spoke with a croaky voice. "How did you find me?"

Only by her voice did he know it was Nayrah. It was a struggle not to cringe at her swollen, distorted features. He estimated it would take about a hundred Terrestrial Rotations to recover based on her current condition. Nevertheless, he studied her and realized that she was too weak to lift a hand in her state, let alone use her Skean powers to defend herself, and it was an opportunity he could not pass up.

"Why is the question you should be asking," he responded.

"I know you are angry with me," she paused to cough up some blood. "You have every right to be; I need you to understand that I had to do it."

"We all have choices, Nayrah; you chose to betray me."

"Gecheana ordered me to kill Zorion."

"I guess she ordered you to use me to do it for you."

"Yes, she did. She knew you could get close to him," she lied.

"I am glad her plan failed."

"I want you to know that it was hard for me to make you do it because I love you."

"Love? You do not know what it is to love someone."

"I cried after I sent you away to kill him. I did not think I would ever see you again."

"Your feelings of regret are of little consolation."

"Tell me, what can I do to convince you that I love you?"

"Renounce your Skean powers and swear never to use them again."

"You do not know what you are asking. My powers are a part of me, just like my body."

"Look at what your powers have brought you. You have hit bottom. I imagine the fall broke every bone in your body."

With a slight smile, she held up her little finger from the bed, "Not this one."

"This is no time for jokes. What is your decision?"

"If I could, I would leave everything for you; even if I tried, it is impossible. I have known the works of darkness my entire life. I was born in darkness, and in darkness, I will die."

"I am sorry to hear you say that."

"We *can* still be together."

“How?”

“Once I recover, I will teach you the ways of darkness, so we can walk in it together and rid Akil of the Saiph, allowing me to claim Zorion’s seat with you by my side.”

“I saw you fight another on the top level. There is still one more Skean on Akil. She will fight you for the position.”

“You speak of Jadell. I can control her. She is my daughter, our daughter.”

“I have a daughter?”

“She is the only one left of three offspring. Otsoa and Va’ron were yours as well.”

“I recently deduced that Thea is your alter ego; I did not suspect I parented any offspring. I suppose Jadell is Yetta.”

“Yes.”

“Why have you hidden this from me?”

“I have never loved Zorion, and I detested the thought of giving birth to his offspring, yet I have loved you from the moment we met, and so it was an honor to give birth to your progeny. After Otsoa was born, I wanted to leave Zorion; Gecheana would not allow it, so I thought it best to hide it from you because I knew what you would do if you found out.”

“I would have told Zorion.”

“Exactly, and Gecheana would have killed you.”

“I thought of leaving you many times, except I could not bring myself to do it. Did you use your powers?”

“Please forgive me, my love. It was selfish of me to keep you as a consort; I needed you and still do.”

“You have robbed me of my life. I could have met someone else who did not live in darkness. I could have been happy.”

“Did I not make you happy, my love?”

“When we were together, yes. The time between our visits was very lonely for me. I hated you for it and myself for not leaving you; at least now, I know I did not have a choice.”

“We can be together. I will give myself to you fully. I will hide nothing from you. Just agree to share my journey. I love you, Olan.”

“No,” he replied flatly.

“What do we do? I cannot live in your world; you refuse to reside in mine.”

Having heard her side of things, he believed she was telling the truth. It only confirmed what he had to do; stop her while she was weak. If he allowed Nayrah to recover, he could not defeat her without Julie's help because she was too powerful. He sheathed his sword, walked over to her bedside, and brushed her hair with his left hand as his right hand found its way into his pocket to retrieve one of his poison darts. As he stared at her with sad eyes, she sensed something was wrong. Unable to flee or even move, she looked at him with raised eyebrows.

"What are you going to do?" she asked tremblingly.

"I am sorry. You leave me no choice. Goodbye, Nayrah."

Olan moved the dart toward her throat and felt an invisible hand grab his wrist, stopping it from moving; he pushed with all his might yet could not get the tip to reach her skin. Looking down at her, he could tell the strain of using the mystic power was taking its toll. Still, he continued to push with all his might. The strength of her mysterious energy surprised him. Even though her injuries severely weakened her body, she had enough power to resist him. It only reassured him that he was making the right decision to stop her now.

"Please! Do not do this! I love you! We can still be together!"

"You are evil, Nayrah. I could never be with someone so vile."

The two struggled for a few hundred heartbeats until Nayrah finally succumbed. The dart moved toward her neck. Although she tried, her body was too weak to fight him. The dart's tip penetrated the skin on her neck and sunk into her carotid artery, releasing its venom. The poison entered her bloodstream, causing Nayrah to gasp in pain. The drug burned as it coursed through her veins. He took her hands and held them tightly as she looked at him with raised eyebrows. Tears streamed down his cheeks as he watched her life slip away. Struggling, she raised her finger to wipe away a tear from his face.

"I forgive you."

Her hand dropped to the bed, but he held her tightly, even after she took her last breath. He occasionally stroked her hair and kissed her forehead until saying his final goodbye. He stood, sighed loudly, retrieved a clean sheet to wrap her body, used the service elevator to the catacombs, and laid her to rest in a tomb the city had reserved for him.

Chapter 104

Earth
Scotland - Edinburgh
May 20, 2452

Larkin was glad to be home and even happier to see Sarah and Sable in front of his house. He woke from the nightmare of losing them to a fire and was anxious to be with them again. Seeing him, Sable ran into his arms. Larkin scooped her up with one hand, repeatedly kissed her on the cheeks, and set her down, so she could return to her mother, who waited for him on the front porch.

Sarah waved for Larkin to join them. Sable tugged her apron so that Sarah would hold her. Sable smiled at him, giggling. He walked to meet Sarah until a strong gust of wind stirred, preventing him from moving forward. Larkin struggled against the tempest, unable to reach them. As the wind blew faster, he saw that they were in trouble. Sarah cried out for him with outstretched arms; the wind would not allow Larkin to move.

The house was ablaze with high flames flickering out the windows. Larkin panicked and willed himself to move forward; the wind pushed him back two steps for every forward one. The flames completely engulfed his house, which exploded, consuming Sarah and Sable; the fire subsided, leaving Sarah and Sable as ash.

He stared at his wife's and daughter's black, powdery statue as the wind took them away. At first, the top of her head dissolved, and the more it blew, the more of her image floated away with the breeze until she and Sable disappeared. Awaking from his nightmare, Larkin jumped from his seat on the jet. Still reeling from the dream, he screamed so loud that it shook the plane.

"Can someone shut him up? I'm trying to land in high winds!" the captain yelled.

The back wheels touched the ground, and the jet bounced, forcing Larkin to fall into his seat; the plane stopped, and Aiden left the cockpit.

"Are you all right?"

Larkin replied as if nothing happened, "Yeah, I had a bad dream, is all. Are we in Scotland?"

"Yes. We're here."

"Good," he looked at Tucker, and they stood, getting ready to leave the plane.

"What do you want me to do?" Aiden asked.

"Stay here with the captain. I'll tie 'em up before leavin'; whatever you do, don't let 'em out of your sight."

Larkin secured the captain and met with the airport owner with Tucker by his side. He was glad to find out that General Bailey's contact helped them. The Regime already paid the owner for a rental car and fuel for their return trip. Before they left, the owner passed on information from General Bailey's contact. The dossier suggested that Dawn had a close relationship with the Royal Duke Holdings Company's CEO.

Larkin adjusted to driving on the road's right side with a few near misses and parked in front of the Holdings Company. As they walked inside, a guard warned them he would have the car towed if they left the vehicle there. Larkin threatened him, so the sentry reversed his position and assured him no one would touch it. Inside, Larkin set his fists down on the security guard's desk. His short-sleeve shirt left his bulky, intimidating triceps exposed. Although the guard tried to hide it, Larkin's predatory instincts sensed his fear.

"What can I do for you?" the guard inquired cautiously.

"I'm looking for Dawn Pierce."

The guard checked his computer, "She hasn't checked in."

"What about the CEO? I heard he has a close relationship with her. Maybe he can tell us where she is?"

"I'm sorry. He hasn't checked in either."

"Where's his office?" Tucker impatiently demanded.

"You can't go up. It's a restricted area."

Larkin ignored the guard, spun his monitor around, and searched for the CEO's office location. As he did, the sentry grabbed the phone, trying to call the police; Tucker glared at him, and he put the phone down.

"Got it. He's on the top floor," Larkin remarked.

"Go. I'll watch things down here," Tucker reassured.

As Larkin stepped off the elevator, the receptionist greeted him and asked for his appointment time.

"I want to see your CEO's office," Larkin demanded.

“I’m sorry, Sir. He’s not here.”

Ignoring her, he searched for the CEO’s office; he also found an office with Dawn’s name on the opposite side, where he searched for any clues as to her whereabouts. Behind him, the secretary followed, demanding him to leave; he ignored her and continued to ransack the drawers.

“Where does she live?”

“I cannot give out that information.”

“Look. She’s responsible for the death of my wife and daughter! Now I don’t want to hurt you, but if you don’t give me what I need,” he paused, leaving the threat hanging in the air.

“Dunnottar Castle,” she blurted.

“Where’s that?”

She gave him directions, so he returned with Tucker to the vehicle, and they sped off to find the castle. About an hour later, they arrived. Once Tucker subdued the guard on duty, they walked inside to find that someone had already searched it.

“Looks like we’re not the only ones looking for her,” Tucker mused.

“You go upstairs. I’ll go down.”

They separated; Larkin did not find anything in the basement, so he checked the first floor, went upstairs, and found Tucker in what used to be an office.

“Did you find anything?” Larkin queried.

“Yeah. There’s a hologram picture of a woman.”

Tucker nodded toward a black disc on the table. Larkin pressed the button, and an image of a woman with long, dark, wavy hair and blonde highlights appeared. The depiction briefly moved as if she was looking at someone away from the camera lens, repeating itself.

“That’s her. It matches her picture in the dossier. I’ll take it with us,” Larkin commented.

“She deleted most of the computer’s data,” Tucker noted.

“Look through it carefully. I ain’t leavin’ till we find a lead.”

“Ah, here’s somthin’. It’s an old credit card receipt. There’s a lot of charges for The Café Royal.”

“That means someone there will know her, so get the address, and let’s go.”

They arrived about 4 PM, Scotland time. It was a long, stressful day, and Larkin felt jet lag. Using his anger, he pushed aside the fatigue and stepped inside. The owner decorated the room with a Parisian-style saloon bar interior. The room had a maroon ceiling with white trim squares, and the white/gray marble floor led to a polished wooden bar, at least twenty feet long. Only a few patrons sat scattered about the room because it was still early.

As they assessed the bar, two young men walked in and went straight to the bartender, who showed them a small pamphlet, which Larkin could not read from his position. The bartender led them to a door, disappearing behind it. Larkin and Tucker looked at each other, nodded, and followed them. The door led to a stairway that went down into the basement. They crept to keep themselves hidden.

The basement was well lit, and they found the bartender fussing with a keyboard. A few seconds later, a portal opened near an adjacent wall. The two young men stepped through the event horizon, and it closed. The bartender started toward the stairs and stopped, seeing Larkin and Tucker glaring at him.

"If you're looking for money, it's upstairs behind the bar. I don't have anything down here."

Larkin retrieved the disc and brought up Dawn's image.

"Do you recognize this woman?"

"Yes, she owns the place."

"Where is she?"

"I don't know. She visits infrequently, and before you ask, there is no set time for her arrival."

"I want to know how to find her. You better start talkin', or I'll contact the Regime and let them know about your portal machine."

"Fine. The woman you're looking for isn't here, on Earth. She's out there somewhere. I don't know her exact location."

"Let me interrogate him, Larkin; I'll get 'em to tell us the truth," Tucker interrupted.

"Hey! I'm not lying. The two young men you saw left through a portal that landed on Pulara IV, on the other side of the galaxy."

"The Regime's portal technology doesn't reach that far," Tucker countered.

"This isn't a Regime portal, and as you have probably already guessed, this bar is a front for a recruiting station."

"Recruiting station?" Larkin wondered.

"Yes. The Milky Way is big, full of solar systems with planets with every kind of society, and the woman you're looking for is out there, somewhere. The only chance of finding her is to join the Abaddonian army. Its territory stretches across the galaxy."

"This guy's pullin' our chain. Let me beat the truth out of him," Tucker threatened.

"Your only other choice is to wait here until she shows up again, and I have no idea if or when she will arrive," the bartender explained.

"What's on Pulara IV?" quizzed Larkin.

"You're not actually considering this?" Tucker marveled.

"What else can we do? If he's telling the truth, she's not here."

"We don't even know him. He could be sending us into a trap!"

"Maybe," Larkin paused and looked him square in the eyes, "If it *is* a trap, we'll get out of it, and we'll return to make you regret ever being born."

The bartender gulped, "It's not a trap."

"Tell me what's on Pulara IV?"

"It's the elite training camp for the Abaddonian army. They'll give you everything you need, including a language imprint enabling you to speak to anyone in the galaxy. Men, such as yourself, could choose any position. I suggest you train to become a pilot, so you can travel the galaxy and have a better chance of finding her."

"I don't know, Larkin. I don't like this," Tucker warned.

For a long time, Larkin thought of what to do.

"Look, if you want time to think it over, come back tomorrow," the bartender offered.

"I'm gonna go," Larkin spoke to Tucker.

"Are you sure?" puzzled Tucker.

"No. Not a hundred percent, but I think it's our best chance of finding her."

"Fine, I'm in too," Tucker confirmed.

"I'll open a portal to Pulara IV immediately," the bartender started working. "After you arrive, you must strip so they can examine you for illnesses. Once you've passed the physical, you'll get your language imprint and start training. Remember, work hard;

your superiors will recognize it and move you up the ranks. The higher your position, the more freedom you'll have to move around the galaxy."

"Once we train, we'll steal a ship and find her," Tucker suggested.

"I don't recommend it. The ships have tracking systems, so they'll find you before leaving the hangar bay," the bartender advised.

"Don't worry, Tucker. We'll figure somethin' out," Larkin said.

"Are you ready?" the bartender asked.

"Yeah, go ahead, open it up."

The bartender repeated his earlier steps to open the portal. Now that he was standing in front of the event horizon, Larkin could see to the other side. It was a room full of technicians and personnel. Armed guards and men dressed in white and grey uniforms were standing by.

"There you go. All you need to do is walk through," the bartender smiled.

Nodding, Larkin walked toward the event horizon with Tucker by his side. Tucker turned to the bartender before stepping through and glared, reminding him what would happen if it turned out to be a trap. They stepped through the portal and landed on Pulara IV; the portal closed behind them, and they began their journey to find Dawn.

Chapter 105

Earth
The Regime - Washington, D.C. - Mercy Hospital
May 20, 2452

Having awakened from a restless sleep, Sofia could not shake the feeling that Vincent was in trouble. Even though her memory had more holes than Swiss cheese, the only sure recollection was of him. A nurse entered the room, and Sofia requested to see him. The nurse agreed to pass her request along. A few hours later, she worried that something had happened to him. The padded restraints started to hurt, perhaps because she kept pulling on them.

A team of doctors entered her room, and she asked about Vincent. None of them claimed to know him and her instincts told her they were lying. She realized they were not there to help her find Vincent; they were there to evaluate her memories, which, after the injection, took about an hour for the MR to complete.

Before it was over, she heard the doctors whispering in the hall, just outside her door. She could not understand everything they were saying but was sure they were talking about her; it made her even more restless. The machine they used started to whine down, so one of the doctors sat beside her.

"We've completed a preliminary review of your M.R. I'm sorry, you've lost about forty percent of your memories."

"Will they ever return?"

"Unlikely, your heart stopped, depriving your brain of oxygen for a brief period; it was enough to cause irreparable damage to certain areas. The bad news is that you kept enough of your memories to go to trial for your crimes."

"My crimes? What did I do?"

"Based on your dossier, you committed enough that you should recall most of them. If you can't remember now, you will in a few days."

"What happens to me until then?"

"You'll stay here for two weeks, and once I'm satisfied that you're healthy, I'll release you to the authorities."

"Will they find me guilty?"

"Yes, I believe you'll spend the rest of your life on the moon."

"If this is my future, please tell me why Vincent hasn't returned to see me."

He hesitated, "I'm afraid he has died in the line of duty."

"What? How did he die?"

"Someone killed him."

"Who?"

"I don't have that information."

"Find someone who does!"

"Please, Sofia. Calm down. It will not help your recovery."

Frustrated, she pulled against her restraints, trying to break free with no success. Before she could figure a way out, her doctor injected a sedative into her I.V. The drug acted swiftly, and she fell fast asleep. Later that night, she woke, took several deep breaths, and searched her memories. The doctor was right; her past returned to her. She wanted to blame Vincent for putting her in Dragon's crosshairs, except she respected him too much to be petty.

Although he did resist her offer to run away together, she understood his decision. She could tell he did not want to turn her in. That hesitation made him the best friend she ever had, which was not a surprise, considering her vocation. She saw only two paths in her future. First, she could lie in bed and wait for the doctor to turn her over to the authorities. Second, she could avenge Vincent. She chose the latter.

She carefully examined her restraints and remembered how to undo the belt-like latch with the toes on her right foot, so she pushed the covers off her body and reached over to her left wrist with her foot. In the process, she discovered her legs were flexible enough to touch the restraints with her toes and remembered her stretching routine. One by one, her memories were coming back. She only hoped her brain kept the important ones.

The latch was tight against the leather strap, making it hard to undo with free hands, let alone her toes; she did not worry because there was plenty of time. After several attempts failed, she had to stop due to leg cramps. Once they subsided, she brought her foot back up and continued to work the leather strap. A nurse paused outside her door to speak with the guard. Frantically, she moved the covers with her feet and put them back up.

The bed covers landed over her body and partially on her left wrist, hiding the work she had completed throughout the night. A few seconds later, the nurse walked in, and Sofia pretended to be asleep. It was not easy to breathe normally, with adrenaline coursing through her veins, making her heart race, yet with all her concentration, she forced herself to take in slow, steady, quiet breaths as the nurse reviewed her vitals.

"Hmm."

Fooling a person was easy; fooling the machine watching her heart was tricky. Sofia managed to take in enough slow deep breaths to slow her heart rate with a little more concentration. Satisfied that her pulse had returned to normal, the nurse left, so Sofia repeated the process, and by early morning, she finally freed her left hand. She unhooked the other restraint and turned off the machines in her room, so the devices would not scream out an alert once she disconnected all the leads attached to her body.

Freed from all the wires and hoses, she reviewed her chart. Within it, she saw a list of antibiotics the doctor prohibited her from taking. Further study showed that the doctor injected her with a new strain of tracking bacteria. She memorized the record, looked for her clothes, and found them in the closet. She walked into the bathroom and changed. She stepped out and saw that the nurse had returned, looking for her. Before the nurse could yell, Sofia ran to her and hit her in the throat with an open hand. As the nurse choked and gasped for air, Sofia removed her outer clothing, guided her to the bed, and bound her wrists in the same restraints that held her. Sofia removed a syringe from the nurse's pocket.

"Is this a sedative?"

The nurse didn't reply.

"You better tell me, or I'll inject it into your throat."

"Yes."

"Where do you keep the antibiotics?"

"There's a small storage room down the hall on the right."

Sofia stuffed a rag into her mouth, moved to the door, and cracked it open. A Regime sentry sat outside her room to ensure she did not escape, so Sofia put on the nurse's clothes and hat, held the syringe in her right hand, and opened the door. Before the guard realized it was her, she jabbed the needle into his throat. He grabbed her wrist, twisted her arm, forced her to fall, jumped on top, and wrapped his hands around her throat to choke her.

The drug knocked him out in seconds, and he fell fast asleep alongside her. She stood and put him back into his seat. Farther down the hall, she saw the other nurse on duty working behind a desk. Carefully, she walked past her, found the supply closet, slipped in, located the antibiotics, swallowed two, put the bottle in her pocket, returned to the hallway, and walked out an emergency exit. *Now I will find out who killed Vincent and make him or her pay*!

Chapter 106

Avalon
At the Equator - Arthurian Resort
May 20, 2452

Standing on the starship bridge, SS Oblivion, Dawn saw Avalon grow on the monitor as her vessel moved into orbit on the morning side of the planet. It was past due for her crew to have a little R & R in a tropical paradise. The turquoise-colored ocean was inviting even from her vantage point (twenty miles from the planet's surface). Thousands of islands dotted Avalon's equator, making it a prime location for vacationers all over the galaxy. Soon, most of her crew, including herself, would be down there enjoying everything Avalon had to offer.

She contacted the flight deck to ensure her spaceship was ready and faced her Chief Officer, Rayvax.

"I'll only be there for a day; you're in charge until I return."

"Yes, ma'am," he replied. "Enjoy your time."

As she walked the narrow hallway, everyone stepped aside and saluted. It took years for her to get the mostly male crew to trust her judgment and instincts as a woman; after a few successful engagements with the emperor's fleet, she had earned their respect. She arrived at the flight deck, and Zadrin was there to meet her. They smiled at each other and moved off to the side where prying eyes could not see them.

"I said we would meet at the hut," Dawn flirted.

"I have not seen you in two weeks. I could not wait any longer," he whispered, just before kissing her.

A few moments later, she gently pulled away, "Not here. There are already rumors about us. I don't want to give them any more gossip."

"I do not know why you pretend. Everyone knows we see each other."

"We must keep up appearances. I am the captain."

"Fine, I will see you at the hut. The shuttle should have us there in a half hour. I will try to sneak away, but they already know where I am going."

"Appearances, Zadrin. That's all I ask," she whispered, and noticing they were alone, she kissed him, "I'll see you there."

Leaving him behind, she climbed the ladder and sat in the cockpit of her fighter. The deck opened below, so she maneuvered the spacecraft through the door and toward the planet's surface. She landed and met with Avalon's governor, who was always happy to see Intransigent members. As usual, he presented her with a few gifts and a glass of champagne.

When the pleasantries were over, she took a shuttle to the island reserved just for her. Traveling light, she carried her bag over the wooden walkway to the hut's deck. Surrounded by water, it sat on poles in a small lagoon. The bungalow featured several glass windows on the floor, allowing her to see the different varieties of fish swimming beneath her. She unpacked, put on a two-piece swimsuit, and opened a beer. Before she finished it, Zadrin arrived. As she said hello, he embraced her with a kiss, interrupting her.

She pulled away, "Would you like something to drink?"

Pulling her back, he shook his head, "First things first."

Having waited two weeks for "alone time" with her, he did not want anything to interfere, so firmly and gently, he pushed her down on the bed, kissing every part of her body. It had been two weeks since their last intimate encounter, and he wasted no time bringing her into the throes of passion. Afterward, they rested on their backs, breathless.

"You *really* missed me," she panted.

"I hoped you could tell."

"Ready for that beer now?"

"Sure."

As she walked into the kitchen, still naked, he smiled, "Have you been working out?"

"Why do you always ask me that?"

"I just thought you would appreciate the compliment."

A few minutes later, she returned with a bottle of suds. The glass was ice cold, just the way he liked it. Within minutes, he emptied the bottle.

"Another one?" she asked.

"No, that hit the spot. I plan to rest for a minute."

He yawned, put his head on the pillow, and his eyelids closed. Seconds later, he snored. Seeing he was asleep, she shook him a few times to wake him.

"Zadrin? Zadrin?" Dawn yelled; he did not answer.

Knowing he would not wake up from the drug-induced sleep for several hours, she put on a wetsuit, goggles, and a mouthpiece that would give her enough air to breathe underwater for at least twenty minutes. It was more than enough time, so she climbed down the ladder into the water, grabbed a Sea-Scooter, and went to the middle of the lagoon. At its center, the pool had an unusual depth of one thousand feet.

On the way down, the sun's light gave way to darkness until she reached the bottom, where lights guided her to the underwater Interstellar Transportation Bay entrance. At the opening, she grabbed the ladder and stepped onto the inside deck like climbing out of a pool. Every room in the station had fresh air, preventing the water from pushing its way inside. The pressure made her ears pop, so she waited until adjusting to her new surroundings and stepped into her changing room.

It was just like she told Zadrin, 'appearance is everything.' She changed and looked in the mirror to ensure everything was proper, and with an approving stare, she studied her black eye makeup. She worked on the design for years. It had two purposes: the first, to bring out the blue in her eyes; the second, and most important, it made her look menacing. To keep her hair from hiding her fierce glare, she pulled it back into a ponytail, which exposed her black earrings. The dress and cape she wore depicted her status.

The unique collection of miniature gold bars embedded in the front of her dress signified that she held the highest rank. Before leaving, she touched the scar on her cheek. Every time she saw it, memories of Thomas came flooding back. Losing him created a void that she could never fill. The longer she lived, the emptier it felt. Pushing away from the melancholy feeling, she walked to the Interstellar Transportation Bay and contacted Ethan, who commanded her ship, *Vandal*, while she was away. It was orbiting Avalon on the opposite side of the planet.

"Greetings, my liege," he spoke over the video comm.

"Send me your coordinates so I can open a portal on the ship's landing deck."

"Right away."

Moments later, Dawn received the information. The computer made the calculations, a green light appeared, and a vortex opened. She stepped through the event horizon, and it closed behind her. Ethan arrived moments after she landed.

"Set a course for Rogue Prime. We must leave at once," she ordered.

"Right away."

Chapter 107

Rogue Prime
Northeastern Hemisphere - The City of Pandosia
May 20, 2452

Standing on the bridge of her starship, *Vandal*, Dawn watched the stars smear across space and time through the forward monitor as the ship moved through hyperspace. Years ago, she instituted a standard operating procedure saying that any ship heading for Rogue Prime had to exit their portals twenty light-years from it. She still had plenty of time to meet with Imperial Majesty Abaddon and return to Avalon before Zadrin woke. The Protocol dictated that the starship should make several random entries through a portal before entering hyperspace to ensure no one followed. After a brief waiting period, the last vortex took them within range of the dark planet.

Millions of years ago, a freak accident threw Rogue Prime from its orbit and slung it far away from its original solar system. Dawn did not know exactly how it happened; she surmised that another world passed by close enough to fling it out into space, leaving it to wander the outer rim of the Milky Way aimlessly without a sun. Although it was tragic for whatever lifeform lived on the planet, it became the perfect place to build Pandosia. Exiting hyperspace, about a thousand miles from the Rogue Prime, Dawn could barely make out the active volcanoes on the planet's frozen surface.

"Bring us into orbit, Ethan. I'm going to the city. Wait for my return," Dawn ordered.

"We'll be in orbit in fifteen minutes," Ethan replied.

Leaving the bridge, Dawn headed for the hangar. Dawn had the idea to build the underground city of Pandosia, and Rogue Prime was the perfect spot for it to flourish. Without a sun to keep its surface warm, all the oceans froze along with the atmosphere, yet it could support life. Dawn chose this planet because of its volcanic activity, which gave Rogue Prime the necessary heat to survive, at least underground.

As she marched through the halls of her ship with purpose, her black cape grandly flowed behind her. Unlike the SS Oblivion crew, the troops on Vandal feared her, and for a good reason. They knew what she was truly capable of doing to anyone who crossed her. Along the way, anyone in her path stepped aside and saluted with fearful expressions. She climbed into her raptor in the hangar, which was combat-ready, just in case of trouble.

When Vandal entered its orbit, Ethan alerted her, and she fired up the engines. Once she disengaged the artificial gravity, her spacecraft lunged forward through the atmospheric force field and into space. She angled the raptor toward the planet and saw Mount Hiri spewing lava eastward into the sky. Whatever magma Rogue Primes' gravity did not bring back down floated behind it in space as it drifted forward into the darkness.

Dawn gave the active area a wide birth to avoid the cooling magma streaming out from the crater, and having cleared the volcano, she sent a coded signal to the control tower below. The moment the landing officer approved her password, two rows of lights guided her to the base of the volcano's quieter west side. As her raptor moved below the volcano's crater, a circular steel plate opened on the planet's surface.

Using her ship's leveling jets, she lowered it to the ground, landed, turned off her engines, and popped the canopy. The platform crew wheeled over a set of stairs, and she stepped out. Looking down, she saw Jika, the emperor's faithful assistant, waiting for her. Having met him on the planet T'Votan, she specifically chose him for the emperor. He proved his loyalty to her by revealing those of his household who planned to betray him.

"Welcome home, my liege," Jika bowed.

"Thank you, Jika. It's good to be back."

He led her to a small electric car, sat in the driver's seat, selected their destination, and the vehicle's automated driving application steered itself as it moved forward. As they drove through Pandosia, she saw that construction was moving forward as planned, making her happy. Workers built structures of all sizes beneath the planet's surface throughout the area.

She watched everyone going about their daily business and smiled with some satisfaction, knowing her significant role in Pandosia's creation. It was her vision of the perfect city. Everyone worked together toward a common goal: to ensure Imperial Majesty

Abaddon succeeded. Over time, it flourished into an underground metropolis, and she would ensure it continued to grow.

They reached the restricted area, where two large, heavy doors blocked their path. Also, four giant humanoids, dressed in elaborate uniforms, stood guard at the entrance. Fierce-looking helmets hid their faces, and their accouterments blended gold and black. The lead sentry walked over and performed a retinal scan on Jika. Upon approval, the doors opened. As they moved forward into the restricted area, the hallway grew dim. Imperial Majesty Abaddon only allowed red bulbs to illuminate the walkway at the temple gate, which was only for Jika's benefit.

"Wait for me here," Dawn exited the vehicle.

Standing before the entrance, Dawn extended her hand, and the heavy steel door lifted upward, staying within the guides, keeping the rest of the fence aligned. She passed through the threshold and released her grip. It fell, causing the floor to vibrate because of its extreme weight; the temple entrance was not as difficult to access. She extended her right hand, allowing the Night Lord's power to flow through her, and the well-balanced, multi-ton stone doors opened without making a sound.

It was dark inside the temple's main room, yet Dawn could see the elaborate decorations. Tapestries of all colors draped from one end of the room to the other. Each had precious stones woven into the fabric with gold threads. Artifacts lined the walls under exotic paintings retrieved from thousands of worlds across the galaxy. These heirlooms were only a few of the emperor's prized possessions. He stored the rest in private museums scattered about his territory.

Before entering the temple, she sensed his presence; inside, she felt his power everywhere in the room. The source of that power emanated from the darkness directly ahead of her. She approached him over the narrow red carpet stretched from the temple's entrance to Imperial Majesty Abaddon's throne.

The carpet rested over a highly polished marble floor. The closer Dawn moved toward him, the more power she felt emanating from him, and at the first step to his throne, she stopped, knelt on one knee, and lowered her head, revering him. Imperial Majesty Abaddon stared at her in the quiet, dark, studying Dawn; sensing that she was anxious to speak, he raised his scepter.

"Rise, Dawn of Darkness."

At his command, Dawn stood to face him. Even without light, she saw his black, hooded cloak. He hid his face behind a mask, and only she knew his identity. Now, so close to him, his power washed over her filling the room. It would bring fear and terror to anyone else; it felt like a refreshing, warm summer breeze to her.

"I sense the excitement in you today. You have not been this happy in some time."

"I have good news, Imperial Majesty. Your plan worked. Jack Mason is no more. Michael took his place as Regent of the Mar Novians."

"Excellent. Now he is one step closer to his destiny."

"He has a wife now."

"You speak of Yanamai."

"Yes, Imperial Majesty."

"You must make certain she does not bear him any children."

"I have already spoken to Stav. He will ensure she does not conceive."

"Good, we cannot risk them giving birth to a Saiph. The galaxy has too many already; his child could be our undoing."

"Have you seen it in the future?"

"No, but as you know, I do not take chances."

"Michael visited one of our educational facilities."

"That was a bold move for him to make."

"He's upset with you for using his invention and has ordered me to map out the galaxy, to show him all the facilities you've built, so he can destroy them with one attack."

"Give him the location of our smaller industrial plants."

"Won't that impede our progress?"

"The delay will be insignificant."

"As you wish, Imperial Majesty."

"Everything is proceeding as I have foreseen."

"How much longer, Imperial Majesty?"

"Patience, my dear. In time, you will bring him to the cave I have chosen, where he will unwittingly eat the moss and become one of us, allowing you to train him in the ways of darkness."

"I look forward to it."

"Once you complete his training, you will bring him before me."

"As you wish, Imperial Majesty."

"Now, what of my weapon?"

"Everything is on schedule. We've begun building the pyramids per your specifications; it is a daunting task and will take years to complete."

"Do not worry. We have plenty of time before I will need them."

"Very well, Imperial Majesty."

"What of my Quantum Disbursement Machine?"

"It is also in the beginning stages of assembly, and we are on schedule."

"Excellent. Once you finish, I will quench all the light in this galaxy by extinguishing every star, giving the Night Lord a foothold in this universe."